ACCIDENTAL WAR MAGE

ACCIDENTAL WAR MAGE

TOMAS J. McINTEE

Podium

Podium

ACCIDENTAL WAR MAGE

CHAPTER ONE

In Which I Meet the General

I will never forget the day I met General Ognyan Spitignov, so it is there that I shall begin my story.

We were still asleep in the barracks when the colonel came in to tell everybody we needed to be ready for a surprise inspection on the parade ground and that a very important person would be arriving at our outpost. He'd been waving a sheet of paper when he told us this, and then he put the paper on a table and rushed off to shake awake the heavier sleepers of our battalion.

I had always been possessed of an extra measure of curiosity, and unlike many of my fellow soldiers, I could read very well. So it was that I was able to catch a glance of the name on the paper: General Ognyan Spitignov. I whispered this to my bunkmate, Vitold, as we hastily rummaged through our locker, looking for our dress uniforms.

"General Ognyan Spitignov? The Butcher of Belz is coming here?" Vitold didn't seem to believe it at first, but his blurted response was loud enough to draw a glare from the colonel, who told us in terms I would rather not write down that we should avoid calling the esteemed war mage "Butcher" to his face. The barracks burst into noise, the hubbub of many soldiers trying to talk at once, and I busied myself trying to find the boxes with our dress uniforms.

Somewhere beneath our regular mechanics' pullovers, our stash of vodka, the playing cards, and that extra tool kit I won from Karlov last week were our fancy parade uniforms, the ones we weren't supposed to touch or get any grease on. Since the supply officer issued them to us last month, we hadn't taken more than take a quick peek at them, and they were still in their boxes. We'd marveled at the deep red color of the capes while carefully avoiding touching them with our grease-stained fingers.

I found the boxes, but as I pulled out the red cape on top, it turned out that my box contained only the red capes—half a dozen in my box and, worse, another half dozen in Vitold's. No fancy coats, no fancy belts, no fancy pants, no fancy hats, just a dozen capes in two mislabeled wooden boxes. It was now my turn to run through my vocabulary of unprintable epithets, though, unlike the colonel, I did so discreetly, under my breath, rather than at the top of my lungs.

Vitold, however, had a practical suggestion.

"Look, Mikolai," he said, "Yuri and Igor have a weekend pass and are passed out drunk somewhere off in town. They will not mind if we borrow their dress uniforms." He gestured with a hairpin at the locker next to ours.

Yuri and Igor were the steam knights who bunked in the next row over from ours; the four of us often played cards together. Between them, they were the thinnest and fattest of the steam knights, which is one reason we knew them so well; they'd gotten new (or rather, newly reconditioned) powered suits issued to them when their unit was rotated to the garrison. Being somewhat nonstandard in size, they had both wanted their suits to be adjusted to fit better. The crew chief wouldn't sign for it without a bribe, so Igor and Yuri decided to cut out the middleman and pay Vitold and me directly.

I thought borrowing our friends' uniforms seemed like a brilliant idea. A few minutes later, I was wearing Igor's too-large dress uniform with the belt looped half an extra turn around my waist, while Vitold, being the smaller of the two of us, was squeezed into Yuri's too-small dress uniform. I kissed my good-luck stone—the one an old lady living out in the forest had given me for chopping wood when I was a young boy—and tucked it under my shirt collar.

We were nearly the last ones onto the parade ground, hustling to join the rear rank just as General Spitignov stepped out of the carriage. He was a very large and exceedingly ugly man wearing a war mage's under-armor harness, and as he stumped around, he muttered to himself as much as to anyone else. Every so often, he stopped to look at someone more closely. I kept my eyes straight forward and my arms rigid at my sides as I strained to hear what he was saying.

After what felt like three hours but was probably closer to ten minutes, he reached our rank and stopped right in front of me. He was taller than most men, able to look me in the eyes without peering upward or downward, and his rune-tattooed arms were as thick around as my legs. I'd met taller men, like my cousin Konstantin, but I'd never met a man who made me feel small and delicate before. He fingered my collar, poked at my chest, then rasped out a word as I started to sweat nervously.

"Name?"

"Mikolai Stepanovich, sir!" My voice cracked.

He paused and then pointed to my hand. I held it up, looking at it, and then back at him, puzzled.

"Sir?"

He rasped out another word. "Grease?" he asked.

I looked down at my hand and at the stubborn black rims underneath my fingernails.

"Uh, yes, sir."

"Good. Not afraid to get your hands dirty." His eyes unfocused a bit. "I like that in a steam knight. Ten-year service badge," he said, waving at my borrowed jacket. "Maintains his own suit personally and regularly, even out here. Loyal, diligent, and willing to get his hands dirty. That's the sort of steam knight I like." He focused again, glanced over at Vitold, looked down at his grease-spotted hand, up at his collar, and then back to me.

"You two are good comrades?"

I didn't know how to correct the misapprehensions of the large, ugly man in front of me without getting into trouble, didn't like him talking about me as if to some invisible third person, and didn't want to endure his halitosis any longer, so I gave the simplest answer I could think of.

"Yes, sir."

This was, apparently, a satisfactory answer, as the general nodded, and moved down along the line. I let out a breath I didn't know I had been holding and watched out of the corner of my eye as the general worked his way down the rest of the line, then circled back up around to the front of the parade ground. He spent a couple of minutes talking quietly to a small weasel-faced man. The lot of us stood nervously as he pointed up and down the line while muttering inaudibly, and then he demonstrated that he could speak above a mutter by dismissing us.

After changing back out of our borrowed parade uniforms and having a late—and cold—breakfast of porridge, we were sent to go work on the battalion's heavy equipment. Apparently, the general was going to take a platoon of handpicked volunteers with him for some hush-hush mission, and the train would be leaving tonight.

I didn't know who exactly was dumb enough to volunteer to leave a nice garrison post in one of the quieter areas of Ruthenia to go off on some hush-hush mission with a war mage of questionable sanity—it sounded like a recipe for getting dead in a hurry—but could they at least have chosen to kill themselves in a way that didn't leave me working for ten straight hours on steam-suit boilers?

Well, at least we were done in time for dinner. Vitold and I were looking forward to this and had a bet to settle. I was hoping that with a very important visitor present, the officers would have rounded up the best cooks in the battalion for mess hall duty, while Vitold was hoping I would owe him ten kopeks for being wrong.

The borscht looked and smelled familiar. Two days ago, one of the new conscripts dropped the mess sergeant's prized box of turmeric into the cookpot while making borscht, turning it a bright yellow-orange color and imparting it with a strange and exotic flavor. The dish showed up again yesterday since nobody with a lick of sense had eaten any, and its repeat appearance today was accompanied by a brusque order announcing that borscht was not an optional part of our meal today. It goes without saying that Vitold, who would eat nearly anything, had already had seconds at dinner both yesterday and the day before—he loved complaining, and it gave him a good excuse.

The bread looked like it had been baked today. I say that not because it looked or smelled particularly appealing, but because never before had I seen rye bread so dense and hard. It looked strange and unfamiliar (unlike yesterday's borscht) and wasn't the least bit moldy (unlike most of the bread we had seen that week). As we headed for our seats, Vitold, who grew up in a bakery, cheerfully informed me that he had made bread just as dense and hard once, when he forgot to add yeast.

When I asked him how he could be so cheerful about the matter, he reminded me that I now owed him ten kopeks. I was fishing through my pockets when I felt a hand on my shoulder, accompanied by a familiar booming voice congratulating me on my bravery and patriotism. I turned to greet the owner of the hand with a sense of trepidation.

"Colonel Illinich! What can I do for you today, sir?" I eyed the colonel warily. He was smiling entirely too widely.

"For me? Ah, I am afraid there is nothing you can do for me. I just wished to congratulate you on volunteering and wish you luck on your glorious mission." The colonel leaned forward.

"Volunteering, sir?" I shot a look at Vitold, who shook his head in wide-eyed innocence. "I don't know what you're talking about."

"General Spitignov was very impressed with you. You have volunteered to accompany him on his mission, since the war mage specifically requested you, by name—and there are no other Mikolai Stepanoviches in the battalion." The colonel gave me a stern look.

Odd, the colonel didn't look delusional. Had I volunteered for something without realizing it? I opened my mouth to object and then looked around the dining hall. No small number of heads were turned to look at the two of us, some sympathetic and some gleeful. I shut my mouth as the real meaning of his statement filtered through my head. That kind of volunteering. As someone who enlisted to avoid being conscripted, I understood that kind of volunteering all too well.

The colonel placed two sheets of paper on the table and spoke more quietly. "These are the official orders attaching you two jokers to Spitignov's command. The train leaves two hours from now. Good-luck."

Vitold and I looked at each other blankly for a moment, shocked. When I looked back at the colonel, he was gone. I broke off a piece of rye brick, dipped it in the yellow-orange stew (I could hardly bring myself to think of it as borscht), and chewed mechanically. It tasted like ashes in my mouth.

"Why me? He didn't ask for my name and didn't talk to me; it was all just you," my formerly inseparable buddy said. "Maybe I can get out of this. I could be sick from food poisoning," he said hopefully, spooning bright yellow-orange borscht into his mouth with renewed vigor.

I read the papers. "Your name is right there. Maybe the colonel wants to get rid of you. You did put itching powder in his boots, after all." I pushed my plate away, my appetite having disappeared. "Do you want to chance having the Butcher of Belz himself mark you down as a deserter?"

Vitold shook his head as he chewed.

"Yeah, me neither. I'll go pack our gear. This one's yours, this one's mine." I passed him one of the sheets and left the dining hall.

My first stop was the mechanics' workshop, where I packed up our tool kits and a few other useful things, and then I hustled back to the barracks. I was surprised I didn't see Vitold there waiting for me. Was he still eating? What was taking him so long?

I packed away what I could into our locker, and in a couple of minutes Vitold came in through the door, carrying a bag.

"Vitold, we're nearly late," I said. He informed me that he had procured a cart so we could ride in style to the train depot, and that we would not possibly be late. I carried the locker out to the cart; shortly thereafter changing places with Vitold, as the mule wasn't particularly inclined to listen to him. Since Vitold grew up in a bakery, rather than a farm, he didn't really have much experience talking to mules. I politely asked the mule if he would kindly hurry on his way, and he did.

We very nearly were late, even with the borrowed cart. The gray sky of late summer's eve was punctuated with a line of smoke and ash drawing near even as we crested the last hill before the depot. At the depot, I could see the giant ugly man standing and scowling as the train pulled up. Most of the soldiers had already been neatly lined up and boarded the train before the two of us finished making it down the hill, where a rodent-like fellow with a clipboard accosted us.

Being a bright fellow, he evidently figured out that we were mechanics from our grease-stained coveralls and the tool kits we unloaded from our cart. He directed us to the task of loading a pile of disassembled steam knight suits into a boxcar. When we were done, we made as if to climb into a passenger car, at which point he informed us that we didn't need to come along, though he appreciated our enthusiasm. After all, they only had enough space in the sleeping compartments for the last two steam knights, who should be showing up at any minute, and our commanding officer wouldn't appreciate our unexpected departure from his battalion.

I told him I had orders to go on that train. He rolled his eyes at me in disbelief and informed me that General Spitignov didn't need any more mechanics, and if my name wasn't on his list, I was not getting on the train to hitch a free ride south to Khoryvsk at the expense of the Imperial Army. I pulled out my orders, waved them in his general direction, and told him that the general himself had personally requested my presence on this mission. He checked the paper against the one on his clipboard, sighed, and waved me and Vitold aboard.

"What was that all about?" Vitold asked, looking at me suspiciously. "Did you just pass up an opportunity to get us out of this? He didn't seem to want to let us on."

"He wanted to make sure our names were on the list, which they are. He just didn't realize we're mechanics. We'd get in a lot of trouble if we stayed behind." I sighed. "Let's get settled in and claim those last two bunks before the steam knights show up. It's going to be a very long ride, and I'd like to get some sleep." Finding the last open pair of bunks proved to be easy—they were right next to the door. We were stowing our gear—or rather, I was stowing our gear while Vitold stared unhappily out a window—when the train lurched into motion.

"I thought there were two more steam knights coming," Vitold said. "Nobody else came down the hill. Guess we're leaving without them."

"Good for us, bad for them," I said. "We don't have to fight anybody for the bunks, and they're on the general's bad side now. I wouldn't want to be in their shoes the next time he sees them."

Vitold rummaged in his mysterious bag and pulled out a flaky pastry of some sort. It looked like something you'd see in a French bakery. "Eat, Mikolai. I raided the officers' pantry on my way out of the mess hall. You look like you're about to fall over."

"Vitold, you're a good comrade," I told him gratefully, and tore into the pastry. It was fluffy, buttery, and had some kind of wonderful sweet filling.

CHAPTER TWO

In Which I Am Railroaded

After a too-brief gray-skied night, in which I could barely hear the snoring of my fellow soldiers over the dull roar of the train, the upper level of the dining car, with its beautiful overlook of the train and of the summer sun over the vast forest, had a view to inspire great love of the motherland. The rail line cut like a knife through the deep green trees, a glimmering steel vein through a vast and open land.

Although the view was amazing, I would have happily traded it for the lower level of the dining car if it came with the expected change of company—sitting next to Vitold and listening to his gripes. The small, weasel-faced man who had accompanied the general on his parade-ground review—and later tried to stop us from boarding the train—was, though approximately Vitold's size, in all other regards his complete opposite.

Colonel Ivan Ivanovich Romanov had consistently aristocratic manners, while Vitold's manners fell in a diverse range from common to crude. Vitold enjoyed cracking jokes, but Colonel Romanov wouldn't know one if it bit him in his nobly born posterior. And while Vitold's company warmed my heart, Ivan sent chills down my spine. He was a terrible man.

Perhaps it was what he had to say to the lot of us; I might have had a better opinion of him if he had been telling us things I wanted to hear, rather than a long series of things I really didn't want to hear.

"To serve General Spitignov," he was saying as he delicately spooned fish eggs on toast, "is to serve the Empire in all her glory. He is harsh and unforgiving but a very great man who does very great things. I am meeting with you today in order to ensure that this company functions smoothly. The general is at his best dealing with a small number of people; and if he must deal directly with the common troops in your squads, he will be very unhappy . . ."

Something about that sentence bothered me, but between the early time of the morning and the surprisingly good food in front of me, I was too distracted to ask any questions and tuned him out as I sat there enjoying the beautiful aroma and appearance of the fine meal. I had just started eating my first piece of toast when a particular word diverted my attention and left me choking.

". . . will be executed by firing squad, unless General Spitignov is feeling in the mood to do it himself."

Wait, what was that? Executed? I swallowed a half-chewed mouthful of toast hastily and asked a question, quietly but urgently. "Sir? Does he really do that as often as people say?"

"When it comes to deserters?" The colonel paused. "Well, yes. So make sure none of your troops desert. You are accountable for everything, and I do mean everything, that they do or fail to do. The general has faith in all of you, which is why he has selected you to lead his troops into battle; so, make sure that your steam knights do not disappoint him."

"My steam knights?" I left my mouth open.

He pulled a worn and folded piece of paper out of his pocket. "I know most of your regular squad was out on leave, but we didn't leave you without a command. We filled in the spots from other squads. You're in charge of steam knight squad number three." His finger stabbed down to indicate one of the boxes near the lower right-hand corner of the piece of paper.

I closed my mouth, then opened it. No words came out, so I closed it again.

"You are Mikolai Stepanovich, right? That's what your papers said. You showed them to me yourself," the weasel-faced man said.

I nodded mutely. My mind was racing, and my appetite had been left behind at the starting line. I pushed food around on my plate until the colonel was done talking about how we could expect to die gloriously for the motherland in some forsaken corner of Wallachia, and then I woodenly climbed down the stairs to Vitold. His inquiries about whether or not I'd snagged him some dessert from the officers' breakfast were met with a blank stare and then a wild look.

"Vitold, I think we need to talk," I said, gesturing toward the door. He patted the chair next to him. I shook my head and pointed at the door. He looked down mournfully at the crust of black bread and smear of egg left on his plate and then followed me out.

The good news, I told him, was that both of us, though especially me, were looking at pay grade increases. The bad news, however, was that we were now steam knights rather than repairmen, and thus could expect that our next of kin would be the ones who would be able to spend that pay.

Vitold took this surprisingly well; which is to say, he did not leap off of the moving train right then and there. The two of us headed forward to the engine car to inquire about the train's schedule, particularly any stops that might be en route. We had to shout to be heard over the racket of the engine as it chuffed away.

"How long until we stop in Khoryvsk?" I asked, leading obliquely toward my desired topic.

"Eh?" The conductor, an elderly chap, seemed hard of hearing, probably from spending too much time on trains like this one.

"Khoryvsk! How long?" I made sure to overenunciate so he could read my lips.

"We aren't!"

"But this line goes to Khoryvsk!"

"We're not stopping in Khoryvsk!"

"When are we stopping, then?"

"Wallachian border fort, in five days!" The conductor held up his hand to forestall a reply and leaned in close to shout in my ear.

"You were thinking of sneaking off? I don't blame you. That's why the general isn't stopping—doesn't want to give anyone a chance to back out. We'll only stop to switch tracks and maybe load coal. You look like bright lads—just keep your heads down, don't provoke the general, and don't volunteer for anything."

"There's been a mistake! He thinks we're steam knights," I said. "We're just mechanics!" He looked very puzzled (and, I thought, might not have heard me clearly), so I repeated myself, with additional hand gestures and more details, trying to outline the story over the noise of the engine.

"Well," he said, "unless you want the general to get angry when he finds out you were fooling him, you have five days to learn to become steam knights. When they pelt you with beets, make borscht."

This was good advice. I didn't really want to make the man who'd already earned the epithet Butcher of Belz angry enough to earn any new nicknames. Maybe we could pretend to be steam knights well enough to come out with our heads still attached to our necks. The two of us set off back toward our compartment.

"I can't believe you didn't steal me any dessert from the officers' mess," Vitold said, pulling something flaky and delicious-looking out of his jacket pocket and biting into it. He continued, words muffled by chewing. "I would have, if Yuri had been the squad leader and I was the one up there. I bet whatever they were serving up there was even better than this."

My stomach growled.

Unfamiliar muscles were sore when I staggered into my bunk after dinner, thanks to an afternoon clunking around in an empty boxcar with a veteran steam knight by the name of Gregor Petrovich. I didn't bother to undress—just took off my jacket and boots. I was fingering the good-luck stone around my neck, about to take it off, when I decided I didn't have the energy to untie the worn leather thong.

I fell asleep with one hand on the stone and the other flung over my head with a pillow to try to block the relentless chuffing of the engine ahead as it dragged the train toward whatever suicide mission the muscle-bound war mage was leading us to. I must have unconsciously been trying to remember the last time my shoulders felt that sore because I had a dream that I was chopping wood endlessly while a little old lady clucked at me disapprovingly, telling me how to do the job properly.

Every summer from the time I was twelve to when I was sixteen, my parents would send me away for a couple of weeks to help out a little old lady. She lived by herself, just her and an old work mech. From what I know now, I suspect she didn't live there permanently but traveled a circuit between several different villages, leading something of a nomadic life. Our village was just her summertime home.

There would be a clattering as of pots and pans outside, and then the little old lady would knock on my parents' door. She would ask my parents about the latest gossip in town, and my mother would send me off to go fetch fresh bread from the baker in town, the expensive kind that had a fine white crumb and was shiny on top. I'd come back to find my mother had cooked up a storm in my absence, and we would have a grand dinner with the old lady; then when dinner was over, she would start complaining about how her eyesight wasn't as keen as it once was and how dark and lonely the road back to her hut was.

My father would laugh, and volunteer my services as a guide through the woods, and so I would take the old lady by the arm and walk her back to her hut, which was over on the other side of the river. What with the short summer nights and how far out in the forest she lived, it would be nearly dawn by the time we arrived at her hut, and she would exclaim that oh, since I was here, would I mind chopping some wood for her?

And how she would talk! It wasn't good enough to say "Mikolai, go chop some wood" and leave me to it—the old biddy had to tell me how to do everything. "Breathe in through your nose now, Mikolai, then chop with the wind coming out through your mouth." "Look at the birdie, Mikolai; isn't it precious? It's so very strong for how little it is, Mikolai. Imagine your arms are wings while you fill those buckets from the stream." It's like she was living vicariously through me, remembering a time when she was young and spry instead of old, wrinkly, and bent over.

So I would chop wood for her and carry water from the stream to her hut until I was too tired, which never took long the first day, since I had hiked all night; and then it was "Mikolai, would you mind staying another day to help me a little more?" Then there would be more chopping wood, carrying water, fixing the roof of her hut, cleaning out the boiler on her work mech, and whatever other chores needed doing.

Eventually, she would send me back home, which was the scariest part of the whole thing, because I never managed to retrace the way that we got there in the first place correctly. It usually took me two or three days to get back home.

I guess it sounds a little strange that she would have a work mech and still need help with heavy chores, but it was a pretty bad work mech—it didn't have any arms, just big chicken-like legs. I guess it was more of a walking cart than a real work mech. Good for carrying things from place to place, but not so good for chopping wood or taking buckets of water from the stream, and mechs usually burn a lot of fuel. Though, come to think of it, I don't remember seeing a lot of smoke from it, so maybe she'd been lucky enough to salvage an arcane engine somewhere. If so, she ought to have sold it—even an old firebox-style arcane engine fetches a good price.

She gave me the good-luck stone that I now wore around my neck on the second day of the second summer, when I was thirteen. It was a smooth green stone with a hole bored through it and a streaky red inclusion that looked like a letter or rune. She got a lot more talkative after that. She would tell me stories in the evening, ask me to imagine strange creatures and designs, ask if there would be rain the next day, and ask what pictures I saw in the tea leaves at the bottom of my cup. She talked about fortune-telling, astrology, and all kinds of faraway places.

I guess she was lonely, living out in the woods by herself. For my part, I treasured the relative solitude; one old lady, however talkative and bossy, didn't hold a candle to a gaggle of siblings, livestock, neighbors, and day laborers as far as nuisance went. That, and it was a change of pace. After that last summer, I saw the old lady once more, just before I enlisted in the army.

I had taken my father's prize mare and ridden out of town in anticipation of getting a letter informing me I was hereby conscripted into the army. There was a warrant out for my arrest. Three days out in the forest, I ran into the old lady, and she asked me what was wrong.

I told her I didn't want to get myself shot. She pointed out that failing to join the army seemed likely to get me shot anyway and suggested that if I hastened to volunteer, maybe I could choose where in the army I would go. She rode with me to the army post in the next town over. Under her watchful gaze, and after a few well-chosen words about my practice with mechanical maintenance, the recruiting officer signed off on my acceptance into the mechanics' corps based on aptitude.

The next day, I met Vitold, a sensible fellow who had never cleaned a boiler before but knew enough about the ways of the world to bribe the recruiting officer into claiming he exhibited "great potential as a mechanic," in order to get him into something with a lower casualty rate than the infantry. The two of us became fast friends, and the rest is history.

When I woke up, I realized the difference between intensive training with a veteran steam knight and chopping wood for a little old lady: Both leave your muscles worn out, but taking and delivering hits over and over again leaves your entire body one giant bruise. My summers with the little old lady in mind, I sat up in the bunk for a couple of minutes, breathing in through my nose and out through my mouth, rubbing the stone and trying to will my muscles to not be so sore and my bruises to not be horribly purple.

Breakfast in the downstairs of the car consisted of boiled groats and was rather less enticing than breakfast in the upstairs had been the previous day. I was hungry, though, so I scarfed my way through three bowls of the stuff. It was also crowded; Vitold, three other members of "my" squad, and I were shoulder-to-shoulder around the table.

Directly across from me was Gregor, balding, with what little hair he had left starting to go to gray. He was a big man, going slightly to fat, with a sallow complexion; he was amiable and a willing teacher, if not especially articulate with words. I thought he would resent my being placed in charge of the squad when he was such an experienced steam knight, but the idea that he should be squad leader never occurred to him. His breakfast came with several slugs of vodka from a flask to fight off the morning shakes he was prone to otherwise.

Misha, sitting on my left, was not especially talkative. He was lean and of medium height. I never learned much about Misha, not even where he got the scars on his face and hands, but I did learn eventually that he was sullen and resentful toward everyone, not just his new squad leader, and that several years had passed between his mandatory term and re-enlistment.

Rumors had it, alternately, that he had murdered a woman in Khoryvsk; that he had been working for organized crime before getting sacked for having sticky fingers and had joined the army for safety; or that his sexual attentions were reserved for livestock of the hoofed variety, and the local magistrate had given him the choice between going back into the army or being turned into feed for said livestock.

The final member of our squad was Ilya. Ilya was a handsome fellow with a quick tongue and a charming smile. He seemed to consider my polite request to come drill with us in the back car to be nothing resembling a binding order; he was far too busy flirting with the redheaded woman at the next table, dismissing me with a wave and a grin.

Drilling wasn't quite as bad as I had feared. If you're a mechanic and working in the repair pool, you've had some practice walking around in steam suits while you test them; and if you have ambitions to become a mechanic officer in the field, you want to be good with them, so you log as much extra time as you can. Officers make more money and tend to live longer, which was enough of a motivation for Vitold and me to develop a sense of limited ambition for advancement to higher ranks.

The powered suit, however, isn't everything there is to being a steam knight. You also have to handle—capably—the weapons of the trade, from poleaxes and shields to small cannons. I thought that using a shield amounted to carrying it around, but there is a lot more to it than that: How you hold it, how you take a hit on it, how you coordinate with the person next to you so that your shields line up. Just carrying it around is awkward enough, given the size and weight of a shield designed to screen shot; add in the rest and it becomes downright difficult.

And the shield was the easy part. The poleaxe might be a distant cousin of a woodsman's axe, but it's longer than a man is tall, and handling an eight-foot pole is an awkward proposition at best the first few dozen times you try it. Loading a gun with powder, wadding, and shot might seem simple under ordinary circumstances, but imagine trying to do so using gripper hands mounted on arm-length sticks operated by squeezing down on handles that pull cables, and that lock in place if you twist the handle without meaning to. They bag the charges, which makes it a bit easier, but it takes practice.

At the end of five days of training, Vitold and I could manage to stay facing the same direction, taking hits on our shields while not dropping the practice poles meant to stand in for our weapons; well, for a handful of minutes at a time, at least. Long enough for Gregor to want to stop for a drink without having knocked us down once, the last afternoon. Ilya and Misha continued on their own projects; Misha cleaned his kit, sharpened knives, whittled, and read laboriously from a little black book; while Ilya seemed to be determined to seek out more pleasant company than the lot of us squadmates.

The train did stop in Khoryvsk, briefly, in the dead of night after two days of travel. I learned from the conductor that they switched engine cars and brought on new coal. When it happened, I woke up in my bunk, hearing only a faint repetitive banging noise. For a panicked moment, I thought I had gone nearly completely deaf, as this was far quieter than the engine had been at any point before; but then the banging stopped, too, replaced by quick whispering, and I saw in the dim shadows a slim figure slipping out of Ilya's bunk on the other end of the car.

If I could hear whispers, my hearing was still good, I reasoned. This meant that the engine was stopped. The next logical conclusion was that the banging noise was the indirect product of Ilya's good looks, the shadowy figure, and the metal bed board of his bunk. I became briefly and intensely jealous of Ilya's good looks. Then the new engine car began to chuff away, and the train jolted forward.

I peered out of the curtains, and that's when I learned we had indeed halted—however briefly—in Khoryvsk. I watched entranced as the train climbed up a bridge to cross the Slavutich River, bringing what seemed like the whole of the city into view. The great city was bathed in moonlight. I promised myself that someday I would see it in daylight. If I survived for long enough.

That promise seemed full of hubris when we disembarked at a fort near the old Wallachian border. We were greeted by a large number of injured soldiers, including more amputees than I'd ever seen in one place before, who were gathered at the depot for the train back to Khoryvsk.

I saw the general staring thoughtfully at the injured soldiers as they boarded their train and we unloaded ours.

Was he counting the missing limbs so he'd know how many enemy limbs to chop off? Was he mourning the tragic losses to the Empire? Was he thinking how lucky they were to have been shipped out alive? Maybe he was wondering what it would feel like to be short an arm or a leg. Unfortunately, all my guesses were wrong, and even less fortunately, I learned the answer two weeks later, but I shouldn't get ahead of myself.

Marching into the fort was the first time I felt like a real squad leader. Colonel Romanov felt the need to impress somebody, so he had us organize by squads, and march in like we were on parade. Before that impromptu parade, I had simply been Mikolai Stepanovich, the misfiled mechanic who had the misfortune to wear a borrowed uniform at the wrong time; afterward, I was Squad Leader Mikolai Stepanovich, the badly dressed buffoon whose squad marched straight through a bed of flowers. A freshly manured bed of flowers, at that.

Afterward, Colonel Romanov gave me a look that reminded me of biting into an unripe apple, and Ilya was positively furious about the state of his boots.

CHAPTER THREE

In Which I Commit War Crimes and Misdemeanors

After an excellent dinner and a festive evening—an unusual state of affairs—we were awoken an hour before dawn to march deeper into Wallachia, covering much of the distance between what had originally been built as a border fort and the recently moved border. I joked that this was so nobody had time to find an excuse to stay at the fort. None of my squadmates laughed; they all thought I was dead serious, even Vitold. At the time, I felt irritated, but upon reflection, that made an uncomfortable amount of sense, given what the train conductor had told us about not stopping in Khoryvsk.

General Spitignov's little army set a hard pace across the countryside, breaking camp before dawn and marching until an hour past sunset. We avoided roads so that informants wouldn't be able to tell where we had gone. This made for rough going, and we seemed to be going every which way—south one day, east another, then cutting southwest, and after ten days, I was beginning to think we were lost.

That's when we found the village. It was small, with several dozen little buildings clustered tightly together and a couple dozen more spread out a bit farther. After the scouts reported this, the general called for a halt and dispensed orders.

A messenger would ride ahead of us into the center of the village and order all the villagers to assemble in the village square. The main body of our force was to surround the village at a distance and ensure that no traitors were to escape, while the general would personally question the villagers about reports of nearby resistance activity. Were there any questions? No? Good, the general told us. He began walking toward the village, accompanied by the mechs he'd picked up at the border fort and one of his dogs.

Properly built war mechs were like armored steam suits, only without the vulnerable human knight on the inside. Instead, they're driven by a powerful elemental spirit bound to a control engine called an elemental cage—a complex but robust array of hydraulics and gears. War mages could direct those bound spirits with no more than a thought and a gesture, but the spirits could be exceptionally literal and perverse when following a non-magical officer's spoken orders.

Given that humans had an unfortunate tendency to die if bathed in steam from a ruptured pressurized line, mechs could be more effective than steam knights, but a proper built-for-battle mech chassis required more complex and expensive machinery and enchantments than a mere steam suit. Some mechs designed for labor were less complex, especially ones specialized for very specific repetitive tasks.

Colonel Romanov told us that he himself would ride ahead to see to it that the villagers were aware of the need to assemble in the village square. He pointed at a captain whose name I didn't yet know (Nikita Egorov), declaring him in charge of the general's honor guard. This honor guard turned out to consist of two squads of steam knights (including mine) and a mounted knight. The cavalryman I did know the name of at the time but have since forgotten, for which I must most sincerely apologize.

The village square was open on one side and boxed in by buildings on the other sides. The general directed us steam knights to stand in a wide half ring along one end of the square, while his mechs were posted in the gaps between the buildings along the other three sides.

"Partisans have been here." The general spoke with grave certainty, his voice loud and clear. "You will tell me everything you know."

The mayor of the village told the heavily muscled war mage that partisans having been here was news to him, and that he was a loyal, if somewhat new, subject of the throne, as were the rest of his darling villagers. Perhaps milord had been mistaken? Whatever milord required, he would be delighted to supply to the best of his humble ability.

The remainder of the conversation between the two was nonverbal. The war mage's enchanted sword swiftly and wordlessly informed the mayor that General Ognyan Spitignov had doubts about his honesty and loyalty. The mayor responded by having his body fall to the ground in obeisance while his head obediently but separately rolled toward the general's foot. The general, strength runes on his arms flaring, picked up the head and punted it over the crowd.

This scene was repeated twice more before the next villager to come forward, a young man, tried something different: He told the general that partisans had come by last week and taken food from the village's stores to feed their troops. He added that they had headed off southeast and were probably very far away by now.

Chop.

There had been some supporters of the partisans among the villagers, but sir had already decapitated all three of them, and none of the surviving villagers knew anything more?

Chop.

The partisans were at this very moment hiding in tunnels beneath the village?

Chop.

The partisans had stolen the village's sheep?

Chop.

At this point, the captain ordered us to load and ready our guns with shot in case the villagers attempted to attack us, and I screwed up somehow. When I brought the cannon back to horizontal after setting in powder and shot, I must have somehow jarred it in a way that set off the phoenix stone; the cannon went off and I stumbled as the gun smacked into me, dropping to my knees. With that, the rest of the steam knights fired into the crowd, the captain shrilly declaring that the villagers were attacking. To this day, I have nightmares about that moment—dropping the breech end of the cannon into my gauntlet and watching the cannon immediately buck back against the armored chest plate of my steam suit. When I looked up, blood and smoke and steam were everywhere, with the captain barking orders at us to load and fire again.

Mechanically, I loaded a handful of grapeshot—I'm not quite sure why—and looked out numbly as the rest of the steam knights fired a second volley. General Spitignov was about to swing at a little old white-haired lady in tattered rags. My stomach churned, and I aimed at the back of his head and fired, hoping that would quell the nausea, but it didn't help. I hadn't seen the gray-haired man pull out his knife and lunge at the general's back, and the poorly aimed shot from my cannon struck the villager instead.

If any of the villagers had tried to flee past me, I would have let them, but none did; standing as I was in the center of the line of steam knights firing at them, they were mostly trying to flee away from my position, where the mechs crushed them like beetles. Those few who tried our line went toward one of the edges. It was over in less than a minute. Ognyan Spitignov grimly stood in the center of the square, coated with blood, bodies strewn around the square. He waved his hand, and one of the mechs stepped forward. I noticed that there was a large bundle of standard-issue foldable entrenching tools tied to one of its smokestacks.

"Captain, I am leaving you one of the mechs. It has instructions to help you dig a burial trench. I do not want the crows to give our position away, so work quickly. Send a runner to fetch me if you find any of the tunnels the fifth villager mentioned. Make sure they are all dead—I want none of them to flee and inform the partisans of our presence. The men may loot the bodies if they wish; I do not care, but let me know if any of them find anything that looks to be tied to resistance to imperial rule."

As soon as the general left, I popped open my helmet, turned around, and vomited until my stomach was empty. Nobody said anything, and it was with a somber mood that we dug the ditch—the mech did most of the work of digging—and tossed bodies in. I found one body that was still breathing, lying very still, pretending to be a corpse; her muscles tensed briefly when I picked her up, a twitch belying consciousness.

"Pretty little thing. Bit of a waste, eh, Mikolai?" When Ilya asked me that, I realized I had been standing stock still for three or four seconds, staring at the limp form in my arms.

"Ilya, shut up," I said, "and get back to work." When I slid her into the ditch, my folding entrenching tool went with her, tucked between her right arm and her torso. Nobody seemed to notice the irregularity, and then Ilya tossed another body down and I lost sight of her entirely.

Crows were beginning to circle overhead; they cawed angrily when General Spitignov showed up again. He had with him a few more corpses and a squad of regular infantry, the latter carrying the former. It was not much later that we left behind a village square that was mostly churned-up mud and blood, with a long mound of freshly turned earth on one side. We hadn't found any tunnels.

CHAPTER FOUR

In Which I Am Bothered
and Bewildered

The next night, I had four unsettling conversations. The first happened at dinner—Captain Nikita Egorov clapped me on the shoulder and told me that General Spitignov had noticed me taking aim on the battlefield.

"Really?" I said, trying to sound casual. I poked a piece of charred mutton with my camp knife, scooting it around my plate. If the general had noticed me trying to shoot him, why was I still alive? Was he just waiting to execute me at a more convenient time? Maybe the captain was warning me so I had a chance to escape the camp before getting shot.

"Well, I had to tell him which of you it was. He's a very observant fellow, the general, but there's not much to distinguish one steam suit from another." The captain lowered his voice to a conspiratorial whisper, and I listened intently, hoping that instructions on how to escape a war mage's wrath would follow. "He's quite impressed. Not many steam knights would have the presence of mind to pick an armed threat out of a crowd of mostly unarmed civilians, or the confidence in their shooting to try to pick off a would-be assassin in close quarters with his target."

The plate of food in my hand suddenly looked much less appetizing. I muttered something about duty and humility, the captain buggered off to wherever captains go when they're not ruining appetites, and I mechanically went through the motions of eating dinner until the plate was empty.

The second unsettling conversation happened after dinner. Colonel Romanov wanted to have a private chat with the squad leaders in his tent.

"I realize that there is some unhappiness among the men at the measures required by General Spitignov, but it is vital that you maintain your troops' loyalty through the end of this mission. The penalty for desertion is decapitation. I would like to remind you that you are each responsible for four other men, and that each of you has four intact limbs other than your head." The colonel's smile didn't quite reach his eyes. "The coincidence of these two counts is one that the general had occasion to remark upon as we were disembarking from the train."

So that's why he had been staring so thoughtfully at the amputees at the depot? I shuddered involuntarily.

"In the effort to maintain morale, I am contributing certain items from the officers' commissary supply that you can use to reward your men for their loyalty and steadfastness today." He handed each of us a paper bag. "It is not much, but to be seen giving encouragement and reward is far more valuable than the reward itself."

Inside my paper bag were a bottle of brandy, some round pieces of hard candy, a long candy bar, a tin of caviar, some crackers, and a round piece of red wax. Presumably, there was cheese inside the wax. I stowed them in various pockets, folded up the brown bag carefully, and set out to go forth and raise morale.

Ilya was busy at work trying to raise his own morale elsewhere in the camp, Gregor had found himself a full bottle of vodka and was already unconscious, and I didn't feel like trying to start a conversation with Misha. So, I waved Vitold and the cavalryman (the one whose name I still can't remember)—over for a game of cards by the fire.

Good, imported brandy shared over cards, crackers, and caviar makes for loose conversation, though we kept it quiet—no need to be overheard. The talk turned inevitably to the topic of the village. I felt like unburdening my guilt.

"I didn't mean to shoot. It just went off and caused all that confusion," I said. "I wish I hadn't."

"Look, Mikolai," said the cavalryman. "Even if you hadn't fired off right then, they were all dead anyway."

"Really?" I frowned and tried to take a swig of brandy. The bottle was empty. I frowned more deeply.

"Did you see that bundle of shovels on that one mech? He had to have packed those before he even decided to go into the village. The general has issued us standing orders to kill anybody who might report our movements to the resistance. Do you think he was going to let a whole village of potential informers live to warn them?" The cavalryman shook his head. "You might have hurried it up a few minutes, but he was going to kill them all anyway."

There was a moment of silence as I digested this datum. It was both encouraging and unsettling—the third of my unsettling conversations of the night.

"I hope we don't have to stop to ask for directions like that again," Vitold said glumly. "Any of that brandy left?"

After a while more of playing cards, the cavalryman declared he was ready to call it a night and left the two of us to tidy up. No sooner were we alone than I heard a faint noise, a jumbled group of clanks like someone kicking a tinker's cart.

"Did you hear that?" I asked Vitold.

"Hear what?" Evidently, he hadn't.

"That noise," I said, waving at the dark woods.

"Maybe one of the sentries tripped on something in the dark," he said, peering out into the darkness.

"Mikolai dearie, you've grown so much taller since the last time I saw you!" said the old lady, standing where the cavalryman had been sitting a few minutes ago and pinching my cheek. Vitold turned around in surprise so quickly that he fell over. "The army has been good to you. Feeding you well, hm?" It was the old lady I used to chop wood for in the summer. What was she doing here? We were the better part of a thousand miles from my home village, and while I knew she traveled around some, that was a long way for a little old lady to cart her stuff. I was taken aback—unsettled for a third time.

"Grandmother, it is very good to see you," I began, standing up. (Editor's note: Particularly in more rural and traditional areas, "Grandmother" is a typical form of address for an old woman. It is most likely that Mikolai was not speaking literally.) I wasn't sure what to say next, so my mouth just hung open for a few seconds while I tried to process what was happening.

How, exactly, was I supposed to tell a little old lady that she had just walked into a camp full of soldiers with orders to kill any civilians who might give away their position inadvertently? Or that she was in a war zone, and we had just massacred a local village, and the locals might want to even the score by killing imperial subjects such as herself?

"Don't be so stiff and formal. Give me a hug, Mikolai. Oh, good, you still have your luck stone; you haven't gone and lost it somewhere. Have you been practicing? You really should, you know." She sniffed at my face and made a sour expression. "French brandy?"

"I'll go wake the sentries up," said Vitold, looking past me.

It was a good excuse for him to absent himself, and as I looked over my shoulder, I wished I had thought of it first. The old woman had been loud enough to get the attention of a certain exceedingly large, ugly, and bald general.

The image of the general decapitating a little old lady flashed through my mind, along with the cavalryman's words: "He was going to kill them all anyway." If we were to leave no witnesses behind, was I about to see this butcher of a man chop off the head of another little old lady?

My stomach tied in a knot as I considered my options. I had a knife; he had an enchanted sword, muscles like an ox, and a lot of practice killing people. I swallowed nervously as he loomed near me, his breath smelling like a rotten battlefield.

"Mikolai, dearie, go make us some tea," the old woman said, making shooing motions, then looked up at the looming monster and pointed at the ground. "Sit down, boy. I'm not minded to crane my neck looking up at you."

To my surprise, General Ognyan Spitignov, the Butcher of Belz, a murderous monster, sat down without a word of objection. He nodded to me, and after a moment, I realized he was dismissing me by concurring with the little grandmother. I hurried off to the commissary tent, where I tripped over a dozing colonel and got into a brief argument with him over whether or not I was authorized to be there, which I won by virtue of being more sober and hence able to finish my mission while he was still figuring out how to stand up.

After making tea and shooing some stray crows out of my way, I made my way back toward the general and my fourth unsettling conversation of the night. Mercifully, the little grandmother from my village seemed to still have her head atop her shoulders, without the slightest sign that she had been through a discussion with the general's enchanted sword. If anything, the war mage seemed to be the nervous one, hunched over and fidgeting with his fingers, eyeing her apprehensively like a child not told the reason he has been called up to the front of the schoolhouse.

Odd. I wondered what they had been talking about. They had stopped when I got close, with the old woman greeting me again and inviting me to come, sit, and talk. I braced myself for the inevitable blast of halitosis-infused air when the general took a sip of his tea and politely thanked me, but didn't smell anything other than the tea, oddly enough.

The general and I followed politely, mostly just listening as the old woman meandered through a range of topics, told a few stories, and then, as our teacups were almost empty, made a little request of me, one that demanded I try to remember what she had taught me.

"Oh, yes, Mikolai, I taught you how to read tea leaves, didn't I?" She patted my hand. "Why don't you show little Oggie your leaf-reading skills? I'm sure he would be happy to have you tell him his fortune."

I managed to refrain from rolling my eyes or letting out an embarrassed-sounding whine. That would be impolite, and it's not good to be impolite to little old ladies—or at least, that is what my parents taught me. In spite of my best efforts to forget the peasant superstitions she had taught me in favor of more practical skills, I found it coming back to me as I peered at the damp blotch of plant matter at the bottom of the general's cup.

"In the past, left . . . no, avoided. Maybe also . . . betrayed?" Yes, that was the pattern. Peering more closely, I added, "The pattern of a wronged woman is amidst the betrayal and departure, athwart. Her soul's unrest leads to the present. She would cry if she lived."

The infamous General Ognyan Spitignov, Butcher of Belz and terrifying war mage, pulled his cup back sharply, looking at it. Evidently, the general was superstitious.

"Little Oggie, let Mikolai finish." The old woman patted General Spitignov on the arm consolingly, and he reluctantly extended his cup again.

I thought I had read all I could read, but when the general jerked his cup back, the tea leaves shifted.

"The present. Found in the woods by . . . a man with a missing heart? It's the pattern for man, but there is a hole in the leaves, the shape of an egg." The old woman peered over my shoulder. I turned the cup and continued. "There is a loyal following, maintained in spite of mistakes."

The war mage frowned, and then closed his eyes, shaking his cup vigorously and holding it out. "The future. Tell me the future."

I looked at the leaves crawling up the side of the cup and decided that they looked something like wings. "I see a dragon," I said. Then I turned my head to the side. "And that your cup is cracked. The dragon is the end."

The general shuddered.

The old woman clucked her tongue and shook her head, then suggested that I clear away the tea service. I used that as an excuse to take my leave of them both and turn in for the night. Clearly, she was in no danger from the general, and I was quite tired. As I was leaving, the old lady said something about unhappy crows to the general.

When I went to turn in, though, I found that Vitold was missing and slipped off into the woods to go check for him. I found him and three of our brave sentries from the infantry hiding up a tree. They seemed worried "it" was still around. After listening to Vitold's description of the "strange, chuffing, long-legged mech" that had snuck up on him and sent the lot of them into a contagious panic, I told him it sounded like he'd made an honest mistake—the little old lady had a work mech that she brought along on her travels to carry her things.

Although it had a mischievous temperament, I informed him that it was harmless and had doubtless put itself on standby mode by now, what with how long the old lady had been sitting around chatting with our general. I may have made some comments about whether Vitold or the old lady's work mech looked more like a chicken. After a little coaxing, I managed to get Vitold to make the bold climb back down the tree and back into the camp through the frightening mech-infested woods.

The sentries were less easily persuaded, saying they'd keep watch from the tree for the rest of their watch. They claimed it was a better vantage point for keeping watch anyway, and they ought to have climbed up the tree to keep watch in the first place. I left them to it and sacked out.

When I woke up, Vitold was shaking me vigorously and telling me that I had slept through breakfast. It was time for us to start marching on. There was no sign of the old lady. When I asked Vitold about it, he said that the only people that had actually talked to the old lady about what she was up to were myself and the general, and nobody had the nerve to ask the general about it.

I told him I hadn't heard any plans—I had just brought them tea, read some tea leaves for the general at the old woman's request, and by the way, did you know that the general seemed terrified of her? What a funny thing for a big man like him, but insanity does take odd turns, I told him, and started to tell him a joke I had heard once about a man and his mother-in-law to try and ease his anxiety. Vitold didn't wait to listen; he rushed off to go round up the rest of the squad before I had gotten more than halfway to the punchline.

When I finally caught up with everybody else, Ilya and Misha apologized profusely to me. I'm not quite sure why, evidently the two of them thought they hadn't been showing me enough respect. We set off through the woods. Some crows circled overhead, cawing plaintively.

I rolled my eyes, irritated. "Angry we buried the bodies so quick, carrion-feeders?" I muttered at the sky.

CHAPTER FIVE

In Which I Go into Acquisitions and Become Diligent

We set out into the woods at a brisk march, initially heading south-east. At the end of several days marching back and forth through the woods in what may have been an intentional search pattern, we found a rebel base. It was a small, unassuming compound, a cluster of low stone buildings. Under other circumstances, I would have assumed it was a monastery or something, but the military nature of the installation was clear, and the soldiers were a dead giveaway.

Gregor, as the veteran of long years that I most certainly was not, identified some of them as professional mercenaries. Based on their distinctive steel helmets, high-quality armor, and equal mix of halberds and arquebuses, they were a free company from one of the mountain cantons to the far west. Other soldiers were clearly amateurs; patriots rather than mercenaries. They were armed with a wider variety of weapons, from longbows and pistols to shepherd's axes and boar spears.

I even saw some sharply-curved sabers, which looked as if they had been left behind by Sultan Alaeddin's men when his troops had been routed by ours in the contest over Wallachia.

The soldiers seemed to have been caught by surprise and readied themselves in great haste; some wore nightgowns or pajamas under hastily donned helmets and shields; others were only partly dressed.

The lot of them were also dead before we got there. I didn't mean that in the way military historians do when they say a battle was lost before a single shot was fired; it's true that there were more of us, and we had steam suits, mechs, and an efficiently murderous war mage on our side, but we didn't need any of those things to defeat them. The crows were already feasting on their corpses when we got there.

I recognized the footprints of the old lady's mech here and there, so we weren't even the first ones to show up after whoever killed the rebels came by; the little grandmother had beaten us to the post-battle looting. Colonel Romanov insisted that we conduct a thorough search for any survivors. We found none, but the low, unassuming buildings were larger than they looked from the outside, dug deep into the earth. There was a workshop, large enough and well equipped enough to take apart and rebuild a heavy mech, and crates upon crates of parts.

The general was very excited, but after examining the labels on the crates and checking through each building, Colonel Romanov was unhappy. The rebels had stored valuable supplies here, but fuel did not appear to be among them, and we were running low. The weasel and the war mage consulted with each other for a while, conferring while the rest of us continued quietly searching for other objects of interest, such as fancy pistols, jewelry, coins, clothes, and other valuables that might have escaped the notice of the unknown killers or subsequent looters, such as the little grandmother.

Colonel Romanov announced that he would lead an expedition to a nearby town to procure fuel and supplies, while the general stayed to secure the base. My squad was one of two steam knight squads that escorted Colonel Romanov and the pack train.

The townsfolk were set astir by our arrival. Some nervous, some wary, some cheerful.

We had emerged from the woods into a farmer's field, and by the time we reached the town proper, news of our arrival had spread to the entire local population. Rumor marches faster than draft horses. The officer in charge of the garrison of infantry posted here rode out to greet us; as he did, Colonel Romanov gave me a stern reminder that all details of our mission were secret, and not to trust anyone with them, not even our fellow soldiers.

No sooner had we marched to the barracks and gotten our boots off than the colonel demanded a quick private meeting with his squad leaders and the commander of the local garrison. He delegated the shopping to my squad; what he and the local infantry officer had to talk about, I don't know. He sent us off before getting into anything substantial.

Ilya and Gregor had already slipped off to some sort of establishment where they expected to find alcoholic beverages and loose women, which left Misha and Vitold at my disposal. Vitold was wearing his newly acquired pistol; it was a pretty piece, with gilded inlays, the sort that a gentleman might wear, formerly belonging to a mercenary officer. A mercenary officer would have to make quite a pretty sum to afford such things, though perhaps the dead man had been given it as a gift directly by an appreciative employer in lieu of a cash bonus.

Misha had found himself a lovely new sword, with a pommel that looked like a hawk's head. The taciturn fellow had apparently been carrying on a lengthy conversation with Vitold about how the ladies like to see signs of class, like a fancy sword, but in spite of his talk, he hadn't the nerve to head out and about with Gregor and Ilya.

Personally, I'd found a pocket watch and a little book bound with a gold clasp on the most unlikely looking fellow—an elderly, balding man whose corpse was dressed in a greatcoat with naught but smallclothes and a bandoleer beneath, wearing fuzzy slippers and a nightcap. Precious little things—even if the other soldiers weren't interested in them, I knew they were valuable.

He'd had a triple-barreled pistol when I first spotted him, the barrels designed to rotate like a pepper mill to bring each barrel's sparking stone in line with the hammer operated by the trigger. Unfortunately, another soldier grabbed it first. A pepperbox pistol is tricky to make and almost as good as a brace of regular pistols, a very impressive gun for the purpose of showing the ladies that you are an accomplished soldier.

Misha, Vitold, and I went about rousting shopkeepers and craftsmen from their dinners and evening entertainment to round up an ample supply of coal—a tedious task—and I resolved to give Gregor and Ilya a firm tongue-lashing for skipping out on the job.

The morning found me instead fuming silently as Ilya received a very warm farewell from a giggling girl; she whispered something in his ear and gave him a kiss. It wasn't as if he was holding up our departure, as one of the horses had thrown a shoe, so I didn't reprimand him for the delay. His earlier disappearance had been without leave, but by that point, I worried reprimanding him for the previous night would just make me look petty and jealous.

One thing caught my eye about the giggling girl: She was wearing a pendant, an amethyst crystal in a silver setting. It looked just like one I'd seen a redheaded sharpshooter pulling off a dead rebel during our loot-ing. Ilya must have won it from the sniper while playing cards and then given it up last night as a gift.

Our return to camp was greeted with enthusiasm. The general had been growing impatient; sitting still wasn't something he liked to do. The cav-alryman had been sent off to report directly to High Command on what he had uncovered so far. In the two days we'd been gone, the soldiers had peeled apart the base looking for loot; only a few dozen boxes remained untouched, piled in the dark corner of the workshop, which didn't look much different from when we'd left it two days earlier.

I was surprised our mechanics had left the workshop largely untouched, but then I found out the general had put them to disassem-bling, cleaning out, and reassembling the boilers on the mechs, one at a time—and the mechs that the general selected were rough-terrain mod-els with heavy boilers. Not a fun job, and not really a necessary one considering the light use they'd been put to since we left the train.

Colonel Romanov decided to silence the grumbling by announcing we would be having a party that night. We had more than we could rea-sonably carry with us on the march, he'd said, so it was fitting to eat and drink a great deal of it tonight.

I woke up in the morning with a fuzzy head and new orders: Captain Nikita Egorov was to be placed in charge of defending the rebel base. He would do so with a single platoon of regular infantry, two steam knight squads, and one mech. Our detachment would remain in place to ambush any rebels returning to the base, which Colonel Romanov assured us must be a vital link in the resistance movement's network. The rest of the force would go with the general on his hunt for partisans.

The general took me aside for a quick word in private before heading off. He told me that in the event Captain Egorov turned out to be a trai-tor to the state, died, or took ill, I would take charge of the defending force, being that he believed I was the most senior of the squad leaders. I hesitated too long to correct this misapprehension.

Nikita Egorov was a plain-spoken fellow, thoroughgoing and hard-working, but with little imagination. His first order of business was to set up watch and mess duty schedules, which he posted by the front door of the main building. He then posted a schedule of drills, "surprise" inspections, and maintenance checks next to them. I and the other squad leaders were exempt from holding watches or taking up mess duty; Captain Egorov believed we would have our hands full making sure our soldiers didn't shirk.

Say what you will about Captain Egorov, but he understood how to keep soldiers busy, even if the true meaning of the word *surprise* eluded him. I spent my spare time working through the little book and investigating the contents of the workshop with Vitold. Being that we were trained mechanics, and didn't like running the risk of being boiled alive by a malfunction, we had been keeping our suits very carefully maintained and tuned already. This meant we had some spare time, provided we didn't advertise its existence to one Nikita Egorov.

It turned out that the workshop contained some very valuable items. I recognized (more from manuals than from personal experience) the parts of several arcane engines as well as elemental cages, mechanically geared control systems smaller and more efficient than the ones in our mechs. It was a treasure trove, and the book I'd grabbed off the dead man with the fuzzy slippers was the key to all of it. It was the diary of the man who I assumed was the project lead, a wizard and mechanic.

It was written in Latin, though not very good Latin. My practical experience with the dead language was limited. My parents had made me sit through lessons when I was younger, and the old lady had some books in Latin lying around her place, but it had been years since those lessons. His handwriting combined with his poor grammar rendered the book cryptic, and it took me a while to make headway, but once I did, the cache of valuable supplies suddenly made sense.

The base was a manufactory of sorts, a site where the partisans could assemble advanced mechanical tools of war. It wasn't meant to be a base of operations for a large number of troops. Those were elsewhere, though the diary wasn't specific about exactly where. The entries of the diary described the development of an increasingly organized rebellion, one that was trying to build its own mechs and recruit or train war mages. The owner of the diary was a wizard himself, though not a war mage.

I didn't want Captain Egorov stealing the credit or, far worse from my perspective as a trained mechanic, ordering me to destroy the "inferior" (but actually superior) imported machinery out of a misplaced sense of imperial patriotism. The value of the machinery lying in the workshop was a secret between Vitold and myself, so far; I hadn't told the captain or even the rest of our squad. The news could wait until the general returned.

On the fourth night, Gregor and Ilya had the midnight watch, and Vitold had the pre-dawn watch alongside a scruffy infantryman by the name of Andrei. I asked Vitold to wake me early, so the two of us could get a head start. I wanted to try to see if I could start up one of the elemental cages, and that was something best done without Captain Egorov peering over my shoulder.

In spite of my best intentions, I woke with the morning sun as it broke through the window, Vitold snoring on the bunk next to me. I rolled out of my bed and prodded Vitold in the ribs, irritated.

"Vitold, you lazy fellow, you were supposed to wake me up!" Not only had he forgotten to wake me up at the start of his watch, but he had gone right back to bed at the end of his own watch, leaving me late for breakfast!

Vitold woke, blinking in confusion at my accusations. He stammered back excuses, and after the two of us had awoken enough to communicate properly, I worked out that he was telling me he'd never been awoken for his watch. I stormed off to find Gregor and Ilya.

Gregor was passed out with an empty bottle at his post up in the little bell tower that served as our watch post, reeking of ethanol to a degree that suggested a surgeon's office. Ilya was nowhere to be seen, and when I checked through the camp, his stuff was missing—his prized boots, his pack, and his personal effects, all gone. I felt a twinge in my left shoulder as I remembered Colonel Romanov's discussion about how the general had been struck by the coincidence between the number of intact limbs possessed by myself as a squad leader and the number of men I was responsible for, excluding myself.

I was very fond of having two arms and two legs. Ilya had deserted us, meaning that there was no longer a one-to-one correspondence between the number of my limbs and the number of my squadmates.

This was a problem.

CHAPTER SIX

In Which I Experience the Pain of Changes of Command

I told Gregor to keep quiet about Ilya's absence. I also told him that Vitold and I would see if we could find where Ilya had gotten off to without getting either of them in trouble; in the meantime, he should assume that Ilya had just managed to stagger down the stairs and gone to sleep in the wrong building.

Gregor told me that Ilya had been drinking with him. Before Gregor had passed out, the two of them had a lengthy conversation about women and life outside of the army. Gregor retold me such a maudlin tale about his own life that it would wash a clown's smile off his face. I thought to myself that if Ilya hadn't been considering desertion before hearing of Gregor's woes, he would have been sorely tempted afterward.

What I told Gregor, instead, was that surely his story would have put Ilya off the idea of women entirely as too much trouble for a soldier. To my surprise, Gregor agreed with me, though I didn't believe it myself. I would have bet a whole grivna of pure silver on Ilya having snuck off for a little fun in town with that Wallachian girl, if I'd had that much to bet with. And if Vitold was willing to take the other end of the wager, which he probably wasn't.

That debriefing done, I spent a few minutes pacing back and forth behind the mess hall, trying to get my thoughts in order. Vitold brought out a tray piled up with toast and hard-boiled eggs and a full samovar and suggested that I retire to somewhere less public to fret. He informed me that the regular soldiers found it unnerving and demoralizing when an officer began pacing nervously, and worse, were the captain to see me, he might find it curious and start asking questions.

We went down to the workshop, and I sat down for a few minutes to wolf down two breakfasts worth of food. Vitold had brought enough out for both the absent Ilya and myself, under the guise that he was bringing back breakfast for the remaining members of Squad Three. The eggs lacked salt and the tea lacked sugar, but the food soon vanished from the tray, and the samovar was emptied of hot water.

It was at this point, staring down at the last cup of tea, that I saw the solution to our problems. Ilya was not, as far as I knew, a woodsman, so we would have a fair chance of tracking him down before he got anywhere. Especially as the crows had been paying such keen attention to us. The carrion-feeders make large predators easy to follow in any woods. We certainly qualified, with the number of corpses we'd left in our wake.

Crows made tracking errant mechs easy, I recalled, having been freshly reminded of my summers with the little grandmother. Something about shiny bits of metal excites birds, and I was always able to rely on the crows to help me find where the old lady's mech had decided to hide. The elemental spirit had been bound long enough to develop quirks of personality, and it was prone to lying in wait in the oddest places while I chopped up a pile of wood, as if it didn't want to have to carry bundles of wood.

Mechs. That was the other piece of the puzzle, I decided. We had to wait until nightfall to slip out of camp. If I went off for a patrol during the day, especially without my steam suit, the captain would ask me why, and I would have trouble coming up with an excuse for why Ilya wasn't going on patrol with me. If I left at night, the captain would be asleep, and I would only have to deal with an enlisted soldier on watch duty, who wouldn't question a superior officer heading off on a patrol at night. He wouldn't even question my taking a horse or two with me.

In the meantime, I had to cover for Ilya's absence during drills, and I had an idea: The mech parts in the workshop were newly manufactured and unused, and I had the diary of the man who was hoping to train a fledgling wizard to use them. He had documented everything, including his musings on what kind of security protocols and binding enchantments would be best to ensure that the mechs stayed in the hands of the resistance rather than being expropriated by mercenaries or captured and reused by the Imperial Army. He'd already summoned and bound spirits to the elemental cages. The only thing he hadn't done was assemble the mechs.

A steam suit is very nearly a mech. With a little work on the internals, I could get Ilya's suit to come out onto the field with the rest of us, even if Ilya was temporarily absent. I just had to make sure the spirits would respond to my orders, and somewhere in the diary were the recognition passcodes I needed to get one of the spirits to respond to my orders.

And they did. The spirit in the first elemental cage I selected responded to my very first attempt at a passcode. It had been bound to recognize a treasonous little quatrain:

A blood-red dawn breaks over Roman soil,
The Dragon's son with us will come and rise,
A purple crown returned through blood and toil,
Let Koschei's greed stay in distant Tanais.

This poem was repeated several times in the little book. I guessed that the owner of the book was fond of reciting it from memory, making it a natural choice for a passcode. Fortunately, I did not have to speak loudly where some other imperial soldier might overhear and misunderstand my reasons for calling the emperor greedy; my first mumbled recitation worked just fine.

Getting the elemental spirit to respond was only the beginning. It turned out that linking the cage together with the mechanisms to control the suit was the easy part; I ended up cutting down to size a smaller metal skeleton that the elemental cage controlled directly, and stuffing that inside of the suit. I couldn't figure out how to put together finer controls to simulate fingers in time, so I just locked the hands in a permanent grasp on the poleaxe for drills. Vitold was very helpful, I wouldn't have gotten the rushed project done on time without his assistance.

When "Ilya" and I marched onto the field to join the rest of our squad in parade rest, Captain Egorov clucked his tongue at us. We were clumsy, he told us, and terribly shameful excuses for soldiers. Who had taught Ilya to hold a poleaxe like that? I should be ashamed of myself for letting such an incompetent soldier in my squad, and Ilya should be very deeply embarrassed.

Or was Ilya still drunk from last night? He knocked on the helmet belonging to "Ilya" loudly with his baton, asking the jury-rigged mech if it was regretting being woolly-headed from how much it had drunk on duty the other night.

At that moment, I realized a flaw in my plan: My replacement Ilya needed to be able to say "Yes, sir" and "No, sir." I recalled there was some trick to throwing your voice, which puppeteers do with their puppets and wished I had learned that particular charlatan's art instead of the more useless charlatan's art of reading tea leaves. It might work if "Ilya" bowed his head as if in shame. That was almost as good as a "yes, sir," and a mumbled response from a hungover soldier would be inaudible anyway above the noise of the boilers.

"Bow," I muttered, then kicked myself, realizing there was no way I could be heard above the boilers without raising my voice, at which point the captain would surely hear. The mech nonetheless obeyed my command in spite of its inaudibility.

When I looked back at the captain's face to gauge his reaction, I found something else to worry about.

There was a little piece of wood sticking out of the middle of the captain's forehead. His eyes were crossed as if trying to look at the feathered fins attached to it. There were four of them, triangular little fins, meant to guide it straight through the air. Red blood welled up around the edges as his head rolled lifelessly back, and his own steam suit began to tilt backward as the body inside it slumped.

We were under attack.

While Captain Egorov had been diligent in executing one duty—ensuring that his troops stayed sharp and ready for action—he'd neglected another. If we were all assembled together for exercises, nobody was posted to keep an eye out for the enemy. Perhaps he had assumed anybody trying to sneak up on us wouldn't attempt an attack when all the steam knights were suited up and ready for action. In either case, he had been negligent, and we were now facing the consequences of that negligence.

I heard a gasp from Gregor as if he had been about to shout something and then stopped himself. This reminded me I was, thanks to my entirely fictitious seniority of service, now the proud commander of our little detachment; I was supposed to give the orders, even if Gregor was more qualified to know what was going on.

I spoke the order I was supposed to give, struggling to keep my voice calm and level: "All knights, form line of battle."

The act of speaking clarified my own emotions. I went from empty shock straight to a burning sense of rage; my voice may have been calm, but my vision was tinged with red. This fury must have leaked through to the elemental spirit somehow because the mech charged straight toward the woods, steam engine whistling as it opened its throttle to full, breaking away from our line.

Squad Two either couldn't hear my order over the noise or didn't think it was meant for them. When they saw the brave steam knight charging past them toward their enemy, they took their cue from him, charging after it with patriotic shouting and a painfully loud clatter of pistols.

I hadn't addressed the regular infantry in my new command, but as experienced soldiers—something I was not—they'd already hastily taken cover and started returning fire into the woods. I say returning fire because the crossbow bolt that downed the captain had been followed by a volley of bullets, arrows, and other projectiles.

War arrows meant for easier prey rained continuously but harmlessly off my armor as the enemy arquebusiers reloaded. I stood in thought. We had two squads of steam knights, a platoon of regular infantry, one jury-rigged mech pretending to be a steam knight, and one imperial war mech that was leaning against the building, its boiler cold. Evidently, Captain Egorov hadn't intended for our drills to include it. My men had divided themselves into three groups, one group scattering like sparrows, a second charging in a berserk rage, and the last four steam knights, including myself, taking a line, the standard response to an ambush based on what Gregor had taught me.

The enemy's disposition was a little more organized. The enemy partisans were armed more uniformly than the dead defenders had been and were mostly in deliberate lines. Front and center were hardened mercenaries, alternating between arquebusiers and halberdiers in pairs. On either side, local rebels alternated between spears and arquebuses, and behind, there were archers, their arrows becoming less accurate as they fired through the rising black smoke. The arquebusiers fired a second volley and then dashed backward before kneeling to reload. The mercenary halberdiers walked back at a more deliberate pace, the flanking groups of partisans pulling to the sides, preparing to surround the heavily armored steam knights. Somewhere in the woods was the crossbow-wielding sharpshooter who'd downed the colonel, and I could see several mounted rebels shouting orders—officers, surely.

Overhead, the crows circled us all.

A bullet pinged off my helmet as the Wallachian arquebusiers fired a third volley, and someone spoke. Gregor, most likely, though in the moment I didn't recognize his voice. "Orders, sir? We have formed a line." The combination was enough to nudge me back to reality and to the fact that I needed to order the squad to do something. We couldn't just stand here taking fire while the rebels cut the other squad to pieces in the woods.

"Axes down," I said, trying to put the hard edge of command in my voice. "Get the cannons and load grape. Support Squad Two with close fire. I'll try to catch up and bring the other knights back here."

The fury kept welling within me. This wasn't fair. We hadn't even seen this coming. Squad Two couldn't even see the enemy halberds on the other side of the trees. The crows had seen it, and they hadn't given warning, eager for battle. My face grew hot and sweaty.

"Go ahead and eat your goddamn fill, carrion-feeders. They're dead already," I muttered under my breath, quietly but intensely, wishing heated words alone could kill as I waved at the birds. "Load and ready!"

We could at least keep Squad Two from being totally encircled, and if they could keep the enemy on the other side of their shields, they stood a chance at surviving long enough. Maybe it wasn't hopeless, I thought to myself as the men behind me dropped canvas bags into their cannons, each bag loaded with approximately half a pound of small metal balls. "Pick shots and fire, as seems best," I said and then started running forward.

Squad Two was already starting to scatter. The crows had come down to feast early and were divebombing both the steam knights and the rebel soldiers. The air was so thick with the carrion-feeders that it was hard to see. The crows weren't trying to divebomb me or my mechanical squad-mate, who was in the center of the great swirling flock, but everyone else seemed to be fair game.

Behind me, I could hear two shots, and then a third, followed by a string of shouted epithets. Gregor and Misha must have fired first, then Vitold. I hoped that the heavy armor of the steam suits would protect them from any misdirected fire; the grapeshot wasn't designed to pierce heavy armor.

The sharp crack of a rifle sounded from up ahead and to my right. A mounted rebel officer's hat flew into the air. Peering into the woods,

I spotted a familiar face in the distance—the redheaded sharpshooter that Ilya had befriended on the train ride. She was perched on a horse with a message tube tied to the saddle, her rifle gripped by the muzzle-end in one hand as she swung a soft mallet in the other, hammering down on the ramrod to force another ball down the barrel of her rifle. She was still wearing the purple crystal pendant I'd seen her take off a dead rebel during the looting. This seemed somehow important, though I didn't quite know why.

I felt a sharp pain in my abdomen and looked down. The back end of a crossbow bolt looked back up at me. It had gone through the steel plate like butter. The bolt must have been enchanted, I thought to myself. This seemed unfair, but I had trouble gathering the strength to be angry about the injustice of it. The world tilted, and I tried to concentrate. Everything went black.

INTERLUDE

A letter addressed to Boris Volkov, Izh District, Northeastern Sector

Dearest Father,

I hope you are in good health. I hope that you receive this letter soon. I hope the censors do not black out too much of it. I have seen five fields of battle since you waved me goodbye on the train south. I fought three of those battles. The others I only saw afterward. Your little girl is a real woman now. I have shot half a dozen of the enemy. Four of them were officers. It becomes a little easier each time.

I am told this makes me an ace. I am told I should expect a promotion if I return home. I hope I do return home. Please do not tell the neighbors I have been promoted already. I am not sure I will be promoted. Our general is infamous for his erratic temper and fear of disloyalty. I am not certain his memory is better than his temper. We have also been running out of reliable officers lately. I fear if the general does not remember, there will be no other officers left who will know to promote me.

I wish I could have written you after the first time I shot a man. This has been my first stop in a town with a good army post since we started tracking the enemy. I am sorry I did not write sooner. But I will tell you the story now of the first time I shot a man. He was not an officer. I do not think he was a real soldier. He had little curls on the ends of his mustache and a light brown cloak with yellow stitching around the edges. He was just running away from the battle. We were ordered to let nobody escape, and he was the fastest runner. I was surprised how quickly he fell down. I dreamed about him the next night.

Last night I dreamed I was shooting targets at the range. Every time I knocked one down, a crow flew out. It flew up to the trees and cawed at me. I wanted to shoot the crows, but I could not. It was a strange dream. We have seen many crows.

I have met many soldiers now. Some of them are brave and handsome. Others are ugly and cowards. There is a little chatty rat of a man among the steam knights who the general said has been in the service for a decade. I think he is only still around because he toadies up to his squad leader. How else does an ugly little cowardly rat a hand shorter than me stay a steam knight?

The rat and his squad leader are an odd pair. The leader is tall, while the rat is short. Skinny, not round. Creepy and cold, not chatty and overly friendly. I cannot understand half of what the leader says. The leader talks all fancy and uses lots of long words. Sometimes, I think they are not even real words. He mutters the eeriest sounding things under his breath. The rat speaks plain. I can also only understand half of what he says. He uses short words but is hard to understand because of his thick western accent. He is very vulgar and common.

I am in town trying to find one of the better soldiers from that squad named Ilya. He is kind and funny. He is not vulgar. He is not creepy and is not a coward. I am certain of it. He has gone missing. The little rat says Ilya deserted. I think Ilya has been captured by enemies. I will rescue him. I hope I make you proud.

With affection,
Your Daughter Katya

CHAPTER SEVEN

In Which I Suffer Durance Vile and Face Death

Four little beady eyes were looking down at me. With effort, I focused, my head throbbing, four beady little eyes condensing into two, framed by brown fur and a set of whiskers. Rodent, my memory informed me. I concentrated, trying to figure out more about the brown rodent. A rat. The rat was looking down at me from on top of a shelf, wondering if I was incapacitated enough to serve as a source of food. I did not think I was a suitable source of food and told the rat as much. But what was I? Who was I? I had a name, I sensed, and with the name would come more information.

A few moments passed in concentration. I was Mikolai Stepanovich, who had received an unfortunate promotion. Wait. Two unfortunate promotions. Three? From a grease monkey to a steam knight was a promotion of sorts, and I had been a squad leader. There had been a battle, and I had been in charge of it, so I must have been promoted again, in fact if not necessarily in name. I squinted upward. The rat had gone away during my moments of introspection.

Yes, there had been a battle. And I had . . . died? I thought about that for a moment. I remembered seeing a crossbow bolt, feeling the sharp pain in my abdomen. I hurt too much to be dead, though. I was hungry, and the stone floor was uncomfortable. Were the dead hungry? I sat up and discovered I was in a small room. My wrists and ankles felt heavy. Running my hands along my body, I felt bandages wrapped around my middle and heard the cold clink of metal as I shifted my hands. Manacles. Prodding at the bandages hurt, so I stopped, letting my arms fall back down with the clink of metal on stone. Doing nothing was the least painful thing I could do. I closed my eyes and focused on that task until the pain faded into blissful unconsciousness.

A face briefly appeared at the little grate in the door. The door opened a moment later, revealing a gaunt young woman with eyes full of rage. She had an imperial standard-issue entrenching tool tied to her belt, along with a knife and a pistol tucked in her waistband. She had half a loaf of bread and a tankard, which she carefully set on the floor beside the door. Then she spat on me, kicked me a couple of times, said something rude, and left, closing the door behind her with a slam.

I clutched my side in pain and digested the new influx of information. Given her accent, I was in Wallachia. Based on her choice of language, she had some reason to believe I was Ruthenian. Her specific choice of words indicated she believed that my parents were not married to each other. I thought about this for a minute. I was indeed Ruthenian, but I felt reasonably certain that my parents were married to each other. It took me a minute to remember them. My father's iron-colored hair, gray and flecked with rust. My mother's kindly but perpetually worried face.

Yes, definitely married to each other, and as I was not their oldest child, there was little doubt they had been already married when I was born. First children are sometimes born out of wedlock to scandal, but never a second child. Half of my brothers had started going bald, two were starting to go gray, and the other was at least married, and it stood to reason that they were probably all older than I was, even if I couldn't quite remember their names.

When I reached for the water, I found that the manacles about my wrists and ankles were chained together through a bolt in the opposite wall. I could barely reach it, the cold steel of the manacles cutting into my wrists painfully while I tickled the tankard into my grasp by my fingertips. I wondered if the girl had meant to place them out of my reach to torment me. The bread was fresh but coarse. The water had a slight acrid tang to it, but I found I was quite thirsty and drank every last drop of it, sucking greedily at the lip of the tankard.

Several hours and one snapped pin later, I had collected most of my wits, was hungry again, and had a new appreciation for Vitold's talents. He made picking locks seem a lot easier than it really was. I also had company again—an older gentleman with a pair of younger men who looked like they were as well suited to the front of the plow as the back of it. The oldster was wearing a silver pin with an amethyst set in it. He offered me a great big tankard of stale-tasting beer.

I foolishly gulped it down. It may have been flat and a bit sour, but I was hungry, thirsty, and tired. He asked me questions. It started innocuously, asking about how I was feeling, had my wound opened back up, things like that. From there, the topic drifted to my background: What was my name? My rank? What did I do when I wasn't busy burning Wallachian villages to the ground and murdering innocent civilians? The questions ranged from the practical to the accusatory.

I wish I could say I resisted interrogation proudly, but it wasn't until the left-hand, ox-like fellow menaced me with a fire poker to encourage a quicker answer that I even realized I was being interrogated by hostile enemies and that I was supposed to give them no answers at all. That sort of stoic heroism was beyond me. Up until then, it seemed like just a conversation, and it would have felt rude to sit there silently. After that point, manners deserted me in favor of trying to get them to stop hurting me.

"I asked how long you'd been apprenticed to the war mage Spitignov," said the old man. "Don't lie to me, boy! It was a mage hunter that brought you down; she told us you smelled like magic, and that's why she shot you. Both of your mechs halted in their tracks after that."

"Both?" I asked, extremely puzzled. Two mechs? I received another painful jab from the ox-like Wallachian's fire poker.

"Playing dumb, Mikolai? It doesn't suit you. We recovered one of them from the scene of the battle. Very cleverly put together; you'd think it was just another steam knight from the outside. You don't match any of the imperial wizards in our files, but I'm not ignorant. I know that the Imperial Army always pairs new wizards with old ones to show them the ropes in the field." The old man glared. "You must be Ognyan's apprentice. They've never assigned him one before that I know of."

"I didn't want to have anything to do with the war mage! Look, I'm just a soldier, he picked me to be part of his special force; I didn't have a choice," I told him.

"Call yourself 'just a soldier' again and Murgu will be unhappy," the old man told me, a gleam in his eye as he waved to his oxlike companion. I realized too late that I had just confirmed that General Ognyan Spitignov was operating a secret strike force in the area. The old man probably hadn't been sure of it before I'd told him, but had only been pretending to be sure that the general was my mentor in order to tease a less specific but more accurate piece of information out of me.

The interrogation continued; whenever I went off topic, Murgu poked me with the fire poker suggestively. If I said something they thought was a lie, Murgu would swing or jab, and that would hurt. The ordeal seemed to last forever, but it was probably only an hour or two, ending when my bandages started to ooze blood, my stomach wound having reopened in spite of the care Murgu took to aim his blows at my limbs. When it was over, I just lay curled up on the floor, crying.

I don't know how much time passed before the girl came back. She didn't say anything this time, just snorted contemptuously before depositing my meal by the door. And so, the pattern began again, repeated for several days. The girl would bring bread and water and take away my chamber pot; sometimes, though not always, she spat on me, kicked me, or insulted me. The old man would come and ask me questions, accompanied by his brutish bookends. Some of the questions were the same, some were different.

They wanted to know what made my comrades tick, what I knew about the general, what tactical doctrines we were trained in, how much coal our machines required for daily operations, and so on. Sometimes, I tried to hold out. Sometimes, I just made up answers to questions I didn't know how to answer.

I wasn't sure how they knew some things, but then I remembered the visit to town and the amethyst pendant that one girl in town had been wearing. A chain of memories and logic clicked together. Before I was shot, I'd seen the red-haired sharpshooter, and she still had the amethyst pendant she'd pulled off a dead rebel. This, in turn, meant that Ilya hadn't won it off her at cards.

This meant that there were two identical pendants to start with, suggesting that the pendant worn by the girl in town wasn't a present from Ilya. It was something that the girl in town had been wearing all along. Finally, the old man had a pin that looked much like those pendants, a brooch set with a polished amethyst. One amethyst was happenstance; two was coincidence; a third was enemy action, a pattern suggesting a common tie between the old rebel, the dead rebel, and the girl in town.

The girl was a rebel as well. Ilya, then, was their other source of knowledge. His desertion had been engineered by the rebels, via contact with the girl in town, and they had gotten information from him either during his overnight stay in town or subsequent to his desertion.

"I should just kill you, Ruthenian," the girl said in a conversational tone. "Yes, I think I will kill you."

I'd been in my little cell for about a week if I could rely on the cycle of meals to give me clues to the time, maybe a few days longer or shorter. The girl who brought me food and took away my chamber pot had never spoken in a civil tone before; she growled, snarled, cursed, and shouted at me in a varied assortment of rude and hostile ways. This was not the first time she'd expressed murderous intentions, but expressing them in a calm and polite tone sent chills down my spine. That, and the way that she held a drawn pistol, handling it thoughtfully. Perhaps it was that which caused me to shiver; it was a new sign of sincerity every bit as alarming as her change in attitude.

"Wouldn't the old man be disappointed if you shot me?" I asked. "He seems to love talking to me." If I could keep her talking, I thought to myself, maybe she would change her mind.

"I'd be doing the captain a favor if I shot you," she said. "We can't let you go, and keeping you around as a prisoner costs us time, money, and bread. None of those are cheap."

I thought she was entirely too young to murder someone in cold blood. "I'm helpless here. Chained to the wall. Are you sure you want to become a murderer? What would your parents think of that?"

Her eyes bored into me like drill bits. "They're dead."

"I'm sorry—" I said, but she interrupted me.

"You lot killed them. Them, my grandmother, my sister, my brother, everyone in the whole village." She pointed the pistol directly at me and continued: "It was a massacre. We weren't even armed. The soldiers brought us all to the village common, and this maniac started chopping off our heads one at a time. Then when we tried to run, the soldiers blocked us in and butchered the rest of us like cattle. The only reason I lived is by playing dead, and I was half suffocated by the time I finished digging myself out of a pile of bloody corpses."

An image flashed up from my memory, involuntarily. I saw in my mind's eye General Spitignov holding his bloody sword high over a little old lady, in the middle of the village square. The square was already spattered with blood, as was the general's right boot.

"I'm sorry—" I started again, but she would not let me finish.

"But you weren't the maniac who chopped my grandmother's head off, so I should let you off the hook? You weren't even there, you never heard of such a thing, so you're innocent? Is that what you're going to say? No. You're all murderers just the same, whether you're the horrid emperor, that giant maniac, or just wear his bloody uniform with the rest of them." She paused to take a breath and aim, her expression settling back down from anger to calm resolve.

"I'm the one who gave you that shovel," I said, quietly, looking down at the entrenching tool hanging from her belt and then back up into her eyes.

Her finger trembled on the trigger. She inhaled, her finger sliding over the trigger. Exhaled. Inhaled. Then she turned and ran away, making a strangled sound of some kind.

For the next several hours, I worried that she would come back with a new resolve to kill me; but she did not return at all. As my attention was fixed on the doorway, the thunderous roar of the explosion behind me took me by complete surprise.

CHAPTER EIGHT

In Which I Am Shocked

The loud boom behind me was accompanied by a wave of heat and debris. Then a beam from the ceiling fell inward, landing on top of the fragments of wall and myself, hammering me into the stone floor with a force that wasn't quite hard enough to end my pain permanently.

I tried to gather my thoughts but felt a sudden jolt from my manacles. Were they enchanted? I opened my mouth to curse in rage and fury, but then there was another jolt from my manacles. And now they felt even heavier. Underneath my shirt, my good-luck charm felt icy cold against my chest. Had I run out of luck? Was I dying?

I could hear gunshots, hoofbeats, and shouting. Someone lifted the beam off me, then pulled me loose from the debris. They said something, but my ears were ringing and my eyes unfocused. Then they shook me again, and their shouting started to make sense.

"Where is Ilya?" A blur resolved into the redheaded sharpshooter. What was her name? She continued. "Ilya! You must know where he is!" She shook me harder.

A voice spoke, deep and emotionless. "Ilya is dead," the voice said. I couldn't place it, but it sounded familiar. It was a little like my father's, only with less warmth, more depth, and a sense of distance. My manacles let loose another jolt and grew heavier yet. The statement made sense, in light of the misunderstandings the rebels had about me. If they had Ilya to question as well, willing or not, their questions should have been shaped by his responses. They would have had different questions to ask as they compared Ilya's answers to mine.

The sharpshooter let go of me, and I fell back to the ground face-first, weighted down by my manacles. "You lie!" she said, and her boots stepped out of my field of view. I heard her voice calling Ilya's name, growing fainter with each repetition.

"Please," I said to the floor in front of my face, "come back and get me out of these manacles. Don't leave me here."

Neither the floor nor the sharpshooter seemed to take notice, but a minute later I heard Vitold's voice. "Wake up, Mikolai, let's get you out of here."

"I can't move," I said, groaning. "The manacles are too heavy." I experimentally tried to shift one. It felt like I was trying to lift a cow.

"Nonsense," Vitold said. He picked one of my arms off the ground, shook it, and then let go. It crashed back down to the ground, the weight of the manacle overwhelming the feeble force of my resistance. "Hm. I guess I better get them off you, though. You must be weak as a kitten." A few moments of fiddling and a few muttered curses about fancy locks later, the weight was gone, and I felt a rush of energy.

Vitold helped me to my feet. I toed the pieces of runed metal on the ground experimentally. They shifted easily. Either they had changed weight, or I had gained strength.

"Come on, Mikolai, we have got to get out of here. The rest of them could come back at any moment." Vitold seemed impatient.

Looking around, I could see that I had been in a small wooden house. One wall and half of the ceiling had collapsed entirely in the explosion. Two horses stood next to the wall. The old man and Murgu were lying on the ground in pools of blood. An inert imperial steam knight suit was lying in the debris, access panels open to reveal the machinery inside. I could still hear the redheaded sharpshooter's voice calling Ilya's name.

I wobbled toward the horses. With a little difficulty, we managed to get on a horse; that is to say, I managed to climb up behind Vitold with his help. The redheaded woman returned and mounted the other horse.

"He's not here," she told us. "I looked under the beds and in the cupboards. They must have taken him to another place to hold him. We ride now!"

This, I dimly perceived, was an order with some haste behind it, as I could hear voices shouting in Romanian from the woods. We were going to have company if we lingered any longer. Vitold leaned forward to urge the horse on, and as the horse accelerated forward, I slid bonelessly off its back, crunching to the ground with the grace of paralytic exhaustion. I may have had some of my energy back, but after my time confined to a cell with only water and a little bread to eat, I was not particularly strong, and my reflexes were diminished.

Ahead, I could see Vitold look back and slow his horse. The returning rebels would catch him if he turned around now. This would not do. But there was the "Ilya" mech, not more than ten yards from me. If only it were turned on. I stared at it longingly, and it burst into life, boiler bursting into full steam from a cold start. The access panels closed, and the mech turned to face me.

I commanded it to come get me as Vitold fought to turn his horse around, and it thundered into motion, scooping me off the ground like a shepherd would with a lamed lamb. The sharpshooter looked pleased and pulled her horse to a halt, slowing to let the mech catch up. I could hear her congratulating Ilya for retrieving valuable equipment and heroically rescuing me, and berating Vitold for saying that Ilya had deserted.

When Vitold started to say "But Katya—", she told him to shut up and that she recognized Ilya's armor.

Katya. That was her name. I made a mental note to myself. The mech helped me down into a standing position. I had a clear head and my feet beneath me, and I decided to clear up the confusion.

"Open your helmet," I told the mech built from Ilya's armor. The helmet popped open, revealing an empty space above the elemental cage, and Katya's mouth dropped open.

"The real Ilya walked off while on a night watch. The rebels had contact with him, and it seems to have been their agent in the town who enticed him to desert. Rationally speaking, he is most likely either dead or cooperating with insurgent forces." Probably dead, I thought to myself, remembering what the cold voice had said.

Katya's saddened face looked like that of a child whose puppy had been trampled to a pulp under the hooves of the horses pulling a nobleman's carriage. I took pity on her, holding up a hand while I tried to think of something to say that would be honest and ease her pain. "I'll promise you this, Katya. If you're right, and Ilya is simply held somewhere, and we find out where, I will help you rescue him, just as you and Vitold rescued me."

A deep, cold voice continued, loud and resonant in my ears. "However, Ilya is dead. When he walked out into the woods, he did so in the dark of night with no decent woodcraft at his disposal. He didn't even make his rendezvous with his rebel lover, but died alone, lost in the woods."

I felt certain that the voice spoke truth, but as I looked around us in the woods, I saw no one else—only me, Vitold, and Katya.

Who had spoken?

It had grown dark, and the mech was low on fuel when we saw an abandoned hut, so we decided to stop to rest. Katya was sulking and refusing to talk to me, so it fell on Vitold to fill me in on what had happened after I got shot with an enchanted crossbow bolt. First, he started a fire and made tea, and then he began his account.

Katya's timely arrival had put fear into the hearts of the rebels, who must have assumed she was the vanguard of a larger force. They'd retreated cautiously but in good order, taking their wounded with them, along with me and the captured mech. My squad had one additional casualty: Gregor Petrovich had suffered a heart attack. He was still gasping for breath when they popped his helmet off, but he died shortly afterward. The rebels' claim that shooting me had stopped two mechs in their tracks made sense now.

Neither of the other members of my squad had been shot through their heavy steam knight armor, but the regular infantry weren't so fortunate. Half of them died during or soon after the battle, including their sergeant; half the remainder were injured, two quite severely. One had lost a leg and another had blown his hand off while trying to reload the platoon's volley gun.

Steam Knight Squad Two, who had charged into the midst of the rebel force in the wake of my jury-rigged mech and then been scattered by the angry crows, died to a man. Most from bullets fired at close enough range to pierce through the weaker parts of their armor. One was killed by an enchanted armor-piercing crossbow bolt like the one that had nearly killed me, and another from an exploding boiler. His one working safety valve had been jammed by a divebombing crow, a freakish consequence of the birds' unnatural behavior combined with a lack of proper maintenance of his equipment.

Katya had orders for Captain Egorov bearing the general's seal. Given that Captain Egorov was clearly unable to receive them, she'd consented to have them opened and read by the corporal of the regular infantry squad, who claimed to be the ranking survivor and therefore in charge.

Unfortunately, they were written in some kind of code and were therefore of little use.

Katya immediately went about organizing a rescue mission for Ilya. Vitold had been unable to convince her that Ilya had deserted but was able to convince her to go to town to search for clues. The two of them went back into town in civilian clothes, leaving Misha and half a dozen injured soldiers to watch over the rebel base.

They did manage to find the establishment of ill repute at which Ilya had met his charming rebel girlfriend. Katya, with all the subtlety of an ox let loose in a shop of laboratory glassware, walked straight in, asked to see the proprietor, and then asked him, point blank, where the rebels were keeping the "handsome Ruthenian prisoner."

The proprietor started, looked down at her chest for a long moment, then back up at her, and told her that the Ruthenian prisoner was being kept in Doctor Onofrei's old cabin, and would she keep her voice down? People could overhear.

At this point in his story, Vitold chuckled and said that he didn't think a good glance at Katya's breasts was worth betraying your comrades. Besides, didn't a man in his occupation have ready access to better ones? The house of ill repute had been quite well staffed.

Katya gave him an angry glare, and I looked over at Katya's chest to see what Vitold was talking about, after which she gave me a glare as well. She was still wearing the necklace. While I wasn't sure I agreed with Vitold's assessment of Katya's more permanent features in the area of her chest, it seemed rude to comment openly on them, so I didn't. Instead, I commented on a temporary feature that seemed important.

"Katya," I said, pointing at the necklace, "were you wearing that necklace when you visited the town?"

She nodded.

"Ah, I see," I said. "He thought you were a rebel because of the necklace."

Katya stopped, put down her teacup, and began to fiddle with the catch of the necklace to take it off, a look of disgust on her face.

"Wait. Don't throw it away. It may be useful, and a good patriotic soldier never throws away a useful tool. Besides, it sets off your eyes nicely," I added hastily.

I'm not sure if it was the appeal to patriotism, the compliment, or simply the fact that I was giving her orders as if I knew what I was doing, but that did the trick. She picked her teacup back up, took a sip, and then nodded. The disgust on her face had cleared away, replaced by a steady lack of any emotion.

Vitold rushed through the rest of the story quickly—figuring out the location of the cabin, getting explosives, and then planning the attack. Mentally, I added up days, and estimated I had spent ten days in captivity.

In the morning, we rigged up a sling for the mech, carrying it between the two horses while the rest of us walked; it was nearly out of fuel. While we nearly encountered rebels in the woods, it was very easy to tell when they were coming, and we simply hid until they passed. With the mech's boiler quiet, the signs were clear as day—to me, anyway. Vitold (being a city boy) was clueless, and while Katya as a woods-wise sharp-shooter surely noticed, she kept quiet, preferring not to talk to me at all if she could avoid it.

We returned to find the base still in imperial hands. The small number of soldiers still occupying it hadn't even made any attempt at keeping a watch; Vitold and I had to go looking from building to building. The corporal seemed shocked to see me.

Misha was nowhere to be found. When I remarked on this fact, the corporal informed me that Misha had gone off to town to fetch supplies, leaving his steam suit behind. Satisfied with this explanation, I told the corporal he should probably arrange for someone to keep watch, and then I retreated to the workshop.

It turned out that Vitold had, on his own initiative, started working on duplicating my work on Gregor's suit and his own suit. Vitold wasn't keen on going into battle in a giant metal target and thought it might be better if he just made himself scarce when battle came around.

The job was only partially complete and he couldn't seem to get any-where with the elemental spirits, but how could I say no to my comrade wanting to stay out of trouble? So, I set to work unlocking two more elemental cages and rigging steam knight suits into mechs.

After a few days of frenzied work, during which I didn't leave the work-shop for more than a minute at a time, Katya showed up one afternoon with a pot of tea. When I asked her what brought her over, she asked me if I would do a reading for her. Evidently, word that I could read tea leaves had gotten around, and Katya was bored enough to ask me to perform parlor tricks for her amusement.

She looked uncomfortable inside the workshop. After a minute, I remembered I had been working nearly nonstop for several days and probably smelled like an old sock.

"Let's go outside for some fresh air and good light, then. It's time I took the boys here out for a walk." I waved at the trio of steam knight armor suits. It was past time to test how good their leg controls were; I'd had to jury-rig the hip joints, so I was a bit worried about their stability.

We went out the back of the complex, where there was a target range large enough to allow the mechs to walk through their paces. We sat, sipped tea, and talked about Katya's life. That is to say that, when Katya asked me shyly if I would read the tea leaves for her, I stalled by asking her a leading question or two and let her do the talking.

She had grown up in a small town near the river Izh, a northeastern tributary of the great eastern Kama River, one of the three great rivers of the Golden Empire. Two great rivers, arguably—the Kama and the Slavutich— were greater than the Tanais, though the imperial capital that gave its name to the river had given it a presence greater than its size. The vast length of the Kama and its dazzling array of tributaries were less important than the central jewel of Koschei's Golden Empire, the city the emperor dubbed a third Rome when he married the princess from Trebizond.

But that is a story I am sure you all know well, and I was telling you Katya's story. She grew up as the younger child of her father's second wife, just five years older than her oldest nephew and her father's third wife's eldest son. Both of those younger boys regularly received new outfits and toys, with hardly ever a hand-me-down, and their birthdays were always celebrated and never forgotten.

Katya had volunteered for the army out of a sense of patriotism and desire for glory, hoping to distinguish herself against the sultan's soldiers in Wallachia. She was promptly shipped the whole length of the empire to a garrison unit in the small town of Muzga, near the Lithuanian border. For the duration of the war against the Sultanate, she was equally far from her home and from glory, but she trained diligently.

And that is all that I can say, for at that moment, I heard distant noises. Katya's voice blended into a relaxing but meaningless babble as I tuned her voice out and concentrated, bringing the distant noises into focus: the rumble of boilers, the steady beats of hooves and boots, and voices, most of them speaking Slavonic. "Katya, do you hear that?" I asked, cutting into her monologue.

She looked annoyed, then stopped, cocking her head to the side. "I do hear it! Mechs, somewhere near. The general must be back!" Tea leaves forgotten, she dashed off, and I followed behind her. If the general had returned, then I should be there to greet him.

CHAPTER NINE

In Which I Lie and Steal

General Ognyan Spitignov. These three words strike fear in the hearts of the Golden Empire's enemies, as well as the hearts of many imperial subjects, including me. This was in spite of the fact that I had been expecting (even at a few dark points, hoping) to see him.

As Katya and I came around the building, followed by my three modified steam suits, the general was talking with a corporal, the senior-most survivor of the infantry platoon. The corporal's voice had a pleading quality to it. Vitold was sitting on a rock nearby, looking pensive, along with the other five members of our little impromptu garrison. Colonel Romanov was standing next to his horse and looked like he had a headache. The strike force had a few new faces but was on the whole smaller.

"General, while my squad has suffered heavily, I have suffered no deserters under my command. Mikolai, on the other hand, well, two of his squad members deserted, and another died from terror at the battle." The corporal's voice wobbled a little bit.

The general looked over past the squad leader's shoulder, and right at me. His face twisted into a caricature of fury, and he exploded into a blur of violent action. I was terrified and didn't know what to say, so I took a step back. I could feel the heat of a trio of steam boilers behind me.

The corporal's head rolled next to my leg. The mouth was still moving, and his eyes were wide with horror. I took another squeamish step to the side. The general spoke softly as he wiped the blood off his sword lovingly with a silk kerchief.

It was easy enough to hear him, the only other sound the rumbling of steam boilers behind me.

"Lying traitor thinks I'm stupid. I can count to five. One here and one there and three more is five. And five is the number in a full squad of steam knights. Five and two and one is eight, and that is more than a full squad. I can add, I can." His eyes narrowed, and he looked directly at me, speaking at a volume that made it clear he was now talking to me.

"I am disappointed that you suffered the traitor to live. You are a ten-year man and should see the signs, but failing to discover and execute a traitor I can forgive today." He shook his head somberly.

"If I executed everybody who didn't execute a traitor . . ." The general trailed off into silence. His eyes briefly crossed as he sank deep into thought.

I think he was trying to work out what would happen if he executed everybody who failed to find and execute any traitors they had contact with, but after about five seconds of thought, he shook his head as if to clear it and wandered off toward the mess hall. Colonel Romanov trailed at a discreet distance, and the newly arrived troops began the process of settling in.

Katya chewed on her lip. Looked at me. Looked at the retreating general and colonel. Looked at the dead body on the ground. She looked a little uncertain.

"Vitold? Katya? I'm sure that the colonel has more questions about what's happened. Why don't the two of you fill him in on the rescue mission, our findings so far about the resistance, and talk to him about the general's misapprehensions?" I turned toward the handful of survivors from the infantry platoon. "We have a few things to talk about."

It turned out that Misha had departed immediately after Katya and Vitold left to rescue me, telling the others that he wasn't going to stick around this hole to see if they succeeded and brought back a man-witch or failed and brought back rebel retaliation.

I explained as best as I could that it would probably be a good idea to just avoid talking about anything that had happened while we were separated from the rest of the strike force and let sleeping dogs lie. If the general had some delusions, they ought to leave those alone and let me handle it, since he seemed to be inexplicably fond of me. I had no more ill intentions toward them than they did me, and I really hadn't intended to get the corporal in trouble. He had gotten himself into his own little mess by trying to blame me.

As I was explaining this, I thought I felt a weight settle on one shoulder. I turned to look, and there was a great big raven looking back at me. I shooed it away and asked the soldiers if they had any questions. They shook their heads as one, their eyes wide.

I supposed it was surprising to them that one of their supposed superiors would admit openly that another one of their superiors was stark-raving mad.

When Vitold caught back up with me, he filled me in on how his little debriefing session with Colonel Romanov had gone, and it filled me with a sense of dread. Vitold had lied extensively to cover up everything. Katya had apparently mumbled a few things about Ilya and became a little more animated talking about the battles, but mostly let Vitold do the talking.

According to Vitold, the colonel was now under the impression that I had taken my newer steam knights, shaken them up, and forged them into an elite brotherhood, sworn to silence, obedience, chastity, temperance, faith, poverty, and a rigorous training regime that required they sleep inside their armor. Vitold had supposedly gone through this routine with me before, but Ilya, Misha, and Yosef had not and were secluding themselves from outside distractions as much as possible.

Yosef was the man who'd replaced Gregor Petrovich after Gregor's unfortunate heart attack. I wasn't sure if he'd borrowed the name from one of the deceased soldiers in the other steam knight squad or invented it out of whole cloth, and I didn't ask. In addition to burdening me with the lies he'd told the colonel, Vitold brought me some useful information—news from the colonel.

All of us would be leaving the next morning, after setting charges to demolish the complex. It was not especially large or defensible, and now that the rebels knew we had taken it over, its limited utility had come to an end. Vitold and I were of one mind as to what that meant: We needed to clear out all the valuable tools and bits of machinery from the rebels' well-equipped workshop. Army-issue tools were just not nearly as well made as these.

Major Alexei Pavlov was nobly born, a chaplain and, by his insignia, a certified alchemist, though his talents as a wizard seemed quite limited. In the time I knew him, he never achieved anything more miraculous than the transmutation of vodka into dilute uric acid, a feat I have seen replicated by many other soldiers of lesser distinction.

Prior to Vitold's fabrication of vows for a holy order of steam knights, Alexei had not been assigned any troops at all, giving him a ready excuse for skipping Colonel Romanov's regular meetings. I hesitate to speculate about the colonel's motives, but after the colonel formally assigned my squad to the chaplain's command, Alexei suddenly found that he was required to attend meetings instead of communing with the sort of holy spirits one finds in the bottom of a bottle.

Fortunately for me, he was profoundly disinterested in getting to know the soldiers under his command, and it would have been difficult for him to care less about our readiness or the state of our equipment. Vitold and I wasted a considerable amount of time practicing speaking in funny voices so that we would be ready to try to fool Father Pavlov. We were worried that as a priest, he might consider himself to have the authority to release a knight from a vow of silence in order to talk with him.

In fact, I would not be sure that he knew the alleged vows at all except for what happened the night before we left the border fort.

That night, vodka was flowing freely in the room that had become the officers' lounge, in celebration of news fresh from the imperial capital: Our fearless leader, the great war mage, General Ognyan Spitignov, was being promoted from brigadier general to major general. The celebrant himself was nowhere to be seen at the occasion, fortunately; but his little friend Ivan Ivanovich Romanov was happy enough to throw a party on his behalf.

The small, weasel-faced senior colonel kicked things off by personally handing out a dozen bottles of vodka to the top-ranked officers. Alexei popped off the top of his bottle, drank directly from it, briefly gestured my way with the bottle, then said he would need to take a second drink on my behalf due to my monastic vows. I might have protested, but the room was crowded and noisy, and I wanted my wits about me.

If the general was being promoted, then perhaps there would be a chance of reassignment while things were getting reorganized. I accepted a proffered glass of rough plum brandy from a grizzled-looking Cimmerian captain and listened carefully. Mail moves no faster than the man carrying it. If mail from Tanais had arrived accompanied by fresh-faced officers, it stood to reason those officers were also fresh from the capital.

On the other side of the room, a young-looking lieutenant colonel with sandy hair was gesturing dramatically. I focused on his voice.

"And the very next morning I saw a ship headed straight in, sails tattered from the storm. I swear, I saw it crash into the pier with my very own eyes. It was the *Ceres*, back from Trebizond. The only man still aboard was the helmsman, dead and lashed to the wheel. The prince was gone—swept away by the storm, they say. The sultan's silver was still packed in chests in the hold." The lieutenant colonel lowered his voice to a whisper. "Luckily, the treaty still holds. My cousin says the emperor didn't care about getting Prince Vlad as a hostage of his own half as much as the silver. The whole point about the prince was just making sure the sultan wouldn't try to use him as a puppet."

As I strained to listen to a voice that was getting quieter and quieter, I noticed someone else was speaking very quietly, barely above a whisper, only halfway across the room. Another senior colonel was talking with Colonel Romanov, looking taller and uglier but otherwise quite similar. They could be cousins, I decided, focusing my attention on the pair of colonels as I took a tiny sip of plum brandy, ignoring the loud laughter of the Cimmerian captain next to me.

They were discussing a different ship, one that had arrived in Fiume. This ship, with firebox-powered paddlewheels and a hull clad in the famous Corsican brass, could be nothing other than a French ship of the line. It had carried a treasure far more precious than the silver Emperor Koschei had received from the sultan: The younger daughter of Leon I, Emperor in Paris, High King over Loegria, Lord of the Seven Great Isles, Protector of Jerusalem and Cyprus, or, in this particular conversation, "Leon the Usurper."

"The emperor is convinced King Janos will launch an invasion right after the wedding," the unfamiliar senior colonel said. "It is said the princess's honor guard is an entire regiment, veterans of the Loegrian campaign, and rumor has it that her dowry included a thousand more new model muskets for the king's own troops. The general's sealed orders are to strike over the border, so make sure the division is well supplied when it goes out, Ivan."

The more familiar senior colonel rubbed his forehead and sighed. "Thank you, Dmitri."

The Cimmerian captain elbowed me in the ribs, and I shook my head, losing track of the senior colonels' conversation.

"Your drink, you want more?" The man was already pouring, making it impolite to answer in the negative.

My first thought had been that if we took apart our steam suits for a full maintenance cycle, Vitold and I might be able to avoid General Spitignov's next forward deployment. However, I couldn't figure out how to avoid revealing the mechanical nature of the other three steam knights in my squad. If we took those suits apart as well, it would be obvious nobody was inside; but if I didn't, the mechs would have to accompany the force without my guidance. The ruse would be up by the end of the first day's travel toward Avaria.

Unfortunately, Wallachian gossip moved considerably faster than an army hauling mechs, steam suits, and many carts laden with fuel. The Magyars sensibly assumed that a division on the move toward the border was likelier to be an attack than a training exercise. Their scouts began harassing us as soon as we began our trek into Avaria. Felled trees and rockfalls blocked the road regularly, bridges were washed out or blown up, and it took a long time to cross what had looked like a short distance through the Sarmatian mountains on a map. Our own scouts didn't always come back from patrol, and sometimes I heard the distant crack of a rifle in the forest.

Days stretched into agonizing weeks. We left some empty fuel carts behind, filled others with wood, stopped for three days to make charcoal, and pushed on with only an emergency supply of proper anthracite coal for real battles. Half of the division's scouts had died or deserted by the time they began to report seeing an enemy army, a force with heavy muskets and light mechs. With a target in sight, General Spitignov pushed us hard.

On the third day, as daylight turned to evening, I could see a flock of starlings swirling irregularly in the air. I looked up at the sky, watching the starlings fly closer and then hesitate, swirling with collective curiosity on the far side of the long, low hill overlooking the road. Somewhere on the other side of that ridge were enough shiny objects to engage the starlings' collective curiosity. Somewhere in these hills was a Magyar army with muskets and mechs. I put the two facts together and panicked.

"We need to load coal and suit up," I shouted, waving the oxen pulling our squad's heavy cart to a halt. "Quickly. The enemy isn't ahead of us. They're on the far side of that ridge."

My authority to give that order was questionable, at least as far as anyone other than Vitold was concerned, but the arguing stopped with a crack of thunder and a cloud of smoke that emerged from a row of innocent-looking bushes only two hundred yards away.

CHAPTER TEN

In Which I Educate the Ignorant

The enemy musketeers fired again, almost synchronized, the deep crack of their heavy arquebuses mixed with the staccato pinging of the bullets ricocheting off my armor.

"Charge!" I shouted the order aloud for Vitold's benefit. I didn't need to verbalize to get our trio of mechanical comrades to rush forward, straight at the enemy soldiers; contrary to my training, it seemed that mechs could understand unspoken orders as readily as spoken ones. At least, the ones I had built with Wallachian parts could; perhaps the imperial manuals were correct and our technology was simply not as advanced.

Steam hissed sharply over the rumbling sound of the boilers as the enemy soldiers broke into a retreat, scattering as they made their way up and over a long, low hill. They were still holding their guns, though, making it an orderly retreat rather than a rout. As we crested the hill, we saw the bulk of the enemy force lying in wait. Somewhere behind us, our own army was lurching into action.

The musketeers who had baited us were already stopped, catching their breath and working on reloading behind a line of pikemen. To one side of the formation, technicians were stoking the furnaces of a pair of mechs, the boilers having been on a low standby to avoid telltale columns of smoke. To my right, toward the head of the column, I could see more formations of enemy soldiers.

If I hadn't known there were more enemies on the blind side of the hill, I would have hesitated as they came into view, and we would have been in trouble. Charging straight in, we had momentum and speed on our side. My mechanical comrades charged with me, aiming straight for the enemy mechs. The first enemy mech had barely finished standing when my jury-rigged mechs smashed into it, bowling it over before it reached full steam and pounding it mercilessly.

The second enemy mech waded into the fray with a murderous hiss of steam. One mighty blow put the pick end of its warhammer in the back of one of my mechs, a blow that would have been instantly lethal to a human steam knight. Vitold and I closed shields together with our mechs, ringing the surviving enemy mech in a semicircle. It would not be able to survive long under the concentrated attentions of our own picks.

Through the thunder of the enemy musket fire, I heard a loud cracking sound behind us, the distinctive report of Katya's heavy rifle. Moments later, I was smashing my pick through the second enemy mech's boiler, the specialized armor-piercing weapon cracking it open with a blast of pressurized steam and water. As it fell, crows swirled around us hungrily, as if the mechanical device's watery lifeblood were actual blood.

When Katya's rifle cracked again, an officer's hat lifted off his head, and the enemy broke in a full rout, abandoning their weapons and in many cases holding cloaks over their heads to shield them from vicious birds that seemed to have decided they didn't want to wait until afterward to scavenge the battlefield. I took quick stock of the situation. I'd need to quickly patch the hole in the back of my damaged mech if I wanted to keep up the fiction that there was a human inside there, and one of the other steam suits was down on the ground. To either side of us, the battle raged.

On some level, I felt certain that two of my mechs were still standing, able and ready to respond to orders; by process of elimination, that meant Vitold, wearing the suit that had formerly belonged to Misha, was in the downed suit. Concerned, I rushed to his prone form, batting away the crows that were already starting to investigate the possible food source.

"Go away," I told the crows, and they did, mostly, except for a few who landed nearby to peck at the dead bodies of those who had been my enemies. Vitold's suit had been pierced in the thinner rear armor. Blood dripped out of the hole. By the sound of his cursing, I could tell he was still alive, but in serious pain. Ordinarily, Vitold could blaspheme pretty creatively, but he was mostly just repeating himself.

I surveyed the scene. There was an enemy officer lying on the ground with a hole in his forehead and a matching hole in his fancy hat, lying ten feet away from where he had crested the hill. That must have been Katya's doing; several other unfortunates had been shot in the back by their own comrades in the confusion, understandable given the volume of fire they'd directed toward us, but he'd been shot from the front, and I thought I recalled seeing the hat take to the air before the enemy broke into panic.

The main enemy force scattered into the woods piecemeal as the general and his mechs broke into their lines. Vitold survived to see medical treatment, and we pieced together what had happened: Katya had accidentally shot him in the backside with her powerful rifle. She said she had been aiming for an enemy and slipped. Fortunately, Vitold had only suffered a flesh wound, and not even that bad of one after the bullet had been slowed down by the armor.

Vitold seemed very put out that his armor couldn't stop a bullet. He said he'd improved it specially, but when I pressed for details he gave a quick distrustful look at Katya and clammed up. We would have to talk about it later when Katya wasn't around. It had been a rough several weeks marching around occupied Wallachia with General Spitignov, and this battle had been particularly hard. Our enemies had been ready for us. They were prepared at what they felt was the best site to turn and fight and were well rested, while we had arrived at the site after a long day of forced marching.

The next night, Katya was off on patrol and Vitold was well enough to show me what he'd done to his armor. There had been several crates of high-grade parts intended for use in wizard armor stored piecemeal in crates in the rebels' workshop among the valuable supplies Vitold and I had made a point of looting. Vitold had replaced the steam boiler with an arcane engine so he could be sure he wouldn't die in a burst of steam. Then he'd installed plates with arcane designs inlaid in orichalcum to try to make his steam suit protect him as well as wizard armor.

After all, wizard armor was specially designed to funnel magic to protect the wearer, right? And he'd even switched out the steam boiler for an arcane engine, lightning-fused actuators replacing the steam pistons. But look what it got him! That rifle bullet should have been no match for steam suit armor reinforced with protective magic; war mages like General Spitignov were bulletproof as far as small arms were concerned, and steam knights nearly were. Maybe he hadn't installed it correctly?

I sighed. Poor Vitold, putting his faith in the goods we'd looted from the rebels and a crude education on the facts of military hardware. We'd had a cursory lesson or two on how to service wizard armor, in case we were ever in a position to assist one of the empire's most prized human assets, but mechanic training hadn't exactly emphasized the theory behind their operation. I started up the arcane engine with the suit's access plate open, testing the connections.

"Let me show you, Vitold. You weren't doing anything wrong. You've done a lovely job, but see here? These inlays? They're not active," I said. "If they were, they'd be glowing. You have to get a wizard to activate them. You don't have any special gifts, do you?"

Vitold informed me he was heir to many special gifts, like nimble fingers and a knack for manipulating small mechanisms, such as locks.

"Um. I meant a sort of magical gift." I gave Vitold a measured look. Was he hiding the potential to be a wizard? Stranger things had happened, though Vitold looked uncomfortable with the idea he might be gifted with arcane powers. He was curious enough to ask how such things were done, though, and I tried my best to oblige.

"To invoke the enchantment, you would touch the runes, like this, and concentrate. Maybe recite some sort of mumbo-jumbo that they teach you in wizard school, I don't know," I said.

I then demonstrated by mumbling the first arcane-sounding thing that came to my mind as I stared down at the runes, which was really just reading them aloud. They had names, and the old lady had taught me how to read these sorts of runes during my evenings at her little hut. It was really just another alphabet, just an old one that didn't get used much.

The runes flared to life, glowing with a distinctive turquoise color. It was fully functional, and I had just activated it.

"Well," I told Vitold, "maybe I was wrong about needing a special talent. Maybe you just have to read the runes aloud. Here, you give it a try. Vitold?" I stood up and looked around, not seeing Vitold for a moment; then I looked down.

Vitold looked back up at me, explaining his situation through gritted teeth with a serious attempt at dignity. Startled by the sudden flare of arcane light, he'd jumped back quite suddenly. Between the vodka he'd imbibed to dull the pain and his upper leg muscles not quite working, this had resulted in him suddenly sitting down, which was not exactly the most comfortable position for a man with an extra hole in his back-side. Would I mind helping him up?

After I'd gotten him upright again, he made a quick sign against evil and told me he didn't really think he wanted to get back inside that particular suit, or even get particularly near it. I helped him toward the sawbones' tent, where he pulled out his coin purse and proceeded to start negotiating with one of the surgeons for an informal increase in his vodka ration.

I left him to it (no need to be seen idling) and went for a brisk walk around the campsite. Walk briskly and purposefully, and people will tend to assume you're on some kind of errand and not bother you, and I needed some time to think without being bothered.

Katya. Katya was already keeping secrets for me and Vitold. I would see if Katya, too, could get the runes to glow. I popped by the command tent, not to visit Colonel Romanov or to bother the general, but because I expected to find the duty officer in charge of the watch posted there. A simple, polite request and I learned that Katya was assigned a sentry post until close to midnight.

I kept myself busy until midnight working on the suit. If Vitold would no longer wear it out of superstitious fear, I would have to wear it myself. Given Vitold's compact frame and my height, that necessitated significant adjustments. After I had finished adjusting the suit, I could start it up with the access panel open and see for myself the glimmer of protective magic coating the outer surface of the armor.

When Katya came back into camp with her watch partner, she was surprised to see me waiting for her; she stopped in her tracks when she recognized me by the dim light of the stars. I smiled brightly at her and asked if she would mind checking over my gun back at my squad's tent. The other soldier gave me a funny look, but headed off into the night as Katya blinked, visibly processing the unexpected request.

I whispered in her ear, softly enough that I felt sure I wouldn't be overheard by others. "Actually, it's something about Vitold's armor, or rather Gregor's old armor, which was his and is going to be mine now, that I really want to show you. But I don't want anyone else to know."

She had a look on her face warring between disappointment and relief, which was soon replaced by guilt. "Is Vitold alright?" she asked.

"The last I saw, he seemed pretty fine. No infection, and he's already up and limping around," I said. Once we were inside the tent, I led her toward the suit and started up the arcane turbine. It was dark but easy enough to locate the orichalcum inlays. I took Katya's hand.

"I'm going to tell you some words to say," I told her, and after I was sure she had gotten them right, guided her hand to the plate.

"Concentrate hard and say those words again," I said.

She looked afraid.

I patted her hand reassuringly. "It won't hurt," I said.

She spoke the words softly in the darkness, and nothing happened. I checked to make sure, and yes, she was touching the plate.

"Curious. Take your hand away from the plate," I said. I touched the plate, read the inscription aloud, and watched them flare to life again. There was still another test to make.

"Katya? Climb inside the armor. I want to make sure of something," I said.

She bit her lip, then obeyed, taking off her coat and climbing into the armor. I helped her with the unfamiliar task. Underneath her outerwear, she felt smaller and softer than I had expected. Her fierce expression, substantial boots, and bulky coat had made her look much larger.

"Close your eyes. Imagine yourself being wrapped in a warm blanket of protective light." Nothing happened, aside from her squinting tightly.

"Touch the plate again and say the words again," I told her. It was a little more awkward with her now inside the suit, but with a little guidance, she reached the plate, mouthing through the words.

"Now imagine yourself surrounded by a field of power. Push the energy outward." Still, nothing happened.

"Interesting. Let's get you back out of this. Let me show you something." I disentangled her from the armor and I climbed in, muttering the incantation under my breath.

"Do you see that?" I asked her.

She nodded wordlessly, eyes wide, face illuminated by the glow.

"Ah. Interesting." I climbed out of the armor. "Get back in and try again one more time. Imagine that light wrapping around you, now that you know what it looks like."

She had a slightly easier time getting in this time. She screwed up her face again, but nothing happened.

"Interesting," I said. That seemed to be the word for tonight, *interesting*. My six older brothers had all been tested by visiting imperial wizards; I had not. Tonight, I had tried to prove that someone else could do what I had done with the wizard armor; I had failed.

I helped her back out of the armor, shut down the arcane engine, and told her very quietly that I needed her to keep all of this a secret. I pointed at her pendant, the amethyst crystal clearly visible to me in the dim starlight that filtered through the tent walls, and told her that the rebels would very much like to know about what Vitold and I had done with the loot from their workshop. She looked past me in the tent, her eyes not quite focused on me.

"I won't tell anyone," she said to the air next to me. "Is there anything else?"

"Don't trust Romanov," a male voice said.

The voice was familiar, and as before, sounded much like my father. I couldn't see anyone else in the tent, though I looked around. Was I hearing voices in my head? Was I going crazy? But Katya had responded to the voice before, and she was nodding crisply right now, a soldier acknowledging an order. A little thrill ran through my chest, and I wasn't quite sure why.

I set aside the mystery of the disembodied voice, as I was tired and had too many mysteries to ponder already, and bid her good night. I watched as she groped around for the tent flap, seeming not quite sure where it was. This looked a little funny since it was right in front of her, but I didn't laugh, just looked on sympathetically. She must be tired indeed to have trouble recognizing it. I thought to myself that she must be running on nothing but fumes and patriotism.

In retrospect, I suppose we were all running on nothing but fumes and patriotism, and I hadn't had much of the latter to begin with.

CHAPTER ELEVEN

In Which I Eat Crow
by Not Eating Crow

We were on the march again, and I had much to think about after that night. I could not help but think about the episode with Katya in the tent and was continually reminded of it as the day ground slowly on. Katya's watch partner was not the soul of discretion; consequentially, a rumor circulated that I had taken her back to my tent for purposes that had nothing to do with gun maintenance and everything to do with her being female.

I suspected (and would later confirm) that Katya found the rumors displeasing; while I outwardly glared coldly in response to the snickers and sly looks, my mind kept drifting back to the surprising softness I had felt when helping her in and out of the armor and the feel of her bare, ungloved hand in mine when I pressed hers up against the runes on the plates of wizard armor. I kept remembering the funny face she'd made while trying to activate the runes and kept puzzling over the strange events of the night.

Vitold had failed to activate the protective enchantments when he installed the orichalcum-inlaid plates on the inside of the steam suit's existing armor plates, but I could believe that was simply him not knowing the words to say or not concentrating hard enough once I'd told him what to say. Katya, on the other hand, had clearly concentrated, had pronounced the same words I had. Not that the words seemed necessary; I could get the runes to flare without speaking aloud at all. Did that mean I was a wizard?

I found that hard to believe. Perhaps, as with the elemental spirit, it was only necessary to speak the incantation once to gain authority, and the protective enchantment could only be bound to one person. My thoughts went back to my captivity. My captors had been sure I was a war mage in training; they were convinced of this for two reasons.

First, their mage hunter had smelled magic on me; and second, two steam knight suits had collapsed when that mage hunter shot me (one thanks to a badly timed heart attack) as if my conscious control was the only thing binding their motivating spirits into action, and I hadn't thought to give them orders about what to do if I fell. The mage hunter might have been smelling the elemental spirit in Ilya's old suit and gotten us mixed up by proximity somehow.

Perhaps I did have some spark of magical talent. Wizards, I recalled, could feel the presence of the magically gifted, and had some way of identifying them. More skilled wizards could detect magical gifts more easily, and stronger magical gifts were more easily sensed. The general was a very capable war mage. I could ask the general if he sensed magical talent in me.

After a few moments of thought on the various directions that conversations with General Spitignov had gone in the past, I decided that asking the general if I was magically gifted was a bad idea. In fact, voluntarily talking with the notorious war mage for any reason seemed like it was a poor choice for anyone, much less a squad leader whose squad included three entirely fictitious members.

I decided that if we happened to stumble across another wizard, one that was neither trying to kill me nor possessed of a tendency toward homicidal mania, I could ask them if I was gifted. If I was, then most likely I had some small arcane talent, barely enough to prod existing enchantments into activating. If I'd had significant magical talents, it should have been obvious before. While I'd never spoken with one face to face, I knew there was an imperial bureau of wizards that went out searching for gifted children regularly.

I wasn't clear on the distinction between war mages and other wizards, but if gifts ran in the blood, the powerful gifts of a war mage surely would only show up in families already filled with wizards—noble families, in other words. I felt certain nobody in my family was magically gifted, neither my father nor my mother nor my six older brothers. I'd never heard of any of my uncles being wizards either, and there were half a dozen of them just on my father's side. The rebels probably didn't understand what made war mages special either; the mage hunter had told them I had some magic about me, and the old man's obsession with the general had led him to guess I was his apprentice.

Other wizards weren't the only ones I could ask, though; animals are supposed to be sensitive to magic on a primal level. Most animals aren't particularly smart, but perhaps I could ask one of the wiser animals if I had some kind of magical talent.

Evening arrived, and we made camp. I politely called over a crow from the trees. No, I'm not a fool. I know that crows are tricksters and that getting an honest answer out of one is a difficult task, but they are chatterboxes and not particularly shy of humans, and the crows were still following our task force. After all, the general had caused them to be fed great fat meals often enough. This one responded to my request with startling alacrity, flying right over as he replied.

Vitold gave me a funny look. Being a city boy from a great big town (well over a thousand souls lived in his hometown; I think I can call it a real city on that account) he didn't understand what the crow was saying. Anybody can talk to animals, but understanding their responses didn't seem to be something most of my fellow soldiers had bothered to learn. Even Colonel Romanov, who did talk to his horse fairly often, seemed not to understand it particularly well.

The crow asked, in a very exasperated caw, what I wanted this time. Then, without waiting for my answer, he complained that I was being bossy again. I suppose that meant he'd been following us for a while, and I'd shooed him off before. In spite of the grumbling complaints, he perched on my shoulder as bold as brass. Crows are clever enough to know that if a well-fed human talks to them in a friendly tone, tidbits of food are likely to follow; crows aren't good eating, so only a very hungry human would try to trap them. The crow asked me again what I wanted, impatience entering the tone of his caws.

Crows tend to get impatient if they don't see any food or shiny objects. I pulled a string of jerky out, holding it securely in my hand, and informed him that I wanted to meet with an owl. He squawked in dismay. Crows, like most birds, are not terribly fond of larger birds of prey. They are, however, inquisitive enough to keep careful track of large predators, so either he or his fellow crows would know where to find one.

The crow hopped back and forth on my shoulder and told me, grudgingly, that he did indeed know where to find an owl. I tossed him the jerky and could see the gleam in his eyes as he launched up into the air. He hadn't actually agreed to lead me to the owl and found it hilarious that I would offer him payment without service. Ah, right. I dug a coin out of my pocket, cleared my throat noisily, and waited for the glint to catch the crow's eye. I then informed the crow that this would be his if and only if he led me to the owl.

The crow landed on the ground, torn. He was clearly thinking to himself something along the lines of *Shiny coin! But owl . . . but shiny coin . . . but owl . . . but . . .*

I told him that he would lead me to the owl, that he would have this bright shiny piece, and he would be happy about it afterward. He called me bossy again, which I took rightly as an affirmative agreement, and he took wing again, this time in a different direction. Every few dozen yards he would perch and wait impatiently for me to catch up. Then he stopped, cawed loudly at a tree, then winged back to me in a hurry, demanding his due payment; which I flicked into the air.

As he flapped by, he told me he and his friends would be gladder to come the next time I called for them and thanked me for the very shiny coin. That seemed unusual, but I suppose crows can be mannerly once in a while.

The owl looked grumpy. It was also quite large. Its wingspan was seven feet if it was an inch, a measure that became clear as it stretched out its wings. I begged it to wait and talk a while with me, telling it that I would endeavor to recompense it for its time and effort. We spent some time communicating, though her side of the conversation consisted primarily of hooting and cocking her head in various directions, as owls are wont to do, rather than using the sorts of sounds that humans do.

I have taken the liberty to set down what was spoken as I or any other woods-wise person would understand our exchange, rather than attempt to transcribe owlish sounds and gestures directly.

"Where is that rascal? I'll have him for breakfast, I will. Damned crows," the owl said, hopping from foot to foot.

"Please, madam, I will have breakfast for you that tastes much better than crow if you just calm down," I told her.

"A human, talking to me? Well, you don't have a gun or a bow. I suppose you aren't a hunter after my feathers. And crow does taste bad," she said.

"They are magnificent, but no, I want to beg some of your wisdom," I said.

"Flatterer. What do you want to know?" She preened herself while I hesitated.

"Well, it's said that owls have the best sight in the whole world. When you look at me, do you see a human gifted with an arcane talent?" Asking the question aloud put everything into sharp focus.

"I should think so. You're speaking with me, after all," the owl said.

"So, what sort of gift is this? What can I do with this gift?" I wanted to know.

"What you've been doing already, and whatever else you humans do with magic. Raise up big humans made of rock and shoot lightning, maybe? Look, I don't know why you think I should know much more than that; you're a talking human, you're obviously magical. I'm a bird, I live in the woods, and I'm five years old. I've only ever met a talking human once before, and he didn't have much to say at the time. Mostly I avoid you two-legged types. You're a bleeding hazard. And a falling-out-of-the-sky hazard." The owl hopped from one leg to the other, growing impatient.

"Thank you," I said, holding out a piece of jerky.

She snatched the offered jerky quickly and then flew off.

I may only have been the second human she'd bothered to converse with, but she had at least given me a solid answer: I was gifted with some kind of magic, something that was obvious to her. Something I was doing already? Maybe to her owl eyes I glowed with magical patterns like a set of orichalcum runes. I suppose I had read too many folk tales where the wise owl gives away the full answer, but part of an answer was better than none. I was magically gifted; just what kind of magical gift I had, however, was open to question.

I walked by the sentry, who didn't seem to see me. It was a moonless night, but he still should have been able to see me clearly by the starlight as it filtered through the trees. I briefly considered giving him a sharp lecture for inattention, as I was supposed to be an officer, but decided against it and returned to my ruminations.

Maybe I was a wizard. Maybe I wasn't. Another wizard could tell me for sure. I was, however, definitely gifted. I'd have to keep notes on anything unusual I'd managed to do, anything that seemed like it might be out of the ordinary. So far, all I'd shown was the ability to make some runes glow. I wasn't even sure if the protective enchantment was effective.

But maybe it was, so maybe I was.

Morale had been low and ebbed lower as cold weather began to set in. I would have thought it impossible to keep the secret that my squad was down to two men, but the other survivors from the detachment left behind to secure the rebel outpost were inclined toward silence and circumspection in the wake of the example of the corporal, and many of the other soldiers were as well. Being under the command of General Spitignov was wearing on the sanity, and discipline was fraying as a consequence.

My "men" not taking off their helmets when assembled for drill, and never being seen outside of their armor, was just one of a very long list of strange things that Colonel Romanov had to deal with. As my steam knight mechs were always ready for action and never far from their wagons when it came time to move, he did not pry too hard. It was not normal for him to socialize casually with men of low rank; he was too busy diligently placing himself between General Spitignov and lower-ranked officers to interact much with regular enlisted soldiers.

The full maintenance of four steam knight suits, three of them heavily modified, kept me quite busy. I spent a great deal of time working on finer control of my steam knight armor suits and working to better understand my magical interactions with what had been originally Misha's suit and, subsequently, Vitold's suit.

After adjusting my old suit to better fit his measurements, Vitold kept himself scarce. I asked him why, once. He said he was busy covering up for our absent squad members and looked at me uncomfortably. I did not press further, and the cold weather crept deeper inside my bones as winter set in.

When the first serious snow fell, we had not seen a town for several days. I suspected we were lost; Colonel Romanov was in an agitated state. The winter weather had thus far been very mild for the season, but food and fuel were running low. General Spitignov believed himself to be in hot pursuit of an enemy of some kind and was pushing relentlessly forward in eagerness for battle.

Our hastily constructed camp for the night was compact, more a huddle of wagons and people mixed in with inconvenient underbrush where snow and ice had halted us; and Colonel Romanov held a meeting in a supply wagon with a man with a thick Romanian accent. As I and my mechanical squadmates had dug in close to the supply wagons, I could hear their voices clearly enough to catch the informant reassuring Colonel Romanov about his own reliability.

By listening carefully, I was able to infer that the informant had come to Romanov to let him know where an army had been sighted—passing by a village just two leagues east of here the day before yesterday. Romanov alternated between suspicion, frustration, and despair.

Previously, I had thought that the general's belief in the proximity of enemy forces was simply another paranoid delusion. Learning that it was not did not reassure me, though. I slept poorly, disturbed by dreams of blood in the snow.

INTERLUDE

A letter addressed to Boris Volkov, Izh District, Northeastern Sector

Dearest Father,

I wanted to write you earlier. When I sat down to write and remembered everything, I cried. The tears made the paper wet, and the ink ran. It destroyed what I said. Today Colonel Romanov has told me he will send me to town with an important letter. This reminded me I had not written since my last letter. I am now sure Ilya is dead. He is one of the soldiers who was with us starting on the train. When our strike force started. There are not many of those soldiers left.

I talked about Ilya in my last letter. I am sorry that I did not tell you I loved him. With all my heart. There. I have said it without crying, so I will be able to mail this letter. I am sorry that I did not tell you I loved him. He was a very handsome man and I wanted you to meet him. It is strange to find love at war. And Mother said I would never find a husband if I joined the army. That a sharpshooter may as well be a widow. Well. Maybe this is what she meant. Soldiers die in war.

Maybe Mother was right.

(Editor's note: Water damage has obscured what may be several more sentences between this one and the next.)

I hope the colonel's important letter asks for me to be promoted. I am sure a promotion for me is not why he sends it, but I hope I am mentioned. I have been a good soldier. Everybody says so, even Vitold, who is like a rat and a very

bad soldier. Who I shot by accident. He said I was too good of a soldier, to repeat him exactly. I think he is jealous. And he is a veteran steam knight! This fact still amazes me. His attitude is so unpatriotic. His squad leader is named Mikolai. I mentioned them both in my last letter. They are very close and love each other well. But they are so different. Vitold is common. Mikolai is myste-rious, and I think he is a noble.

Secretly. Maybe a bastard noble. But very well born. He is educated and looks young for how old he is and speaks with such authority and everyone treats him with respect. They do not like him. They do respect him. I under-stand the difference. You told me about it. Now I have seen it with my own eyes. With the general. And with Mikolai. And I want to be liked and respected. Both at the same time.

With love,
Katya

A letter addressed to [REDACTED]

After the [REDACTED] *in* [REDACTED] *and* [REDACTED]—*remember that little episode, my old friend? I do, and you should never forget that I* [REDACTED]—*I hope you trust in my good judgment and discretion. It drives me crazy that I can't talk about this with the general, because I don't want to set off his paranoia; the frothing lunatic is as likely to have me executed as anyone else.*

But I am certain I have a soldier who is not who he claims to be. He claims to be "Mikolai Stepanovich" and presented himself as a ten-year vet-eran of the steam knights, accompanied by his friend, "Vitold Szpak," who has apparently accompanied him for some years. The two are very familiar with one another. The former is a tall, gaunt man with a long, narrow nose, bright blue eyes, and dark wavy hair. The latter is a short man, on the edge of being pudgy, with straight medium-brown hair and medium-brown eyes.

Neither has the characteristic build of (nor any of the sorts of scars common in) the steam knight corps, though they have gained several since boarding the train. They are sloppy in formation and combat, though their continued sur-vival suggests to me that they are veterans of some kind of training. We picked them up at [REDACTED] *on* [REDACTED]. *I have since written back to the keeper of records at* [REDACTED] *asking for a complete listing of every* steam knight who has been posted at [REDACTED] between [REDACTED] and [REDACTED], and neither of their names are anywhere on the list.

Yes, you might suggest that it is sloppy record-keeping, and I agree in advance that the records I received were in poor order, but you would think that a solid veteran of the corps would likely be recorded. I sent letters to [REDACTED] and [REDACTED], asking if they remembered any steam knights by those names, and they have also sent replies in the negative. I suspect that whoever these men are—and their names are likely assumed ones—they are not in fact genuine steam knights, and their identities are fabricated. This leaves the question of who they are, who is paying them, and who aided in their disguises.

I have enclosed good likenesses of them. "Mikolai" speaks with an accent that sounds like it comes from some hut deep in the middle of rural Ruthenia, but his vocabulary is too extensive and his diction much too polished for that to be anything but an affectation. He's fond of melodramatic pronouncements and starts outlandish rumors about himself to keep the troops fascinated with him.

I've heard that he can see straight through walls, trees, and the thickest dark of moonless night; that he and the general had tea with Baba Yaga one night; that when he walks through the wounded, he avoids looking at the ones that will die in the night, while those he speaks to will be on their feet in the morning; and all sorts of superstitious nonsense. Mikolai's troopers, of whom I have only been able to talk to "Vitold," obey him like his words were that of God Himself speaking to His most loyal crusaders, and he has managed to get the general himself to trust him. I can't get the man to trust his breakfast to be loyal to the plate it's lying on, but he trusts "Mikolai" to be loyal somehow.

I can clearly place "Vitold's" accent as being from one of the larger Polish settlements on one or another side of the Lithuanian border; it is strongly regional but he is clearly unfamiliar with life outside of towns. The man couldn't tell planted turnips from weeds and is clearly inexperienced with both dogs and horses. On the other hand, it could be that he is a much better actor than "Mikolai;" perhaps is even really the master pretending to be the servant. I feel I may be forced to take matters into my own hands soon.

Colonel I. I. Romanov

CHAPTER TWELVE

In Which I Stuff Stockings

The village had been abandoned before we got there. This took place long enough before our arrival that the fresh coat of powder blowing across the ground didn't show tracks, but it can't have been much longer than that.

It was obvious to me at a glance that nobody was left in the village, but Colonel Romanov ordered a full company of troops detached to conduct a house-to-house search anyway, while General Spitignov and the main body of the force continued onward to a fortified manor that was supposed to be nearby.

Major Alexei Pavlov volunteered his two steam knight squads to guard the infantrymen. I am not sure why, but I think he wanted an excuse not to accompany the general into battle. For once in my life, I was grateful to "volunteer," as my preference was to be as far from the halitosis-infused madman as possible.

The search ended up taking a long time. By the time we were done, it was dark gray out and raining, the sort of indecisive winter rain that meets the snow on the ground and negotiates an agreement somewhere between slush and ice. The sun would be setting soon, at which point it would become pitch-black and the thin layer of semi-liquid slush would turn rock-hard and slick while rain turned to sleet.

So we stayed inside various huts within the village for the night. The hut I picked for my squad had stockings hung out to dry by the fire, a platter of half-eaten cookies, and even an ewer of milk on the table, a thin layer of ice over its top, evidence that suggested the villagers had fled the village in great haste. We ate the cookies and milk.

Well, to be more precise, I ate the cookies and drank the milk, while Vitold made an accounting of our fuel. Vitold didn't trust the cookies or the milk, and freezing rain had soaked through one of the spare canisters of fuel. Some of our coal was now wet, which would make it hazardous to load and burn. You don't want steam underneath the boiler, just inside of it, and an untimely explosion of steam could lead to a frightful accident.

After a moment's consideration, I loaded the damp coals one by one into the stockings. That way, the water would drip away, without leaving the coals frozen to the floor in the morning or risking setting the hut on fire, both of which seemed like possible outcomes if I spread them out to dry in front of the fireplace overnight.

We hunkered down inside our armor for the night, parked next to the fire for extra warmth. The door no longer quite fit over the doorway after we'd marched through with steam suits, which made it a pretty drafty place. The enclosed shells of the armor would stay reasonably warm even if the fire died in the night.

I felt very lucky for my choice in the morning when I awoke to the loud roar of gunfire and the worrying sensation of a bullet pinging off my armor. Through the cracks and fresh holes in the door, I could see mounted arquebusiers with sharply curved sabers at their sides. They looked like Magyars, their guns smaller and lighter than the heavy French muskets I'd faced earlier. Having loosed their first volley, the arquebusiers were firing in ragged singletons as they reloaded, trying to murder us from safely out of reach.

Behind us, on the other side of the thin walls of the hut, a presence loomed, and I could hear the muffled roar of a heavy mech boiler at work. Not good news. Before I finished taking stock of the situation, half the infantry that Colonel Romanov had detached to search the village were dead, and the other half were cowering in fear and silence behind cover. We were outnumbered two to one in living bodies, caught with our boilers cold, and the enemy had a heavy mech—a great big monster holding a mace meant to batter heavy armor to pieces.

I had, once before, started a cold mech with nothing more than a mental plea, while being rescued from captivity. Remembering that feat, I exerted my will, deliberately reaching and pushing, hoping that whatever talent I had was strong enough to awaken multiple fires at once. The boilers of my three jury-rigged mechs fired into full life with a cough and a roar. They grabbed poleaxes and were soon thundering toward the enemy at top speed.

The arcane engine on my own suit woke with a hum, not needing the same kind of warm-up time as a conventional boiler. Muffled swearing to my left and a ragged gurgle indicated Vitold was starting his boiler up by more mundane methods. I picked up a cannon and loaded it, and there was a pause in the gunfire. I walked out of the hut, cannon ready, taking in the scene.

A heavily armored man on horseback caught my eye. His plated mail and that of his horse were inlaid with orichalcum, an old-fashioned style. In one hand, he held a saber; in the other, a leveled double-barreled pistol. At the other end of the leveled pistol Colonel Romanov kneeled, his hands in the air, unarmed and unarmored.

There was a deep crack as the pistol fired, and the colonel fell over, the hole in his forehead as wide as his gaping mouth. The enemy leader looked over at me and spoke quietly to a subordinate, his words barely audible over the noise of battle.

"That one," he growled. "Mark him. Hidden in that armor, he could be the prince we've been hearing rumors about, for all I know. Make sure he does not escape."

The Magyar words were thick and harsh, and I wondered if I had misunderstood the unfamiliar tongue, my book learning leading me astray. Perhaps what I thought was "prince" meant "commander" or something of that sort, and he had mistaken me for the general.

He raised his voice, switching to crude and badly accented Romanian—it was not my native tongue, but I had heard enough of it from locals to tell it wasn't his either. "Surrender and live, wizard. Keep birds and die."

Wizard. That meant I was one. Perhaps he was as well.

He switched back to his native tongue, shouting orders too fast for me to follow, and then singing words that blurred into each other indistinctly. A shot from the other barrel of the wizard's gun bounced off my armor and the mech lumbered forward, slowly accelerating as the wizard chanted.

I fired at the heavy mech and dropped the cannon as I backed away, grabbing a shield and a pick from the supply cart I had parked next to the hut. The cannonball dented one of its shoulders severely but did not slow it in the least as it barreled forward. I ordered two of my mechs to come back to me while the third helped keep the surviving enemy infantrymen busy.

They weren't fast enough. I raised my shield desperately as the enemy mech's mace came swinging down at me. The sharp shock of the mace rattled me, and I felt the jolt go down from the suit's arm into mine and on down to the ground beneath me. The runes inside the armor flared brightly, turning the inside of my visor a brilliant shade of turquoise as the protective enchantment cushioned the blow; I was alive, though I was several inches lower to the ground than I had been before. The force of the blow had driven me through the upper crust of snow and frozen ground, and into the soggy mud below.

Rattled but still alive, I swung back with my pick, the heavy point biting into the chest plate but not striking deep enough to damage anything vital to the functioning of the machine.

Ahead of me, the chanting intensified, and the next blow struck my shield hard enough to bring me to my knees. Arquebuses coughed behind me, my surviving comrades having gained the courage to fire blindly from cover.

I risked turning a moment to shout back at the troops behind me.

"Aim for the enemy wizard," I ordered. Sounding decisive in battle would help them find their nerves, and while the wizard was protected by armor and enchantment, both of those had limits.

The chant reached a peak and ended. Searing yellow light flashed around me, and the crows dispersed, flying away with confused cawing.

"Your magics are no match for mine, Ruthenian," said the enemy wizard, speaking quietly in his native Magyar dialect. A bullet struck his armor, which held with a flare of yellow light and a sound like a sack of coins dropped on a table. I could hear him as clear as a bell through the noise. One quiet voice among a racket of explosions, the roar of steam engines, and the clangor of metal on metal stands out all the more, does it not?

I replied heatedly, but my words were not as hot as the fire that he called down from the sky with his next chant. Nor were they as hot as the boilers in my own mechs as they crashed into the much larger enemy mech, poleaxes jabbing in with all the momentum they could muster.

The enemy mech, taking full advantage of its greater size and more solid engineering, picked up one of my self-propelled steam suits and threw it not simply into but through a hut. Then it took another sideways swipe at me with its mace, which sent me to my knees and jammed the actuators in my left shoulder. It then followed up with a great overhand strike. Unable to move my shield up, I hastily interposed my pick; the shaft of the weapon snapped in two under the force of the blow.

It raised its mace again, and I winced, closing my eyes against oncoming death. When it didn't come, I looked again. The machine had come to a shuddering halt in a rising cloud of steam, and there was my good friend Vitold, tossing a length of metal tubing into the snow, wrench in hand, climbing down.

I was in the process of congratulating him when there was a crack from a gun, and he dropped to the ground limply. I looked up; there was the enemy wizard, his freshly reloaded double-barreled pistol smoking as he rode toward me. Fury coursed through me; I rushed forward, shield locked in place by my frozen shoulder actuator.

The enemy wizard paused for a moment, confused as to why an unarmed wizard would charge forward, and then I crashed into his horse. A noble beast it might have been, but even the noblest of steeds will have trouble keeping its footing after a collision with hard steel plate and nearly half a ton of steam suit behind it. Its rider found himself flung about and then shortly afterward on the underside of the unfortunate horse.

"Surrender and live," I shouted at him, echoing his own words from earlier.

For a moment, I didn't think he had heard me over the screaming horse and his own pain, but then he shook his head. As the enemy wizard slowly raised his pistol, I turned to interpose the shield held in my locked arm. There was a loud bang. Turning back, I discovered he had chosen to shoot the second barrel of his pistol not at me, but at himself. Looking up, I saw the rapidly vanishing forms of enemy troops fleeing into the distance—and also the approaching form of Vitold, bloody and limping unevenly but alive.

"You're alive." In my state of shock, I felt the need to state a fact that Vitold certainly already knew.

Vitold informed me that he felt that, after having been shot in the shoulder, it seemed wise to pretend the shot had been lethal, so as not to attract additional attention to his easily punctured hide. When I inquired further about his appearance, I gathered that he had felt it would take far too long to start up his suit, which would only serve to make him an obvious target, and that as he'd attempted to exit the battlefield quietly, he had found himself unnoticed behind the enemy mech. The access panels were unsecured, and it was child's play to climb up to remove certain key components from the enemy mech without being noticed.

An unarmored man climbing up the side of a hostile mech in the middle of a raging battle to sabotage it is a brave man indeed, and I told him so. He responded by saying that he must have been seized by some variety of temporary madness. Perhaps the enemy wizard had cast a spell on the imperial soldiers to remove their sense of self-preservation. This seemed unlikely to me, but I didn't press the matter.

Two of my jury-rigged mechs were nonfunctional, and we had a pile of dead and wounded. With one Colonel Ivan Ivanovich Romanov numbered among the dead and my direct superior nowhere to be seen, I took it upon myself to assume command of the situation. It seemed the natural thing to do. As a leader of a squad of steam knights, I may not have technically outranked the infantry captain, who had spent the entire battle hiding in a vegetable cellar, but she didn't seem inclined to object.

I sent a messenger off on the colonel's horse and put the rest of the survivors to work. The wounded needed to be moved into warm, dry shelter and their wounds treated; the perimeter of the village needed to be fortified and a watch posted; and the battlefield needed to be searched carefully for the wounded and for loot.

I found a survivor from the other steam knight squad, trapped underneath a beam in a barn that had been collapsed by rocket fire. He and his comrades had been sleeping in the loft.

I ordered the arms and armor of the fallen gathered into one pile to be divided fairly and usefully among the survivors, and the bodies of the dead to be brought to the village square and laid out. Vitold went to work fixing the broken machinery; the infantry officer to assembling the wounded in one place; and I tramped back and forth, carrying things and people hither and thither with the aid of arcane power provided by an advanced lightning flux engine.

A glitter caught my eye—a gilded hilt. The hilt was attached to an odd-looking sword I had seen in the hands of a gray-haired enemy soldier, whose body now lay broken in the snow and mud. The blade was straight for a section, and then bowed into a sudden curve, pushing forward and then hooking back. From a distance, the blade had looked like it was fancifully and wastefully gilded along the blade; up close, it was revealed as brilliantly polished bronze, showing some sort of complex patterning.

I picked it up, inspecting it. The hilt was styled as a pair of serpents ready to strike, a pale pearlescent stone anchoring the pommel. It was a weapon worthy of an officer, though the exotic-looking bronze sword was probably destined for a future as a mantle decoration. What soldier in the field would want such an oddly shaped weapon? Not only was it awkwardly balanced, but if I remembered correctly from my books, bronze weapons were inferior to steel ones.

The blade flickered, and my lucky stone felt warm. Were those irregular patterns writing? I held the blade up in my right hand to catch the morning light, inspecting the blade at an angle. My lucky stone suddenly felt as cold as ice; everything went dark quite suddenly.

CHAPTER THIRTEEN

In Which I Ask the Time

I blinked and then looked around wildly. Yes, it had become dark all of a sudden. A slim waxing crescent moon shone gently through the ruined village, and the stars were shining. Who had stolen the sun from the sky and turned it into night? I went to the barn, where I had told my comrades to put the wounded, finding Vitold napping just inside the door in a chair. I woke him with a shake.

"I'm awake, I'm awake!" he protested. "Oh, it's you, Mikolai." He put down his pistol. "You scared me for a moment there."

I asked him what had happened, and why everyone was asleep. He informed me that he had intended to keep a watch, but must have dozed off, and he was very sorry, but he didn't think we'd be attacked again so soon, especially what with me standing there like a terrifying gargoyle. I had never realized Vitold thought I was ugly, so I felt the need to ask further.

"Vitold, I don't think my face is so terrifying as to scare off an army, and while you are right about—" I stopped myself, connecting the facts in front of me. "Vitold? How long was I standing there?"

He told me that I had been standing there the entire day and at least some of the night, holding up the sword and surrounded by an eerie glow. I'd scowled at the sword like a statue, he added, the sort those fancy types tend to put on their buildings—fierce expression, martial stance, and all. Did I know what he meant? Was gargoyle not the right word for that?

I reassured Vitold he had indeed remembered correctly what a gargoyle was, and that I did as well. His mention of the sword reminded me that I was still holding it. I remembered that the hilt had been shaped like a pair of serpents twined together, their heads curled apart to form a crossguard, a pale pearlescent stone anchoring the pommel between the curled tips of their tails.

However, when I looked down at the handle in my grasp, it looked instead like a crow, the blade emerging from the crow's head. The crow's spread wings formed the crosspiece and its grasping talons the pommel.

Strange. Had someone switched out the old man's sword for another one? That seemed unlikely. I didn't remember seeing any other swords so finely decorated, much less ones with such an oddly shaped bronze blade. The enemy wizard hadn't even had a sword, though much of his gear had been decorated with orichalcum or gilded with gold. It had to be the same sword I'd picked up from the corpse of the old man.

The enemy wizard leader had confirmed my status as a wizard, in a way that nobody else could: Seeing me through his own senses as a magically gifted individual as I fought against him, commanding my mechs without words and shielded by wizard armor. I had felt, too, that he was a wizard just by looking at him. And if he had indeed been a war mage, I probably was, too; war mages had no peers on the battlefield.

Whatever had just happened with the sword probably also had to do with my newly discovered magical gifts, but I didn't want to think on those matters for too long or too hard. It was late, every muscle in my body was sore, and I was exhausted. I went to sleep with the sword still clutched in my hand.

The next day, the messenger returned, along with the well-bred horse that had once belonged to Colonel Ivan Ivanovich Romanov. He was escorted by Katya and a dog wearing little snow boots and an armored harness, which identified him as an honorary sergeant of the Imperial Army. The messenger had a sealed message tube, which he handed me without delay. I eyed the personal seal of General Ognyan Spitignov with trepidation for a moment, then broke the seal open. There was a small dried scrap of hide, pulled and twisted into a rod, and a rolled-up piece of paper. I tucked the twisted piece of hide into a pocket and pulled the paper out of the tube, unrolling it.

Hopefully, the general was in an understanding mood and willing to forgive my lateness to rendezvous with him at the manor, considering we'd been attacked by Avar soldiers. They may not have had new-model

French muskets, but they'd been quite deadly enough with their older arquebuses.

"Dear Comrade Wizard Mikolai Stepanovich Yagin," it began, a form of address that puzzled me mightily.

Everything except the "Mikolai Stepanovich" part was rather startling, in fact. Wizard? Yagin? Dear Comrade? This was the same General Spitignov who thought that being diplomatic involved waiting to behead people until after he had finished enunciating his demands, rather than swinging immediately. We were neither peers nor friends.

But we were, I supposed, in the same army, even if we did not share the same sense of purpose. And if wizards can sense each other, the general might have known I was a wizard, even if I hadn't. So "Dear Comrade Wizard" made some sense. I had no idea who the Yagins were or why the general thought I might belong to that family. My family didn't even have a surname.

I forced myself to read onward. The general proceeded to congratulate me for my unswerving loyalty to the state and my "dedication to maintaining Secrets of State in Tightest Confidence." He praised me for having "surprising mental flexibility and quick learning for a Man of your advanced Age and long Years in the Steam Knight Corps." He apologized for having to cut my training short. My what? Training? The general thought he was training me? I wasn't quite sure what to make of that.

Evidently, he was being recalled elsewhere by "orders of the Highest Security of State." As those orders did not explicitly require him to bring his task force with him, he was leaving behind the wounded and anyone else who would slow down his travel plans. In accordance with his travel plans, he had "a Mission, which my most puissant Facility of Intelligence divined was Necessary for me to take Initiative to order you to embark upon at whatever Cost in Blood is Necessary."

I was to join with the wounded he had left behind at the manor, and after repairing or disposing of disabled soldiers and damaged war material, take all steps possible to root out and destroy support for Wallachian rebels among their close ethnic kin in the eastern part of Avaria—not, he clarified, to conquer and subjugate Avaria, as "such is Unfortunately Forbidden."

He would, he finished, leave me one of his dogs, named Yuri. This was, the letter assured me, a singular honor, a token of his appreciation for my loyal service to "the Imperial Cause and State Security." The last line on the page was a string of nonsense words written in runes, which flared as I read them. It was a latent spell, one activated by the simple act of silently reading the letters.

For a moment, I thought I smelled the general's distinctive whiff of halitosis; and then there was a burst of fire. I flinched, closing my eyes; and when I opened them, I was holding only ash, and my gloves were singed. The messenger was looking at me with wide eyes, his mouth opening and closing as he tried to form words, unsure of what to say. Katya also looked surprised but was biting her lip, holding in her own questions. Vitold and the other soldiers busied themselves, conspicuously looking in every other direction but at me.

As for me, my anger and frustration were as warm as the smoldering ashes in my hands, and it was plain on my face.

I heard a snuffling sort of noise, then looked down. There was the dog, sitting on its haunches at my feet. Unusually for a dog, he didn't seem concerned by the pyrotechnics that had just taken place less than a yard away; he was looking up at me, a doggy sort of smile on his face. He thought I had something he wanted. After a moment, I remembered the twisted-up piece of hide and fished it back out of my pocket.

"Yuri?" The dog barked again, recognizing his name. I tossed him the scrap of hide. It's hard to be angry at a dog, and my mood eased.

The messenger was surprised when I told him General Spitignov had assigned me command of the mission; particularly since he hadn't known that the illustrious general had received orders requiring his imminent removal from our vicinity. The messenger was also surprised at my field promotion. Evidently, that was something the general had felt was important and therefore deserved to be kept secret.

The messenger swallowed nervously and glanced quickly at Katya, who was busy biting her lip and looking at me intently. As she was intent on me, she ignored the messenger's questioning look completely, neither confirming nor denying this shocking piece of information. Yuri interpreted the messenger's fretfulness as a sign of impending treachery and advanced, growling menacingly.

"Yuri, heel," I told the dog. He gave me a mournful look and padded back to my side. "Good dog," I said, patting him on the head. I drew myself straight and looked the messenger straight in the eye. "If I'm not accurately representing the contents of that message, I'm sure the general will take a personal interest in correcting the error when he finds out. Do I look like I want to pick a bone with the general?"

Behind me, I could hear cawing, and the light of day dimmed a little. The crows were back in force to come pester us. Obnoxious birds. The messenger shifted uneasily as if he wasn't sure how to answer my rhetorical question. Flighty fellow. I took a deep breath and made my first command decision: We would move out immediately, or as quickly as we could get everything on the road.

When I had been placed in charge of a small detachment of men by circumstance, digging in with the wounded men and broken machines and asking for someone else to come sort it out seemed like a brilliant way of dealing with being put on the spot. Now I was the someone else who needed to sort it out, and there was nothing to be done but move the wounded and broken and connect up with the rest of the strike force as quickly as possible. There were three reasons.

First, this was the site of a pitched battle. Many of the enemy had escaped, and word of our presence was surely spreading. If more soldiers were in the area, they might gather a greater force and strike again. For that matter, the carrion birds had announced our presence to any other interested parties. Rebels, bandits, scavengers—everyone within miles surely knew a bloody battle had happened here. Our mission was one that would be most easily accomplished if we kept the balance of information on our side.

Second, I wasn't sure our mission was entirely legal or that my command status would stand up as legitimate in front of a board of inquiry. The message implied that the general had assigned himself the mission, and their recall of him might have been intended to prevent serious retaliation from Avaria. I needed more information, and I wasn't going to get it sitting around in the ruins of the village.

Third, if the general hadn't seen fit to inform the messenger delivering my orders that I was to assume command of the force, he might not have seen fit to inform the men he'd left behind at the manor either. If I didn't move now, the rest of the strike force could very well decide to move on without me. If I was, in fact, in legal command of the strike force, I could be held responsible for anything they did, in which case I needed to get there before they did anything precipitous.

My mind made up, I strode around, pointing my sword this way and that as I gave orders. I never realized before what a useful thing it is to have a bright, shiny stick to gesture with when ordering about men and heavy machinery. Perhaps this is why officers often have shiny swords. Katya followed in my wake, trailing behind me with an uncertain expression on her face and an unasked question on her lips.

I asked her about it, once, and she said that she could wait until we were alone to talk. There wasn't really any privacy to be had while moving around heavy machinery and wounded men and getting them all moving along the road in approximately the same direction, and so we didn't talk about whatever it was at all.

Once we got on the road, I asked Katya if she would do me the favor of making sure we didn't have anyone following our trail. She gave me a salute, mounted a horse, and rode off. I didn't see her again until after we arrived at the manor, rejoining the main body of the strike force. I had meant for her to simply ride a circuit of the battleground making one last check, but I had not been specific.

When I sighted the manor, I was pleasantly surprised to find it largely intact. Vitold had a low opinion of the building. He remarked to me that he thought it looked like a bordello, that the walls looked too thin to keep the wind out, and that the entire thing looked like it was about to collapse from a lethal combination of dry rot and sheer ugliness. It was, he finished, a death trap, and a single volley of fireworks would quickly transform the whole thing into a collapsing pile of flaming wood.

How the man could grow up in a town full of buildings and not see the solid stonework beneath the garish mauve and crimson veneer, I don't know. The windows on the first two levels had clearly been designed as arrow slits originally. The building was perched on top of a hill and surrounded by mostly open fields, though shrubs were creeping up on it and vines had grown up the sides of the building.

This was as defensible a building as I could hope to find, in other words. Militarily, if not necessarily aesthetically, anyway. I couldn't contest its ugliness and said as much to Vitold. Over time, the building's garish look would grow on me, but on first encountering it, I thought it was inexcusably hideous.

When I met with the officers who had been left behind, I discovered that word of Colonel Romanov's death had apparently not spread; they asked me for his whereabouts and seemed very surprised to find that I was claiming to have been given command by order of the general.

Given that some of the officers substantially outranked me, this surprise wasn't unreasonable; nor was it unreasonable for them to ask to see personally what the general had written. I told them as much, apologizing for the unfortunate way in which the note self-destructed. I tried to gloss over the margin by which they outranked me in the normal chain of command and spent most of my time reminding them of precisely how unreasonable General Spitignov actually was.

After a short discussion of the folly of provoking the infamous war mage needlessly, the officers appeared to come to a shared conclusion. Each of them had no desire to be placed in the position of ultimate responsibility, where they would be held accountable to both the general's whims as well as to the official regulations of the army. This was even more true when the general's whims stood in contrast to standard doctrine.

CHAPTER FOURTEEN

In Which I Am Confounded

The strange thing about rumors is the way in which people work hard to turn them into fact. I anticipated being hard-pressed to explain why Ilya, Gregor, and Misha had not shown themselves in person or as corpses during the battle, and that Vitold's web of lies would fall apart. I spent some effort preparing myself to explain everything and found that my thoughts turned with inevitability to fleeing very far away and assuming a new identity.

What I did not anticipate was that the other surviving steam knight from the battle with the Magyar soldiers would swear up and down that Gregor Petrovich had initiated him into the special society that my squad had formed, and that a dozen steam knight troopers would likewise join him and put themselves ceremoniously into the state of avowed silence and isolation that most of my squad appeared to be practicing.

They refused to speak with anyone but me and the fellow members of their respective squads, except as required by duty. They isolated themselves in constant drill; when required to stand watch, they did so in full armor, and they spent a great deal of time meditating when they were not pestering me with questions I could not answer. I had mixed feelings about it, but if I didn't answer a question, I would later hear that Gregor (or, more rarely, one of the other two dead men from my squad, Ilya or Misha) had offered some answer to them.

Since some of the fabricated answers were outlandish, I resolved to address questions if I could, in spite of my ignorance. The absence of my three dead squadmates (and therefore their idleness) and the occasional appearances of their purely mechanical replacements (surely, such could not be always mistaken for having human occupants?) proved not to be an issue. Instead, the issue was the way in which they seemed to be getting into a remarkable amount of mischief. My dead and absent squad members were overworking themselves by proxy, somehow held responsible for the scheduling of inconveniently timed or placed steam knight drills, interfering with normal disciplinary procedures, and passing on assorted words of questionable wisdom to their more junior brethren.

Instead of searching for ways to keep idle soldiers busy, we had a real labor shortage; the men were busy cutting firewood and burning charcoal to keep up with the fuel demand. Charcoal is much lighter than coal but burns just as hot and with less ash; using only charcoal for drills let us save our limited coal reserves.

Instead of having to deflect questions about where my squad members went, I had to answer a pointed question from an infantry officer about why Ilya had led two squads of steam knights in drills early one morning. Katya gave me a strange, hopeful look when the officer asked that question.

I sighed and turned back to the officer who was complaining to me about Ilya. I neither confirmed nor denied the existence of Ilya to the officer, simply stating that I would talk to those responsible for scheduling a rather noisy rock-breaking exercise an hour before dawn on the grounds immediately outside and below the room the officer had claimed for her own. In the meantime, if she felt too tired to be the duty officer tonight, she was hereby excused to take a nap.

The rest of that particular day dragged on. The fresh-falling snow, reports on the rat extermination project . . . There were a few precious hours I managed to salvage for myself in the workshop we'd set up, working on the mechs and my heavily modified steam suit. Once I felt too tired to do any more work, I ate a late, cold dinner and dragged myself off to bed.

As I was just getting settled, I heard a knock at my door. Yuri looked up, sniffed, then put his head back down. I made up for his lack of growls by grumbling to myself as I lifted myself out of bed and to the door. I found Katya on the other side of it. What was Katya doing at my door? I waved her in and closed the door. There was no need to feed the rumor mill by having her standing around outside my door for any longer than necessary.

"Did Ilya come back?" She had that look on her face again. Pleading. Hoping. Worrying.

"No, Katya. I don't know who was pretending to be Ilya. Maybe Vitold? Maybe someone just wanted to put the blame on one of my troops and figured Ilya wouldn't have a good alibi." I patted her shoulder gently. "I'm sorry."

"Are you sure that he is . . ." She caught herself and looked into my eyes for a moment. She faltered and looked down. Her shoulders hunched, and she made a small choking noise, her face straining into a stoic blank.

I gave her a hug and she returned it, hard enough to hurt a little. She buried her face in my chest, breathing irregularly. I felt sure she was sobbing, though she was too proud to show her tears. I didn't ask her what was wrong or what I could do to fix it; I just held her.

Her grip around my abdomen eased from painful to merely firm after a minute. I started gently stroking her hair, from the crown of her head down to her shoulders, in what I hoped was a reassuring and calming way. Her breathing slowly settled back into a regular pattern; and once it achieved complete regularity, she rubbed her face on my shirt. Then she loosened her grip on me and stepped back to look up into my face. Her eyes were red and puffy.

"Just . . . hold me?" she asked in a very small voice. "For now?"

I did, and after a time, fell asleep holding her. She may have fallen asleep first, but I didn't want to disturb her to check.

A knock sounded from the other side of the door. Three heavy raps, imperious. I woke to find myself alone in my bed. Casting my gaze around the room, the only other living being I saw was Yuri. The dog was sitting next to the bed, silently looking at me.

"Just a minute," I said.

The door was locked from the inside. I had made sure of that last night, and the bolt could only be operated from the inside. Logically, then, Katya had not left the room, yet she was nowhere to be seen. This was curious, though fortuitous given that I had company banging at my door. I unbolted the door and opened it; it was the colonel in charge of supply, and he wanted to talk over a few things before breakfast. Fairly boring things. I had trouble focusing my attention on what he was saying.

I reassured him that I was confident in his ability to keep us well fed and that I would look into sending out a shopping expedition. When that didn't seem to end his litany of complaints, I suggested pointedly that he should probably be supervising the serving of breakfast, lest the portioning be improperly managed. I ushered him out of the room, and then firmly relocked the door. I took a long, deep breath, looking out the window to the snowy landscape below. The master bedroom of the manor was on the highest floor, so I had a very good view of the surroundings.

The window had metal shutters, but those I had left open; they were positioned outside the lovely glass window. The first two floors simply had shuttered arrow slits, but up on the highest floor there were glazed windows, affording a view without a draft. Decadence had its points, I had to confess. Being inside a toasty warm building while gazing out upon the lovely snowy fields was a novel experience and a pleasant one. We'd been there for three weeks, and I still found the contrast between warmth and winter landscape fascinating.

Exasperation put aside, I still had a puzzle in mind: Where was Katya? I checked under the bed, in the closet, and then inside several pieces of furniture I doubted were large enough to conceal a full-grown man but might have been small enough for Katya's petite frame. No Katya.

"Katya?" I asked, experimentally, and thought to check the canopy of the bed. No Katya hiding on top of the canopy, or in it. Had I dreamed her entire visit?

I stared at the bed. It would make sense, I thought to myself, and then spied several long red strands of hair on a pillow. These were the wrong color and length to belong to me or to Yuri. I picked one up, gently, and held it up to the dog.

"Do you know where she is?"

The dog sniffed at my hand experimentally, then jumped up on me, putting his paws up on my shoulders and leaning on me.

"Yes, the girl who was lying on top of me last night."

I sometimes wished Yuri was a lot more talkative. The general, or whoever he trusted the training of his dogs to, preferred that they keep quiet, especially while indoors. This pantomime routine was less than ideal.

"Where is she, boy?" I said.

The dog spent some time sniffing around the room, making a great show out of being thorough to try to impress me. I went back to the window and turned my back to him. I knew better than to encourage his theatrics by paying attention to them.

After a minute, Yuri joined me at the window, putting his paws up on the sill. He made a quiet sort of whuffling noise, a softly mumbled statement that the lady had gone out. Wherever "out" was.

He then pressed his nose up on the glass, then yelped in an undignified fashion when he discovered how cold the surface of it was. He looked at me, worried about being punished for making a loud noise or, I realized, possibly for talking aloud in the first place. I chuckled and scratched him behind the ears, reassuring him that I wouldn't punish him.

"Let's go get some breakfast," I said.

After some weak tea, rubbery eggs, and gritty toast, I was both more awake and more understanding of the colonel's complaints. I called together an officers' meeting, with the addition of Vitold, who decided that he could leverage our friendship to poke his nose into the meeting in spite of his lack of formal rank. At the meeting, I discovered that in addition to the developing shortage of edible foodstuffs, there was some grumbling in the ranks about pay and leave.

We spent the whole morning hammering out a list of problems and trying to figure out the connections between them. One central problem was that we had no money; the general had taken the pay chests with him when he'd left. Money could solve other problems, too. With enough of it, we might be able to acquire supplies locally on a more informal basis. Morale would improve substantially if soldiers were paid.

Another issue was that while nobody was eager to question the general's orders, our mission was, at best, difficult and, at worst, illegal. The part where the general expected us to hole up at the manor and deal with wounded soldiers and damaged equipment seemed reasonable. However, the general had been recalled, and imperial authorities might have expected his troops to come with him.

The solution was to send a handful of men on fast horses back across the mountains. If we were lucky, we would get orders to make our way back to imperial territory. If we were less lucky, we might still get money to deal with our other problems. The supply colonel sat down with me and drew up the appropriate pay requisition forms, forging the deceased

Colonel Romanov's signature in several places on the theory that it improved the odds of success.

I spent the afternoon down in the workshop, while Vitold and the officers ran about putting together the expedition and sending it out. Vitold had begun the process of turning my old suit—his new suit—into a fourth mech, and it was up to me to finish the job. Katya, contrary to what had become her usual practice, didn't come watch me at work. As she was not an officer, I had not been alarmed by her absence from the officers' meeting. As the afternoon wore on into evening, though, I developed a measure of concern. When Vitold came down to tell me dinner was to be served shortly, I brought the subject up with him.

Vitold told me that she'd ridden off with the supply colonel and a handful of other skilled scouts. He'd thought nothing of it. She was a good rider and had spent a good deal of time scouting out the surrounding countryside, making her a natural choice for the mission. Two other sharpshooters had gone, along with a well-born scout who was supposed to be something of an illusionist.

I'd never seen the alleged illusionist succeed at making anything appear or disappear, so I personally doubted he was any more magical than Major Pavlov. Where, I asked Vitold, had Katya been? I hadn't seen her this morning at breakfast.

"Don't know when she set out, but she came riding back in just after lunch," he said with a shrug. "Didn't ask her neither. She was in a foul mood after I passed her the orders. You'd think she'd be happy to be going back across the border, but I know not to throw rocks at a hornet's nest. Especially a hornet I've seen shoot a man in the head without a crack in that poker face of hers."

"Ah. What's for dinner?" I asked, tactfully changing the subject; a wise choice, as Vitold was decidedly pessimistic about how edible dinner would be with the departure of the supply colonel. His griping ended up costing him a kopek when I took the other side of the inevitable wager; dinner turned out to be much more edible than breakfast, in spite of the absence of high-level supervision.

CHAPTER FIFTEEN

In Which I Read Mail

I begin this segment of my narrative with a letter, which Katya brought to me when she and the others returned. (Editor's note: I was provided with the original envelope and document. Postal markings on the envelope indicate it was mailed from a train station in Lviv; the remains of the seal and the markings appear to verify Mikolai's claims that this letter was labeled as an urgent military dispatch.) The supply colonel had been concerned with requisitions and had come with a train of mules laden with supplies, but Katya had a letter she wanted to send home, so she had collected the mail to bring back with her. This particular letter was addressed to the deceased Colonel Ivan Ivanovich Romanov, and Katya had thought that meant I should have it.

Dearest old friend,

My apologies for not writing sooner, but the investigation required some additional efforts beyond that which I normally command. Fortuitously, I received news of the recall of a certain general, which should distract him substantially and therefore open your options considerably. This letter will probably not arrive until after the general has received his recall orders, but if he has not, you should be aware that he has or shortly will receive orders to do so.

This should afford you the opportunity to separate with your trouble-makers—make some sort of logistical excuse to temporarily separate the general from his new favorites and then arrest M.S. and V.S. Execute them if they resist, bring them straight to Tanais if they can be chained up without losses—take the fastest horses you can and leave the general in doubt as to what has happened. Do this without delay; do not allow them to send any communications.

M.S. cannot be anything other than an enemy spy, and V.S. his bought man. Subsequent events indicate that members of their cell, or additional cells of their organization, are likely in communication with them; this suggests that they are part of a substantially larger organization. I am alarmed, and I suspect it will be your head and mine if it continues. The post from which they came caught fire the day before I arrived to inspect records in person and conduct interviews. Coincidence? I think not. Coincidences of this nature simply do not happen.

My investigations demonstrate that there is no record of M.S. or V.S. enlisting in the steam knight corps anywhere. Neither is recorded as being commissioned as officers per records in Khoryvsk, Tanais, or Kazan. I went as far as to check through training records at the military academy. While there are several M.S.'s in the various records, unsurprisingly—common given name, common patronymic—I have eliminated all of them from consideration based on age, physical description, or their location being clearly accounted for.

V.S. I have identified, in spite of his absence from regular army enlistment records. He is from Lviv in western Ruthenia, not far from the border with Lithuania. Records indicate he disappeared from his hometown at the age of fourteen under suspicion of a string of petty thefts and a couple of more serious burglaries. The fourth son of a baker, he was apprenticed to a local machinist for several years before running into trouble with the law. The machinist provided positive identification based on the sketch you provided, as did several other locals. His association with a spy marks him as a traitor to the realm, but if his loyalty is simply to coin, it may be possible to convince him to exchange testimony for leniency in sentencing.

As a bonus, old friend, you should be out of Wallachia fast enough to miss the fireworks. You will probably hear rumors about the prince being alive after all—I cannot confirm this, but half of Yalita was set on fire, and Sultan Alaeddin may decide that the undying emperor has betrayed him.

—I. V. T.

I looked up at Katya. "No, I'm afraid it doesn't say anything about commendations or promotions."

Her face fell. She bit her lip and glanced over at the colonel in charge of supply, who was impatiently giving both of us the hairy eyeball.

"Well? What does it say?" he asked, an edge of belligerence in his voice.

I couldn't blame him for being in a sour mood. Here he was, rightfully of rank to command a battalion of troops himself, and I was, as far as he was concerned, a jumped-up squad leader with delusions of grandeur. On the other hand, while I sympathized with his anger, I couldn't exactly show him a letter that demanded my immediate arrest and recommended a prompt execution.

"I'm afraid I can't tell you that," I said, folding the letter back up.

The colonel blustered for several minutes about how it wasn't right that an impudent enlisted soldier would have denied his request to open the letter immediately, that he had a right to know what the letter said, and that he wanted Katya flogged for insubordination—maybe even shot—but he was a merciful fellow; flogging should be good enough. The woman needed to be taught her place and to respect rank, didn't she? And wasn't he a colonel? The blustering continued, meandering onto a few more subjects before dying out. Throughout his entire tirade, I kept my face completely still. At the end, I raised one eyebrow.

"Is that all?" I asked, my voice taking on a sharp edge.

Katya was trembling and turning white. The colonel shrank in on himself under my stare and nodded very slowly and gingerly.

"Is your name Ivan Ivanovich Romanov?" I asked.

He shook his head. Obviously not.

"Are you, by any chance, the commanding officer for the force to which Ivan Ivanovich Romanov is posted?" I asked.

He shook his head again, a little more slowly this time. He may have been, on paper, the senior surviving officer in our little strike force now that the general had left, but he was not in charge.

"I know that you are quite familiar with regulations. Please take a moment to recall the regulations pursuant to messages marked like so, addressed to an officer in the field, that happen to be important dispatches involving state secrets." I wasn't sure what those regulations said, but I was guessing they involved dire consequences. I let that hang in the air for a moment.

The colonel said nothing.

"Say 'thank you' to Katya for preventing you from making a mistake." I made a little shooing motion with my hand.

His eyes wide, he stammered out an apology to Katya and backed out of the room, nearly tripping over the doorway.

Katya had stopped trembling and was returning to her normal color, alabaster rather than ghostly.

"I did insult a superior officer," she said, very quietly. Uncertainty crept into her voice. "I called him stupid. I called him greedy. I also called him ugly. It was very not respectful."

She was now looking at me with some confusion. I could see a question floating in her eyes: Wasn't she supposed to be punished? She had done a bad thing! She clasped her hands behind her back and looked up at me, waiting to be judged.

"It's okay, Katya," I said. "You can apologize to him later, after he's calmed down. But when he wanted to read the letter, you were right to tell him no."

I shouldn't have reminded her of the letter. Her eyes snapped to my pocket, full of curiosity. I spoke again, quickly and with some uncertainty of my own.

"It's better that nobody else knows what's in that letter. Even you, Katya." As much as I liked Katya and wanted to trust her, handing her a letter marked as an urgent military dispatch talking about arresting and executing me didn't seem like a good idea.

A thought darted across my mind. The locked door. A week ago, I had woken up in this room with my bed smelling of Katya, her hair on my pillow, and a door locked soundly from the inside; a puzzle left unsolved. I trusted Katya—had to trust Katya—to not reveal the death and desertion of my comrades to the general, but I did not understand her very well at all. I did not know how, much less why, she had stolen away quietly in the night.

She was about to shuffle out the door when I asked her to wait and told her that we had other things to discuss. I shut the door and locked it, then sat down on the bed, bringing us nearly eye to eye as she stood stiffly.

I needed a few minutes to gather my thoughts, to understand her motives; so, to pass a little time while I did that, I asked her to describe the trip from her perspective. I added that I did not entirely trust the colonel's thoroughness or priorities. The reason was a factual one, but my nods and thoughtful expression lay over the face of a man sifting his memory for clues about a redheaded woman rather than a man paying attention to what she was telling him.

After a while of this, I decided that I really needed to ask her directly if I wanted answers; so, the next time she stopped to sift through her memory, I took action. I took hold of her hand and squeezed it gently, then spoke up.

"Katya? I think that's enough about the trip for now, thank you. I was wondering," I cleared my throat, still working out how to phrase the question in a way that didn't sound like an accusation. "If I could ask you a question of a slightly more personal nature."

She stared blankly back at me for a moment, then opened her mouth to reply. However, she was interrupted by a loudly barking Yuri.

Odd. Yuri was usually very quiet inside. I looked over at him and he barked again, looking out the window. Strange men had arrived. Looking out the window, I saw the strange men were carrying arquebuses, bows, pikes, and long-bladed spears, which looked like someone had stuck a sword on the end of a staff. And there was at least one woman with them; she was clad head to toe in shining steel plate with intricate orichalcum inlay and was pointing her sword, mouthing something I couldn't hear before closing her helmet. A man who looked similar enough to be her brother or cousin held up a banner of arms.

A purple gem was set in a pearled band wrapped around her helmet, a symbol of her sympathies. I had the sense (how, I did not know) that she was a wizard—could feel that there was some kind of link between her and several nearby mechs. The machines were lumbering forward at full speed, camouflage nets falling off as they pounded ahead under full steam, revealing bold blue, yellow, and red paint—what I would later learn were the colors of the House of the Dragon. There were other machines as well, low squat machines, which I could only think to describe as walking guns, but those were not linked to her.

We were under attack. Taken entirely by surprise, I stood there staring, trying to get a good handle on how many of them there were. The rebels must have followed our people back from their supply mission, launching their attack while my soldiers were busy unpacking cargo. And, judging by the bottles my soldiers were dropping as they scrambled below, they had been busy with a little impromptu celebration to mark the return of wine rations to their diet.

Suddenly, I felt myself being roughly jerked away from the window; Katya was diving to the floor, pulling me with her. We landed between the desk and the wall. There was a crash of shattering glass and breaking wood, and a draft of cold air flooded into the room. When I made as if to rise, confused, she pulled me back down. My heart pounded, and I swear I could nearly hear hers over her fierce whisper.

"Stay down; they have sharpshooters with rifles. One of them spotted you in the window." Katya's white-knuckled grip on me eased up when I nodded assent.

Several more bullets pinged into the room, and there was another crash as the lamp on the desk hit the floor. Yuri barked frantically, promising to rip the enemy gunmen to pieces. I smelled smoke. Katya went crawling for her rifle, left resting against the wall (she never seemed to want to let the thing out of her sight, a habit I was now suddenly glad of); I crawled toward the door.

The locked door. The very solidly locked door, whose lock was conveniently located at shoulder level. I could see a bullet lodged in the wall lower than the lock. Keeping the rest of my body as low as possible, I slowly reached up the wall toward the lock. I instinctively yanked my hand back at the same time I heard a loud ping; an unseen marksman had fired. There was a thin red line on the side of my hand, courtesy of a very near miss that had struck the bolt I was reaching for instead of my hand.

Lucky me, I thought to myself, and then I looked closely. The bullet had smashed the handle off the bolt, and bent the bolt in its housing, but the Avar aristocrat who had the lock installed had placed a very high value on privacy—the piece of high-quality workmanship remained securely attached to the wall and door. I would need a hammer and a chisel to open that bolt now.

"Door's jammed," I told Katya.

A bullet pinged off the chandelier. Katya popped up and fired back, then ducked back down. She looked back at the door as she reloaded her rifle, hammering a new round in as quickly as she could.

"That was a nice shot," she said, staring at the damaged bolt. "Lucky for him. Not lucky for us."

"Unless you know of any other ways out of here," I told her, "then we're trapped in here."

"If we weren't being shot at," she said, "we could climb out the window."

"Is that how you vanished last week?" The question left my mouth before I thought twice. The words dripped with accusation and annoyance.

"I needed to go think. Alone." Katya sounded hurt and defensive. She pounded a new round down the muzzle of her rifle with a bit more force than strictly necessary, the ramming rod bending slightly under the impact.

It sounded like battle was being joined outside. I could hear explosions, the clatter of metal on metal, and the screams of those dying, as well as those who wished they were dying. Yuri started barking again.

"I'm not angry at you," I shouted angrily.

I realize that shouting at someone angrily to tell them that you aren't angry at them tends not to be terribly convincing, but in my defense, modern warfare is loud, as are barking dogs. As Katya crawled under the window to the other side, working toward a better position, I considered our options as best as I could.

We could climb out the window and get shot at. We could take pot-shots at the large number of riflemen outside, distracting them while they fought with my troops, and then get blown up once they thought to pitch a grenade into the large open window. We could hide under the bed, and likely survive the battle that way. However, I doubted I would be lucky enough to survive being captured by Romanians a second time if they won; and if our side won, I would face charges of cowardice and probably get executed. None of these options seemed good; we needed a distraction. I grabbed hold of Katya's calf to get her attention.

"Wait a minute," I told her.

I fished through my pockets, coming up with a handful of coins, and lobbed one in a high arc outside the window as hard as I could. The crows would already be gathering in anticipation of carrion; and if I could get them distracted and excited, perhaps they could serve as a decent distraction.

A cawing noise; there was a lone crow perched on the windowsill. I had the attention of one; others would soon follow.

"Katya, give me all the coin you hold within your possession." My voice sounded distant but calm. A feeling of detachment settled on me.

She looked at me warily for a moment, then complied. With both of my hands full of coins, I stood and pitched them upward and out the window, a bullet whizzing by my head as I did so. A storm of crows dove down from the sky, snagging the coins out of the air even as the metal bits began to fall. Greedily, playfully, they took and traded the shiny pieces with one another. I could barely see the other side of the raucous black cloud of crows. It had worked better than I had hoped, but I could not expect it to last for long. We had to move fast.

"Climb now," I told Katya.

She shouldered her rifle and clambered out the window with enviable grace and speed. Yuri jumped up, putting his paws on the windowsill to watch. I yanked back on his collar. Like most young war hounds, he was very excited at the prospect of battle and was probably ready to do something foolish, like trying to climb the wall after us. I would rather he didn't get hit by a stray bullet.

"Yuri! Go under the bed! Stay there until I come back!" I pointed firmly.

The dog whined, disappointed, but slunk slowly toward the bed. I hastened to follow Katya.

I followed her up the wall as best as I could, watching closely to see the handholds and footholds she used. Her admirably well-toned aft end disappeared over the edge of the roof and was replaced by her concerned-looking face as I struggled up the last few feet. She offered me a hand up; familiar with the physical principles of action and reaction, however, I declined to take it. I thoroughly outmassed her, and a drop from this height would do neither of us any good, I reasoned. However, after I pulled myself over the wall surrounding the rooftop garden, I noticed the rope she'd tied around herself and fastened to a dwarf maple and decided against giving her a lesson on the principles of natural philosophy.

I should take a moment to describe the roof of the manor. Originally, the top of the manor was flat, an open area surrounded with crenelated walls about waist-high, intended primarily as a prepared position for defenders to rain arrows or rocks down on any attacking force. Later, a roof was installed on stilts above the walls, so that people walking about on the upper floor would be shielded from the weather.

More recently, most (though not all) of the roof had been taken out and replaced with the framework for an enclosed greenhouse garden. This garden was not complete—there was no glass in the wood and metal frame, though there were plants in the garden. It wasn't clear to me if glass had ever been installed, if it had been removed during the evacuation of the original residents, or simply smashed during a prior battle or raid. Finally, a small dome—an observatory of sorts intended for astronomical or astrological purposes—sat defiantly perched on top of what little remained of the older roof, supported by a combination of iron pillars and truly audacious architectural engineering.

Since it was winter, the garden was mostly barren and brown; the dwarf maple tree had no leaves—a sad little skeleton of a tree trapped in a pot. Katya and I did not find the garden empty of life, however; there were a pair of mortars there, diligently lobbing shells toward the army below. The mortars, in turn, were fed and tended by a small gang of enlisted men. Presumably, they were doing so by command of the lieutenant, who was currently peering thoughtfully through a looking glass.

There were also some sharpshooters at work, doing their part to reduce the rebel menace a single well-aimed shot at a time as they moved from merlon to merlon around the outer edge of the roof, taking care not to linger in one place too long. One sniper lay slumped against the wall, missing half his head, a gruesome reminder that the other side had sharpshooters of their own.

Near the observatory, I could see the supply colonel arguing with a mechanic about something, gesturing up at the dome. I didn't want to know about what or why. I did, however, want to take stock of the battle, now that I had a chance. It looked grim; we'd been taken by surprise and were struggling to hold back the enemy long enough for the troopers in steam knight suits to get their boilers going. A pair of our mechs had been loaded with charcoal and activated to help move the heavy loads from the carts, but they were taking a heavy beating. And then there was the enemy wizard. She was practically dancing across the battlefield as she directed the rebel army and its war machines against our walls.

"I'm sorry, would you repeat that?" I asked the lieutenant. He'd been asking me something.

"Sir, do you have a plan?" The lieutenant looked ill at ease, though the question was a fair one for him to ask.

I considered his question. Our strategic choices consisted of trying to hold the manor, fleeing, or throwing ourselves on the mercy of the rebel commander. The second and third options involved putting large quantities of imperial military equipment into rebel hands, just the sort of thing to get me executed for cowardice or dereliction of duty. The third also involved becoming a rebel prisoner, something which I had experienced already. I had no desire to repeat that experience.

"Well," I said as a particularly loud crash sounded from below us, several tons of mech collapsing into so many pieces of scrap, "I believe we should fight."

The lieutenant gave me a funny look.

CHAPTER SIXTEEN

In Which I Am Challenged

I left the lieutenant with orders to keep the shelling going at full rate until and unless the mortars started to glow red-hot from being fired too often. He was, I informed him, free to use his discretion in guiding the fire. It isn't clear to me when I learned it was a good idea to tell people to do exactly what they seemed to already think they ought to do, but this was one of the earliest times I recall doing it. The lieutenant straightened up taller and prouder, happy to know he was already doing exactly what he was supposed to do.

I cut the colonel's argument with the mechanic short and asked if he would do me the kindness of fetching additional ammunition for the brave fellows firing from the rooftop. Then I told the mechanic to go fetch buckets of water and sand and try to make sure none of the soldiers blew themselves up or started any fires while firing the mortars. I didn't bother asking what they were arguing about.

The sharpshooters I left to their own devices, or perhaps in truth to Katya's devices; she exchanged a few quick words with them.

I brandished my sword dramatically for the benefit of my military audience, uttered a few words that may or may not have been inspiring, and then paused. How much patriotic fervor could an antique bronze sword infuse in modern imperial soldiers? I resheathed the awkward blade and hastened down the stairs. Katya followed behind me, trailing discreetly in my wake. On the lower levels, chaos reigned. I forged my way through, pretending to be as purposeful as possible. A grubby mechanic rushed toward me.

"Workshop's this way, sir!" He panted, catching his breath for a moment before he jogged off.

What was in the workshop? Oh, right. My armor and the other mechs. Having been given a good idea, I ran after him to the workshop, where Vitold was working on babying the mechs' boilers up to full power. I climbed into my armor, told Vitold to stand clear, and flexed my mental control, revving the warm boilers of the steam knight armor suits to full steam in moments. It was easier than it had been before. Were the elemental spirits growing to know and trust me, or was I growing stronger? I started to close up my armor, rediscovered my sword, made a few adjustments, and then finished the job. Awkward things, swords.

If I didn't know better, I would swear it was trying to blood me with the more decorative parts of the hilt. As I tested the joints and pressure lines with the helmet open, I considered the wisdom of wrapping the sword up with some padding. I mused to myself that if I were a real officer, I would have had a lot of practice pushing it out of the way, fiddling with it, and keeping the thing out of the way, but I wasn't a real officer. I'd never owned a sword before.

Good thing I didn't need to use the thing in battle. I grabbed my poleaxe out of its nook behind me, the heavy weapon light as a toy to the powerful artificial muscles of the suit. I let my mechanical brethren take the lead and was pleased to see soldiers cheer as we marched out of the workshop and toward the main entrance. The enemy had driven us back against the walls of the manor, forcing us into a defensive posture; now we would sally forth. I tromped out in tight formation with my mechs and pointed my poleaxe forward, bellowing something vague and forgettable which, at the time, I thought was suitably patriotic sounding. It was probably drowned out by the noise of the steam engines.

There were three small problems with my glorious charge.

The first problem was that there was a friendly heavy mech just outside the doorway struggling with a pair of lighter but more agile enemy mechs; the heavy mech was taking orders from a particularly valiant crew of mechanics, who were very bravely hiding behind a pile of crates off to the side of the doorway. The lot of them were shouting conflicting commands at it as they boldly cowered low to the ground under cover, tool bags held over their heads protectively against the chance a bullet might manage to curve around the wall, take a high arc over the crates, and plunge down at them from above.

If discretion were the better part of valor, these mechanics were among the most valorous soldiers the Golden Empire had to offer. I think the elemental spirit driving the mech was having some difficulty understanding what orders to follow, if it was following orders at all. It was simply standing in place and waving its weapons around in a vaguely threatening manner, making it difficult to pass safely. So, our dramatic charge had to slow and turn as we passed the friendly heavy mech and came around to the side of the pair of enemy mechs.

The second problem was that in spite of the armor, the crows recognized me as the generous fellow who'd been throwing shiny things around upstairs, and they started diving down to ground level as soon as I stepped out the door, engulfing me in a sea of black wings and greedy cawing. Crows are very clever and learn to recognize the faces of humans, and humans are something they often gossip about. Crows you have never met will know your face and know if you have been kind or cruel to them. I had, unfortunately, placed myself in the former category, and one of the greedy pests must have been watching through the window of the workshop, letting the rest know that the man inside that armor suit was the same as the man who threw the shiny coins out the window.

The third was that the enemy wizard had sensed me coming, her arcane senses warning her of my approach. While I stood in the middle of the milling crows regretting my earlier generosity, she unleashed a powerful blast of force that slammed me against the stone wall of the manor. My poleaxe broke, the haft snapping just below the head; only the protective magic of my armor saved my bones from a similar fate. For several seconds, my attention was split between trying to regain an upright position and providing direction to my mechs. One I called to follow me; the rest I directed at the enemy mechs in the entrance before they finished off the friendly heavy. Crows cawed hungrily, their cries audible over the ringing in my ears.

A hail of bullets rattled off my armor as I lurched to my feet, looking at the wizard who had tried to smash me like a bug. I could feel her hate like a palpable force. The deep crack of Katya's rifle sounded behind me, a familiar note in the hymn of battle. The man waving the banner dropped to the ground like a sack of beets, the flag standing by itself for a brief heartbeat, balanced precariously on end before it followed him to the earth. The wizard's concentration wavered as she glanced back at the man, her sword dipping toward the earth involuntarily.

One of the enemy mechs, a heavy, dropped the tip of its own much more massive sword into the dirt, turning in perfect unconscious harmony with her body. The death had taken her off guard, and her link with the elemental spirit driving the machine's hydraulics was so intimate as to defy separation. She shook herself, and then she and the mech both spun in place, pointing swords at me with the same synchrony. A bolt of fear shivered through my heart, and I grasped the broken shaft of my poleaxe in both hands. The rebel wizard shouted one word as she stalked forward, waving a sword that was now glittering with runes.

"Butcher!" she shouted.

Whether she was confusing me with a different imperial officer or simply saying that I was a vile murderer wasn't clear to me. What was clear was that she intended to kill me. The hate in her voice, the hate in her eyes, the hate just filled the air between us. I was an imperial officer; I was responsible for this latest death, for the fall of the banner she fought under, both literally and metaphorically, and for the death of her kin. Perhaps this man, and likely others before him. For this, only my death would sate her, and probably only for a little while.

The crows were starting to drift back toward me. I needed to buy time for my mechanical comrades to catch up with me. I turned around.

"Go bother her for a change," I shouted at them through my helmet.

Then I (perhaps taking inspiration from my valorous comrade mechanics) cranked my suit's arcane engine up to full and sprinted to keep distance between myself and the rebel wizard. Pressure valves strained at their limits as hydraulic pistons slammed. Bullets rang off my back as the enemy soldiers focused their fire on me, realizing I had been singled out by their commander as a special target. The raucous cawing behind me sounded angry—the enemy wizard had stopped to slice at the birds.

I also needed a weapon; something other than my sadly headless poleaxe. A sharp pain in my back reminded me that I had a weapon; it was just inside my armor. I raised my arms up, then pulled them directly inward, disengaging them from the armor. This left my suit's arms up and out of the way and my own arms in position to scrabble around for the sword and open my helmet. I think I nearly dislocated my shoulder trying to get the awkwardly shaped sword out through my opened visor. I did gouge myself with the hilt, one of its talons tearing a bloody scratch from my neck up past my ear before the sword plunged into the dirt.

I stopped my headlong run, put my right arm back into place to control my suit's arms, and overbalanced, lurching forward as I tried to grab for the sword. There was a flash of light just as I swung the visor shut with my left hand, the enemy wizard blasting me into the air. To one side, I could hear the approaching footfalls of a heavy enemy mech, and then I hit the dirt, a blinding flare of turquoise light reflecting off the inside of my helmet.

I called my other mechs forward to me. One of the enemy light mechs was a pile of scrap metal already, and the other was retreating steadily from the entrance, away from the friendly heavy mech. My fellow imperial soldiers were now advancing under cover as best as they could, the crates, wagons, and boxes from the shopping expedition finding new purposes as bullet-blockers.

As I searched for my weapon in the dirt, I found the sheath first, and then I saw the sword itself. Red blood seeped around the edges of the talons, leaving me wondering how much I had bled. The wings of the gilded crow were also spread wider than I thought I remembered, and the blade was glittering very brightly in the sunlight. The blood tracing down the cross-hatching of the grip made the shaft look like it had scales. Interesting, I thought to myself. A loud crash of metal on metal not five paces to my rear reminded me that I didn't have time for a close inspection of my weapon. I spun around.

The enemy heavy mech was standing over one of my mechs, its massive sword raised. The collision of the two war machines had gone poorly for the smaller one, which was mine. Beside it was the enemy wizard, sword in one hand, pistol in the other. I lunged; there was a clatter of metal as the enemy wizard parried my clumsy blow. The next thing I knew, she was in my face, her blade ringing off my helmet. The edge of her sword was not well suited for smashing through heavy armor, and the enchanted armor absorbed the shock with little trouble. She darted back out with a frown on her face.

I felt the mech's elemental cage crack as the enemy mech's much more massive sword smashed into it, close to a hundred grivnas of tempered steel creasing armor plate like paper. I took a cautious step, readying my blade, pointed at the enemy wizard, then swung hard to the side at the heavy mech, hoping to catch the machine off guard and throw it off balance. If I could knock it over, I could escape.

The ancient bronze blade sliced deep into the hardened steel. The heavy mech lurched drunkenly, its control systems disrupted by the blow. I followed up with another blow while it was staggering, a high overhand swing that cut down between the enemy mech's shoulders, biting into its control systems with a flare of deep green light. As the enemy mech toppled, I felt a sudden surge of pain across my left side, my muscles seizing up without my control.

The enemy wizard had come up behind me and severed one of the flux transmission cables of the arcane engine with a powerful lunge, the point of her enchanted blade proving equal to the task of puncturing a weak spot in my armor. I knew exactly which hydraulic line she'd been lucky enough to stab; the left leg of my armor would be stiff for the rest of the battle, the actuators unpowered. I turned, pivoting backward on the frozen leg. My other three jury-rigged mechs were rapidly approaching, but at the moment only the crows kept the enemy soldiers away. I swung at the woman wildly.

She parried again, riposting smoothly. The tip of her enchanted blade dug into the gorget of my armor for a moment before skittering off. The crows swirled around us, pecking harmlessly at her armor as I swung back, but she was already darting away, giving an order that directed a fresh volley of bullets in my direction. A hail of bullets battered my armor.

The arcane engine that powered my armor was damaged, I was bleeding from several places, and the protective enchantments that kept me alive were starting to fail. However, I still lived, and the attention I and my mechs had drawn had cost the enemy dearly; each of the scattered bullet holes and dents in my armor represented a bullet that was not sent to pester my less well-protected comrades. More steam knights were advancing from the manor.

A few shots pinged off my mostly intact rear armor. I've watched new infantry on the training field; standard imperial practice is not to teach them to aim, but simply to load and fire repeatedly. It is not the most efficient practice when it comes to the consumption of gunpowder; nor is it especially comforting when unaimed fire clips you from behind. With the possible exception of the enemy wizard, however, the enemy's armor was not as good as mine, and they were taking casualties.

Then the front door of the manor opened, revealing a dozen steam knights, and the enemy soldiers faltered. If four out of the first five steam knights were still standing after having withstood the brunt of their fire, what could they do against a dozen more steam knights? The artillery landing on their flank and the unnaturally aggressive crows did not much help. The aggressive birds were trying to harvest eyeballs from men who were still standing—usually such attention is reserved for corpses, or at least the helplessly injured.

Had they known that my mechs had enough spent bullets rattling around their inner works that their legs sounded like shaking coin purses whenever they took a step, perhaps they would not have been so discouraged. The real steam knights weren't protected by enchantments as I was, and they had fragile flesh and bone on the inside.

The enemy wizard dashed back and forth along their lines, trying to inspire them, her agile form seemingly untouchable in its shining shell of form-fitted wizard armor, but she could not halt the tide. I watched an enemy officer drop out of his saddle; watched as his fellow cavalrymen turned deaf ears to her shouts and their backs to the battle. Our dead lay mostly behind crates and walls, shielded from view. Many of their mechs had gone down, but nearly all of our steam knights were still standing.

I lurched forward with my squad, keeping up the illusion of pursuit as best as I could with a stiff leg and an engine on the verge of failure, my mechanical comrades waving their poleaxes menacingly. One bold squad of enemy halberdiers did rush us, their combined efforts putting Misha's old suit on the ground. I felt nauseous as my makeshift weapon ripped through one of them, cleaving up from his armpit to the opposite side of his neck. I watched sickly as his head hit the ground, helmet falling off. He had brown hair, a goatee, and a surprisingly well-combed mustache; the calm expression death imposed on his face seemed out of place in the chaos of the battlefield.

Then I was swinging again, striking at a man whom I'd thought was already dead but who was now rolling over and trying to work his arquebus with his one remaining arm. In the distance, I could make out the bright form of the enemy wizard astride a horse, and then in a different direction, Katya, perched up on the roof, aiming. She held her aim for a minute and then lowered the gun, a gesture of mercy. Katya slung her rifle over her shoulder, then patted her hip. Squinting, I could make out what she had patted: a bag at her waist.

It was over but for the screaming, the looting, the taking of prisoners, the cutting of throats, from mercy or malice, the salvaging of enemy machinery, and the reckoning of what it meant for our mission. I didn't feel like dealing with any of those things. I sat down and began to look over my weapon.

The bright blade had not so much as a bloodstain on it, though my armor was spattered to the point of looking mottled brown. The crow that made up the gilded crosspiece of the weapon—I now noticed it was a slightly pudgy crow with a bulging belly; how had I not noticed that before?—looked about as cheerful as the real ones did right now. I guessed that a well-made sword, being a smooth piece of metal, didn't need cleaning after a battle. It must have dripped itself clean while I wasn't looking.

I had a vague feeling I was supposed to oil it or something, but being a mechanic rather than an officer, I'd never really been taught about the care and feeding of swords. Sword steel was made differently than tool steel, and I had rarely dealt with any sort of bronze at all.

CHAPTER SEVENTEEN

In Which I Speak of Devils

It would be overstating matters to say that Vitold surprised me. I gradually became aware of his presence and his reproachful look. Evidently, someone needed to bring the steam knight armor suits inside, and he didn't trust anyone else to do the task. I wondered how well Vitold's thin fiction about Ilya, Misha, and Gregor's continued existence would hold up now that half our command had witnessed them having holes shot in their suits that would kill a living man. Not to mention, Vitold was supposed to be my squadmate, too, and he had been in the workshop the whole time that his suit had been fighting.

I waved the three functional steam knight armor suits to work; Vitold's former suit helped me walk back to the workshop while Gregor's and Ilya's carried Misha's between them. Vitold walked with us openly, looking over the damage and commenting. He didn't like how slow I was limping, and when I said that I hadn't broken my leg, he decided to stop for a minute to examine my suit.

"Oh, I see. Yeah, can't just patch that until we get this thing pulled apart, and I don't want to do that until we're back in the workshop. Do you think she was aiming for that?" Vitold said, indicating the puncture in my back.

"I don't think she knew the machinery well enough to know what she was aiming for," I said, "but I think she was aiming for that little spot. Scary woman. I hope I don't meet her again."

Vitold snorted. "I thought you liked the spooky women, Mikolai."

"Whatever gave you that idea?" I shook my head, puzzled. "I wouldn't want anything to do with her even if she weren't trying to shoot me. Did you feel the sheer hate she puts out?"

Belatedly, it occurred to me that the sheer presence of hate I'd felt from her might have been something that only I, as another wizard, could feel. I knew wizards could sense each other, and I'd begun to sense other wizards myself; maybe that sense extended a little further than knowing who was and was not a wizard. All Vitold would have seen was a woman in armor, directing the enemy troops. I concentrated, closing my eyes, consciously trying to feel around for the beacon of hate, but she must have been too far away. I could feel neither her burning hate nor her.

"Mikolai? Are you listening to me?" Vitold waved his hand in front of my face. "You're a bit spooky yourself, too." Evidently, he had continued the conversation about me and scary women; after turning my attention inward, though, his words had just blended in with the noise of the boilers around me and the cawing of the crows as they scavenged.

"Sorry. Tired after all this." I waved my hand at a nearby corpse. "I don't like it."

"That's what I'm talking about. One of the things. Speak of the devil," he said as a familiar woman on horseback approached and dismounted next to us. Her horse was breathing heavily. What did Katya's approach have to do with infernal beings? Vitold's statements didn't make much sense to me, likely because I hadn't been paying attention to what he'd said earlier.

"Should I put together some men and go after them, sir?" Katya was crisp and formal. "I counted twenty-one of them, sharing nineteen horses. It should not be hard to catch them up in a few days of riding."

I thought for a moment. The enemy wizard could return later, with more troops. On the other hand, she had a head start and was likely on friendly terms with the Avar authorities. Possibilities whirled through my head and I jumped to a decision. There were other things we could be doing, aside from trying to chase down a defeated rebel wizard who had raised a force of Wallachian sympathizers in the Romanian-speaking part of Avaria.

"No," I said, then explained the reason for my decision. "Even if she had noticed your gesture of mercy, which I doubt, she's not the surrendering type, and any force we can move quickly enough to catch her and the other survivors at this point will be too small to deal with any reserves she may have refrained from committing to this battle." I hadn't seen any wagons or mules loaded up with coal at the battle; logic suggested it was unlikely she left her supply train unguarded.

"Gesture of mercy? Sir?" She seemed genuinely puzzled. Had she not heard me over the noise of the boilers?

"When you refrained from shooting her?" I mimed raising a rifle and then lowering it without shooting.

"I forgot I had not reloaded, sir." She looked down and patted the empty bag at her hip. "My ammunition was out. I killed eleven men today," she added, a note in her voice that could be taken as hopeful or pleading. She stood there expectantly, the noise of four active boilers filling the space between us.

After a moment of wondering what she was waiting for, I fumbled out a useful order for her. "Tell the men I want the dead stripped of everything. And I mean everything. Take the clothes as intact as possible." I looked down at a corpse. "And have them washed. The clothes, not the bodies. The bodies I want burned. I'll be in the workshop."

She looked crestfallen for a moment, then mounted back up and rode off to relay my orders to the men scrounging around the battlefield. I watched her with some interest, then took note of the blade at her side. Sharpshooters, like officers but unlike regular arquebusiers, were issued swords as a matter of course. Perhaps she could instruct me in the use of swords and how to care for them properly. They seemed quite different from axes. I was reasonably sure that an axe blade would have needed cleaning at this point, but an axe blade would also have been caked with drying blood; the bronze sword wasn't.

I looked over at Vitold. He was shaking his head.

"Spooky women like you, too," Vitold said, leaning in close so as to be heard without being overheard.

The pieces came together in my mind: Vitold thought Katya was spooky. When he said "speak of the devil," he had been employing metaphor, much as my aunt in town refused to talk about the little old lady I chopped wood for in the summertime or even tell me if she had a name other than "Grandmother," on the superstitious grounds that naming her might cause her to show up. The attention of demons and devils and the like are supposedly drawn by mention of their names. It's a silly peasant superstition, really—as any educated person ought to know, the rituals for summoning demons are a little more complex than that. (Editor's note: This comment marks the end of a page in the original manuscript. Mikolai's manuscript contains marginal notes, which are numbered, either providing addenda [which I have chosen to insert directly into the text] or illustrating a point visually [the limited capital available for print-ing this publication precluded the use of engravings in this edition of the work, so these have simply been omitted]. The last marginal note on this page is numbered 71; the next marginal note is numbered 74, indicating that there is some material missing from the manuscript as I received it.)

Aside from all that, the basic point that I came to understand then and there was that Vitold didn't like Katya, and in fact was a bit frightened of her. Just because I was friends with both of them did not mean they liked each other; this would later prove important. I didn't really know how to respond to Vitold saying that Katya was spooky or suggesting that Katya had a particular liking for me. She was, of course, my friend, and I counted her as having saved my life, but Vitold seemed to think there was something more between us.

As Vitold and I finished our hike back into the workshop, I noticed that other soldiers were taking note of the serious damage to Misha's old suit as it was carried in—it was halfway crushed and full of bullet holes. I thought they were taking note of the lack of telltale blood dripping out, but then I noticed the respectful looks sent Vitold's way and the murmured congratulations and wide eyes.

They were, it turned out, most impressed by how Vitold had man-aged to survive his suit being so thoroughly wrecked, having somehow mistaken Misha's suit for his. One steam knight even joked that Vitold was tougher than a steam suit and that the suit should wear him for pro-tection in the future.

It is amazing how far men will go to bend reality to fit a lie.

On my way into the workshop, I left an assortment of instructions. In addition to repeating the instructions I had given Katya (strip the bod-ies of the dead of everything, including clothing, burn the dead, wash the clothes), I left instructions that steam knight squads were to be in armor in shifts for the night. This was so we would have a quicker response if the enemy proved to have immediate reinforcements; I did not suspect this would happen, but those orders, orders for the watch to be doubled, orders to take care of the wounded, et cetera, all served to reassure the troops and officers under my command that I had a good grip on the situation.

By the time I reached the workshop, I was thoroughly tired of it and left instructions that I was not to be bothered, short of the resumption of hostilities. I wanted to put blood and war out of my mind for a while. I wanted to work with metal and machines constructively, rather than destructively. I also wanted to get a good look at this weapon of mine. There were too many puzzles about it.

When I outlined my ideas to Vitold, he went enthusiastically to work disassembling the least damaged mech (his original suit, as it so happened).

He didn't ask to help with the sword, nor did I ask him to; his discomfort was obvious. On close inspection of the weapon, I myself became uneasy. I carefully laid it on a workbench and inspected the blade. There was something written on it; remembering my blackout on the day I had found the weapon, I stepped back, retrieved a looking glass, and examined the lettering at a greater distance, making sure not to touch the weapon. The words that were written in orichalcum inlay on the bronze blade were crude and cryptic:

> *By willful light and wrath has slaved he me,*
> *With blood and prayer aimless in him.*
> *Thus bound my hunger fast to raven grim,*
> *For I am chained to feast and fight with glee.*

It didn't make much sense, and it didn't sound familiar. I thought back again to when I had first seen it and how I thought it had a handle shaped like two serpents then. Then a gaunt crow, and now a fat one. Perhaps that memory had not been mistaken; perhaps this had been a snake-handled sword once, the one I remembered seeing. If that was the case, the sword must have shifted. I wasn't sure, but even the blade looked larger to me.

It was a puzzle I wanted to spend more time on, but that was time and energy I could not spare. The weapon had served me well today, and that was that. I had work to get done—modifying and rebuilding a steam knight suit and attempting to assemble at least one working elemental cage out of several wrecked ones. Vitold turned in sometime around midnight; I kept working for a while. After I caught myself falling asleep, and nearly planted myself face-first in a coal bin, I decided it was time to call it a night. I staggered upstairs and into my bed.

In the morning, I awoke and noticed three things I hadn't when staggering sleepily into my bed: First, the shattered window had been boarded up, so it was still fairly dark in the room. Second, there had been a note left on my pillow. This was now adhered to my face; evidently the ink had not been completely dry when I rolled over onto it. The note was thoroughly illegible—smudged and smeared beyond any recognition. Third, Yuri wasn't there; an unusual occurrence, as he usually followed me everywhere and, I recalled, I had last seen him here.

I was scrubbing my face clean of ink when a knock sounded at the door. It proved to be the lieutenant who had been directing the mortars in battle the other day. He had dark circles around his eyes.

"Sir?" the lieutenant asked me. "The prisoners have been asking for their clothes back. They have been making quite a racket."

"Prisoners?" My mind stalled for a moment. It took me a minute to think back and remember that some of the enemy's troops had surrendered. "Asking for their clothes back?" I repeated his words back to him. "We have a bunch of naked prisoners downstairs." The tone of my voice was that of a statement, but the meaning carried a question.

"Yes, sir, we were told you wanted the enemy stripped of everything, including clothing, and the clothing washed." The lieutenant's tone was measured and even. "We obeyed your orders to the letter, sir." His eyes were full of questions.

I had ordered the prisoners stripped? I thought back. I had ordered the dead bodies stripped. There had been some creative interpretation somewhere along the chain of command. Perhaps, I reflected, I had made a mistake in leaving orders that I not be bothered.

"Fyodor," I said, for that was his given name, and I was inclined to be familiar. "Return their clothing to them and give them my apologies for the misunderstanding. Tell them"—I paused for a moment, searching for something diplomatic to say—"that I simply intended to offer them the option of having their clothes washed, but a mistake in translation was made." Translation not from language to language but from person to person. "It would be very helpful if we could secure their voluntary cooperation for the next phase of our operation."

"Next phase, sir?" Fyodor apparently couldn't keep all his questions penned up in his eyes.

"Yes, the next phase." The prisoners hadn't played a role in my plan originally, but they could help a great deal with its successful execution.

I had a quick breakfast, during which I met up with Yuri and Katya. The former was bashful and the latter reproachful, which I thought was strange. I had forgotten Yuri and left him hiding under the bed, and he had every right to look reproachful, but he looked bashful. Katya was in some fashion responsible for the misinterpretation of my orders, giving her every right to look bashful, but instead, she looked reproachful. I suffered their respective bashfulness and reproachfulness without comment.

When the lieutenant returned from placating the prisoners, I told him to compile a quick dossier on the prisoners based on what he and the other soldiers had learned while guarding them and to bring it to me in the little library as soon as possible. I wanted, I told him, to interview the prisoners before lunch.

CHAPTER EIGHTEEN

In Which I Face Treachery

The little library was a small, windowless room on the first floor. From the empty bookshelves lining the walls, we had deduced that it was a library; there was a larger and grander one up on the third floor; though it, too, lacked books. It had two gorgeous chairs, a small table, a desk, and several lamps; the chairs were a little too large to fit comfortably through either of the doors to the room. Presumably, some workman had assembled them inside the room, or one of the doors had been removed to facilitate their entry.

The fact that the room was small and had two doors exiting into two different hallways was important for me to stage this correctly. I did not want the prisoners to talk to one another after being interviewed or even to know what had happened to the previous interviewee. I had seen first-hand what happens when soldiers are filled with ignorance; ignorance had fueled all sorts of whispers about me behind my back. I wasn't entirely sure what all the rumors were, but they seemed to have generated a great deal of unwarranted fear and respect.

The lieutenant was swaying on his feet a little when he delivered a short stack of papers to me.

"Fyodor, how long have you been awake?"

He stammered something about having gotten a short nap after dinner the previous day. I suggested he get some sleep on his own terms before sleep caught him unaware and set its own terms of engagement.

I passed on orders to bring the prisoners by one at a time, starting with the apparent leaders, and busied myself leafing through the papers and reading about our prisoners. I was out of uniform, wearing a stark but expensive-looking ensemble of black clothes salvaged from a miraculously overlooked closet up on the fourth floor.

I was seated in one of the chairs; Katya stood at my left shoulder, and Yuri sat on my right side. We had loaded the shelves with what books we could find, along with an assortment of other things (weapons, papers, tools, and the like) to give the impression of long occupancy. My sword leaned in one corner, not for any practical purpose, but because it served as a reminder that I was not someone to be trifled with. Also because I didn't want anyone else to touch the thing and wind up getting caught in a trance the way I had been the first time I took a serious look at it.

The first prisoner they showed in was one of the foreign mercenaries; purportedly the most senior one.

"You are called Torvald Bauerstein?" I asked.

He nodded.

"Speak up," I said.

"I am indeed Captain Torvald Bauerstein," he said. "The ranking officer of the Bauerstein Company." He muttered something in a Norse dialect under his breath.

Yuri growled dubiously, baring his teeth.

"Ah, you don't believe he's telling the truth?" I asked Yuri, and then turned back to the man, switching to my best book-learned Norse to make my point. "Let us speak unpolished truth. Lives lie on the table like coin."

To illustrate my metaphor, I placed a silver Avar denarius on the table, pushing it forward with my finger. I let him see the coin and then cocked my finger and flicked it. It chimed musically as it bounced on the floor, spinning unevenly. I waited as the coin wobbled to a complete stop, and let the silence hang over us.

He swallowed. "Junior Lieutenant Ragnar Rimehammer, third-ranking officer of our company before today. Our number two took a mortar shell to the face. I volunteered to pretend to be the captain in case you were going to execute the officers. They said that—" He stopped himself.

"I'm sure your cousin appreciates your loyalty," I said dryly, taking a shot in the dark. The widening of the lieutenant's eyes was encouraging. "I'm afraid the question isn't about the disposal of officers alone." I steepled my fingers and let him draw his own conclusions about what that statement meant. "I am, however, hiring, and your contract with those amethyst pendant people has collapsed."

I opened a drawer on the desk. I placed in front of him a small silver bowl, a quill, a penknife, and, after a moment, a sheet of paper. The paper announced, in Norse, that the undersigned individual swore loyalty and secrecy, and would be compensated appropriately at the end of the term of service, not to exceed one year or the completion of the mission. The wording was vague and, I hoped, a little ominous. I dripped several drops of a clear liquid into the bowl from the flask.

"I am not at cross purposes with you or your distant homeland. If you wish, simply nick yourself," I gestured at the bowl, "and sign." I gestured at the contract.

"And if I don't wish?" Ragnar gave me a hard look.

"It is your choice to sign or not sign." I shrugged nonchalantly.

"What happens if I don't sign?" His request for details was understandable.

I ignored the question entirely, letting the absence of a reply speak for itself.

He slowly reached for the penknife and contemplated it for a moment. Yuri growled. Katya stiffened. Tension filled the air, but I continued to feign indifference. After a few moments, the Swede sighed and pricked his thumb, squeezing out two drops of blood into the bowl. He set the knife down, picked up the quill, and signed his name in blood.

Having Ragnar's real name and rank sitting there on the paper was helpful in dealing with the rest of the Swedish mercenaries. He was second in command and had been trying to pass himself off as the captain of that company, after all; the display of his willing cooperation and honesty worked to reassure the rest of them. One by one, they each signed the contracts I prepared for them and were sent to assemble in the main hall.

The last was their real captain, an older fellow who walked a little unevenly, his surviving foot taking a larger share of his weight, a preference ingrained over the last two years. His name was Felix Rimehammer. He took in the fact that I had signed (perhaps I should say "impressed") his company out from under him with equanimity and even cracked a brief smile when I asked him to add his title of captain to the front of his signature.

I told him that I would brief everybody at once on our plans as a unit after I was done dealing with all of the prisoners. He gave me a careful, measuring look.

"I look forward to learning more," he said. "Though I wish I were on a kinder side of the puzzle you present."

The process of dealing with prisoners got a little trickier after that. The Swedish unit had surrendered as a group and survived largely intact, including two of its three officers; the other surviving soldiers were a mix of at least two different smaller mercenary outfits and an assortment of independent fighters with varying loyalties. Some were from Wallachia, some from Avaria, and others from elsewhere in Western Europe.

The second Romanian-speaking prisoner I met with was a young aristocratic-looking fellow by the name of Radu Odobescu. He had refused to answer any questions about who he was and where he was from beyond giving his name, but his name and his native fluency in Romanian made his origins clear enough. If I knew more about the Wallachian nobility, his name might have been enough for me to know where he was from, but all I know is that he was the first to reject my offer of employment.

"It is your choice to sign or not sign," I told him, gesturing to the penknife with finality.

He picked it up, looking it over; and then suddenly lunged at me, taking me by surprise. His lunge was stopped short, for as quick as he was, Yuri was faster, a furry blur full of growling teeth bowling him to the ground. A rasp to my left sounded, Katya belatedly pulling out her sword to protect me. Radu stopped struggling, and Yuri stopped biting, content to stand over Radu's prone form.

"Is he still alive?" I asked.

Katya bent over him for a few moments, then stood back up.

"No," she told me, beaming with confidence in her answer. She fished a greasy rag out of her pocket and started wiping something red and sticky off her sword.

Radu's body had gained some additional perforations in several places; a fact that explained both Katya's confidence in her medical assessment, as well as the state of her blade. Under the circumstances, I could not find a rational fault with Katya's enthusiasm; the fellow had been trying to kill me, after all.

"Ah," I said, collecting my wits about me. "Well done," I said to my protectors, then patted each of them in turn on the head.

A moment later, I remembered that head-patting was not a traditional form of commendation for humans of the army, but Katya looked fit to split her face with her smile. No harm done, I thought to myself. I suppose she took that in the spirit it was meant rather than as an insult. Then I poked my head into the hallway to call for a couple of soldiers to remove the body.

The next time one of the prisoners tried to kill me, I was not taken completely by surprise, and jumped out of the way, knocking my chair over and toppling backward over it in a most undignified fashion that sent my face into the base of a set of shelves behind. The shelves then buried me in a combination of knickknacks and books and left me with a cut from the cavalry saber that had been displayed on a stand.

Katya acted more quickly this time, flailing wildly at the would-be assassin with her sword. He put up a remarkable show for a man with limited armament, ducking away from the wilder swings and parrying others with a stool in his left hand, the penknife held low and loose in his right hand as he waited for a good opportunity to counterattack.

Yuri, barred a safe shot at the man's throat by Katya's wide swings, lunged at his belly, grabbing a mouthful of flesh and intestines, the latter spooling out as the man staggered away from Katya and dropped his stool. He blocked one more blow with the penknife in his right hand, but no more than that as she chopped into his left shoulder, forehead, and then neck. Katya dragged the body out and then returned with a pistol appropriated from one of my officers, evidently considering her sword insufficiently lethal.

The third would-be assassin also went for the penknife. I tried to grab it back from him, meaning that my left ear was singed by the flash from Katya's pistol. After that, I resolved that I would sit farther back out of the way and let my bodyguards handle it, but no other attempts were forthcoming. In retrospect, I think that most of the troops who had great personal enthusiasm for the Romanian cause had either fled or died rather than surrender.

That, or the bloodstains on my bodyguards and on the floor in the room were obvious enough of a warning that future attempts were likely to fail.

I had bloodstained boots and a stack of contracts signed in blood. The coppery tang of blood seemed to follow me into the great hall as I walked to the head of the head table—a seat that in the manor's dining hall was elevated a step above the rest of the head table and two steps above the lower tables.

Katya and Yuri trailed in my wake. The mercenaries waited with evident trepidation and my imperial comrades with evident anticipation. From the faint whispers I heard, the rumors were flying fierce and fast around the lower tables. I would have blamed Vitold, except he was sitting quietly at the high table with the other officers. A neat row of coins sat in front of him; I was not quite sure why, but whatever the reason, Vitold had a smile on his face as he counted them.

"Our mission has been to track the rebels down, root down to their secret bases of strength, and to destroy them at the source upon their own ground." This should not surprise anyone, but I wanted to state it carefully in those terms.

"That ground is not here in Avaria." I raised a hand to still the sudden babble of confused voices, a mixture of consternation and surprise emanating primarily from my imperial comrades.

When silence fell, I continued. "We have gathered crucial intelligence in our operations here; where before we struck at the hands and feet of the rebellion, we may now seek to position ourselves for a strike at its neck. As our commanding officer made sure to impress on you, our mission has always been served by operational security. In order for us to strike at those manipulating and supplying the rebels from afar, we must be a hidden blade, one that does not show the emperor's undying hand. Our new recruits have already sworn secrecy in the firmest terms."

Several nervous former prisoners touched the fresh knife pricks on their hands or arms nervously, looking around. One looked ready to vomit.

"We will, as far as anyone outside our chain of command is concerned, simply be a band of sell-swords operating together under contract. Each of you will be developing a cover identity. To the degree that our supplies allow"—and by that I meant the salvage from our last battle—"you will be afforded new arms and armor and new uniforms, or at least modified ones. Everything must look foreign, salvaged, or both. This will be most difficult for the steam knights."

Vitold frowned sourly. So did the steam knights. I continued my speech.

"We have a number of experts in the use of our new armaments, and in the deportment, habits, and hobbies of mercenary soldiers. They will be accompanying us and will be integrated into our force until such time as their contracts expire. Integrated completely, I might add, at the level of the smallest squads. I am satisfied with their guarantees of loyalty."

I waved at the clumps of mercenaries, sitting in tight little groups together around the hall. I was not actually so sure of their loyalty, but the more confident I seemed in my ruse about blood oaths, the more effective it would be. It would be enough if they believed they were bound by magically binding contracts.

"We will depart this location within a week to continue our mission elsewhere. I expect by that time each of you has a cover identity that will hold up under scrutiny, clothing that does not look like it was issued to you by order of the emperor, and at least one new friend with whom you feel honored to fight back-to-back against great odds. Your officers will have further, and more specific, orders for you later."

Over the din of dismissed soldiers taking their leave, I heard the soft sound of metal sliding on wood and a musical clinking—Vitold pushing two coins across the table to a smiling lieutenant and pocketing the rest with a broad grin of his own. The supply colonel had a sour look on his face, an expression that grew even sourer when I told him I needed him to arrange to produce good forgeries of various documents, and that he was responsible for putting together the necessary sewing circles to tailor our imperial uniforms into less regular garb that could pass for private issue.

The following excerpt is taken from the first chapter of *Ragnar Rimhamar, Gentleman Adventurer*, with permission of the publisher. The discerning reader may note that there are a number of differences between Mikolai's version and Ragnar's version of the events described herein. Some of these differences may be due to translation, but I am unable to reconcile some of the discrepancies. I leave it to the reader to do so.

I will never forget the day that I met Mikolai Stepanovich, so it is there that I shall begin my story.

He was taller than most, and in proportion to his height slenderer than most as well. Where another man of his status and seniority might have allowed himself the comforts that fill a man's midsection to rounding, Mikolai's waist could be seen as narrower than his hips. Lest you mistake me, his figure was not feminine; this was not a case of womanly hips on a man. Mikolai's hourglass was the hourglass of a wolf, asymmetric and gaunt.

This was my first surprise; we had been captured by what we thought was the army of the Golden Empire, and I had been led to expect that its officers were usually shaped like bears, shaggy and round. The guards had spoken of him in hushed tones, and so I thought he would be some giant bear of a man, so big that putting him in a customized suit of steam knight armor was the only option.

Instead, the dog sitting next to him looked like it weighed more than half of what he did. It was a large dog, but still, I am not speaking of a man of great bulk. It felt a little irregular to be left alone in the room with the enemy commander, his dog, and a tiny slip of a woman who must have been his mistress.

After my introduction, he stopped to have a little conversation with his companion. Not the woman, the dog—he asked the dog if it thought I was lying. Pluck me bald if the dog didn't seem to think it was having a conversation with him, too.

Then I got my third surprise: He spoke my native tongue, or nearly spoke it. His dialect and accent were unusual; not so much foreign as archaic, like the ancient dvergr who visited my family when I was eleven. Not quite Danish, not quite Swedish, but something similar to both.

"Let me and thee speak unpolished truth," he said. "Lives lie on the table, coins unspent." To demonstrate exactly what he thought of coins left unspent on the table, he flicked a silver coin across the room. It chimed when it hit the floor, an indication of its purity, but he didn't seem to much care. Just sat there, waiting for me to tell him the truth.

I spilled out my real name and rank in a spurt of nervous energy, then tried to explain why I might lie to him. In particular, I told him that I was worried about the real captain's fate as a prisoner. Maybe not the best excuse for what was really a routine bit of obfuscation. Ragnar, I thought to myself after blurting that out, now you've practically accused his country of routinely violating the conventions of civilized war; you're in for it now.

He didn't seem to care about the accusation. "I am sure thy father's elder brother's second son doth appreciate such concerns of thine," he said. "Though I fear the question of disposal pleads over more than officers." He paused meaningfully. "Despite mine concern, I seek to hire. Wherefore our situation, betwixt thou and the amethyst unfathered, contractual obligations lie dead and buried."

Mikolai's precise knowledge of the exact relationship between the captain and myself was my fourth surprise. If he knew that much about us, he didn't need to ask for my real name; it was just a test of my honesty. My surprise explains how long it took me to notice he had suggested very obliquely that he was willing to kill all the prisoners.

His threat and his profanely creative metaphor, which I could only guess was meant to refer to the nobles bankrolling the effort to restore princely rule to Wallachia, underscored the gravity of the situation; I felt like I was being interviewed by a mountain king, not some apprentice wizard on his first field mission.

That was how the intelligence officer had described Mikolai: As a novice with no known history, attached for some unknown reason to the Butcher of Belz for practical training. A negligible threat, a mere accessory to the presence of the better-known imperial officer, and easy prey in his absence.

His troops, as I mentioned, had a very different opinion; they held him in the sort of esteem reserved for things both great and terrible. Fear and respect ran in alternating currents, and they spoke of him in whispers more often than aloud.

Those same feelings, fear and respect, were running through my own breast as he offered the knife and bowl to me. "The silver of Sweden lies separate from the vein of coal I seek," he said. "Thou need not forswear thine silver in the taking of mine; slice thy thumb and write oath with it."

"What if I don't want to sign your contract?" I asked, ice running down my veins.

"Thou hast the choice," he said.

"What will happen if I choose to decline your offer?" I pressed. He didn't say anything, but his eyes flickered. I looked back around the room and saw the coin on the floor. He had already told me everything, and he was not going to waste any further words while he waited. The choice was mine, as much as I had one.

"If you have lied to me about your interests," I told him, "or if you cheat me and my men of just compensation, I will have your blood in trade for mine." I snatched the knife, swiftly slashed my thumb, and signed fiercely.

CHAPTER NINETEEN

In Which I Do Not Sleep Alone

Integrating the mercenaries and my regular soldiers on the squad level was a task easier described than accomplished. None of the mercenaries were familiar with the operation of steam suits, and I wasn't interested in getting any of them too curious about how the machines worked. The Swedes, similarly, were reticent about their self-propelled guns and claimed that their sword staves did not mix well into a formation of pike and shot.

I asked the supply colonel to return surviving mercenaries' weapons to them and to issue other captured equipment to squads of soldiers on the basis of recommendation by any imperial squad leader or officer. He flatly told me he was too busy with the job of writing up paperwork and to pass it to someone else.

In the end, I put that job on the shoulders of the highest-ranking surviving infantry officer, a captain. She would be responsible for the issue, or reissue, of captured mercenary weapons which, in the case of living mercenaries, should be generally returned to their owners. I gave her a list of names of every non-Swedish mercenary and told her to assign each one to a partner from among her troops. Each pair was to be assigned to duties together, and she was to encourage them to get to know one another somehow.

She accomplished the assignment of partners in an expedient fashion by taking the list of names, pulling out her company roster, and pairing them off down the line. Since her company roster was organized by squad, and her company outnumbered the surviving non-Swedish mercenaries by a factor of two, this meant that only half of the squads were initially assigned mercenary members, and the others were understrength by comparison.

The other part of the job—tracking the issue and reissue of captured equipment—she delegated to a lieutenant. This turned out to be a particularly unenviable task, as when we had stripped captured mercenaries of their weapons and equipment, we hadn't kept records of which pieces of equipment belonged to each mercenary or, for that matter, which pieces of equipment had been taken off of dead mercenaries in the field and which had been taken from live prisoners. This resulted in some disputes over ownership of equipment.

Having delegated the task of integrating the mercenaries with the regular troops, at least for the moment, my chief worries were supply and desertion. I was more worried about desertion. The mercenaries' loyalty was questionable, and imperial conscripts had not much more reason to be loyal to the Golden Empire.

The real risk with deserters wasn't the loss of fighting force; I could barely pay or feed the soldiers I had under my command. Desertion would ease our supply issues. My worries instead focused on other armies, both the Avar army and the army of the Golden Empire. The letter to Ivan Romanov made it clear that the charade I'd been forced into had attracted enemies inside the Golden Empire.

While deserting might have been a good choice for our rank-and-file soldiers, I was too visible, too prominent. I couldn't sneak out if I wanted to, with or without Vitold, my unfortunate comrade in deception. My officers were constantly coming to me with problems and suggestions, and Katya followed me as faithfully as Yuri. Her loyalty to the Golden Empire seemed pure and simple. I felt sure that Katya would track me to the ends of the earth if I managed to slip out—to rescue me again if she thought I was loyal or to shoot me in the head if she thought I was not.

The discerning reader may have put together that, in a certain technical sense, I was deserting—I was simply bringing an entire company of imperial troops with me or, more precisely, a severely depleted battalion. I was taking initiative well outside of what I would have been permitted, even had I been a full general, much less my actual rank. My authorization consisted entirely of a generous interpretation of a letter from a madman, a letter which no longer existed as anything other than a pile of ashes, except in my own memories. I was pinned between my own troops and my lawful superiors.

Katya's wrath wasn't the only thing that stayed my hand from the saddle and from abandoning the madman's mission; I also found myself wanting her good opinion. It was addictive, having this serious and deadly woman beam up at me with a bright smile, hanging on my every word, and faithfully assuming that everything I did was both very clever and for the greater good. She really was a very attractive woman, once you washed the blood off her hands and put a smile on her face.

It is true that as a sharpshooter, Katya had not literally gotten any blood on her hands during the battle or any other battle I had seen, but Radu Odobescu kept living on in my dreams. For several nights in a row after it happened, I watched Katya cut his throat over and over again. Each time, the butchery was messier, and each time I startled awake, I could not help but think of how much more metaphorical blood coated her hands.

My fears of desertion peaked on the third day of preparations; a pair of mercenaries had gone missing during the night. They were found in the afternoon by a patrol, their dead bodies twisted with agony. They were missing their eyeballs and covered with small scratches. Mystic writing, if you believed the rumors, which I did not. Thorns will scratch up a body in all kinds of funny ways as branches and twigs are bent and snap back into position, and soldiers are a superstitious lot at the best of times.

What I thought most likely was that they had bedded down amidst a clump of holly bushes for cover at night after having made a meal of their berries, which are (in spite of their bright and attractive appearance) somewhat poisonous. They had crawled back out of the clump as they suffered, and scavengers had eaten their eyes after they died from a combination of poison and exposure to winter weather. There were many other possibilities, too, such as snakebite, spider bite, or eating some tasty-looking but poisonous mushrooms. The list of ways for people to get themselves killed in the woods that were more likely than death by mystical forces was a very long one.

After dinner that night, Katya told me she feared that someone would try to kill me during the night. The rumors worried her; evidently, there was talk that the only release from the blood oaths binding the mercenaries to my service was death, and she thought someone might try to make that my death as opposed to their own death. This, she pleaded with me, worried her greatly, and she asked to spend the night in my room. On consideration, it seemed like a reasonable request, so I granted it.

As I listened to the supply colonel drone on about the progress he'd made in committing enough acts of forgery to, as he put it, justify leaving him in a cell until the Mongols came back—he was, I gathered, not happy with his assignment—I reflected on my folly.

Sometimes, staging drama for the purpose of impressing people can backfire. How was I to know that a couple of soldiers would wander off in the night and get themselves killed by mysterious means? Whatever natural force had killed them as they blundered around in the woods at night, I was now thought to be responsible for it. I had sown seeds of superstitious caution to inhibit betrayal; I was now reaping a whirlwind of superstitious terror and panic.

Even Vitold was giving me strange worried looks. That hurt; we had been friends since our enlistment, buddies through our training, and bunkmates in the garrison where we'd been stationed. I'd helped him into and out of trouble as he'd played pranks on a wide range of victims, from the barmaid in town to high and mighty colonels lording it over us enlisted peons. We'd learned to operate steam suits together, gotten swept up into this whole affair together because of a too-clever borrowing of dress uniforms, and now he looked at me like I was something not quite natural.

The colonel was looking at me expectantly. He had stopped talking while I was thinking.

"Very well, colonel. I expect you will have finished the remainder of the papers tomorrow and checked them over personally for any mistakes."

When he opened his mouth, presumably to resume complaining, I cut him off with a curt wave of my hand and then looked around the table at Vitold, the colonel, and the other officers. They looked back at me.

"This meeting is adjourned," I said.

I couldn't take the stares and whispers any longer. I retreated to my bedroom, Yuri dashing ahead of me on the stairs and Katya lingering a respectful several steps behind. I made sure to lock the door behind us, drew tight the curtains, and moved a chair in front of the door.

Katya dragged an end table next to the bed and laid her rifle across it, along with a pistol and her sword, all pointed at the door. She perched on the bed next to the pillows, inspecting her weapons closely for readiness.

I crawled under the covers and lay still with my eyes closed, trying to quiet the thoughts that whirled around each other in my head, an unhelpful and repetitive circling, like a dog chasing its own tail. Even Vitold, I thought to myself. Even Vitold believed the rumors. I opened my eyes, and looked up at the woman sitting next to my head, the woman who had watched the contracts being signed and had seen my totally mundane preparation of them. Did she believe the rumors, too?

"Katya, do you think I caused those men to die?" I asked.

She looked down at me, bit her lip, and hesitated. My heart skipped a beat.

"I do not know how magic works," she said. She paused. "If you did, they must have deserved it. And you are good." Another pause. "You are a good man, and I like you." She was, in her own way, trying to reassure me that she was my friend.

And I, for my part, was reassured by that. "Thank you," I said, and very soon after fell asleep under her protective watch.

CHAPTER TWENTY

In Which I Fail to Keep My Lips Closed

I woke up to discover that sometime during the night, I had decided Katya's lap would make a better pillow than the bags of cloth filled with goose down designed for the purpose. She was still more or less sitting, head leaned against a bedpost, lightly dozing and startled to full wakefulness when I lifted my head. The dark circles under her eyes, the rapid blinking, and her difficulty attaining a completely vertical position convinced me she had not fallen asleep quickly but had been sitting vigil until sleep had ambushed her sometime early in the morning.

When I pointed out the various evidences of her exhaustion, she shifted from talking about how she was still awake and had merely dozed off just for a moment to claiming she felt fine and well rested and was ready for another day full of dutiful wakefulness and watchfulness. By this point in our conversation, I was up and about and dressed for the day; and she was still sitting on the edge of the bed, listing visibly to one side.

"Katya," I told her, grasping her by the shoulders and shaking gently, cutting off her meandering account of how she didn't actually need much sleep, "I'll be fine for breakfast. You should sleep."

While she worked on figuring out how to rebut this, I gently picked her up, laid her down flat on the bed with her head on a pillow, pulled the blankets back up over her, and tucked her snugly in.

"There you go. Now go back to sleep. That's an order," I said with mock ferocity.

Then, on a sudden impulse, I bent down and kissed her on the forehead. When I straightened back up, her eyes were closed and she was breathing evenly; if not fallen back asleep, at least making an effort to pretend, which in her current state was very likely to lead to the real thing anyway. I watched her for a few moments and then quietly went off to breakfast, Yuri trailing in my wake.

An awkward silence descended on the high table upon my arrival. It began with a respectful fall into silence as everyone turned my way, and when I sat down at the officers' table and started eating without a word of greeting, the silence continued for some time; no one felt like being the first to breach it. Truth be told, I didn't mind being able to focus on the food for a change rather than being distracted by the business of command or my officers' attempts at polite small talk. We would be leaving soon, and the quality of the cooking would not improve when it was done in the field instead of a real kitchen.

After clearing my plate, I decided to go straight into business.

"Well," I said, "Fyodor was in charge of the night watch, so everybody is here who will be here. Let's just get started, shall we?"

We usually ended up having an informal officers' meeting for a short period of time after breakfast. Inevitably, one or two officers needed to go take care of something in the wake of breakfast, and the officer in charge of the late watch would be sleeping, barring an emergency of some kind. That still left most of the officers at the same place at the same time, something that wouldn't happen again until dinnertime.

"That redheaded wench, what's her name, not going to be here this time?" Ragnar was still working on learning the names, faces, and ranks of everyone, but he was trying.

"Katya didn't get much sleep last night; I told her to sleep in," I said, then immediately wished I had put that another way.

The knowing grin Ragnar flashed to his cousin and the quick elbow jab told me that the rumor mill was going to be grinding at full speed with grist for a fresh story about how I had kept Katya up all night. This would probably turn into a graphic description of fraternization somewhere along the grapevine, bearing as fruit a variety of lewd jokes. I briefly considered correcting Ragnar's misconceptions to nip that shoot in the bud, then remembered something I had heard early during my training as a soldier about fraternization within the ranks and proper military discipline in general.

I had been told (by way of contrast with how the soldiers of the Golden Empire were supposed to be) that mercenary companies were rife with discipline problems; fraternization of that sort, in particular, wasn't unusual. Katya had an unusual amount of unofficial authority in spite of her lack of official rank, and that sort of combination would make a lot of sense if we were thought to be personally involved. It would add a touch of verisimilitude to our facade as a mercenary company, and it would be all the more plausible if the rest of the company really believed it.

On the other hand, rumors spread unpredictably. Vehement denials sometimes draw more attention to the issue than simply ignoring them, so perhaps if I wanted to keep it in the realm of scurrilous half-believed rumors rather than taken for certain fact, ignoring it might be better. My unwise remark and Ragnar's immediate inference would only draw so much attention and might not even be remembered after all of the officers had made their best attempt to fill each other's brains with minutiae. If I corrected Ragnar's misconception, it would be remembered by most of them.

Having come up with conflicting but convincing reasons to keep silent on the issue of Katya, I focused back on what was being said. Vitold was giving a progress report on our efforts to cosmetically alter the steam knight suits and mechs to make them seem less like official imperial military equipment and more like a grab-bag of mercenary machinery. Battlefield salvage was a useful source of parts, and we had even inherited some intact mechs with our mercenaries. Unless Vitold could get some more qualified mechanics, we would have trouble finishing the job quickly, and we didn't want to wait long enough at the manor to get attacked again.

I dumped the job of searching through all the soldiers for suitable assistant mechanics for Vitold on Fyodor and Ragnar. Ragnar had worked alongside the Romanians for some time; he also had a sort of peculiar cachet among my own troops that sprang from a combination of his outgoing personality and his status as the first of the mercenaries to sign on with me.

As for Fyodor, he was one of the infantry officers and thus immediately familiar with the largest share of our troops. In addition to this, the infantry captain had handed Fyodor the job of distributing the mercenaries' equipment back to them; going through making lists of everyone's possessions leaves you with impressions of a great many of them. For that matter, the requests for equipment our own troops made of Fyodor gave him a better idea of what talents they thought they had other than those the military had told them to use.

The more senior Rimehammer, I noticed, had a sheet of paper out and was taking careful shorthand notes. Halfway through the supply colonel's litany of complaints, he made a marginal note, highlighting the fact that the supply colonel had given two very different figures for our diminishing supply of vodka. He gave the supply colonel a curious look.

The supply colonel continued without appearing to notice and launched into his next complaint. He was deeply concerned with the fact that we were feeding the wounded and former prisoners three-quarters of a full standard ration of food just like everyone else, instead of the third of a standard ration of food he felt they would be able to minimally survive on. He seemed rather put out that we had not simply executed the prisoners and been done with it; feeding them generously wasn't helping our supply situation any.

After the meeting ended, I reported to the workshop personally to put in my own contribution of skilled labor. I was also hoping to mend fences with Vitold. Our easy camaraderie had foundered, run aground on the rocks of my strange new abilities and rank during the storm of our mission. I wanted to reassure him I was still the same old Mikolai he'd played countless games of cards with, drunk with, made silly bets with, and gotten into mischief with.

We were working on reassembling a damaged elemental cage, a relatively quiet task, when I realized I was wrong. I couldn't tell myself, much less Vitold, that I was the same old Mikolai. After the miles and months that had passed since our idyllic days at the garrison, I was a different man. War had changed me, left its stamp on me; I had faced its horrors and come out with bloody hands gripping the reins of command. Vitold, too, had been changed by the war, but in a very different way. If I was riding the wolf so it could not turn upon me, he had climbed up a tree and was hoping the wolf would go away.

The innocence was gone for us. We could not simply joke around and pretend that our service in the military was a temporary nuisance requiring us to live temporarily in a great big house full of other unhappy men in the middle of nowhere, or that our combat service drills were purely theoretical in nature. Pranks were no longer delightful and funny relief from boredom, but instead, potentially deadly distractions. And Vitold could not forget that I was now his commander—and a man who commanded fearsome, unnatural powers.

The best that I could do was to tell him I was still his friend in spite of being a new and different Mikolai. Even if I seemed strange, I was not a stranger. In response, he grunted and asked where the three-quarter French inch wrench had gone, as the three-quarter Avar inch wrench didn't quite fit.

After cleaning up and getting lunch, I went upstairs to check on Katya. I found her awake, though lying in bed. I think the sound of the door opening awoke her.

"Good morning," I said, and she responded in kind.

After some brief inquiries as to her alertness, sense of well-being, and a successful bid to interrupt her profuse apologies by handing her a sandwich and an apple and telling her to eat breakfast, I recalled my own breakfast. In particular, I remembered that Ragnar had noticed her absence. My unfortunate choice of a truthful but poorly worded response to his inquiry about said absence also came to my mind.

Katya deserved to know that the rumors were likely to return; I also wanted to convince her that the best course of action was simply silence. This, I thought to myself, was going to be difficult. Katya was in many ways a fine soldier, but she was not well-equipped to handle social subtleties.

"Katya, you remember those rumors that were going around camp after that night I had you in my tent trying to make the rune plate light up?" I asked with a little trepidation.

She nodded and made a vaguely affirmative noise through a mouthful of food.

"Well, it seems like some of the men know you were sleeping in my room last night," I said, glossing over the specifics. No need to get Ragnar (or myself!) in a particular spot of trouble for my poor word choice. "So, those rumors are probably going to be starting back up again. And . . ."

I held up a hand, trying to formulate a diplomatic way of saying this. I didn't want her to think I was the sort of man who wanted her to suffer, and I remembered that she took the rumors badly before. How could I tell this woman that I wanted her to just let her reputation be dragged through the mud in order to bring the mercenaries and the regular soldiers together, and to help lend an air of mercenary disorder to the way the company acted?

She looked at me silently, swallowing.

"Well, in the light of everything that's been going on lately and how this mission is going, I was thinking that it might be better if we just . . ." I hesitated again. I wasn't about to tell her to lie outright. She was charmingly honest, and I doubted she was any good at lying. Katya swallowed, put the remaining half a sandwich on the end table next to her sword, and looked at me apprehensively, waiting. After a little while of groping around for the right phrase, I thought I found the right way to put it.

". . . if we just allow the rumors be taken for truth." I thought it was a neutral phrase. Her reaction took me off-guard, and she covered the distance between the bed and myself with remarkable speed, considering that the blanket ought to have slowed her down a little bit. I closed my eyes and flinched away from her attack.

I could taste lingering notes of pumpernickel and cheese as I staggered back from the impact of Katya's body slamming into mine, her arms wrapping around my neck and her legs wrapping around my waist. The tastes were, I soon realized, because I had left my mouth open, and Katya was kissing me vigorously. She had not quite tackled me as much as climbed up me, though the speed with which she had done so made for little difference between the two; and I found myself returning her kiss before I knew I was doing so.

My arms were around her, supporting her and embracing her, the slender curves of her body apparent to the touch in a way that was not visible to the eye through the rumpled uniform she had slept in. My heart kept hammering, for a reason other than anticipation of attack. She pulled her mouth away from mine for a moment.

"I am happy you also want the rumors to be true," she breathed in my ear. She nipped at my earlobe and kissed her way from there down to the base of my throat before locking her lips back onto mine.

I thought back to the previous night—the very quiet, very earnest, almost whispered statement of "You are a good man, and I like you." To the beaming smiles she had been giving me lately. Vitold, talking to me after the battle, telling me he thought I liked spooky women and that they liked me, too, and how he seemed to be referring to Katya. She had taken my hesitancy for the hesitancy of a shy man confessing his love in the most singularly awkward way possible. "Just allow the rumors to be taken for truth," I had said. That hadn't been my intention, I thought, and then I started to pay attention to what I was doing.

While I reflected on Katya's thought processes and emotions, I had continued to respond and react to her passion without conscious effort; we were now both on the bed, and articles of clothing were being thrown in the general direction of Yuri, who was looking decidedly uncomfortable about the whole affair and was retreating backward, toward the closet. I should have been thankful he was not barking.

Perhaps I, too, had feelings that extended beyond friendship, I thought to myself, reminding myself of the impulsive kiss I had laid on her forehead this morning, the way I lit up inside when she smiled at me, the way that she drew my eyes even while climbing over a wall in the middle of a raging battle. Even, so long ago, the shock of discovering her softness and smallness in the dark as I helped her in and out of my armor. We both truly did, I realized, want the rumors to be true; with the good lieutenants rounding up plenty of helping hands, my own hands could be easily spared from the workshop to help turn false rumor into solid fact.

And with that last thought, I shifted the whole of my focus to Katya; the two of us spent the afternoon, in its entirety, on the enterprise of making up for the time we had lost to military propriety, misunderstanding, mourning, and miscommunication.

When we had worn ourselves out several times, it came to my attention that the sun was sitting quite low in the sky, that we were both quite hungry, and that the small army I was purportedly in charge of might be starting to get itself into some kind of mischief or mishap during the period in which I had been thoroughly preoccupied instead of closely supervising my fractious officers. As focused as I had been on Katya, I would have missed anything less obvious than the manor house burning to the ground.

This last worry, it turned out, was misplaced. Since I had left them all with clear orders (something I had clearly failed to do several days before, in dealing with the prisoners) and then stayed out of the way afterward, my officers had impelled the men to heights of efficiency and productivity that surprised me pleasantly. There was an important lesson about leadership here, which I was beginning to learn, though it would take me more time to master it: Great leadership comes from knowing how to delegate, and half of knowing how to delegate is knowing when to step out of the way.

The job of disguising our hardware was, for one wonder, mostly complete, or at least the more difficult parts were. What little remained could be accomplished in the field or explained, easily enough, as the use of battlefield salvage in field repair and refit. It would be obvious on close inspection that a modified heavy mech had been originally built in Khoryvsk, but with enough parts and weapons replaced or rearranged, they would pass readily enough for battlefield salvage.

The most difficult part had been rehousing the elemental cages so that they would not be recognized as being from the Golden Empire. The elemental cage is the most valuable part of a mech; but also the most difficult to recycle from a disabled mech salvaged from your enemies, as they are generally secured against unauthorized use. Without the correct passcodes, compelling the elemental spirit into loyalty is impossible, and there is no way to read those codes short of tearing the cage apart. The easiest thing to do is melt down the orichalcum and rebuild the whole thing from scratch.

The rest of our equipment was, while not completely refurbished, already beginning a remarkable cosmetic transformation. Even Yuri had new equipment; Ragnar presented me with a set of armor for Yuri cut down from the barding for a mercenary's horse—which did not miss the barding, as it had not survived the fight. Yuri sniffed at it dubiously. He'd come with an armored harness, one that marked him as an honorary sergeant of the Imperial Army.

I thanked Ragnar, Vitold, and Fyodor for their fine work. I had learned by then another valuable lesson of command: Rewarding good behavior with praise seemed to be as effective with officers and soldiers as it did with horses and dogs, a curious commonality between man and beast.

That evening, I addressed my troops in the dining hall.

We would, I told them, be leaving the manor behind the next morning. We would not be coming back to it in the foreseeable future; instead, we would be making our best pace northwest, crossing the northern part of the Sarmatian range and out of Avaria, somewhere near the border between Lithuania and the various petty princes who answered to the Emperor in Oenipons. The great forest there was wild, reputedly home to ogres and witches. It had stopped the Romans from going any further north in times of old and helped limit conflict between Vilnius and Oenipons in more recent times.

This route would be safe because our enemies would not expect it at all. It would, I cautioned them, be slow going, especially since we could not expect to come by much coal, meaning that the mechs and steam knight suits would need to spend most of their time riding on carts. We would make charcoal along the way and use it as a field expedient to the best of our abilities.

The supply colonel and I were all too aware of our coal problem and had spent a great deal of time talking about it. The northern Sarmatians were not a place to buy coal on the civilian market; there was little organized settlement of the area. Even if we stumbled upon a village with an adequate supply, local prices were unlikely to be particularly reasonable. We might be able to "expeditiously requisition" (or more accurately, steal) their coal anyway, but that would draw attention to us.

The supply colonel and I were both dubious of charcoal as a field expedient; him, because he didn't understand that using charcoal didn't harm our machinery, even after my assurances to the contrary; and I, because I knew how long it would delay us—stopping to fell trees and then turn the wood into charcoal in the middle of potentially hostile territory seemed unwise. Charcoal is a fine fuel that burns more cleanly than most coals, if you do not mind the fact that it is half the density; you will burn through a full bin of it quite quickly.

I didn't want to lecture the troops on the tight supply situation, so I moved off the topic of coal and charcoal after mentioning it just that once and left them with a reminder that our cover identities would be all that stood between us and the opportunity for a heroic last stand. While I was, I told them, confident in their ability to heroically die to the last man, I would rather we not put such a matter to the test. After the speech, I had a lengthy talk over dinner with the other officers, going into the nuts and bolts of our departure and planned route.

I wanted to avoid attention from Avar soldiers. One of our recent recruits, a nobleman with a French name and some sort of kinship claim on a Wallachian estate, explained to me at length that King Janos's marriage to Emperor Leon's daughter somehow meant that the king of Avaria would not send any troops over the northern Sarmatians. His explanation included a family tree, which I cannot remember and will not attempt to reproduce.

After the end of a dinner that lasted until quite late, Katya and I went back up to bed, where we held one another close and talked (well, whispered more than talked) late into the night about anything but strategic or tactical plans. We talked about home and family, about food and drink, and about cats and dogs and weather.

CHAPTER TWENTY-ONE

In Which I Steel a Hart

In the early morning, I held Katya close, stroking the smooth muscles and curves of her back as she sleepily nuzzled my collarbone. I had awoken with the first light of dawn, but I did not want move from beneath Katya's warm and cuddlesome weight or rush her into full wakefulness and the cold air.

"I think I shall miss comfortable bedding," I said.

Underneath the warm blankets, Katya's body, and mine was a bed fit for a prince, or at least a decadent Avar noble with wealth that was fabulous as measured by my humble Ruthenian sensibilities. The massive wooden frame and deep down mattress would be nearly as difficult to transport as an inert mech and far less easy to justify taking with us.

She stirred. "I wish I could send another letter home," she said. She was, as I eventually realized, much more open with her feelings when not entirely awake.

On the one hand, I wanted, on some level, to be a fair commander of my troops, including Katya. I wanted to have my cake of impartiality intact on the shelf after having devoured a Katya-sized slice of it with my highly unprofessional acts of fraternization. Perhaps I should say more than one metaphorical slice, we had fraternized very thoroughly.

I had talked to the other officers about the idea of sending a courier with a mail bag during our last meeting, impressing on them that I believed even a message sent through military channels was likely to be compromised and lead to the immediate failure of our mission. I had not explained that this was in part because some highly placed officer had decided I was a liability and told Colonel Romanov to kill me, but it did make a great deal of military sense. Spies could find out a great deal from correspondence, and I had ruled out the sending of letters in no uncertain terms.

On the other hand, I could also remember how happy Katya had been when she had a chance to send a letter back to her father the last time and how many times she had told me that she hoped her father had gotten her letters. The idea that she might simply vanish without her father knowing why or where she had fallen upset her a great deal.

And I had eaten my Katya-cake already. I had eaten several slices, licked the icing off the rest of it, eaten the other slices, and then scraped all of the crumbs off the table and sucked them down. Gorging myself was now leading to indigestion—a belly-deep pain at her sadness. If only we could just send a message directly to her father, without having to deal with the risks of being located through the mail system . . .

An idea hit me with the sudden force of a thunderbolt.

"I have an idea for how to get a letter to your father safely," I told her, "but we will need to hurry."

"Really?" She perked up into full wakefulness immediately, up on all fours and looking down at my face with a brilliant smile that sent a jolt of good feelings all the way down my body. This left me more tempted to stay in bed, though not at all tempted to go back to sleep.

"Really," I said, giving her a friendly squeeze. "You'll have to get off of me first, though, so I can get out of this infernally comfortable trap of a bed. Get up and write quickly."

The sun was just rising when we picked our way down the stairs, her blowing on her letter to help the ink dry more quickly, and me carrying an extra bag with Yuri's old armored harness. Yuri followed, wearing his new armor—I'd had the time to put it on him while Katya worked on her letter. The two of us got onto Katya's horse, leaving word with a harried-looking captain that the army should get started on its way, whether or not we returned before they had finished emptying the manor; we would, I assured her, be able to quickly catch up.

I told Yuri to behave and stay with the nice captain, and that we needed some time to ourselves in the woods. He growled something disparaging about humans in heat as he trotted over to the captain. Most likely, he was still upset over the fright we had given him by suddenly kissing each other (it looked to him rather like Katya trying to bite my face off) and the way in which he had been subsequently pelted with flying clothing.

We rode through the woods until I spotted what I was looking for—a stag. He saw us at nearly the same time and froze, waiting to see if we approached nearer, hoping that we hadn't noticed him. Stags are a curious mixture of skittish and bold, but with as much cause as they have to worry about hunters, the former quality almost always surfaces first when they see someone two-legged approaching.

"Hold, good sir stag," I said. Stags can be quite pretentious animals, and it doesn't hurt to flatter them. "We are not a-hunting today, but we were looking for you. I have heard you are swifter than an arrow."

He snorted, dubiously, and reminded me that he was not at all swifter than a bullet, and that my companion had a great big gun.

"Ah. It is a very nice gun, quite big. A great deal heavier than hunters use on stags," I told him. "You see how big it is? It needs to be that big to punch through the armor men wear. Why, if you had armor, the little rifles hunters use would scarce slow down a great runner like yourself."

The stag pointed out, reasonably, that men make man-shaped armor, that stags make no armor at all, and that stags didn't carry things to slow themselves down with.

"I have armor, here, that a stag could wear." I shook the bag. "A noble stag could wear such armor, and give all the hunters the slip. It is made for someone with four legs, like you, and moves with you. It is meant not to slow you down at all, and is much lighter than you might think. And as you are already so fast and so strong," I added, engaging in grievously dishonest flattery, "you would surely still be faster than a lame hunter's horse, hobbled with a whole hunter sitting on top of him. Why, if you are as noble a stag as you seem, I would be a horrible man if I did not gift you this armor, to make sure you live to breed many noble and beautiful fawns."

The stag preened, my praise scoring direct hits to his pride. He was indeed so noble and so fast that he deserved such a gift, he agreed, and was even so noble as to allow a talking human to give him gifts. A less noble stag, he informed me, would refuse gifts from men due to their base suspicion.

"There is just one thing, though," I told him, sighing heavily.

A catch? The stag was dubious, engulfed with the base suspicion that he had just denied having. Trading was beneath him, he reminded me.

As a noble stag, he could hardly be expected to do anything in exchange for the gifts due him. If the armor was to be some kind of payment, a noble stag would reject it on principle.

"Oh, I wouldn't dare to try to bribe a noble stag," I told him. "It's just that my woman, here, and I have been talking. She has doubts you have the stamina for a real journey." I might have been stretching the truth a little, there; when I explained the plan to Katya, her eyes did fly wide a few times, and I felt confident that a stag was capable of traveling quite a distance if he cared to. Making him want to make the journey was the difficult part.

The stag rolled his eyes and raked the ground with his hooves. He found those doubts offensive and infuriating; injurious to that most valued possessions of stags everywhere, which is to say pride and reputation. He then spent a little while posturing and posing, each successive boast more expansive than the prior.

"Don't expect to convince her like that. She's a very skeptical sort of person. Why, I don't think she would believe in her own ability to ride from here to her father's house if she hadn't come all this way from the other direction," I said, stretching the truth a little more by papering over the fact that Katya had traveled south by train. "She's only seen you just standing there like a four-legged tree. I can't really blame her. You know the ways of hinds when it comes to harts."

I worried that my dig might be a little too subtle. Would the stag pick up that I had just insinuated that a mere domestic mare, saddled and with a human woman strapped on top of it, could ride farther than he could run? Would he think that the does he wanted to impress might somehow hear of his failing to meet the challenge of a fellow female—a human hind?

Tossing his head, the stag protested at great length and boldly pronounced that he could run there and back in the time it took her fat pony to waddle that way carrying her fat, discolored, flat-faced, thick-legged, bipedal, and furless derriere, with time to spare.

Fortunately, Katya didn't take offense at the insults the stag flung in her direction with a toss of his horns; she did a very good job of pretending she couldn't understand a word that the stag had said. She deserved congratulations on maintaining an expression that was nearly completely blank—perhaps slightly puzzled, but neither offended nor impressed. Faced with a human female's disdain and prompted by my comparison, he reacted just as he would with a dubious doe: He demanded the opportunity to prove himself.

I gave him directions to Katya's father's lands and bade him wait while I gave him his gift first. I had scratched Katya's father's name into the armor; and as I strapped the armor onto the stag, I attached a message tube to it, also addressed to Katya's father. I told the stag he could leave the tube on her father's doorstep to prove he had been there.

His athleticism wasn't the main barrier, but I didn't tell him that. I thought it was at least as likely that he would be shot or captured by some curious hunter somewhere in the Golden Empire, likely in Ruthenia but perhaps in Khazaria, after he was lost and tired from the long run to the east. Hopefully, any such curious hunter would forward the message to Katya's father via more regular means.

At a minimum, I could feel confident that the stag wouldn't decide to tear up the message and use it for nesting material. The stag also wouldn't decide that he'd rather keep the shiny message canister for himself. A bird might have been faster, but deer don't have a love of shiny objects or have a nasty habit of shredding up paper to line their nests with. After I finished fastening the armor, the stag gave us both a contemptuous look, then dashed off eastward at a flat run. I walked back to Katya, still seated on her horse, and mounted back up behind her.

"I cannot guarantee the letter reaches your father," I said. "But I doubt any spies are watching the woods for messenger deer."

Katya turned around in the saddle, reseating herself backward, and then proceeded to express her gratitude (or perhaps just pent-up affection) with considerable vigor and enthusiasm.

Several letters mailed locally within the Izh district

To My Dear Neighbor Boris,

My steward says he found the most curious visitor at my manor the other day; what he claims to have been a deer wearing armor. It was waiting for him outside the back door, apparently; I am having him fitted for false teeth while his broken bones heal. From the hoof-shaped dent in his forehead, he is lucky to be alive.

He was clutching a message tube in his hand when the maid found him, and the tube had your name on it. He informed me that the deer had been wearing it around its neck before it attacked him, destroying his favorite crossbow, breaking both his arms and one of his legs, cracking his rib cage, breaking his jaw, knocking out half of his teeth, and concussing him before running off.

I thought this meant that the deer had come from you, somehow, and was intending to write you an angry letter demanding restitution for the damage wrought by your creature (the doctor's bills and putting my steward out of service for at least the next several months, if he is not crippled permanently), but my little nephew opened it up while playing with it, finding a letter inside. The letter was addressed to you from your daughter Katya.

The letter has been enclosed, along with a list of expenses related to its delivery. In the future, please discourage your daughter from making use of messenger deer (whoever heard of such a thing?) or at least arrange for them to show up at your estate instead of mine.

—Ljubomir Ignatovich Vladislav

My very dear Konstantin Borovich,

I hope you are well in Kazan! I write to tell you that I heard several most amusing rumors, with hopes of enticing you to return back for at least a little visit. The cloth factor's daughter is pregnant, for one, and everybody is busy guessing who the father might be.

Speaking of fathers, the other amusing rumor I have heard says that your father has been terrorizing Ljubo with enchanted livestock. An alternate rumor says that one of your relatives has come back from army service and shot some of Ljubo's men for poaching on your family's lands. In either case, Ljubo came to town and visited both of the local lawyers about filing a suit. I gather Karlov gave him the brush-off.

—S.

Dearest Konstantin,

It is always business with you! Surely your business can survive a week or two without you watching over it like a mother hen? Tell them you have family matters to deal with—it would be true! Ljubo's lawsuit has attracted attention; a mage came here from Kazan asking questions about it. It did not take him so long to get here! You could take the train almost all the way here, like he did!

Imagine, a mage lodging in our little town! My uncle has been running himself ragged! I think he is from the Ministry of Internal Affairs—he has a skulky sort of look about him and pokes his nose around like he hasn't a worry about getting it knocked in. He spends a lot of time asking about some girl Katya—a cousin of yours in the army, I think? It is hard to keep track of all your relatives, Kostya!—and waving around pictures of men in the tavern. He is investigating, he says, some "irregularities." Katya's supposed to have written the letter that launched the lawsuit, Ljubo swears it was carried to his door by a deer.

—S.

To Magister Igor Vladimirovich Topylov, whom this matter may concern:

As far as I know, my youngest half sister is missing in action and probably dead. Your indelicate inquiries into her fate have upset my father, aiding and abetting that villain Vladislav. The Vladislav letter is of course a forgery intended to upset my father, whose health can be expected to have become delicate at his age. The Vladislavs have a long history of dishonest dealing, and Ljubomir is but the latest of a long line of cheats, drunks, wastrels, and ruffians. In what sort of drunk and debauched state he must have hatched this ridiculousness about a deer carrying a letter is nearly as far beyond my comprehension about how a Magister like yourself might be taken in by such a farce!

I can testify that Katya never mastered her letters; any letter purportedly written in her own hand is therefore a transparent forgery. She was never a particularly bright child but was, however, loyal to a fault, and I will not stand for you smearing her name by spending evenings in local taverns, showing them pictures and asking if anybody had ever seen her in the company of this or that man, or implying that she might be seen in their company in the future. I demand the satisfaction of an apology to our house for the insults you have aimed at our family's honor. Were I a younger man, I would certainly be demanding satisfaction in a much more direct and permanent fashion.

—Konstantin Borovich

In Which I Face Fear and Give Offense

What had been planned as a short detour to find a stag turned into a lengthy detour without much conscious intention. When the sun set, we set camp and resolved to catch up to my battalion the next day. Surprisingly, they had chosen to follow my orders with alacrity instead of waiting for us. Katya wondered aloud if they had meant to leave us behind, and I assured her otherwise with more confidence than the situation warranted. We spent two days following their trail before a storm hit; after the storm, it took us a week just to find the trail again, and much longer before we caught up.

When we did catch up, they were stopped in a mountain pass, officers deep in argument. A group of hollow-faced soldiers carried loaded arquebuses as they stood nervously around a pair of supply wagons. After Yuri barked to announce our arrival and ran out to greet us, we were made to feel welcome and I immediately found myself busy with matters of command.

The infantry captain we'd left Yuri with didn't feel like she had quite enough authority to boss around the other officers beyond earnestly repeating what I had told her; they seemed to be sharing her doubts. The colonel in charge of supply was theoretically the highest-ranking officer in our force; while he and the other officers accepted that General Spitignov's orders placed me in charge of the force in an unusual rearrangement of ordinary matters of rank and seniority, he was unwilling to deviate further from protocol.

To him, it wasn't clear that the most junior captain in our army had the authority to issue new orders in my absence that more senior officers might need to obey. It certainly wasn't clear to either the supply colonel or said captain. This was unfortunate because, in spite of his seniority, the supply colonel was not a person I wanted to leave in charge of matters in my absence, as he didn't seem to be inclined to make any decisions I agreed with. (The inclination was mutual.) My army needed its officers sorted out into a proper and functional pecking order so it could function smoothly in my absence.

This matter also wasn't clear to the Swedish captain, who didn't feel that his contract had placed him under the orders of anyone who wasn't me, up to and including the supply colonel. The supply colonel and the infantry captain both agreed that the various mercenary officers should answer to both of them, but Captain Felix Rimehammer felt otherwise. He objected strenuously to both the supply colonel's ration cuts and the infantry captain's nervous requests for the command codes for his self-propelled guns.

I spent the rest of the day smoothing (or in some cases plucking) various ruffled feathers among the officers as we rode through the cold, wet snow. For now, the ground was still frozen and hard, and I wanted to put the miles on before ice turned to mud. If this happened before we reached a railroad or a navigable river, the thaw of ice into mud would make it quite difficult to take the wagons cross-country. A shut-down mech is a heavy load for a wagon even on a good road; in mud, it is a recipe for immersion.

All the little details of supervising a force on the move weighed down on me. Whenever any two soldiers from different units (or officers from the same unit) had the least difference of opinion, my own opinion was needed to resolve the matter. And then there were the real problems— horses throwing shoes, fixing burst water pipes, clearing trees spaced too near to let the larger carts through, and all the other necessary tasks required to keep the entire circus going in the correct direction all at once.

When evening fell, we set camp, felling trees to make space and create a secure perimeter. My throat was hoarse, and I was reduced to whispering until the watch schedule had been put together for the night. After that I snuck away in silence, pen and ink still clutched absently in my hands, escaping to Katya's little tent to evade further attention. It was a snug fit for the two of us, but after a few minutes of quiet wriggling, we managed to fit ourselves comfortably inside and around the tent, blankets, kit, and one another without too much damage to any of those things. Yuri had to be satisfied with parking his furry self right outside the tent, as there was no room for him inside.

When I dozed off at long last, it was with the warm, friendly weight of Katya weighing upon my body and the cold unfriendly weight of my worries weighing upon my mind.

I dreamed about organizational charts and ice melting into mud. About running out of fuel. Of sinking carts trapped in peat bogs. Organizational charts chained to sinking carts trapped in peat bogs, with the severed heads of my officers swinging off their branches instead of names and ranks, with a mysteriously dry, open trench full of corpses waiting ahead. Then I looked away to the east.

General Spitignov was there, trying to chop down a tree. On top of the tree, there was a cave, and a man came out of the cave. The man was dressed in red; his hair was long and flowing, his mustache was thick over a bare chin, and his eyes were intense. On top of the man's head was a felt cap rimmed in small pearls, with a great, dark purple gem set in a sunburst topped with a crescent moon made from larger pearls. The stranger turned back into the cave with a swirl of his cloak, and in the shadows of the cave, there was a movement as of the stretching of a bat's wings.

Then I saw a woman's head impaled on a stick; at first, it was Katya's, and then it became the head of the girl whose life I had spared in the massacre. Then it became the head of the little old grandmother, whose name my aunt had refused to ever tell me, which then came alive and started talking to me between sips from a floating teacup; but I couldn't comprehend what she was saying because it was in a language I didn't understand.

I pulled my sword from the ground and began to carve on a tree. I couldn't understand her words, but I could see how and where the charts, their inky-black limbs struggling in the mud, had broken and failed; where the heads were tangled; and which ones fit better the yokes that tied them to the carts. And peat—there was something about peat. I took off from carving the tree to cutting out squares of peat and hurling them on top of the carts, watching them float higher in the water under their added weight, a paradoxical reversal of the normal order of things.

Then I turned back to the tree and the head. The head was gone, leaving a half-empty teacup, which I drank, and then I went back to slashing the bark, carving into it a diagram. It was a network of arrows and short words, the words written in runes that I could not read. This did not bother me; I didn't need to read them, only to write them down. When I finished, I walked on top of the water, across the water, following a trail of golden coins to the ocean. Then a raven, which I suddenly realized had been on my shoulder all along, cawed and took wing.

I awoke in the predawn gray with a sudden understanding of what needed to be done and a picture of the rank structure I needed to impose on our disorganized force. Feeling this understanding was ephemeral, I grabbed for my pen, sketching the image before I could lose it, inking down a tree of names, ranks, and units. We needed three things: coherent function, the appearance of being a single unified force, and certain senior officers' authority neutered.

My fears that I would forget the solution before I had finished writing it down were grounded; even as I blew on the ink to dry it, I found myself surprised by what I saw. Had I not been so quick to write it down, I would have surely forgotten it. Then the diagram wiggled under my breath, and the blanket slid down a little further away from the drying ink, revealing the gentle swell of a hip.

"Mikolai, that tickles," Katya said, her voice a little muffled. "What are you doing?"

Have you ever tried to persuade a woman to stand naked out in the snow so you can get a better look at what you wrote on her backside in ink?

I cannot say I recommend it. My experience to date suggests to me that women are not fond of being used as writing desks, not fond of cold air when they are sleepy, and, last but not least, not fond of being exhibited nude in public places. It is not my claim that your arguments will necessarily fail; but rather, whether or not you succeed, you are likely to find that a certain amount of unpleasantness ultimately results from the request.

Katya, bundled up in her coat, rode off in a sullen mood, leaving me word indirectly that she would be scouting ahead along our intended route. This explained her absence from the officers' meeting after breakfast. I did not actually learn of Katya's quiet exit until after the meeting was over, though it happened before the meeting had gotten anywhere. I simply thought she preferred not to sit through yet another iteration of the diagram inked on her back and had ducked out to avoid a terminal case of boredom.

The officers' meeting ended up running for half the morning as the army grew restless. Before the meeting was halfway done, I had begun to sympathize with General Spitignov's method of dealing with insubordination. Have you ever tried to persuade a senior officer to adopt the pretense of being a lieutenant?

As you might expect, this is another thing which, rather like asking a woman to stand naked out in the snow so you can get a better look at what you wrote on her backside, is likely to result in a certain amount of unpleasantness. I had a compelling set of reasons ready for the support colonel's demotion.

First, I said, in the interest of forced integration, I would make Captain Felix Rimehammer, the most senior of our newly recruited officers, nominal second-in-command of the force. However, while Captain Rimehammer would be nominally second in command, he would be placed in charge of only the logistical apparatus.

His role in logistics necessitated placing him over the supply colonel; naturally, with the supply colonel being junior to someone called a captain, this necessitated calling the supply colonel a lieutenant for the purposes of operational security. He would naturally continue to draw appropriate pay but would have a respite from the stressful task of dealing with the complex logistics of a force equipped and organized in a very ad hoc fashion.

Vitold was also moved to the supply division, also at the rank of lieutenant. I joked that this was to keep an eye out for the Swedish captain accidentally wrecking our machinery. I hoped Vitold understood that, underneath the quip, I really did need him to keep an eye out on the newly demoted colonel. The apparent favoritism involved in the combined demotion and promotion produced a large volume of objections from the supply colonel, as well as a lesser volume of complaints from other imperial officers.

The combat troops would be divided into three groups, each a company within the battalion. The young infantry captain would be placed in charge of the main infantry division, which included the main bulk of the soldiers, and which needed, still, to be fully integrated on the squad level. I pointed out to her that this was in effect a promotion, roughly doubling the number of soldiers under her direct command.

The heavy armor company—steam knights, mechs, and the well-armored Swedes with their sword staves and self-propelled guns—would be placed under the command of another imperial captain, an older gentleman supplied with not much initiative of his own but with more intelligence than the supply colonel, which I did not note aloud. I wanted our fuel-burning war machines used cautiously and cleverly if I was absent; if I was present, I would likely take direct command of this unit myself.

During the circumstances of actual combat, I said, Captain Rimehammer and the support division were to consider themselves subordinate to the heavy armor division and the senior imperial captain, even if the Swedish captain was nominally senior outside of combat. The other captains—two imperial captains and a pair of mercenary officers claiming the rank—were ruthlessly demoted to acting lieutenants.

This was greeted by more objections from the supply colonel and the demoted captains in question, though the elderly captain of the heavy armor company and the young infantry captain remained prudently silent in the face of their good fortune. So, for that matter, did Captain Rimehammer, in spite of his earlier objections to taking orders from anyone other than myself—and the junior officers, who saw opportunity in the demotions.

Military officers like their hierarchies to be neat and orderly, but for the most part, the Ruthenian officers not being directly demoted were, at this point, satisfied with the idea that "nominal senior" meant "not really senior," while Captain Rimehammer seemed fully cognizant of the fact that I was still handing him an unusually large responsibility, considering the nature of the relationship.

The supply colonel found this particularly irksome, pointing out he was now being placed under the orders of a more junior imperial officer (the elderly captain) and I found myself needing to go back over why I'd placed the colonel under Captain Rimehammer in the first place, with the addition of trying to diplomatically emphasize the fact that if he had been placed in charge of the heavy armor unit, he would be unable to concentrate his full attention on logistical matters.

Fortunately, everybody was running low on spirit for further argument by the time I introduced the third company, which I called a "cavalry" company, in spite of the fact that not all the soldiers in it were mounted. It was an undersized division, including all our more irregular troops. I had put all of these under the command of a single mercenary officer, who I announced had the rank of lieutenant.

Katya, I added, would be his direct superior as my fourth captain. There was a brief round of muttering about favoritism at the promotion of an absent sharpshooter to captain, with all of the senior and formerly senior officers loudly deploying reasons why the third company should be under their command instead. Then I said that given the nature of this command and the fourth captain's habit of operating solo, as she was doing at present, I expected the newly promoted Lieutenant Gavreau to be in frequent communication with the other three captains.

And with that, the demoted officers seemed to come to the conclusion that Katya was a captain in name only, and in practice, simply my bodyguard and bedmate with no real authority of her own, while Gavreau's real commander was one of the other three captains. Later, I learned that each of my other three captains had reached the same conclusion, which proved a recipe for disaster.

As for me, I would style myself by the rank of colonel and strongly encouraged the officers to start referring to me as "the Colonel." Lieutenant Gavreau appended that I should perhaps not go by "Mikolai," suggesting the name "Marcus," as generically Latin, something that could belong to someone anywhere from Loegria to Lithuania. This seemed fine to me, and I agreed. At some point later, someone (I do not know who) decided to start appending a surname, and I became "Colonel Marcus Corvus."

After another several rounds of questions and gripes (in many cases related to worries that the round of demotions would lead to reductions in their pay), I ended the meeting and ordered the army put on the move, following our advance scouts who, in turn, followed the markings left by our newly unwittingly promoted captain. I had hopes that the promotion, even if it was only a promotion in name, would leave her happier than when I had last seen her.

The diagram I had drawn on Katya's back in my sleepy moment of inspiration hadn't included her as a captain. It had included the mercenary lieutenant, but the diagram placed him directly under my command. She had actually been entirely missing from the table of organization and equipment I had drawn on her back; I hastily added her later in the morning when I noticed her absence from it.

In truth, the demoted officers' assumptions had been correct. When I had drawn up the chart, I had not been thinking of her as a military officer; just as my indispensable and adorable self-appointed bodyguard and bedmate. Now that she was absent, I missed her presence sorely, both as an officer at my right hand and as a woman at my side.

CHAPTER TWENTY-THREE

In Which I Deal with Matters of Grave Importance

As we proceeded down from the Sarmatian peaks into a low valley, home to a lazy and boggy bend in a well-frozen river, I could only assume that it was Katya who marked off hazards and left a clear trail for us to follow; her angry pace left her far ahead of our other scouts, and she did not return to camp for several nights. Yuri tried his best to keep me company, and Vitold started to talk to me again, but neither dog nor man was the same sort of company as Katya had been. I felt lonely in spite of spending none of my waking hours alone.

Scouts reported sighting strange mounds of earth upon which trees did not grow, a mile off the track that Katya had marked as passable. Katya's marked trail swung wide around the mounds, though it was not clear why she had chosen to do so; she had left no particular signs of explanation. More solid-seeming ground was likely; as it was, the frozen ground creaked alarmingly beneath our mechs and horses, and the worry that a singularly warm day would bog us down deeply in mud was ever-present.

The cavalry lieutenant seemed surprised at my enthusiastic reaction to the news of the mounds. To his nobly bred sensibilities (bred, I rather suspected, on the wrong side of the sheets somewhere in Wallachia), unexplained mounds meant ancient barrows, and ancient barrows meant unearthly haunts from half-remembered childhood stories. The wild forest was a frightening place, a setting for tales of woe, and by no means a popular travel destination.

My more humbly bred instincts suggested that mounds meant people likely lived nearby, and people meant fuel we might be able to purchase.

This was a great deal more important than fanciful stories. The simple fact, colder and harder than the creaking ground beneath us, was this: We were burning fuel far too quickly in our attempt to drive our way through the swamp before it thawed. We needed more fuel, and sooner rather than later.

I had a further suspicion (a glimmer of audacious hope, really) about the possible nature of the mounds, which I explained to him as we rode to the site.

"I have read that in bogs, peasants sometimes cut and burn the earth itself, after pressing and drying it. Something about the way the sediment forms makes it flammable; this type of earth, known as peat, burns hotly. Some natural philosophers have theorized, on grounds of alchemical analysis, that it is the most raw form of coal, and that should peat be dried enough and compressed firmly enough, it might eventually form brown coal. A few alchemists have gone as far as to classify peat as the lowest grade of coal, below lignite."

The lieutenant pretended to listen as I continued to outline the thermal characteristics of the various types of coal, talk about how peat compared in the grand scheme of things as a fuel, and some of the alternate theories about the formation of coal. It was helpful for me to say these things out loud, even as the words passed in one ear of the lieutenant and out the other.

When I arrived at the vanguard of the main force, I held on to my optimism. There were holes in the frozen earth and piles of earth beside them; it looked very much of a piece with the illustrations I had seen of peat mounds in a book on the alchemy of fuel. As we drew even nearer, though, I had to guess a second time. While the mounds (there were three of them) looked very much like they were formed from pressed slabs of earth stacked so as to drain, the lower parts of their sides showed brown grass growing on them, poking out through the layer of snow covering them. These stacks had been here quite some time, the lieutenant pointed out, and reasserted his opinion that if they were the work of men at all, they were burial mounds, not some strangely burnable earth.

On closer inspection, I decided that my first impression was correct. They were stacks of peat, cut and pressed and stacked to dry years before; but whoever had done it had failed to collect them after all this time, long enough for vegetation to start reclaiming the peat, creeping up waist-high along the sides. I dismounted to get a good estimate of the quantity and condition of the fuel, and when I walked around to the back side of the hill, I found another hole at the base of the mound; this one a dark gape torn in the earth, distinct from the neat geometric cuts made by those harvesting peat.

Interesting. Peering in, I could see the broken skeleton of a man below. Our mysterious peat collector, I thought to myself. It was obvious that he'd managed to find a cave the hard way and had died either on impact or starved to death after. The lieutenant dismounted and joined me.

"See anything?" he asked.

"Nothing other than the obvious," I said, pointing down at the hole. "My guess is it's a natural cave system."

"We don't need to go in, do we?" The lieutenant's apprehension was visible.

I made a snap decision. The lieutenant was afraid of going into the cave; this was an opportunity to impress him with my own courage and build his trust in my judgment as a consequence. I asked him to fetch me a rope, told him I would go down and take a look to see how large it was, and how stable the hill looked from the underside. It wouldn't do, I told him, for us to lose a wagonload of peat by collapsing half the hill as soon as we brought more weight on top of it.

As he fetched the rope, I realized that my excuse was a good one on geological grounds—cave-ins are chancy, dangerous events for anyone above a cave, as well as anyone inside of it. I may have been fishing for an excuse, but I had hooked a sound reason. We tied off the rope to a tree, and I climbed down the hole with a lit lantern hanging off my shoulder.

It wasn't really dark enough down there to require a lantern, but I appreciated the way the lieutenant had rigged up a carrying sling for the lantern so I could readily climb down the rope with both hands, and I felt it would be undiplomatic for me to refuse his helpful addition to my gear. The girlish shriek from above as the lantern swung sideways and briefly illuminated the ground directly below me reminded me of two things: First, the lieutenant was worried about finding barrows. Second, that the poor unfortunate peat-cutter at the bottom of the hole was in a skeletal condition.

I planted my feet on the ground, then peered up. The lieutenant had disappeared. Fortunately, he hadn't taken the rope with him. I took a deep breath to calm myself, and then another one to prepare myself to yell at him to come back with the appropriate amount of dignity.

What actually came out of my mouth was a little bit different—an inarticulate scream only marginally more masculine sounding than the lieutenant's. The reason for this difference was simple: A bony hand was grabbing my ankle. And by "bony," I do not mean merely slender; I mean completely devoid of flesh.

The lieutenant's reaction seemed now much more reasonable, if not particularly valiant. As I jerked my leg forcefully to try to get it away from the grasping limb of the departed peat-cutter, I saw no signs that this hill was undermined by a natural cave system; but rather, proof positive that it was built up around a barrow mound of great antiquity.

"You have come to rob the wrong king," rasped the barrow's original occupant. It took me a minute to realize what was being said; his Latin sounded different from how I expected Latin to sound. Perhaps modern scholars get the language subtly wrong; perhaps it was simply that he lacked flesh and blood lips; perhaps it was not his native language to begin with.

My first reaction, on being accused of being a grave robber, was to deny the criminal charge. As I started to do so, I realized that I had every intention of robbing the dead. That is, I meant to rob the dead peat-cutter of the produce of his labor, sitting up on the hill above. Then I started to deny I had any intentions of disturbing a grave and realized, as I did, that would be false as well. Having seen the skeleton below, I had every intention of disturbing what I thought to be an accidental grave by descending into the hill.

In retrospect, my first reaction should have been to start climbing; I was outnumbered and surrounded by hostile forces. Whether or not the occupant's claim to royalty was overblown, he was clearly important enough to have been buried with a number of servants; and I had the space of about a dozen heartbeats between the moment the peat-cutter grabbed my ankle and the moment several of his servants laid hands on me. Maybe I wouldn't have been able to climb quite fast enough to escape them; it's hard to say. My heart was beating at a lively enough rate that those dozen heartbeats were not overly long in measure; and while I am by no means in poor physical condition, climbing up a rope is one of the slower ways of escaping a dangerous situation.

The traditional heroic reaction from the stories I'd read would have been to pull out my sword and cut my way free, shouting out battle cries involving God, Christ, various saints, the Christian god, some pagan god or goddess, my emperor, some lesser liege lord or, at the very least, my own glorious heritage. However, I came from a humble background, which left me well versed neither in bladework nor in suicidal folly.

I know that, given my decision to climb down in the first place, you may have doubts about the latter, but I would argue that was simple folly on my part, and not even much of that. How many ancient, haunted barrows are there in that wild bit of land between Avaria, Lithuania, and the empire ruled from Oenipons, which referred to itself as "sacred" and "Roman"? Finding this one was a stroke of exceptionally poor luck.

So, instead of playing the hero, I did exactly what those of us of less lofty birth have been doing when confronted with a noble (or in this case, royal) temper tantrum: I apologized and begged for mercy. While, of course, trying to underline the utility of my continued survival.

I had a large number of things I could apologize for. My ignorance of his name and dominion. Disturbing his rest. Stepping on his subject while panicking about being grabbed. Being of low and base birth. My atrocious Latin accent. It was not, I am ashamed to admit, difficult to bring myself to the point of tears as I asked him how the humble soldier Mikolai Stepanovich could be of service to his most royal highness. I think I may be allergic to grave dust.

But I am getting ahead of myself. Let me tell you what I learned while prostrating myself, apologizing profusely, and letting the man talk. On the subject of his dominion, he proudly proclaimed that in life, he had ruled over ten thousand subjects and lands so vast that you could ride all day on a fast horse without seeing the end of them.

A patriotic hero would have scoffed and called him a kinglet with pretensions to grandiose titles, told the dead king that his long-vanished kingdom would barely merit marking on a map, and boasted of serving an emperor who ruled hundreds of times as many people and lands that would take a year to ride across. I expressed astonishment that I had not heard of his reign or his kingdom, and after a little more conversational maneuvering, determined that he had never heard of the Avars.

"Christ's mercy," I exclaimed, fishing for a little more information. "Your most royal highness, I beg again for your forgiveness. I should have realized you were one of the revered great lords of the days before the Avars. Only such a lord would have such a marvelously shiny crown."

"You're one of those Christ-cultists?" he asked, curiously biting the hook I had trawled in front of him.

This dated his last exposure to the outside world a little more precisely and allowed me to play for more time while I explained that Christ-worship had become quite fashionable, first in the Roman Empire and then later spreading to many of the surrounding peoples after Rome fell.

There's something daunting about trying to trick someone in the neighborhood of a hundred times your own age; how can you come up with something they haven't thought of? I could just hope he hadn't spent much of his idle time in the tomb making contingency plans. What does a dead king do while he sits in a tomb for a couple thousand years? Do the undead sleep? Do they play knucklebones for decades on end?

I know that if I were stuck in a barrow, conscious but dead, I'd spend some time coming up with detailed contingency plans. That, or start digging.

A dark shadow flitted in through the hole, and a raven landed on top of a skeletal servant, perching on its collarbone. Ravens, as you might expect from their role on the battlefield after the fighting is over, are not particularly frightened of dead humans.

"You're right," said the raven, cocking its head and peering through the gloom. "It is a very shiny crown."

"Ah," said the king. "I see the birds are eager for your flesh to become carrion. As interesting as the stories you tell me are, I really should get on with having you killed. Kneel. I will grant you the boon of being killed by my own hand; it will be mercifully quick."

He rose up from his throne, rings glittering on his fingers as they wrapped around a hammer made of a silvery white metal and accented with precious gems. No workman's tool, that hammer, but the weapon of a proud noble with a strong arm.

As the king walked forward, I could see out of the corner of my eye the raven's head, nodding in time with the king's step as it turned its head, eyes tracking the bright gold circlet perched on top of the ancient skull.

I knelt in seeming obedience, hoping to surprise him when I dodged out of the way. As merciful as a quick death might be compared to the alternatives, I was hoping for mercy that spared me from execution entirely; I would rather have a painful chance at life than a nearly pain-less death.

Can the dead be surprised, or is that a biological reaction of some sort? There was much I didn't know about ancient undead creatures living under hills. Maybe I should have asked the lieutenant to tell me his old bedtime stories.

CHAPTER TWENTY-FOUR

In Which I Am Forgiven

I could feel the hairs on my neck raise along with the hammer above me. Though I was looking at the floor, I could sense its presence. As the hammer started to come down, I dove sideways into a roll.

A loud squawk sounded, and a cry: "Stop the thief from escaping!"

I ran around the outer perimeter of the barrow, hoping to evade pursuit and grab the rope. When I turned, I realized I wasn't being chased; skeletons were climbing up the rope, and a black feather was floating down from above.

The king was furious, but for the moment, his fury was not directed at me. I felt unreasonably indignant for a brief moment: How dare they forget about me in favor of a new thief to catch and kill? Unfortunately, his soldiers were blocking the only exit I knew of. I continued my circuit of the barrow, looking outward, hoping to find a tunnel, but no such luck. I slowed, then stopped. Perhaps if I held very still, the dead king would not realize I was still here.

"You. You brought that black bird here." The king directed his empty-socketed gaze directly at me.

No tunnel, and the dead king had not forgotten about me. I pleaded ignorance. Why, hadn't he himself said that the carrion birds were eager to see me dead? It was just his poor luck that the carrion bird also found shiny things interesting and worth flying off with. No accounting for priorities—perhaps the raven hadn't been too hungry today. While ravens aren't picky about their fare, they can be distracted by other things. And, I added, that had been an early bird, one too impatient to wait long enough for a man to die. Surely, if he killed me, far more birds would come later to pick my corpse clean. I paused to look around mean-ingfully at the barrow; there were other shiny things around, I noted.

"No birds came to feast when he came." The king gestured at the broken-limbed skeleton I'd nearly landed on and had definitely stepped on repeatedly while trying to escape his grasp.

"And he took his time about dying." He made this pronouncement with the authority of a death sentence.

I continued to argue for my innocence, suggesting that perhaps the birds hadn't realized there was a pit here. Or were too shy to approach it until after they realized there was nothing living down here that might try to eat them as they dined. Flying down into a dark hole is not a par-ticularly sensible move. And now that one had come here, I added, more were sure to follow. Ravens do talk to each other, after all; they are quite gregarious birds. I concluded my arguments by expressing doubts his soldiers would be able to hunt it down before it had spread the gossip about all the shiny things down the hole. His only hope lay in consulting an expert on birds, who might be able to work out a way to deter them.

"And would you, then, claim to be such an expert?"

The humble soldier Mikolai Stepanovich (yours truly) admitted that he perhaps did know a thing or two about birds and asked how he could serve his most royal highness. Tears welled up in my eyes—partly, I think, the effect of the grave dust I had gotten in them when I rolled. As I said, I think I may be allergic to such stuff. I then commented that I expected more birds to show up at any minute, so if his most royal high-ness permitted, I would aid him in his plight before a plague of birds set upon him and his men to strip them of all valuables.

The king seemed skeptical; then he heard cawing, drawing nearer; then the light from the hole darkened. The king ordered the hole blocked with a stout shield, but dozens of birds flew in before the skeleton bearing the shield could finish making his way up the rope. The birds attacked the dusty old skeletons of his servants, swirled around the cave, and gen-erally made nuisances of themselves.

One even dropped a fur-lined hat, as if adding insult to the injury of the theft of the crown. However, soon enough, the soldier with the shield made his way up the rope; and the hole was blocked, leaving the barrow dark. Too late, I realized that my shoulder was coated with lantern oil and sprinkled with broken glass, and that the lantern had been crushed and gone out.

It was very dark in the cave. From the chaos I witnessed, I think neither the birds nor the skeletons could see each other well in so little light. Soldier struck soldier; bird collided midair with bird. Seeing this, I hunkered down and covered my face with my arms, hoping to wait out the chaotic violence by staying as far out of the way as possible.

There was the ringing of metal on metal; the clatter of bone, the scrape of talons, the whooshing of feathers, the cawing of birds, the loud crack of a rifle, not too far off, and the angry shouting of the king as he fended off the would-be avian jewelry thieves. I tried to sort out the din in my head, and then light broke back into the barrow, seeping in around the edges of my arms.

I risked a quick look. The skeleton holding the shield lay shattered on the ground in a pile of scattered bones, a cut length of rope laying on the ground around him. The tip of a rifle waved over the hole, but evidently whoever was on the other end of it couldn't see into the barrow, even with the light from outside pouring in, because they made neither a comment nor a shot.

Whoever they were, they were alive—or at least more recently so than the king. In a moment of inspiration, I stripped to the waist, swiping my undershirt over the oily patch on my coat. I then wrapped it around my hatchet and set it on fire with a match. This may sound like an involved process, but believe me when I tell you I did it in less time it than would take me to explain what I had done aloud, and my torch soon illuminated the barrow.

As the torch lit, there was one last squawk, and then silence. In the torchlight, it was clear that the fight with the birds in the dark had cost the king some of his servants and soldiers, their bones prized apart by beak and talon or by each other's weapons, the survivors bearing numerous scratch marks. The king himself, however, was unharmed. He was surrounded by a ring of dead birds, each bearing the mark of his hammer. The fight was over. He was turning his head back and forth; taking stock of the situation and, if my experience as a commander is any guide, counting his casualties. He was not pleased.

"Maikoli Stenapovek," the king said, mangling my name to a nearly unrecognizable state, "I do not know by what foul and unnatural magics you have brought these birds upon me, but I will end you."

It didn't seem particularly fair for an undead creature to accuse me of foul and unnatural magics.

I was armed with a hatchet, the efficacy of which was altered (not particularly for the better) by the fact that the head of it was wound with a burning oily shirt. The dead king was holding his favorite weapon, the one he had been buried with. Even if it was an ordinary weapon, he knew it like it was an extension of his own arm—and what ordinary weapon shines like polished silver while having the hardness of tempered steel? I was not even sure what type of metal it was made from. He could swat nimble birds out of the air with it while blindfolded.

I would be lucky if the flaming shirt of my torch didn't unravel mid-swing. Even had I been holding an enchanted axe with the sharpness to fell a tall pine in a single swing, I was no great warrior of the ages, nor had I a hundred lifetimes of bored practice in a sealed tomb during which to refine my technique. It was all I could do not to make a fool out of myself on the battlefield with steam-powered (or, more recently, flux-powered) armor on, and I did not have that mechanical enhancement to rely on now. I was, nevertheless, willing to fight for my life. I saw no other alternatives.

I thrust my makeshift torch at him with a fierce yell, and I was amazed to see him stumble backward, with a sharp deep crack that sounded as loud as a cannon in the quiet room. Then I heard another loud crack, not quite as deep, and a hole appeared in his robes of office. He looked around warily; another sharp crack. I could not resist looking up. The rifle barrel had returned, along with a pair of pistols and a spot of red hair. Then both vanished, and there was a sound of hammering as Katya worked at pushing another bullet down the barrel of her rifle.

"Foul sorceress!" the undead king shouted. "What devil's bargain have you made, to throw thunderbolts with that wand? No human wields such magics on her own! Or are you human?"

He did not seem fully convinced that Katya belonged to my species. It took a real effort to keep my attention on the present after briefly noting to myself that this confirmed my earlier estimate of his age. I held the torch high, trying to provide better light. The rifle dipped down, and there was another loud report; the king's skull dropped to the ground, still talking.

"Maikoli Stenapovek, I forgive you. I did not know you were a slave to a demon walking in the skin of a woman."

His body hunched forward, holding the hammer to the side while he groped around for his skull. He couldn't quite see what he was doing; his skull had rolled to face the wall when it landed. There was another sharp crack, and his skeletal body tumbled to the earth in two pieces, spine severed. He, in his several parts, began flailing about in blind panic.

I stepped forward cautiously, then started trying to smash the bones with my hatchet-torch. After the first few blows, the torch part had been extinguished, the blade having severed enough of the burning cloth that it fell off, no longer secured in place. The last thing the king's skull told me was to free myself from demonic influences, to fight the foul and unnatural magics that left me a pawn to a fiendish mistress. I sighed heavily.

"Would that I could have talked to him without him trying to kill me," I said to myself out loud.

I had so many questions I had wanted to ask. It is not every day you meet someone over a thousand years old. It is one thing for some old country grandmother to tell you tall tales about the days of yore, but another entirely to hear it from someone who had been there. As old as the little old ladies are, I doubt that many of them (any, even) are more than a hundred years old. More likely, they just start to forget how old they are and begin to confuse stories they've told about their younger days with stories their own elders told them once upon a time.

For example, I remember the little old grandmother out in the woods telling me a tale about when Khoryv sailed up the Slavutich with his sister and two brothers. She told it as if she had been there, even though that took place many centuries ago. The logical conclusions are either that she was a bit confused, or that she was simply reciting the story word for word as it had been told to her by her own grandmother, who had heard it from hers, and so on, passed on from generation to generation.

I decided to risk whatever curses the pulverized king might rain down on my head and filled my bags with jewelry before I headed up the rope. I also took his hammer. I'm not sure whether I intended it as the rightful spoils of war or if I wanted to make sure he wouldn't have it with him if his bones reassembled themselves. Both reasons came to mind afterward.

If he did regenerate from his smashed state, he would surely want revenge. If we had merely inconvenienced him, rather than destroyed him, and he climbed out of the hole to chase us down and revenge himself upon us, I didn't want to leave him his favored weapon. How do you kill what's already dead? My education was sorely lacking in this area, and I hoped it wouldn't prove an important deficiency later on.

Katya asked me if I'd retrieved her hat. Evidently, a bird had snatched it from her, and she had ridden hard after the bird until she saw it fly into a hole. The hole, she told me, was one with me down inside of it, surrounded by the undead, in the process of getting myself messily killed by those undead. And her back was still stained from the ink. She'd washed it, she informed me, several times, and her undershirt would never be the same. And would I please not get myself killed in a dark hole in the swamp? Please? She liked me. She meant she really . . . well, really liked me. And she cared if I got myself trapped with a horde of ravening undead.

She buried her face in my chest. She really, really cared about me, she informed me, her icy cheeks and nose pressed against my bare chest, hugging me tight. The chill wind whipped across my back, reminding me I'd left my coat behind as well. She mumbled something nearly inaudible and entirely into my chest, then took a deep breath.

"Katya?" I said, cutting her short.

As warm as my heart felt on hearing her work up the courage to say what she meant, the rest of my torso was experiencing a contrasting sensation, and I was beginning to fear frostbite.

"I know. I love you, too." I picked her up and kissed her firmly before setting her back down.

"I'll be back up with your hat and my coat. Hold this," I said, handing her the hammer.

"And this." I emptied the bags and pouches tied around my waist, leaving a pile of jewelry at her feet.

"Oh. And this." I handed her the somewhat singed hatchet.

I descended into the barrow once again, this time risking a careful look around before I descended the last stretch. For the moment, it was quiet in the barrow. Although I was tempted to refill my bags again with more grave goods, I didn't linger any longer than necessary to quickly pull on my coat and her hat, climbing back up the rope with all due speed.

CHAPTER TWENTY-FIVE

In Which I Compare Lieutenants

Peat fires are terrifically smoky. I felt like I was painting ARMY RIGHT HERE in great big letters of smoke across the sky every time we fired up the mechs on a peat load.

Charcoal loads, due to the lower fuel density, need more frequent reloading than coal, but burn more cleanly and at a similar temperature. Peat loads not only needed more frequent reloading than coal but required adjustments to the boilers, careful attention in operation, and more frequent cleaning. It was inconvenient and difficult, but good, hard anthracite coal, glossy and black, was in short supply and best reserved for an occasion of combat. We had a small reserve remaining from our Ruthenian supplies, and only slightly more of the brown coal we'd scavenged locally in Avaria.

We pressed on from dawn until dusk each day, and a little beyond, as fast as we could drive the men and machines. I was as eager to put miles between us and the desecrated barrow as I was to get us onto proper roads before the winter passed and mud arrived. While I wasn't familiar with the area, my experience had always been that springtime meant deep mud. Luckily, the weather had taken a turn for the colder.

The cavalry lieutenant claimed the cold snap was the chilly vengeance of disturbed barrow-wights haunting us, and that he had dreams of the undead chasing after us, ghostly fingers drawing frost out of the air with the chill of the grave. His superstitious nature had been reinforced by the episode with the undead. While I disliked the effect of his stories on morale, I could not bring myself to chastise him for spreading the stories under the circumstances. As far as he knew, they were true; and I was not sure they were not true myself.

I carried the dead king's warhammer on my tool belt opposite the bronze sword. Its pale, silvery-white metal stayed bright as polished steel, even though I didn't polish it; its gleam was marred only by the frost that collected on it in the cold air. My good-luck stone, too, was collecting frost. After Katya managed to catch her arm in the cord while sleeping one night, I had begun to take it off before turning in. Additionally, with it being cold from the night air when I picked it up in the morning, I didn't feel like putting it next to my skin; so, it went on outside my shirt, where it collected frost.

All of these things would frost overnight inside our tent, even if I wiped the frost off them before going to sleep. Katya's rifle didn't frost at all, I suppose because she oiled it regularly. With the two of us packed tightly together in there, we stayed warm enough. I didn't make a big deal out of the fact that I stopped sleeping in the big command tent after Katya's return, and neither did anyone else. If anything, it made the command tent a better command facility; the watch officer no longer worried about disturbing my sleep, and my sleep was only disturbed if there was something that couldn't be handled by one of the other officers.

The older Rimehammer cousin, Felix, whom I had promoted to executive officer of the battalion, was not as talkative as Ragnar, but he was very good at getting people to listen to what he had to say and took his position as second in command outside of combat very seriously. It was as if by hoarding his words, he made each one as precious as gold by means of scarce supply.

Not even the supply colonel (in his new role as supply lieutenant) was immune to the power of this effect. It didn't stop him from drinking to excess while off duty, but his episodes of blustery insubordination and attempts to exert his former authority as colonel would halt abruptly with one or two sharp words from Captain Rimehammer.

Felix's written reports were another matter. Whatever reservations he had about speaking too many words aloud, he seemed to have an unlimited eagerness for written documentation. His notes and reports were meticulous, detailed, and might have run us out of paper by the end of the trip if not for the fact that he had made a very thorough accounting of supplies and consumption rates and arranged for the manufacture of more paper. The supply colonel was not happy with the repurposing of some of the cooking equipment to make a paper press.

To be more precise on the subject of interruptions, soldiers under my command disturbed me late at night exactly twice in the days following my brush with undeath and Katya's return to camp. The first time was not what you might expect—not some bold or drunk or desperate soldier seeking his commander's attention on an urgent problem. It was the red-headed soldier in my sleeping bag who woke me up with a protest I couldn't quite understand. She was at least halfway asleep and speaking directly into my armpit, which is not nearly as good at hearing as my ear; moreover, her mouth was close enough to my armpit to impede proper diction. The only thing I could make out was a tone of complaint.

"What did you say?" I asked, reasonably, shifting around to unmuffle her mouth.

"Hammer too cold. Throw away," she mumbled incoherently.

I wasn't convinced she was awake, much less being reasonable, so I shut my eyes and worked on getting back to sleep.

"What you need a hammer for anyway?" She said this clearly and distinctly.

"Alright, I'll leave it elsewhere tomorrow night," I promised.

Looking around in the dim light of stars filtered through the fabric of the tent, I spied a canteen that was likely the real source of her discomfort—it was cold and hard and had moved during the night. Likely, she'd rolled onto it while asleep, woken up, and gotten confused.

Nevertheless, the hammer, as shiny as it was, probably didn't need to be crowded into our small tent with us. Two people were a tight enough fit even without our gear, and I really had no practical use for the hammer—just an irrational worry that if I took my eyes off it, I would see it again soon. In particular, I worried I would see it in the hands of a deadly undead warrior king. Rationally speaking, since he hadn't caught up with us yet, he probably wouldn't ever catch up with us; either he was bound to his tomb or smashing him into little bits had gotten rid of him for good.

The second time I was disturbed in the middle of the night was later that same night. I awoke to the sound of Lieutenant Fyodor Kransky (the artillery lieutenant) nervously swallowing as he walked toward our tent.

He breathed in deeply, as if to shout, then paused. I guessed that he was working up the nerve to wake me. His unease was surprising; I had thought he was among my boldest officers. The cavalry lieutenant was superstitious; Vitold was prudent; two of my captains were old men, old enough to no longer be so bold; and Ragnar had signed a contract in blood. I had not given Fyodor a reason to fear me.

"What is it, Fyodor?" I asked, starting to rummage around in the tent, locating my boots.

I assumed that whatever business he had with me, it would be important; and it was unlikely I would be able to deal with it from inside the warm, snug tent with a winsome woman snuggled up with me. Given the weather outside, donning some clothing (boots in particular) seemed necessary.

He startled, as if surprised I had known he was there. He swallowed again, steadying himself before answering my question.

"Ah. Sir, we've captured a spy."

In spite of my head start, Katya awoke so quickly and completely at the mention of espionage that I think she could have beaten me out of the tent if it had more room, and if I hadn't already been blocking the exit. The tent wasn't large enough for me to pull my boots on comfortably without already being half out of it, but Katya was fully dressed and peering eagerly over my shoulder before I stood up.

By the time I arrived on the scene, the spy had already confessed, identified his employer, and detailed his mission. Several times. From the parts I heard as I came into earshot, he was working for . . . Emperor Koschei himself? The Castilian Inquisition! Perhaps Emperor Leon? No, obviously Emperor Sigismund II. And his mission was to . . . assassinate King Janos? Poison General Spitignov? Steal our secret recipe for hardtack? Track us through the swamp? Sabotage our mighty mechs? Flush out treasonous activity by Cimmerian conspiracists intent on overturning the Golden Empire from within?

Fortunately for him, none of his confessions were clearly understood (much less believed) by his interrogators. In his terror—an understandable state, given that he was tied up and several enlisted men were waving around pointed and heated objects in a threatening manner at the direction of the elderly captain of the heavy armor division—he had reverted to his native language and was speaking at an incredibly high speed and pitch. While I assessed the situation, he started getting creative. I don't think there is a Purple Pants Syndicate or an Order of the Divine Machinists' Trade Union, but the spy confessed to working for both of them.

I say fortunate because the old captain (in truth, middle-aged, but this is old in an army in the field) had very little sense of humor, and would have taken those last claims as an attempt at levity. Attempts at levity were, in his book, a capital crime. However, he had managed to reach the rank of captain in the Imperial Army without ever having to learn any of the dialects spoken in the Gothic Empire.

"Stop waving those around for a minute," I said firmly in Latin. If the man was educated, which I suspected was the case, he would understand that.

Then I repeated myself in Slavonic—stiffly accented Slavonic, deliberately trying to ape an accent that I thought a mercenary from the western cantons might have. I hoped this would be a subtle reminder that we were supposed to be a ragtag mishmash of several wrecked mercenary companies welded recently into a single entity. After the hot pokers and sharpened knives were whisked away, the man stopped confessing for long enough to take a deep breath, and I switched to my best approximation of Gothic. I had never practiced it aloud, only read it, so I had little faith in my pronunciation.

"I have trouble believing you are on that many payrolls," I told him. "You're not nearly well-fed enough for that."

His eyes bulged, and he started to jabber out a series of apologies and abasements.

"Save it for later. I'm sure this is all just a simple misunderstanding," I said, switching back to Latin. I wasn't quite sure how to say "misunderstanding" in Gothic.

"However, we do need to understand the reason for your presence in our camp." I untied his hands and handed him a biscuit.

"Fyodor? Bring me tea," I said. "Two cups."

The man eyed the biscuit with a combination of wariness and hunger.

"It's not poisoned. If I wanted to kill you, you'd be dead already." I crossed my arms and waited.

The biscuit disappeared very quickly. A few crumbs were ejected along with a cautious expression of limited gratitude. I pulled out a handy prop.

"This is a very special hammer. I want you to look at this closely for a minute."

The man peered at it. He licked his finger, then attempted to rub off the frost from the head with the same finger, likely to try to read the inscription. His finger stuck fast, unsurprisingly, and he let loose with a stream of curses. This was ideal. I couldn't have hoped for a better turn of accidental foolishness. I then deceived him in the best way possible, using nothing but the truth.

"Quiet. If you utter a knowing falsehood while in the grip of justice, things may go badly." A true enough statement, if slightly misleading. "This hammer is very dangerous," I added. Also true. I had seen it wielded very efficiently. "I would hate to see your arm freeze off." I really would hate seeing that. I didn't expect to see it, but technically, I was still being truthful.

I stared at him for a long moment before speaking again. "You should tell me the truth, the whole truth, and nothing but the truth when answering my questions. Do you understand me?"

"Yes," said the man, soberly and in stiff ecclesiastical Latin.

Some of the soldiers were starting to look bored and restless. After assigning them the mission of scouring the area for any companions, equipment, or tracks the man might have left behind, I questioned the man carefully. He admitted to having left behind a cart outside of our camp, and that when caught, his intentions had been to load said cart up with a quantity of our provisions and machinery, which would keep him fed both in the short run and earn him money once he'd made another visit to civilization. He'd worked as a salvage mechanic in the armies of the border lords in the Gothic Empire a few times and knew the parts would fetch a pretty penny.

Had he not been convinced that he was under the compulsion of the threat of having his arm frozen off if he was evasive, I probably would not have gotten the full story about his employment history—he had been fired twice, both times on suspicion of theft. The second time had involved being fired *at*, as well; that particular employer had owned a pistol with gold inlay, and upon recovering it, felt gripped by an immediate need to make sure it was still working by loading it and firing it at the would-be thief.

"You don't appear to be very good at thievery," I remarked. "Would you work for them again if they would have you?"

He would, he admitted. A few good, solid imperial marks would go a very long way toward keeping his belly button and spine at a safe distance from each other. Marching all over the country and having to work in mud, rain, thunder, and artillery fire was not his idea of a good time, but the lords weren't too picky about who they hired. They always needed more men who knew which end of a wrench to whack a malfunctioning machine with. He started waxing rhapsodically on the subject of the regularity and quantity of military chow, and I felt pity well up in me.

Okay, I should have known that if he was a decent worker, he would have been able to find his desired civilian employment, but faced with a hungry and unemployed man wandering around in the wilderness, who wasn't actually my enemy as far as I knew, I made the decision that felt natural.

"Look. We don't pay as well as a prince. Mercenary payrolls aren't as regular or as reliable as all that. But I'd be willing to give you a second chance. We need mechanics, too, you know? Just keep in mind, we know you have sticky fingers, and you know that you aren't any good at getting away with it. Close your eyes."

I muttered some ominous-sounding gibberish and splashed hot tea over his stuck hand, which he jerked back reflexively. Then he opened his eyes. After discovering his finger still attached, he thanked me profusely for my mercy and swore undying loyalty, honesty, and diligent workmanship.

"So, did he say who he works for?" Katya couldn't contain her curiosity any longer.

"He works for us now," I said.

This earned me several incredulous looks. I hefted the warhammer thoughtfully. The incredulous looks disappeared, diplomatically pointed elsewhere or replaced by simple concern. The story of the hammer's origin had been spread very rapidly by the cavalry officer. The lieutenant's ghost stories often featured the wilderness, and various elements of those stories kept attaching themselves to the story of how I had obtained the hammer.

"Ragnar?" I waved over the Swedish lieutenant.

"Yes, sir?" Ragnar maintained a steady face.

"Our little friend here is joining your cousin's section as a mechanic. Basic grade. See that he fills out the appropriate paperwork."

As my fingers absently traced patterns in the frost on the warhammer, whimsy struck me. I beckoned the lieutenant closer and handed him the hammer.

"It's a rimed hammer," I said under my breath in Norse, by way of explanation, "and it is yours now, Mister Rimehammer."

There was a flash of lightning in the distance, then a crack of thunder, and the flurries of snow turned to light rain. Ragnar's eyes widened and he stammered out a very formal and stiff expression of thankfulness.

"Also, your cousin should know that our little friend here has a history of trying to make off with inventory, which is what brought him creeping into our camp in the first place." I said this in Norse as well, still speaking quietly so as not to be overheard.

Ragnar's expression of surprise was replaced with a sour look.

INTERLUDE

The following excerpt is taken from *Ragnar Rimhamar, Gentleman Adventurer*, with permission of the publisher.

The thief was babbling his fool head off in an unintelligible Gothic dialect. What sort, I don't know—his Latin had been hard enough to understand—but Mikolai seemed to know, and after addressing him, first in Latin and then in what I thought was probably a Ruthenian dialect (I couldn't make it out very well), he started talking to him in more or less the same language.

As much, that is, as one could tell. The high-pitched and high-paced jabbering was nothing like the deep, harsh, and measured words that Mikolai uttered. I couldn't get a clear look at what was going on between them, on account of the darkness; but then I saw a flare of white-ish light, and when I poked my head in, the man's hand was glued fast to the hammer of the barrow-wight king, little rivulets of ice creeping up his arm.

Had the thief tried to snatch the artifact from him?

Mikolai said something that left the thief looking pleadingly at the heated tongs that Corporal Banks was handling.

"I think you can put those away now," I whispered to her.

She startled, dropping the tongs into the dirt, where they hissed.

"Shit! You startled me!" She paused and looked at me. "I mean, shit, sir?"

I waved aside the formality. I could forgive the way her obvious lust for me left her fumbling for the right thing to say. Professionally, sleeping with one of the enlisted soldiers in my cousin's command seemed like a bad idea; though on a personal level, her interest was flattering.

"What do you think they're saying?" I said.

I was keeping it down to a whisper so that my superior officer, the colonel, wouldn't take notice. Colonel. A pretty pretentious rank for a mercenary who commanded a short battalion rather than a full regiment, but I wasn't going to question it. The man was downright terrifying, one of those war mages who was worth a battalion by himself, and I think his original rank in the Golden Empire was something close to equivalent to that anyway.

"I don't know. Sir," she whispered back, putting special emphasis on the last word.

I watched, fascinated, as Mikolai released his spell on the thief's arm and pronounced him part of the company.

"They're like insane children," Corporal Banks muttered under her breath.

Mikolai pointed at me, addressing me in his archaic Norse speech.

"Lieutenant Ragnar Rimehammer, attendest thou me," he said. "It is fit that this man be into thy father's eldest son's brother's second son's company's mechanic-platoon inducted as a machinist of meanest rank. His records ought be filled by his hand or by discussion with him."

"Sir, yes, sir!" I tossed off a casual salute.

He beckoned me closer, holding out the hammer. "I grant unto thee this hammer as a boon. It fits thy name as a hammer rimed."

Hesitantly, I grasped the enchanted weapon. Thunder rolled in the distance, and chills ran down my spine. I could feel the magic flaring out from it, freezing the rain around me as it fell, little pellets of ice bouncing off my boots.

"Thank you, sir!" I clicked my heels.

"Also, I must tell thee this; this man hath confessed to theft of one pair pistols, and also of an elemental cage; and that is but the times that he was caught. His intent was similar upon his first approach to thy tents."

Mikolai gave me a look I could not interpret immediately; I decided after a minute that it had been an apologetic one, but that I had never seen him looking apologetic before. I passed the job of bringing the bad news to my cousin to Corporal Banks, who did not appreciate being exiled from my company, and cursed out loud as she realized hers was the short squad of mechanics and probably would be assigned the extra pair of hands, complete with sticky fingers attached.

As for myself, I had a magical hammer to examine. I had never owned a warhammer before; the sidearms used in my cousin's unit were either swords or axes, the latter having considerably more use as a tool in the field but the former having a bit of prestige. It was longer in the haft than a hatchet—not quite a two-handed maul. In spite of its length and weight, it swung surprisingly easily in my hands. The long grip, I realized, was one meant to accommodate a user who slid his hand to different positions, closer and further from the head; you could fit two hands on the grip at once for power, or a single hand for longer reach.

Snowflakes swirled around the hammer in unnatural eddies, illuminated by a silvery glow as they orbited the enchanted artifact. A truly priceless artifact that, for reasons I could not fathom, had been simply given to me. Mikolai had offered the justification of whimsy fueled by the coincidence of my name with the tracery of frost on the hammer's head, but I felt sure there was some deeper purpose behind it. Thoughts of Corporal Banks's problems and sticky-fingered Goths left my mind as I tried to grasp the implications. I resolved to speak with my cousin about it; perhaps he would better understand what it meant.

I went to sleep a happy man.

CHAPTER TWENTY-SIX

In Which I Guess Twice

A warm spell and a bout of rain left us wading through mud for three days. Those who had griped about the constant cold now complained instead about the constant wet and were joined by the more winter-hardy members of our company. The would-be thief settled uneasily into our company under the wary supervision of the Rimehammer cousins.

The older of the two was particularly annoyed. That first rainy afternoon, Felix said more words to me than I'd heard out of him since we'd first met, and every one of them was a word of complaint related to his newest subordinate. After the captain had pointed out a convenient spot to bury a body for a sixth or seventh time, I decided to have a little conversation with said subordinate.

He was struggling to keep up on the march and had fallen a bit behind; he was nearly at the back of the column. I found him letting his pet pigeon out of its cage for some air while he took a short break from wrangling his cart through the churned mud the rest of the army had left behind. It was a very tame bird, not the least bit alarmed about being handled, and the man released it without a care in the world, seeming to fully trust that it would come back.

In spite of that apparent trust, it did wear a little collar with a tube attached; and there was a little scrap of paper in the tube. I heard it rustle once as the pigeon's wings beat, unrolling the paper just a little bit to fill the tube more completely; a faint but clear note among the music of the pigeon's wingbeats, heartbeats, and his crooning about how much he liked to fly. Pigeons, as you may recall, are not noted for their cleverness or for having much of a vocabulary to express themselves. This one was some variety of overly domesticated pigeon: very pretty, but with half of what little brain pigeons normally had lost to inbreeding.

Presumably, the paper named the bird's owner and gave the address of one of his more sedentary friends or relatives to whom to bring the bird in the event it managed to get itself lost. The bird seemed intent on trying not to get lost—it started jabbering about making sure it knew which way to go home before it was even out of sight. How stupid does a bird have to be to need to remind itself which way to go to get back to the person who feeds it, and before it's even out of sight? Wild birds usually have a little more sense, even pigeons. I cleared my throat, and the man jumped in surprise, both of his feet sucking nearly clear of the mud at once.

The sudden movement brought Yuri's attention back to the man—he had been watching the bird fly off with the focus of a hungry predator watching a tasty feathered snack. Yuri growled at the man. I patted Yuri on the head and told him to shush, then addressed the man.

"Given the dislike the captain has taken to you," I said, "I shouldn't be surprised if you change your mind about working with us. I won't hold it against you if you decide to part ways with us with the next town you reach, but we won't force you out of the company."

I paused, remembering the terms on which he had left his last several employers, and added a caveat.

"Well, unless you give us a reason to do so. You do understand that I will not tolerate theft any more than Captain Rimehammer will?"

The man told me that he could deal with being thought of as a kleptomaniac. He deserved it, even; it would be penance of a sort for his past sins. He cared about earning the captain's good opinion and pledged to be a diligent worker.

"I appreciate your positive attitude. Just remember, you have proven yourself no good at thieving. Stick to being a mechanic and you'll make out much better in the long haul." I picked my way forward through the column, back toward the front, carefully avoiding the deeper ruts and holes. Difficult to believe that this had all been frozen solid just the day before. The speed with which the ground had thawed was an affront to my northern-bred weather senses. I had been aware of the need for haste, but it seemed unnatural to have ground frozen solid enough for a mech to walk over it one day, and then simply mud the next, with not even a crust of frozen ground; no patches of ice, no piles of snow, nothing but the wet rain, mud, and the smell.

The smell was the worst part. I had feared mud. I had considered mud. I had not realized that the mud of foreign lands would smell so bad. Perhaps it was a matter of acclimation—I was used to the scent of Ruthenian mud, and this mud smelled subtly different. Yuri's fur was caked with it after taking several spills. The weight of my boots doubled from their extra layer of clinging mud; I left them outside my tent that night, only to find them full of water in the morning and nearly ruined.

On the second and third days, we took everything that could walk out of the carts, including the mechs, and pressed forward burning peat. I had to take point to find solid ground, and we had to go single file if we didn't want to get any heavy machinery stuck in the mud. It was an exhausting ordeal, but we did not lose any machines or men to the mud that way.

We did lose one pet bird, though. The pet pigeon never returned. I assumed this was the result of a wild bird of prey having noticed the dumb domestic bird and deciding it looked appetizing.

It was still raining lightly when we made our way onto solid ground the morning of the third day of warm weather. Morale was low. Fuel was low. Many of the soldiers had picked up a ragged wheezing cough. Everybody was bone tired. Even the cavalrymen up on their horses were spattered with mud from head to toe. Only those of us inside steam suits had been spared mud-soaked skin; in our cases, the mud was simply all over our armor. I made the executive decision to clear out a section of trees, build fires, and set up camp while there was plenty of daylight left; the people, horses, and machines of our little army needed a break.

I was strongly considering spending another couple of days camped there, though I didn't want to promise that until the scouts had gotten a good look around.

"Sir, the trees bleed when we try to cut them." It was one of the soldiers detailed to clear trees.

I had been about to take my armor off but decided I couldn't spare the time. I hurried over. I saw no blood anywhere; several trees were partway hacked through. Sap oozed from the edges of some of the cuts. I allowed that a color-blind man in the grip of superstitious frenzy might have managed to mistake it for blood.

"See the blood, sir?" The soldier pleaded with me hopefully.

Several squads of soldiers stood around nervously, axes in hand, but not chopping. They looked wet, miserable, and frightened.

"No," I said. "Sap, yes, but no blood." I held out my hand for an axe; one of the soldiers handed me theirs, and I chopped away. The soldiers flinched and cringed.

"See? Just ordinary sap."

"And the screaming, sir?" The soldier was holding his fingers in his ears.

I gave him a hard look. Then I gave the tree a hard look. It was chopped halfway through. I pulled back my armored fist and slammed hard, the powered actuators of my armor lending my shove extra force. The tree cracked and fell.

"Does that sound like a scream to you?" I glared fiercely at the soldier.

"Sir! No, sir!" The soldier snapped off a frightened salute.

The soldier busied himself, as did the other troops. A weedy-looking fellow in a white cloak grimaced in frustration, shaking his head, and then vanished as he stepped behind a boulder. I realized too late that he was not one of my men, which explained the fact that he was idling rather than helping set up camp.

I walked over and looked more closely at the boulder. There was something unnatural about the man's disappearance. I couldn't see any signs of a cave that he might have vanished into, nor any tracks at all. The woods had a reputation for playing host to witches and ogres and all sorts of wild things. It dawned on me that he might have been a local playing some kind of trick on my men, trying to drive us away from his home.

However, he hadn't looked like a merry prankster out for a laugh. He had looked deathly serious. I had the feeling he would be back and with something more substantial in hand than phantasms with which to frighten superstitious soldiers. So, as the scouts began to report back in and say they found no signs of any hostiles in the area, I ordered double watches and the construction of barricades and cleared fire lanes.

The men grumbled, but these woods had a terrifying reputation, and the precise structure of my company's chain of command meant that I could refer vaguely to "reports" with only the cavalry lieutenant knowing it hadn't come from one of the scouts. Said lieutenant privately put forward the suggestion that my paranoia could wait until the next day, after the men had rested.

"Lieutenant, I appreciate your input," I said.

Then a voice continued, sounding like my father, and I found myself unable to finish the sentence the way I'd originally intended. "However, the enemy is approaching from the west." I found I was pointing up to the sky. Was this voice mine? Was that what I sounded like?

As I looked up, I could see carrion birds had begun to gather, along with storm clouds, and I shook my head to clear it. "Lieutenant, I need a full load of coal in every mech, stragglers rounded up and brought back in, and as many of those barricades finished as possible."

After the lieutenant slunk off, Vitold lowered his voice to a level I could barely hear over my own idling arcane turbine. "Did you really mean that, Mikolai? Or was that just to get them all hopping out of your way?"

"The birds see bloodshed and carrion in the near future," I said. "And see over there? Past the second low hill? The trees moving?"

"Trees move in the wind, right?" Vitold was still a city boy at heart.

"Not quite in that way. That particular sort of vibration is different, and those trees are in the lee of the hill. Footsteps of something large and heavy, like a mech, will shake the trees like so, for several hundred yards; you can see the vibrations are shared alike over a wide area, yes? There's no sign of smoke, though, so whatever the heavy element of their force is, it doesn't burn coal." I peered off into the distance.

Vitold frowned. "I had best get to work then," he said.

"Ready for a feast, birds?" I asked the sky rhetorically, as the lead rank of the enemy slowed under the cover of the trees. Presumably, they were readying their weapons as their leaders took stock of the situation, waiting to shoot until after they had assured themselves everything was going to plan.

The birds did not wait. A horrendous cawing filled the air and black feathers flew as they tried for an early dinner, attacking men armed with bows, javelins, and axes—a few on horseback but most on foot. By the time the strangers had recovered from the surprise of the avian assault, Lieutenant Kransky was directing shells into their midst. While some officers might have described his decision to fire without my express orders as premature presumption, I soundly approved of his initiative.

The men retreated, leaving behind scattered dead and an alert army. I sent word to hold ground and be ready to fire on their reappearance; they had not fled but were merely regrouping to synchronize their assault.

Having been denied the advantage of surprise, they would instead hope for the advantage of overwhelming force, striking all at once.

We readied ourselves, our own heavy armor closing up in tight formation. I stood front and center with the mechs, the steam knights anchoring the left side of the line, a choice that made me concerned with my own safety but that appeared to have a strong, positive effect on morale, while the Swedes anchored the right side. Our artillerists reloaded and waited for the enemy to reappear; our infantry dispersed behind the cover of hastily constructed barricades; and our cavalry waited in reserve to counter any attempts at flanking our position.

The rumble of the clouds overhead sounded like an echo of our guns. The wind whipped the trees, not quite disguising their unnatural motion as the enemy's heavier forces moved forward.

I waited. Waiting is the difficult part of fighting. To ease the strain on my arms, I locked them in place, twisting the catch of the manipulators sideways. This kept the pointy end of my weapon toward the enemy and my shield steady. The unnatural motions of the trees came closer, yet I still saw nothing above the thick underbrush. Whatever massive devices or creatures were nudging the trees out of their way were no taller than men.

The lucky stone around my neck suddenly grew cold as a white-cloaked figure stepped up on top of a boulder, holding up what I thought to be a copper-clad spear. The mage (I could sense he was such) shouted as he thrust the spear skyward once, twice, and then a third time. Blindingly bright lightning connected him with the sky.

My eyes flinched shut. For a brief and optimistically naive moment, I thought that in his hubris, the cloaked war mage had brought divine vengeance down on himself. Then deafening thunder erupted all around me.

CHAPTER TWENTY-SEVEN

In Which I Am Shocked Again

At the time, the thunder seemed to simply overwhelm my ears, a continuous explosion of sound lasting for several long seconds. Later, I realized that the sound consisted of more than a hundred separate explosions happening at once, the magically guided strike of lightning acting much the same as a phoenix stone, sparking off the powder inside of the sealed firing chambers of pistols, arquebuses, and even cannons.

Many of those guns were pointed in the general direction of the enemy, but even had they been well aimed, it was too early to fire a volley that would shock the enemy. Worse, few of the arquebusiers had been braced to fire; at least half dropped their guns as a torrent of rain fell from the sky. Heavy droplets hissed as they hammered the flaming wreckage of a cart that had hosted a half-empty barrel of gunpowder; the fortunate news is that only one cart had gone up.

The boulder shifted beneath the white-cloaked wizard, lifting him upward as a great fanged head tore loose from the dirt. To the left and right, two other heads curled around. It was a great serpent, as big as a poor peasant's hut and as long as a rich man's dacha, with three heads and six pairs of legs, and it roared angrily.

Out of the forest pounded two great serpents, each bearing another cloaked rider—a second dressed in white and one dressed in gray. Thirty-six massive legs pounded the earth as the serpents and their wizardly riders drew nearer. Each held what looked to be a copper spear but was perhaps better described as a lightning staff.

"Hold!" I shouted, raising my sword horizontally above my head with one hand and my shield with the other.

"Hold!" Ragnar echoed to my right, waving his newly acquired hammer, which was building up a layer of ice in the rain. "Set and brace!"

"Set and brace!" I shouted over my left shoulder, belatedly remembering that was what infantrymen were supposed to do in the face of charging lancers.

Behind me, the regular arquebusiers were in chaos, some scrambling for their guns and others remembering that it was time to cast their guns aside and use their fork-rests as military forks. Those who boldly went without forks, either due to laziness or confidence in their ability to aim and brace, had cause to regret their choices.

Although the serpents had caught my eye first after I reopened them, the serpents and their riders were not the first to meet our line of steam-powered machines, steam knights, and stalwart Swedes. That particular honor belonged to the first rank of enemy warriors, who wore bear-skin cloaks with naturally attached bear-head hoods. The men howled with a thirst for blood and savagery, rushing into our lines as quickly as the wind itself. (Not as quickly as the winds you sometimes find on the sea in the great storms that roll across the ocean, but near as quick as the winds in any storm I had yet been in. I have been in many more by now—but I will get to that later.)

We took their charge standing. I might have fallen over if not for the fact that when I staggered backward, a mech or steam knight behind me—I don't know which—shoved me forward. The tip of my sword dug into the dirt, sticking. The man who had smashed into me went down with a poleaxe in his gut, then a man wearing an exotic-looking white bearskin stepped over him and delivered a powerful blow on my upraised shield. I could see Yuri clinging to the man's rear leg, doing his best to try to distract him.

I had my mechanical comrades chop at him at the exact same instant I yanked to free my weapon from the dirt; and with that end free, I had the leverage to pull the blade sideways and up, cutting through the man's torso. The light went out of his eyes and he collapsed.

I raised up my weapon in triumph and let out a wordless cry. Six months ago in the safety of the barracks, I would have thought such a gesture silly and dramatic, but I had learned my lesson about the importance of morale on the battlefield. My troops would be encouraged by the sign of my victory. The curved bronze blade on the end of my weapon glinted in the light, clean and bright in spite of having been drenched in blood moments earlier.

I could feel my magic singing in my veins and then a familiar lurching sensation. Familiar, as I had felt it before; the Romanian wizard had sent me flying with an angry gesture, and this felt similar in all regards except for the direction. I kept my feet on the ground this time as I was pulled forward; casting about, I saw the white-cloaked man gesturing, his hand dragging just as I was being dragged.

I opened my senses in full to the force dragging me, focusing on it as I was pulled up next to the wizard's serpent. Perhaps I should say the serpent's wizard rather than the wizard's serpent—even today, I do not know which was the junior partner between the two. The serpent clumsily bit down at me once, twice, and then a third time, finally connecting with its third head, the force of the bite breaking several of the joins between armor plates.

Yuri stood beneath me, barking ferociously as the serpent flung me in the air.

In spite of the ringing in my ears, the sharp pains in my chest, an inability to inhale, and the blood in my mouth, I remembered how to tie a snare one-handed. The old lady in the woods was particular about what she thought was the proper way to tie snares. I imagine arthritis has a way of focusing the mind on efficiency of gestures.

Getting your face pounded into the ground by a fifteen-foot fall also focuses your mind on the efficiency of gestures. With that motivating me, I propped myself up with my shield and twisted my right hand before pulling it inward from the grip control, freeing it to gesture without dropping my weapon. I stared back at the cloaked man, tying an imaginary snare with my hand and throwing it outward. Magic tingled in my fingertips as I remembered setting snares for rabbits in the summer. I pulled and he flew to me, startled.

"Two can play at that game," I said, and swung my arm.

The blow should have taken his arm off, but the serpent interposed one of its foremost limbs, taking on the force of the blow aimed at its master or pet. (Again, I am not sure of the nature of their relationship, and I apologize.) The white-cloaked man launched himself into the air, his cloak flapping in the wind as he flew away from me.

By the time I was fully upright again, I had mechs packed in behind me and serpents in front of me; between friend and foe there was no room for me to do anything but stand and fight. It was brutal and bruising for me; it was deadly for some of my comrades. Blood, coal, and gears littered the ground under my feet, proof that a house-sized serpent can tear a steam knight in half between two of its heads.

Trapped in the thick of things, it was hard for me to follow what was going on in the rest of the battle, and I had no chance to make anything I said heard. I struck as hard as I could at the joints of the serpents' many limbs, braced myself, and raised my shield at an angle to deflect a mighty blow and live a little longer, again and again. Black spots filled my vision as I gasped shallowly for breath. Then the serpent in front of me fell, and I could see the field of battle.

We were now in the forest rather than in cleared area; either we had driven the serpents back into the trees, or the trees had grown up around us, and I took that as a good sign. Then everything went white, and I took this as a bad sign. I called (and, more importantly, signaled) for a halt.

Then everything went white again. Where was the wizard? A third bolt struck, and I cast about, looking for the source. There, a flutter of a familiar white cloak. He was raising up his staff, and the clouds were swirling in response. At my feet, Yuri lay still, and I was filled with rage—pure, deep, and simple rage.

I opened the throttles of my mechs—the pair that were still standing, which were Ilya and Vitold's old suits—and the three of us pounded together toward the man up on the hill, who was waving his stick, lightly armored warriors scattering before us. The terrible cawing of thousands of crows drowned out the thunder above and even the sound of the boilers of the steam knight armor suits next to me.

If a murder of aggressive crows had attacked the natives of the forest earlier, what swirled in the space between myself and the white-cloaked wizard was a massacre of black birds, numbering a flock of flocks. The beating of so many wings stilled the wind, turning it into a storm of isolated breezes wavering back and forth through the trees. The eddies within the storm told me the enemy mage was still ahead of me, keeping low to the ground as he beat a retreat; I could not have known otherwise. Even the rain struggled to reach the ground directly through the swirling birds.

Lightning cracked, splitting a path through the birds, leaving the smell of sulfur in my nose, my hairs standing on end and my vision wavering; but we continued our charge up the hill. As we neared, the man stepped behind a tree and was gone. My mechs and I smashed into the tree anyway, the trunk cracking at once upon impact. I could no longer sense his presence, but I raised my weapon to the sky and called out to tell him what I would do to him if he troubled me again.

When I had finished shouting myself hoarse and taken several quick shallow breaths, I looked around. Most of the enemy had fled. Most of those who had not fled had died, and of those who lived, most bore marks from the talons and beaks of the feathered foe. I saw only one who seemed to be still trying to fight, his empty, bloody eye sockets explaining why he had not realized the futility of his intentions; as he waved a spear menacingly in my general direction, his head erupted in a gory spray, and the audible crack of a rifle proved to me that the cawing of the crows had settled to a normal level. I would not have been able to hear it before.

The crows were all over, but not many more than you would expect scavenging a battlefield. Had I imagined the storm of birds? Watching Katya ride up to the dead man, checking her accuracy, and then jerk fearfully back when a crow hopped over to the body, I suddenly became certain that others had also seen and heard the storm of birds. I opened my helmet, taking in the scene, and waited, letting the rain rinse sweat from my face.

The first to join me on the hill was Yuri. A little unsteady on his legs and with crossed eyes, but still alive. Say what you will about General Spitignov, but the man knows how to breed dogs. Loyal and as tough as nails. Yuri growled grumpily at me, grumbling about how I had run ahead too quickly and that his fur had gone all pokey. I scratched him behind the ears, underneath the armor, and called him a good doggy, and he soon forgot why he was growling.

Katya was next, having steeled her nerves, riding slowly through the trees and up the hill, letting her horse pick its way around the dead bodies. She still tensed stiffly whenever a bird flew too near but didn't let it show in her face. "Go let the men know you are still alive," she suggested, waving back toward the camp. "And do commander sorts of things," she added. "Mikolai?"

"Yes, you're right," I said, and she looked relieved. "I should go be Mikolai, the commanding officer. Colonel Marcus, I mean. We should be practicing with my new name."

She frowned. "I would rather have Squad Leader Mikolai," she said, with an edge to her voice. "Or Brevet-General Mikolai."

I plucked her off her horse into a big hug, scratched her behind her ears, and told her she was a good girl. She looked confused and unsettled. I made a mental note that humans and dogs are not quite as similar as I had thought earlier, and then kissed her thoroughly instead. She would, I informed her, have Brevet-General Mikolai in her tent that night, but for now, he needed to be Colonel Marcus.

I set her back on her horse, and we headed back toward the camp together. Either the kiss, my acceptance of her advice, or the sights of the carnage left by the battle had her smiling brightly along the way. I hoped it was the first of those things.

CHAPTER TWENTY-EIGHT

In Which I Raise Concerns

It was not long before we met with friendly soldiers; I had not run that far afield after the enemy weather wizard. The soldiers snapped to attention and stammered something incoherent; I told them to go back about their business. I thought to myself that this conspicuous display was a sign of respect for my decision to fortify the camp and prepare for battle in the face of doubts from my subordinate officers.

If Katya had been worried about the other officers making a mess of things in my absence, she had worried needlessly. The other captains had matters well in hand, and the elder Rimehammer checked with me to make sure I approved of the captains' decisions. Resuming the march was out of the question; we had wounded, prisoners, a fortified position, and were collectively exhausted. He did suggest that I give a speech before dinner and wanted me to sign off on dispensing an alcohol ration and a double dinner ration. I agreed with those suggestions readily.

While I was out and about camp, I noticed that some soldiers would turn white at my approach and that whispers rose up behind me. Stories were being told of my performance on the battlefield when my men thought I could not hear them. According to the first version I overheard, I had chopped off all three heads of one of the great serpents with a mighty swing, vaulted over its body in a single bound, and screamed to a herd of rampaging bears in their own tongue that my birds would devour their bodies and I would devour their souls, that the sky had turned black as night, raining with equal parts blood and water afterward.

Preposterous.

The natives had retreated with much of their force, including at least one wizard and two great serpents—one of the latter having left behind one of its three heads and several of its dozen legs. The rain washed the blood from the battlefield in gory red streams. Mindful of the risk of disease, I had the bodies dumped into a hastily dug trench, mechs fouling their furnaces burning peat to do the necessary heavy work before night fell. The cool, the damp, the weariness from battle; none of it meant a true halt from work, not unless we were willing to risk more lives for the sake of a little extra rest.

I gave a speech in the mess tent as promised; I do not remember how well it was received. I tried my hardest to leave them with the impression that I was deeply satisfied with how well everybody had worked together. I was sincere in my praise: This was the first major battle we had fought since bringing the mercenary survivors of the rebel force into our fold, the first since I had completely reorganized our force. Many of our officers were commanding troops they had never commanded before, and conversely, many of our troops were following officers they had not followed before.

Many of our soldiers, further, had been using weapons they had not taken into battle before. Many of the arquebusiers, freed from proper imperial doctrine, had left off carrying their forks with them, especially those who had salvaged lighter guns.

For all that they had been rearmed and reorganized, they had acquitted themselves well. True, the foe had thought they would take us by surprise, and they had not; their attempt at a sudden first strike had been hampered by the birds. But the foe had come in numbers, on their own home turf, backed up with weather magic, powerful serpents, and men whom most of my soldiers seemed to have genuinely mistaken for actual bears in the heat of the moment. (And, after burying the bodies, for magical shapeshifters.)

In spite of all those things, we had few of our own to bury compared to the foe. And by that, I was impressed. What I held myself back from saying was that I was still not sure if our mission would come to anything at all. I had found myself strapped to a raging bear when the general had been recalled and had driven the bear forward whenever it seemed I might be prepared to fall off. My accidental impersonation of an officer had spiraled out of control.

I was acting well outside of my orders, even the highly irregular ones that General Spitignov had issued. I felt sure the general had meant for us to stay in Avaria and that his commanders had meant for him to bring his entire army back with him when he was recalled. Our journey was as much motivated by my desire to stay ahead and away from people interested in arresting or executing me (such as the late and unlamented Ivan Ivanovich Romanov and his mysterious correspondent "I.V.T.") as it was by any desire to accomplish something useful on behalf of the Golden Empire and our undying emperor sitting on his throne in the city he called Rome-upon-Tanais.

I had exceeded my authority by a large enough margin that the Ministry of War might consider my subordinate officers traitors for failing to mutiny against me. Was I willing to put a small army of men, women, and the odd dog at risk of death in battle just to have a chance at keeping my own neck clear of the noose? By the time I finished my speech, my smile felt forced; inside, I was no longer celebrating our survival, but wracked by guilt over the mortal danger I had brought to my comrades.

I had even nearly managed to get a dog electrocuted, I reminded myself as Yuri begged shamelessly for table scraps. There is something about seeing animals suffer that cuts at you, even when war has numbed you to most human suffering. I grappled with my conscience as I packed in dinner, my smiles feeling more forced as the meal wore on.

After dinner, I spent some time talking with prisoners. Or, rather, trying to talk with prisoners. Most of them were not well educated and spoke only their impenetrable native dialect with a few words of Gothic and other languages used for trade. They were also remarkably uncooperative when it came to explaining why we had been attacked. I gathered that they viewed us with hostility, and that the "white wizards" had told them where we had camped and that we had great riches for the taking but learned little else. I suspected they knew little else.

The one weather-wizard we captured (one had escaped my wrath, and another had been killed) had learned Latin with a Romanian accent and Slavonic with a Gothic accent. In spite of her greater vocabulary, questioning her didn't give me much more information. She was the one who had worn a gray cloak and was surprisingly young. I got the sense from her answers that the gray cloak was the mark of a novice who hadn't yet earned the right to wear white and call herself a white wizard.

She was quite talkative, but most of what she said was useless. Grandiose threats, pleas for release, offers of mercy if released, a lengthy string of insults, and then, after a crow interrupted our conversation to complain about how quickly the dead bodies were buried (I told it off and shooed it away), she curled up into as small of a ball as her bonds allowed and babbled terrified nonsense for the rest of the time I was there.

Ragnar told me later that after I left, they were able to get her to stop babbling in terror. Once calmed, she expressed a very different attitude, one that was very cooperative and humble.

When Katya and I were at long last curled up in our tent together, she asked me what the great General Mikolai was thinking about now. I didn't say anything for a while. Holding her in my arms, I recalled that this woman was one of the people whose lives I was putting on the line in place of risking a line around my own neck. My conscience was relentless, and after a minute of guilty reflection, I admitted to her that the "great General Mikolai" was feeling very doubtful at the moment of both his purported greatness and the utility of his mission.

Even as I said that, I remembered that Katya was also someone whose ideals and sense of patriotism approached fanaticism. Would she shoot me if I told her the whole truth? I believed that she loved me, but I did not want to test that love against her sense of duty to the Golden Empire. Whichever force won out in that test could break her heart, and if it was duty that won out, it would leave a bullet in mine. What could I say to her further without provoking that test?

She took my moment of silent concern over whether or not she would be trying to kill me in the near future as a continuation of my concern over the value of the mission, and she gave one of the longest speeches I had ever heard her make, whispered quietly enough into my ear that only I could hear. (Well, Yuri, being a dog with very keen hearing parked right outside our tent, could also hear Katya, but I am not sure Yuri understood her very well.)

"Fighting rebels in our own lands is good. Bringing the fight to them is better. Cutting off their money is best. We have enemies, and those enemies give money to rebels because it is what the rebels need most. The rebels use mercenaries to fight. Those mercenaries will not fight if the money is interrupted. The rebels impress and train unhappy people.

Training and arming people takes money. Cut off the money, and the rebels must become bandits to keep fighting. Then nobody likes them and they lose."

She punctuated her whispered speech into my ear by nibbling said ear. I conceded aloud that she had a point, and my conscience eased up enough to tell her she had raised my morale back up. Her response to that was mostly nonverbal and pushed our conversation through a hard turn onto the topic of other things raised up by her, and then shifted into a thorough demonstration of our appreciation for one another's continued survival and affection.

CHAPTER TWENTY-NINE

In Which I Do Not Lie

After the battle, we spent the next three days resting in our camp and burning wood into charcoal in large batches. Tree-felling parties went heavily escorted in case the locals returned, but the only locals we saw were those few we were holding as prisoners. What, exactly, we were to do with our prisoners was unclear. I found myself in the grips of a dilemma.

I wasn't inclined to execute prisoners in cold blood, however savage and unprovoked their attack on us had been. Nor could we dispatch them to some convenient fortress to be held there; nor were they of any use to us out here in the field, simply an inconvenient encumbrance. I wasn't ready to hand them bows or guns and ask them to go hunting, though the idea had occurred to me. Simply letting them loose would reinforce the enemies that attacked us.

Food was rapidly becoming an issue of some concern. Very few people were willing to set out on hunting expeditions deeper into the dark forest filled with hostile bear-men, weather-wizards, and great serpents; most of our scouts were kept busy keeping an eye out for the enemy. Katya and I were familiar with a few edible wild plants, but teaching others to identify them correctly was a time-consuming process.

Captain Rimehammer jokingly suggested that we should have butchered the dead instead of burying them. (At least, I think he was joking.) The food supply situation wasn't that bad—yet—but careful rationing was needed if we couldn't locate supplies inside the forest. Spring may have been on the way, but we could not count on some springtime bounty of edible plants and animals emerging in the next week.

Katya was of the opinion that we should simply slit all the prisoners' throats and be done with it; most of the rest of the soldiers I heard expressing opinions on the subject more or less agreed with her. The prisoners were savages who barely spoke any words of any civilized language. According to rumor, at least some of them were shapeshifting bears, leaving the humanity of the rest in question.

Earlier, I related that "Colonel Marcus" eventually became "Colonel Marcus Corvus," and it is time to elaborate on how that came to pass. The arcane acolyte we had taken prisoner, the one with the gray cloak, freely admitted that she was very afraid of "Colonel Raven." That is to say, "Colonel Corvus." The first time I heard it come out of her mouth, I wondered if it referred to someone else; the second time, I started to wonder why she was calling me by the name of a bird; and the third time I heard it spoken, I turned around and asked the lieutenant speaking with her where the term had come from.

Nobody was willing to take credit for the term and I wasn't sure if the acolyte had invented it or if it had been in common circulation behind my back. Our magical prisoner had given up on grandiose threats and insults and focused instead on pleading for mercy, promising that she could be very useful to us if we didn't kill her, a subject upon which I had failed to be particularly reassuring. Being that the other officers were aware I had not yet made a decision on the disposition of the prisoners, none of the people willing to talk to her had reassured her on the topic either. In spite of the fact that she was likely the most dangerous prisoner, she was also the best liked as far as most of my soldiers were concerned.

It was true that she had joined our company in association with an army of howling savages trying their best to kill us. However, unlike the howling savages in question, she could speak clear Slavonic and Romanian. She was also an attractive young woman. Those were in short supply in the area at the moment. The acolyte was perfectly willing to talk for hours on end with any man assigned a shift as officer of the watch. This display of patience from a woman was something many of the men hadn't experienced since joining the army, and it bred a certain level of fondness for the neophyte weather-witch.

Vitold was, at first, of the opinion that we should probably let her live, sympathetic to an attractive young woman in duress. On the second day after the battle, I told him that I was very certain she did have magical abilities and had been trying to use them in some subtle ways when she thought she was unobserved. I joked that she might have bewitched him into being friendly. He brought an iron wrench up to his forehead for a moment, then suddenly frowned and told me he wanted to weld her inside a mech's boiler and fire it up.

Passionate fellow, Vitold. Katya disagreed with him on pragmatic grounds, pointing out that the boiler would need to be unsealed and cleaned out afterward. She was still of the opinion we should simply slit *all* the prisoners' throats (including the witch) and be done with it. After all, it was not as if we could keep an eye on them after letting them go to make sure they wouldn't cause more trouble, whatever they might promise.

That gave me an idea of what to do with the prisoners, though I was hesitant to explain it in case I wasn't able to pull it off. On the third day after the battle, I went for a ride in the woods with a handful of shiny copper kopeks, freshly polished in an alchemical solution—the brighter they shone, the better they would work as bribes, as I intended to hire help that didn't care about the face value, but rather, how shiny they were.

I came back from my ride through the woods followed by dozens of crows and ravens of several varieties. The birds waited patiently while I climbed into my armor, fetched the weather-witch to act as an interpreter, and then went to the enclosure where the other prisoners were kept. They waited nervously, some growling savage oaths under their breath to try and put the best face on whatever their final fate was. I told them to be quiet and then stood there staring them down until they complied.

We let the prisoners out one at a time. Each time, I held up a bird, greeted the prisoner in as friendly a fashion as possible given that I was armed and wearing heavy powered armor, and said that it would be best if they chose the path of friendship and of staying out of my way while my army marched through the forest. There was, I told them, nowhere they could not be seen by the birds.

Then I would release the bird, who would fly up, caw out a few choice threats at the liberated prisoner, and circle them a few times as they walked (or ran) deeper into the forest. I didn't expect the birds to keep up their watch for long, but given the fear they seemed to inspire, I thought the show would help put the locals in the mind to spread the right rumors about us.

Every time one of them saw a corvid winging through the woods, he would worry he was being watched. I wanted it known that we were merciful and not here to try to conquer the woods, but simply to pass through. I also wanted it to be known that we were dangerous enough that tangling with us unnecessarily was a poor idea.

Four days earlier, I would simply have preferred to pass through without notice, but having already clashed once with the white-cloaked wizards and the local inhabitants, I thought it certain that the white-cloaked wizards, at least, would be tracing our passage through the forest by magical means. We could not hide from them, but we could try to convince them that another attack would be a very bad idea.

As the second to last prisoner jogged into the woods, looking over his shoulder every several seconds, Katya rode over, asking if we would kill any of our prisoners at all. She looked pointedly but pessimistically at our remaining prisoner, the acolyte who had called me "Colonel Corvus" to my face. What was I going to do with her?

It was an interesting question, one which I had spent entirely too much time thinking about during the previous night. I looked over to where Vitold was working on a mech. The mech was opened up all the way for maintenance, the boiler wide open and large enough to fit the acolyte's slight body.

The acolyte looked at me, appearing more like a terrified teenager than a mighty mage. I locked eyes with her. Fyodor swallowed nervously, shifting from foot to foot. Vitold frowned and opened the hatch to the mech's currently cold furnace, patting it like an old friend. Katya looked around vigilantly at our surroundings instead of at me and the last remaining prisoner, making her perhaps the only person doing their job at the moment. Everybody else was staring at the two of us.

"You are free to go," I said, affecting a bored tone. "If you really want to go, that is."

I shrugged, as if not seeing why she might want to leave the people who had taken her captive as a prisoner of war.

The weather-witch blinked. Fyodor breathed a giant sigh of relief. Vitold made a sour face. Then Fyodor caught wind of my second statement and looked hard at the woman.

"Of course I want to go!" she said.

She took an experimental step toward the woods, then another, and looked back, pausing. She was clever enough to suspect some kind of trap.

"And no following me." Her tone was somewhere between a command and a question.

"No need to worry," I said soothingly. "I don't care about you any more than your mentor does, and it's none of my concern if you go tromping back to him empty-handed."

She crossed her arms. "My master cares about me! He's a very important man."

"I am sure," I said, in my least convincing tone of voice. "Most of you apprentice wizards never make it, but I suppose he could be attached to you. Maybe he's been waiting anxiously to see if his weakest acolyte has the teeth to chew herself out of a cage or the wits to make herself helpful. Either way, you're failing his test right now."

I yawned. "However, if you say he cares about you very deeply as a person, he'll give you another chance. Just tell him to keep away from our line of march, and convey my apologies in advance for any disruption caused by our passage. Clearly, there are parts of this forest he wants outsiders to stay out of, but I don't know which. We'll just blunder on through and destroy anything that gets in our way."

I made little shooing motions with my hands, the sort a genteel young woman might make to unsuccessfully discourage a goat from testing the edibility of laundry on the line.

She took it in much the same manner as a goat in such a situation and bit down hard on the bait. If anything, she seemed encouraged by the shooing motions telling her to run along.

"You wouldn't! You shouldn't!" She was angry and fearful.

"Well, I'd rather not, to be honest," I said. "I'd rather detour around any rituals he has in progress, the lairs of the great serpents, and so on, but I don't know these woods too well. I just want to pass through here and make my way to the Gothic Empire. But you don't want to stay with us, you're distraught from your confinement, and you probably don't even know the woods well enough to guide us through, so just run along. I'm sure you'll grow up to make a fine weather-witch someday."

I let bored contempt drip from my voice. I decided against another shooing motion as being a little too over the top and simply turned away, walking purposefully back toward camp.

"Wait!" Thumping footsteps behind me announced that the acolyte was hastily following.

Katya unslung her rifle, and I winced inwardly.

"I changed my mind," the acolyte said. "Please let me come with you."

I held back a smile. We had a guide to help us find our way through the forest. One who probably thought that she was spying on us on behalf of her superiors, which she certainly would be doing. She might betray us or try to lead us into a trap if she got to thinking she was especially clever, but I would deal with that if it came up.

"Fyodor," I said, signaling to the artillery lieutenant. "Escort the young lady here to the command tent." My voice hardened a little, and I looked him in the eye. "Try to make sure she doesn't cause any trouble for us humble mercenaries."

My statement was intended to be a reminder that our cover was to be maintained at all times. I wasn't worried about the weather-wizards knowing half of us were regularly enlisted in the army of the Golden Empire, but practice makes the master, and we were not yet masters of acting like a mercenary battalion.

Lieutenant Fyodor Kransky saluted sharply and hastened to obey. He was unquestionably fond of the young witch, something I had worried about while making my decision the previous night as I had looked down at Katya, clinging affectionately to me through the unconsciousness of sleep. I was reminded it cut both ways. Young women often have a fondness for handsome young men.

After the two of them left, I climbed onto a wagon and out of my armor, letting the boiler cool, and then I went off to find the would-be thief we'd enlisted earlier—his name was Ehrhart. As I came up to him, he hurriedly hid his diary. The man was an avid diarist; when he thought nobody else was looking, he'd often sit there, gazing thoughtfully into the distance, writing in his little journal. I had a suspicion that he was writing poetry and didn't want to be thought unmanly.

Pretending I didn't see the bound leather diary he had just jammed into a tool kit, I discussed with him a small favor he could do for me. I would have asked Vitold, except for the hostility he exhibited toward the acolyte. Vitold might flatly refuse, drive her off, or even arrange for an "accident" to take care of her. I did not think him a murderer by inclination, but the taking of life had become less exotic to both of us.

I wanted someone to help keep an eye on the acolyte. Fyodor couldn't keep an eye on her all the time, and while I thought him a loyal and talented officer, it would be unwise to trust him to report anything I needed to be aware of. Ehrhart, on the other hand, was the sort of fellow who didn't trust easily, and he was on the smaller side, sneaky and a keen observer. He also never had to stand watch; Captain Rimehammer didn't trust him enough.

This made Ehrhart a perfect choice for spying on the acolyte while she was around the camp. To my surprise, he found the idea agreeable, even to the point of volunteering to help step in and distract the young acolyte if she seemed to be engaged in some subtle mischief and I was busy. He knew enough about complex machinery to invent a credible claim to need an extra pair of small but steady hands to complete some routine maintenance task.

He looked a bit nervous during our conversation, probably because Yuri kept growling at him. Yuri's love for Ehrhart rivaled Vitold's love for the acolyte.

CHAPTER THIRTY

In Which I Am Troubled by Love

The man I had appointed lieutenant of the cavalry rode into camp, the acolyte clinging on behind him. Fyodor stared at the two of them, jealousy creeping into his eyes. If the acolyte was to show our scouts what routes to take, she would have to work with our scouts closely. Quentin Gavreau, lieutenant of the cavalry, found the girl keenly interesting for many of the same reasons Fyodor Kransky, lieutenant of the artillery, did. The last week had been full of an increasing number of hostile stares from one lieutenant to the other as we made our way through the forest.

Perhaps if I had simply made the acolyte Quentin's responsibility instead of Fyodor's in the first place, Fyodor would not have seen enough of her to make an issue out of it. Why hadn't I? The simple answer was that I hadn't been as sure of the cavalry lieutenant's intelligence or reliability. When I had dreamed up the new command structure, I had confidently assigned him a degree of responsibility greater than (and a degree of supervision less than) nearly any other mercenary officer. Captain Rimehammer had more responsibility but was also much more closely supervised by officers of the Golden Empire.

Fully awake and cognizant, on the other hand, I had trouble identifying the reasons my dreaming self had for putting him in such an independent role. Quentin was arguably either French or Romanian, depending on how seriously you took his inheritance claims. In either case, he was from a noble family with allegiance to at least one liege lord, whose interests were not aligned with those of Emperor Koschei. Pointedly, he had volunteered to take up arms to liberate Wallachia from the yoke of the Golden Empire; his ultimate loyalties were dubious.

Instead of worrying that the acolyte might compromise the loyalty of one of my officers, I was worried about the loyalty of two of them. Worse, I was worried that they might come to blows with one another. The two of them might try to kill each other in a duel or some such nonsense.

The acolyte may have been raised outside of and with contempt for civilization, but in spite of her general hatred for humanity, she was still human and no less young and foolish than either of my lieutenants when it came to matters of the heart. After years of isolated study under the watchful gaze of old white-cloaked wizards, she seemed to enjoy having a pair of handsome young men vie for a greater share of her attention, encouraging both of them.

According to the younger three of my elder brothers, most young women would find it flattering to be the center of two rival young officers' attention. When I suggested this was just normal behavior for the acolyte, however, Katya bristled angrily, telling me it wasn't right to lead two men on at once.

Katya had a most unflattering view of the young woman. I hesitate to write down what she said; suffice it to say she suggested that the acolyte had moss growing in certain unseen places (between her ears, and also between her legs) and that the acolyte would be charging two kopeks per ride as soon as she figured out what a kopek was. When I objected and told Katya that the girl had probably not spent much time around human men near her own age, Katya responded by hypothesizing that the acolyte had a history of inter-species conjugal relations.

I let Katya know that according to the former thief's reports, the young lady slept alone, but she waved away that information when I presented it, insisting it was only a matter of time before the acolyte's bedroll turned into transient housing for an assortment of men. I may have made the mistake of alluding to the potential impropriety of our own relationship when I asked why she was so angry with the acolyte; after that question, she grew very quiet and very still for the space of a dozen heartbeats. Then, she informed me that she was going to go check on the sentries while I enjoyed (or rather, failed to enjoy) a tent to myself.

Katya didn't come back to the tent that night; in the morning, I learned she'd slept for a little while in the command tent, then rode out at dawn for an extended patrol. I had six cups of tea during an extended breakfast, which was stretched over the course of three meetings. The first meeting was with Katya's three fellow captains; the second was with a certain pair of lieutenants to let them know that their rivalry had not gone unnoticed and had better not escalate; the third was a meeting with Vitold about Captain Rimehammer's fuel consumption calculations and how many mechs we could afford to operate while on the move.

Vitold and I also talked at some length about Katya, about the insanity of war, and about what we might want to do at the end of our term of military service if we got out of this alive—and did not simply go straight from the army into prison. I talked of seeing my family again and returning to the peace of the countryside; Vitold talked about becoming fat and respectable somewhere, owning an estate or perhaps just a bakery, and how much easier baking seemed now that his life experiences had expanded.

It felt good to unburden my troubles on Vitold. While he had his own troubles to burden me with, I think the burdens weighed lighter on both of us after we shared them; and our friendship seemed to grow a little bit closer to what it had been before we boarded that fateful train.

At the end of the meeting, I stared down at the bottom of my teacup, but no matter how I turned it, the leaves would not tell me a happy story. Betrayal from an unexpected quarter, death and dismemberment stalking ahead, a road full of teeth, a caged bird with its wings clipped. According to the tea-leaf reading techniques I had been taught by the little old lady during those summers in the woods, the omens had been terrible every single morning in the forest; I was beginning to understand the superstitious worries that plagued the soldiers as we started into the deep and sparsely inhabited woods.

I suppose even the fact that I was back to reading tea leaves was a sign that I was growing nervous. I am not inclined to put much credence into such silly superstitions, but the tea leaves were right in front of me and added to my sense of constant danger. In spite of the terrible omens, though, we had not yet run into any difficulties since the battle, and we were making very good time with our guide's help. Our scouts had, over the past week, found some signs that we were being watched, but the inhabitants of the woods remained elusive. More good fortune.

The scouts found no sign of those that day, or the next, at which point I began to worry. Not about being attacked, mind you, which seemed less likely in the absence of signs of probable enemies, but about Katya. I tried to quash my worries as irrational; Katya was no more likely to get lost in the woods than a goat was to get indigestion. As far as danger was concerned, she was one of the most dangerous people I knew. She was much more likely to bring misfortune to someone else than to fall prey to it herself. Love, I decided, leads us to folly. I resolved to have faith that Katya would return when her anger had cooled.

Several wagon loads of provisions had been emptied on the march, and we filled one of them with a contraption intended to manufacture charcoal while simultaneously driving a steam engine. We would put wood in, and it would simultaneously burn wood down to charcoal and push itself forward at a slow but steady walking pace, provided the terrain wasn't too rough. Now we could process some charcoal on the march, stretching our resources further. It wasn't the most efficient device, either as an engine or as a charcoal kiln, but there was no shortage of wood for us to turn into charcoal.

Working together with Vitold on a simple and useful machine was a pleasure, but even that pleasant activity could not take my mind off what (or rather, who) wasn't with me. Even as my mood fouled, Vitold's improved as he considered the long-term effects of even a modest rate of charcoal production while on the move.

My third night in a row sleeping alone was filled with dreams of an unrestful variety, and I woke before dawn, unable to go back to sleep. Instead, I sat and watched the dawn with aching eyes—bloodred fingers of the sun's first light trying to push through the thick cover of the forest canopy then stabbing into the ground as it found gaps. I was not alone; the acolyte sat a cautious distance away, seemingly wanting to talk about something but she appeared unsure how to broach the subject.

Vitold brought me a mug of tea and word that we would be able to get on the move shortly. He took one look at the acolyte and then shot a questioning glance at me.

I made a very small shrug as I accepted the tea and began to sip at it. Nothing really to be done but ask.

"Something on your mind, miss?"

She hesitated, glancing at Vitold, and stood up.

"Um. Nothing important, sir," she said. Then she hastily headed back toward the main part of camp. I watched carefully as she left, trying to guess what had been left unsaid.

"I preferred Katya," Vitold told me quietly, giving me a sharp look.

"It's not like that," I told him as I watched the acolyte leave, smiling a little at the way Vitold jumped to conclusions.

I could still remember him calling Katya a "spooky woman." Vitold was just the sort to prefer the devil he knew to the devil he didn't. He may have thought Katya a devil, but he would much rather I be with her than take up with the awful acolyte.

"There's nothing between us. I think she just didn't want to ask for advice while you were around," I added.

Or, it occurred to me, forgiveness for stirring up trouble, or permission of some kind. Rumors flew swifter than most birds and were generally more colorful. My discussion with Fyodor and Quentin might have gotten back to her in a form that gave her cause to worry.

Vitold frowned. "You've got that thinking look on you, and I saw you watch that devil girl's butt as she walked off. She's trying to enchant you, just like she tried to enchant me. Touch cold iron and think of Katya instead. She's probably in trouble somewhere by now. Maybe dead," Vitold said, giving voice to the worries I had tried so hard to suppress.

I let his first misconception slide in favor of his second, shaking my head. "Katya is the deadliest woman—deadliest person, perhaps—that I know. She rides like a tick, shoots like a standing man at a full gallop, and is woods-wise enough that she won't lose her trail. We haven't run into anything more dangerous than a disgruntled badger since the locals' attempted ambush. She'll come back when she's not angry at me anymore."

Vitold clasped me by the shoulder. "Mikolai, she took three days of rations for the trail," he said, his tone appropriate for a funeral.

"It's three days now," I said, my brow furrowing for only a moment as I reviewed my memories, breaking into a smile. "So then she'll be coming back soon." Vitold's sense of humor had gotten more subtle, I thought to myself.

"Katya takes three days' worth of trail rations when she goes out for a single day's ride," Vitold said. "I asked her why once. Felix had been griping about spoilage lately and short supply. Katya told me that if she thought she would be gone three days, she would pack a week's worth of food if she could. Just in case." Vitold crossed his arms.

"Oh," I said.

There was not very much else I could say without looking like a complete idiot. My heart sank as my mind raced through the possibilities. She could still show up, having been delayed by foreseeable complications—investigating a curious trail, resting a lamed or injured horse, et cetera. She would not starve in the woods; indeed, she could easily start foraging for herself. But she hadn't meant to leave for more than a day.

Unless . . . perhaps she had decided to leave for good and didn't want to arouse suspicion by checking out more supplies than usual. I shook off the thought. The only relationship Katya was willing to court with desertion was shooting people who did it. What if she had run into trouble, too much trouble for one woman—however deadly she may be—to handle?

I stared down at the tea leaves in my mug, swirling the last dregs of fluid. The tea leaves plastered against the edges of the mug in a pattern suggesting the painful dismemberment and death of a loved one. The memory of an old lady's voice echoed in my ears, talking about how the future was mutable but signs of it could be seen reliably in many places.

"Damn peasant superstitions," I growled to myself, flinging the mug violently away from me.

The tin mug struck a tree and bounced off, halfway crushed by the force of the impact. Vitold started, surprised by my sudden motion; Yuri raced after the mug, fetching it and depositing it at my feet. I patted the dog on the head but passed the slobbery and dented mug to Vitold instead of throwing it for Yuri to fetch again.

"Sorry," I said to both of them, standing up and shaking my head.

I headed back into the center of the camp to talk to a certain lieutenant of the cavalry. He wasn't able to tell me much more about Katya's intentions, just that she'd ridden out ahead of us and wasn't back yet. She'd left some markings along the way to point out fresh water and the location of a blackberry hedge. I gave him some rather brusque instructions on finding her trail and catching up with her; he muttered something in Romanian about hypocrisy and fraternization, and I decided not to let it pass.

"Quentin, I don't care about fraternization so long as it doesn't impact the mission. I don't care if you get a werewolf pregnant with a litter of a half dozen puppies so long as it doesn't slow us down. You and Lieutenant Kransky could share one large sleeping bag between yourselves and our friendly, local weather-witch at the same time for all I care."

By the end of that statement, I was speaking with a raised voice. I stepped closer without moderating my volume.

"However, the two of you cannot duel with each other, whether with pistols and swords, or, as you have done so far, trouble-making and words. You will treat your fellow officer with due respect and consideration, and you will keep your temper not only leashed but kenneled until it is housebroken."

I glared down at him from a close distance.

He hastily saluted and stammered out an affirmative mingled with a couple of "sirs" before rushing off to follow my orders about finding his immediate superior. Then the captain who was Fyodor's direct superior came over to chat. Cued by jealous rivalry, fraternization, and perhaps Vitold's comments about how I should not think about the acolyte's posterior, I found myself taking notice of the fact that the officer in question was a healthy woman not too many years older than I was.

I tried to push that awareness out of my mind, feeling vaguely disloyal to Katya for having noticed in the first place as we found a quieter corner of camp in which to have a private conversation. The subject was fraternization, her subordinate Fyodor, and the chain of command, and I readily conceded that yes, she would be well within her rights to bar Lieutenant Kransky from intimate fraternization with the acolyte, or his fellow lieutenant, or both simultaneously. Although not a woman easily disconcerted, I think at least one of those possibilities took her off-guard; she had some difficulty formulating a reply past a "Yes, sir."

I also quietly let her in on the reasons I had made the decision to assign Fyodor as the girl's watchdog, and discussed what I knew about the neophyte weather-witch. When we walked into the mess tent together, I caught Vitold giving me a sharp look, reminiscent of earlier that morning. The cavalry lieutenant also took note; he turned to give the two of us a speculative look, the corner of his mouth pulling a little, reminding me of his mutterings about hypocrisy. I frowned sourly at them. They both quickly looked away.

INTERLUDE

From the diary of Quentin Gavreau

Today it is January 6. My little sister Septima gave me a small book for Twelfth Day, bound in the new style, and she says I should fill it by writing every day about my adventures.

Today is January 7. It has been very quiet, but my little sister says I should write every day until I have filled this book.

Today is January 8. I think I will save paper until I have something to say.

Today is my birthday! And it has been wonderful. Sunny, bright, and perhaps a little too warm, but that is late spring for you. My stepfather gave me a honeycomb pistol; my mother gave me a horse; and I am to be fitted for mage-tempered armor at an expense of thirty livres out of my mother's dowry. It is time, my stepfather says, for me to go out and claim my inheritance in the faraway land of the Vlachs. It is unlikely my grandfather left other heirs, and the sultan's grip on the land has been loosed.

The honeycomb pistol is a marvel. It is set with a separate phoenix stone in each of six chambers; the whole assemblage rotates like a peppermill, a steel rod filling the seventh chamber as an axis. There is a striker that activates only the bottom stone, which can be removed for safe loading or travel. And the whole thing is a work of art—gilded and engraved with my name, with a carrying case of Loegrian leather that is supposed to be charmed against premature discharge. (More importantly, the case has polished leather pegs matched to the barrels to hold in shot—if you round each shot with gunner's wax to keep the powder from dripping round the edges, the whole thing can be carried fully loaded.)

My mother says I must study the political situation and practice, of all things, lance work, saying they are old-fashioned in the eastern lands and I will reflect poorly on my stepfather and the Gavreau name if my lance work is poor. It is as if the Century War had never occurred, which I suppose is true for them.

It has been a week since my birthday.

Having followed my mother's advice, I now understand there is some degree of uncertainty about who my future liege might be; Vladislav the Dragonslayer fled to Rumelia, and has two brothers. His predecessor (Vlad the Dragon) left behind four living sons, the eldest of which was kept in the sultan's court and has now been sent to Tanais, but the others are probably somewhere in Avaria or possibly the Gothic Empire, both of which I must cross if I am to become a <u>boyar</u>, which seems to be the Vlach word for <u>baron</u>.

The Vlachs call themselves Roman, and I should have an easy time learning their tongue, for it is like Latin, but the Magyar language is difficult and I must practice it two hours daily while I travel. We will take nearly the whole length of the great Istros River. My little brother is clamoring to come, and my little sister says I should write every day. I promised I will tell her the whole story when I come back.

I shall have with me letters of introduction addressed to a second cousin once removed in Transylvania and a first cousin twice removed in Pesht. With luck, one of them will help me connect with my inheritance.

Being fitted for a mage-tempered cuirass is a frightful affair! They proof it fitted, to show off how good their tempering is! I flinched, but the pistol ball left only a little mark, scarce a dent.

There is so much that I should have written while I was traveling up the Istros, but today I remembered that I had this diary with me. Everyone is atwitter here with the news of Princess Marie's engagement to King Janos. My stepfather's sister's husband is a third cousin to the Empress herself, and I had no idea the Emperor was arranging such a thing, but it has made it a fine time to be French in Pesht. It is also fine news to write home with; Emperor

Leon has stolen the march on Emperor Sigismund, who has been trying to marry his line into the Avar throne for two generations!

My cousin was happy to receive me and eager for news, and she introduced me to her grandson's friends right away. They are all sorts of politically interested and cosmopolitan, and they, in turn, introduced me to Erzsebet or Elisabeta (depending on which language she has been addressed in), who is a powerful mage and says she was promised to marry the Dragon's son when she was small.

She has been raising funds and asking for volunteers, and I was able to purchase the commission of an officer in the New Wallachian Army for only twelve livres after telling her of the particulars of my situation—the Imperial Army charges a round hundred for the privilege of being a cornet in the cavalry, so this is a very good bargain! I will write more later. The train is here.

Not content with massacre within Wallachia, the Golden Empire has sent its soldiers over the Sarmatians. Elisabeta says this is the final straw—and so, even though it is winter, we are riding to support the Avar army. There is perhaps some hope that if we show strength in his aid, King Janos will openly support the cause of a rebellion against the oppressive rule of Emperor Koschei.

I am so very grateful that my honeycomb pistol was engraved with my name—I think if it had not been, it would have gone to a greedy Cimmerian rider. That I have been given it back makes me grateful, for which I feel guilty. The battle went disastrously. Elisabeta was in fine form with her enchanted blade and her spells, but we were assaulting a fortified position with an inexperienced force that did not have full confidence in its commander.

In addition to the advantage of a fortified position with snipers and cannon on the heights, they had more heavy armor—sixteen steam knights afoot—and a war mage of their own, one with command over beasts and dark terror. The Manual at Arms of the New Model Army says that the moral is three-quarters of the battle and the physical one quarter; Elisabeta struck at one-quarter, and the enemy mage at three-quarters, so a quarter of them died and three-quarters of us fled in terror or surrendered.

This has been an utter disaster, and I am not sure why I am even writing this down. I feel ashamed to say I surrendered. I have given my parole and then some, and I am afraid I may be forsworn. Elisabeta will surely hate me if she sees me again. And what am I to tell my little sister?

CHAPTER THIRTY-ONE

In Which I Make Substitutions

The horse shifted restlessly under me, whickering his discontent quietly under his breath. A draft horse is not quite the same as a destrier, or heavy warhorse, though in the better-bred and better-fed cases, the humble workhorse can often match the proud destrier for size and strength. The draft horse I was riding was the largest and heartiest one we had.

There were several other differences between destriers and draft horses. First, a destrier is accustomed to running, cantering, and moving at speed; a draft horse usually doesn't plod faster than a walk under human command. It is not that they are not capable of running at all, but simply that they usually don't do it while pulling a load or carrying a rider, to which they are simply not accustomed at all.

That brings us to a second difference. Draft horses pull loads, destriers carry them on their backs. The draft horse was strong enough to bear the weight of my armor and strong enough to pull a heavy mech by himself, given a stout wagon and a well-laid road; but he wasn't used to having anything heavier than a harness or the occasional mischievous youth perched atop his back, and he found the sensation mildly vexing.

A third is temperament. A destrier in an unaccustomed job would have been more than mildly vexed; draft horses are bred and trained for calm natures. The draft horse was neither spirited nor eager for battle. His phlegmatic temperament combined with a vein of sensible cowardice was something I found reassuring. The horse felt much like I did about the matter: Voluntarily marching into battle was for idiots and fools. (Since I have been known to march into battle by choice, I suppose the draft horse had a higher opinion of himself than I did.)

I was doing just that at the moment. I was riding after the scouts who had tracked Katya's trail down past the blackberries, almost certainly to battle, even if I was no more of a true warrior than the draft horse. I should explain at this point that the scouts had, on careful investigation of Katya's trail, found signs of a struggle and of a large party moving through the woods. The trail of trampled and broken underbrush was obvious enough when I happened on the scene late in the morning; enough so that I gave the cavalry lieutenant a sour look.

How had his scouts not noticed this trail the first time they had ridden across it? Were we not in the wild woods, known for everything from witches to barrow-wights? Were the scouts not tasked with aggressively seeking out any signs of potential hostiles? Surely they had ranged out this far a day or two ago. I did not wait for him to come up with excuses; I waited simply long enough for Yuri to sniff and bark twice, telling me that he'd picked up Katya's familiar scent—old but weak—along the line of flattened bushes and broken saplings.

I called him a good dog, and he capered about next to me, pleased by the praise, barking happily. The draft horse, over ten times the size of the dog, nevertheless shied away from Yuri nervously before I told him the dog would behave himself and to move along. One thing about horses, even draft horses, is that they have great faith in humanity and a self-sacrificing nature. The horse obeyed me without complaint, faithfully taking my word that Yuri wouldn't start trying to bite at his ankles and belly.

In the Imperial Army, complaining is a sacred ritual, observed at least as often as all other religious rites combined. I suspect that mercenaries are mostly coreligionists in this regard, for the muttered complaints of the platoon trailing in my wake blended together as thoroughly and as indistinctly as vegetables in a pot of borscht that has been reheated for three nights in a row without any fresh additions. Quentin's company of cavalry started to range ahead on their speedier mounts. Mounted infantrymen, perched on mules liberated from the supply train, trailed behind me and my plodding draft horse.

Perhaps I should explain the mules. I had asked for a band of volunteers to reinforce the cavalry company after the initial report had come back from the scouts, reporting signs of violence. We could not afford the fuel to push our heavy armor company at high speed to catch up to them and make a rescue, and could not possibly move our supply train so quickly. Men afoot, though, could keep pace with the draft horse I was mounted upon—if, that is, they had someone to show them how to move quickly through the woods.

Then Captain Rimehammer pointed out that those left behind could get by, for a little while, having the mechs pull carts on charcoal fuel, sparing some of the smaller mules without slowing down appreciably. The mules were not combat mounts by any stretch of the imagination, but they could be coaxed into carrying men at a fair clip, even if they were not battle-trained. The infantry captain promptly "volunteered" those of her men who could sit a horse, and we were off.

That platoon was now being commanded by Fyodor, in spite of the fact that his regular platoon, the artillery detachment, were not coming along, and also in spite of the fact that he was, at best, an indifferent rider. He was a stoic one, though; his mule complained more than he did.

In fairness to Fyodor's mule, it had a heavy and awkward burden. While Fyodor himself was by no means fat, he had packed a rocket launcher and a significant number of reloads, and it was a worse burden than most of the other mules had to carry. Most of the mules complained nearly as much; they were cleverer than my draft horse and no less favorably inclined toward the idea of being ridden to a battle.

As I would learn later, Fyodor had been inclined to stay with his men, until a certain cavalry lieutenant suggested within earshot of a certain comely acolyte that Fyodor was staying back at the camp with the cowardly hope that said cavalry lieutenant might fall in battle. All I knew at the time was that Fyodor had volunteered loudly and eagerly for the duty, which made him an ideal choice.

It was close to noon when a scout reported in to say they had found a campsite; unoccupied, but with noteworthy features. The scout seemed uncertain about what to tell me as he led me toward the campsite. He thought it had been occupied for several days and that the force which captured Katya had joined with others at that campsite. After a little hemming and hawing, the scout, showing unusual squeamishness for a veteran soldier, said he'd found a pile of singed bones littered around the fire.

Bones that had been gnawed upon.

He suggested ogres. We were in the wild woods, and more tales were told of ogres and witches within them than barrow-wights and weather-wizards. I was inclined to agree with him, based on the apparent success of my diplomatic initiative with the locals; they would have come in much greater force, or not at all, if they wished to risk the wrath of "Colonel Raven."

When Yuri reached the campsite, he stopped and gave me an alarmed look, barking to inform me that he'd scented a second ogre. This news surprised me, since I hadn't realized he had come upon the scent of a first ogre, and that the trail of broken and trampled underbrush I'd thought left by a dozen men had been left by a single large manlike creature. A few short questions later, I had a good idea of what we were up against.

What did ogres want with a captured human soldier? The bones suggested one ominous reason for taking Katya, but inspecting the scattered bones gave me cause for relief. They looked to be the bones of a horse. I could recognize a hoof, and the skull of a horse, very unlike that of a human.

The fate of Katya's horse, then, was clear; the ogres saw no use for the beast, so they'd cooked it over a fire and ate it. I could see some bones were singed and had cut marks on them. I stared at the firepit for a minute, contemplating its circular shape. The firepit was deep with ash and ringed with stones. This was not, then, a temporary campsite, but a regular one, used on a routine basis. Had Katya been roasted over that fire, and her bones simply left elsewhere? I looked carefully for any sign that might tell me whether or not Katya still lived, but saw nothing.

I slowly convinced myself that she must still be alive, returning to the way the horse bones had been treated. If the ogres had bothered to butcher and cook the horse, they had an ample meal of meat in them. Katya was a dainty morsel in comparison. If the ogres felt comfortable leaving a pile of bones behind from dinner, they would surely have left all of them there, and I would have found something to recognize—inedible hair, a scrap of clothing, a skull, something.

Yuri smelled her scent—her sweat and fear—in the campsite, and voiced his concerns.

As I dismounted from the tall draft horse, I had to be careful of an overhanging branch, and looking at it, I saw something important: a ruddy, brown stain on the branch, contrasting sharply with the lighter brown of the bark. The color of dried blood. Startled, I sat back down on the horse heavily, with a loud clatter of armor. The gelding nearly bucked in sheer surprise at the sudden impact of a heavy mass of steel.

I spent a minute calming the horse and then asked Yuri to come jump up. I caught him and hauled him up, holding his keen canine nose up to the brown stain I had seen on the tree. He growled, letting me know that yes, it was blood; yes, human blood; yes, Katya's blood. I let him down and stood up in the stirrups to take a closer look at the branch with my keen human eyes. Hemp fibers clung to the bark, and wear marks, suggesting that rope had been tied around the branch and something heavy dangled from the rope.

"Yuri, is there more blood on the ground down there? Maybe some bits of hemp rope or fiber?"

Yuri barked out a loud affirmative, excited and anxious. It was strong enough that it couldn't be from earlier than yesterday morning, Yuri told me with confidence.

She had been here! Here, and alive enough to bleed, tied up and hung from the branch, almost certainly. I was deeply relieved she hadn't been eaten for dinner. Then I realized that she had been hurt, and bleeding; I was filled again with worry and rage.

Fyodor gave me a strange look, shifting uncomfortably on his mule.

Yuri growled, telling me with the scents as fresh as they were, the ogres couldn't have gotten too far, not in such a short time, and especially not on foot. They had, he reminded me, eaten the horse that he could smell. Besides, he added in a sudden burst of canine genius, the horse could only have carried one of them at best.

"You heard the dog as well as I did," I told Fyodor, gesturing broadly. "It's perfectly clear what happened here. They tied her up and hung her from this branch here. Maybe to torture her. Maybe so she wouldn't sneak off in the night. Maybe to make sure she wouldn't be eaten by a bear while they slept."

He gave me a careful measuring look before shaking his head and setting his mule into motion. The other soldiers followed suit, coaxing their mules into motion, some with more success than others. After several minutes' ride, Fyodor brought his mule up to my draft horse and cleared his throat.

"Ah, sir, begging your pardon, but all I heard back there was some barking and growling," he said. "It may be perfectly clear to you, but I must confess to being puzzled, sir. But if you say so, I will take your word for it."

"Don't understand dogs?" I asked. "I hadn't figured you for a city boy, Fyodor."

"I'm not, sir. My family's estate is a full day's ride from Khoryvsk, out in the countryside," he said. "But I can't talk with animals. Never known anyone who could, sir."

I stared back at him in disbelief.

He flushed suddenly when he realized he had just called his superior officer a liar by accident. "Excepting yourself, sir." His face was a study in conflicting forces.

I turned around and took in the faces of the soldiers trailing behind us. We had not been speaking quietly, and by the expressions on their faces, I could see that not a one of them had understood Yuri either. For the first time, I considered the possibility that perhaps being able to understand animals was something uncommon, even unusual.

I could not help but come to the conclusion that there was something terribly strange in the world if most of the people who talked to animals (which includes most who ride horses, hunt with dogs, or even simply feed pigs) were carrying out what were, in their view, one-sided conversations. That people, as a rule, talk *at* animals but not *with* animals. This seemed very strange to me. Then again, noble humans tended to do the same with non-noble humans, talking to them but not with them.

Having paused in thought to consider Fyodor's words for a long minute, I brought my attention back to the present. When I had turned around, my horse had stopped, and when my horse had stopped, the mules (being clever enough to know I was in charge of this expedition) had also stopped. I needed to stop thinking about the nature of humanity and nobility and instead focus on the issue of pursuing the ogres and retrieving Katya.

Hopefully, they would return Katya without a fight. If things went badly, many people would die.

CHAPTER THIRTY-TWO

In Which I Order My Soldiers to Kill

If Katya were here, she might have told me that sending a quarter of my entire battalion (to be specific, the understrength cavalry company and what part of my infantry I could mount on muleback in a pinch) after a single scout was foolish and wasteful. This wasn't going to help me achieve my claimed mission and ran the risk of serious losses, far more serious than a single scout.

Then again, had she shown any such signs of calculation when she rescued me?

I thought back to my dark days in captivity in the hands of the rebels, my time spent chained to the wall and staring down the barrel of a pistol as an all-too-young girl tried to work up the nerve to execute me. The rebel girl had lost her nerve, but I had no illusions about where I would have been if Katya hadn't ridden out to save Ilya: buried in a shallow unmarked grave. She and Vitold pulled off a rescue against great odds to save me.

The grave of the ancient king came to my mind as well. Katya had ridden into danger to save my life then as well, appearing from above like an avenging angel to smite the undead. All she knew was that a bird had stolen her hat, and when she arrived to find a hole full of undead terror, she didn't flee, as Quentin had; instead, she entered the fray and saved my life. Again.

I thought back to the crushed look on her face when she discovered that Ilya was dead; I thought back to our time together and the love she had shown me, and I shuddered. Katya had saved my life more than once, against terrible enemies and terrible odds; she was my lover and my hero rolled into one petite package. I had to save her, or avenge her if she was beyond saving. The cost did not matter.

This is why people make infernal bargains, even when they ought to know better. Sometimes, price is not an object. I kicked my draft horse to a canter, and the mules followed suit, startling several of the riders. A tickling sensation danced along my arms, in tune with the branches brushing mules and riders; I mentally pulled at what felt like a thread inside of me, and the sensation eased. The men whispered to each other superstitiously, and I realized I had spurred the placid draft horse to a full gallop.

Sooner than I expected, we caught up with Quentin, who had posted himself halfway up a hill. He startled when I cleared my throat to get his attention, nearly falling sideways out of his saddle. Evidently, he hadn't seen us coming. I was beginning to reconsider Quentin's suitability as an officer in charge of reconnaissance when he redeemed himself by giving a full report on the position and disposition of the enemy. He had scouts posted around them; the ogres had stopped by a stream on the other side of the hill and were presently enjoying a midday feast of freshly caught boars.

He had not, he added, spotted Katya, or at least, not an intact Katya. He allowed for the possibility that Katya might have been in a stewpot, or divided up into unrecognizable portions. One of them, he pointed out, was at least twice the height of a tall man, and there were a dozen of them, a piece of information that I might want to become aware of and which he thought ought to lead me to reconsider confrontation.

I told him I already knew I was dealing with ogres; though I didn't mention I hadn't dealt with ogres before. I dismounted, and between Quentin, myself, and Fyodor, we sketched out the camp and a plan of attack. First, we would lead the mules and the draft horse over there, a safe distance from the action, and I would convince them to stay put. The rest of the men would stay just behind the crest of the hill while I alone advanced along the stream, offering parlay. I did not say it, but this would also allow me to see if Katya was present but hidden; at that moment, I trusted my own eyes more than those of Quentin and his scouts.

If the ogres returned a still-living Katya to me without incident, all would be well. If they attacked, or if I gave a signal to indicate they were not going to return an intact Katya to me, it would be time to lead a charge down the hill and have bloody vengeance upon them. Quentin and Fyodor exchanged a quick look when I said that, and then looked up. Crows were starting to circle, either in anticipation of leftovers from the boar feast or in anticipation of leftovers from battle. Quentin expressed doubts about the wisdom of taking on massive ogres without mechs on hand. Fyodor joined in, pointing out that we had no cannons with us, only arquebuses and pistols.

I gave them both a look and told them that if I died, they should feel free to retreat. Until and unless that happened, however, I commanded their support, and I had every confidence in their ability to shoot one ogre to death while I handled the other eleven if necessary. When Fyodor pointed out that only half of his men had brought halberds, I allowed that perhaps it was better that he and the best arquebusiers of the lot parked themselves on top of the hill with arquebuses steadily aimed on hook-rests while Quentin covered himself in glory with a cavalry charge.

When Quentin started to talk about how the ogres were massive enough not to be ridden down by horse, I allowed that perhaps the first thing should be a concerted volley of fire from Quentin and Fyodor's men alike, but that the cavalry and every man with a halberd should follow down the hill quickly. This was, I reminded them, only a contingency plan. Ogres are more intelligent than many give them credit for, and it was entirely possible they simply had Katya tied up somewhere out of sight and were willing to release her, given a little bit of negotiation on my part.

I had a pouch filled with coins and jewelry for exactly that purpose, but I expected instead to die. As much as I tried to cling to a thin sliver of hope, I was coming around to the belief that Katya was dead. My heart's desire was not to live, but instead to extract a blood price for her death. I eased myself quietly down the hill to the stream, out of sight of the ogres, and then walked downstream right into the middle of them.

The one I guessed to be the leader, the shortest one, had a familiar-looking rifle slung across his back. A fine weapon for hunting even large game, like boar. Katya's weapon. I could see easily enough that Katya herself was not there; and when I quietly whispered the question to Yuri at my side, his answer was a simple negative, confirming what I saw: He did not hear Katya, nor could he smell her.

Ogres will eat anything. For a moment, everything in the world stopped, and my last thread of hope snapped.

I waved my sword in the general direction of the ogre leader, the curved bronze blade gleaming brightly as it cut through the air.

"You! You! Die!"

I had intended to say something a little more intelligent-sounding, but as it turned out, I had been rendered inarticulate with rage. The last sliver of hope had snapped and apparently had taken with it my ability to communicate like a civilized human. Jabbing my sword in the air at the ogre while shouting monosyllabic words was as close as I could get.

The curved blade glittered in the light, the crow-shaped crossguard looking gaunt and hungry. The leader got as far as "What do you—" before my men took my gesture as not only the signal to fire but also as the designation of a target. Bullets saturated his position, sending him jerkily toward the ground. The other ogres bellowed as if in sympathetic agony, lurching to their feet.

He was fast and tough; I will give him that. He had Katya's rifle out and fired it at me as he bled on the ground before I reached him. The bullet pierced all the way through my armor and into my shoulder; then I arrived and stomped on his face, holding his head to the ground while I parted it from his body. The ogres howled, and the cavalry thundered downhill among a rain of lead shot.

My armor rattled with the sound of pellets striking it from all directions. I waded forward into the mess, my blade flashing brightly in the sunlight. The tallest of the ogres, the giant that had so worried my lieutenants, did the most sensible thing and ran away; most of his smaller kin stood and fought, proving that they were every bit as stupid as us mere humans.

Every time I struck one of the ogres with my crow-crossed blade, I felt a surge of fresh energy flow through my arms. My rage shifted from roaring fury into a perverse sort of exultation. Yuri trailed behind me, guarding my flanks as I pushed forward into the enemy ranks, leaving me the freedom to swing the blade in wide arcs, faster and faster. The ogres did not fall without resistance. They struck me with heavy blows, but aside from one wielding a particularly heavy club, their blows did little to slow my progress.

That one knocked me off my feet entirely one time, leaving my ears ringing. As he bent over to see if he had killed me, however, a bolt of canine ferocity sailed over me and tore out his throat, buying me the time I needed to roll back onto my feet and stand. Some screamed; some prayed while their guts spilled out on the ground; one died with a lance through his eye socket before I could get to him.

A buried part of me felt sickened, even as I reveled in the rising tide of energy I felt surge through me with each fallen foe. Had Katya screamed and prayed as she died? If she had, they had not had mercy on her. I pushed the sick feeling away, burying it deeper as I cut and thrust again and again, the curved blade of my sword a gleaming talon spraying blood with every movement.

Then there were none left to kill; they were all dead or had fled. I swung reflexively several more times as I scanned for foes, then grounded the tip of my weapon in the bloody mud as I surveyed the scene carefully, the flood of energy slowly fading from my limbs.

A dozen of my men were either dead or wounded, and half as many horses. Two had fallen while trying to gallop downhill, taken out of the action by reckless riding rather than enemy bullets or blades. The enemy dead were as numerous as our own casualties, and, on average, several times more massive.

I was coated with gore; even the blade of my sword, which usually seemed to drip itself clean when I wasn't looking, was coated all the way from the tip past the bloated bird with an obscenely bulging stomach that served as a crosspiece between blade and haft, and the gore had even spilled several handspans down the haft from the cutting edge of the blade.

I picked my way toward the fallen leader, taking Katya's gun and a pair of surprisingly elegant rune-carved pistols from his headless and bullet-ridden body. Near him, another ogre proved to have a reinforced box in a satchel, about the size of which one might place a severed head. I picked that up, too, thinking I might find just a head in it, and nearly overbalanced; it was heavy for its size.

I whistled for the draft horse. He came, dragging with him the bush he had been tied to. Fyodor came over and asked a question. I am not quite sure what it was, but when I met his gaze eye to eye he tripped over himself backward. I am not quite sure what I said to him next, but I gather it had the effect of putting him in charge of rounding up the soldiers, seeing to the wounded, and distributing appropriate rewards. As for me, I walked into the stream and knelt, rinsing blood off my armor before mounting, because the smell was making the draft horse uneasy.

I began to talk. Not with the horse, or with Yuri, but with myself. Or perhaps more accurately at myself, because I had plenty of cause to harangue myself and little to say in response to my own angry words. There were good men and horses dead today because I had gone charging in for vengeance. And now that I had my vengeance, what was it worth? A pair of pistols, a box, Katya's rifle to send back to her father with a sad letter? A pile of dead men, horses, and ogres? More danger and disarray?

All of this had happened because I had been careless with my words and driven her away from me. I could not even bury her body; she was eaten and gone. I had gone completely insane; I had enjoyed the butchery of the battle and I was talking to myself.

"Poor little Ognyan," I said to myself with irony, remembering the broad and halitosis-ridden general. "Now, poor little me."

After the battle with the ogres, I understood better how a man becomes a monster, better than I wanted to. I wanted Katya back. I wished to myself that I could at least lay her body in a grave.

Yuri growled indignantly at me, interrupting my monologue just as I was beginning to repeat myself. He knew where Katya's scent had been, and it hadn't come anywhere near where we had killed the ogres. If I wanted to dig a hole and put Katya into the dirt, he could help me find her. I told my horse to follow the dog, then closed my mouth and resolved silently that I would deal with this like a sane and civilized man. The world had enough insanity in it already.

CHAPTER THIRTY-THREE

In Which I Return to the Scene of a Crime

Yuri led me back the way we had come, back to the campsite, where he stopped and sniffed about with care, spiraling outward from the fire. Every so often he would pause, going inward or outward for a bit, excited by something. I dismounted and left my armor standing to cool, giving myself and the horse a chance to relax, standing by the tree where I had found the bloodstain. I stared up at the branch and let my thoughts drift for a little while and then came back to the present. Yuri was gnawing on a bone by the campfire.

"Which way was she taken from here, if not the way we went?" I asked Yuri.

Yuri dropped the bone and looked up at me. I reminded him that he had been seeking Katya's scent. Yuri told me that while her scent entered the campsite, it didn't leave it. He asked if he could go dig a hole.

I sat down heavily and waved him away from the bones, telling him yes, he could go dig a hole. I went to the task of slowly sorting through the bones, looking closely to see what bones might belong to Katya. After several painful minutes of staring and realizing I didn't really know that much about human anatomy, I began assembling the skeleton of Katya's horse, using my own mount as a guide. Katya's horse was much smaller but shaped similarly. I had to shoo Yuri away from the bones when he took a break from digging.

At the end of this exercise, I had a two-thirds complete horse skeleton, with a small pile of smaller bones, mostly cut or broken into fragments, that I was less sure of. The skull of the horse had been cracked open. There were no identifiably human teeth or skull fragments, which reminded me of the head-sized box I had picked up on the battlefield. I went over to my horse and retrieved the box. It took me a little while to smash the lock open with my tools, brute force and hardened steel substituting for the more sophisticated measures that someone like Vitold might apply.

The box did not contain a severed head. It was thickly insulated and padded, the interior smaller than the exterior. A glittering medallion with a double-headed eagle stared up at me at the top of a varied collection of coins, catching my eye; there were also papers.

A later accounting would show that the papers were quite valuable and of considerable interest, with several letters of credit neatly folded up, along with, of all things, a letter of marque and reprisal from the Kingdom of Loegria, now part of the domain of Emperor Leon I, and a letter of commendation for a bold mercenary knight. There was also some jewelry.

There was no way to know if perhaps one of the smaller ogres or a half-blooded kinsman had seen service as a mercenary and marine traveling the world, or if all of it had been stolen from travelers in or near the forest. The coinage was diverse, a broad sampling of the surrounding world; there were even several gold coins and one of the little orichalcum crowns minted by the short-lived Spider King of France, the visage of Louis the Last as bright and crisp as the day the coin was minted.

At that moment, though, I was uninterested in reading through the papers or sorting through the coins; instead, I set the box aside. I almost hurled it away in frustration, but after reminding myself of my resolution to act like a sane and civilized man, chose the more sensible path of closing it (to the degree that the broken clasp permitted) and carefully stowing it back in a saddlebag.

Logically, the fact that the head-sized box that I had half expected to carry a severed head didn't contain a severed head should have made me happy, but instead, I was simply frantic and confused. I shooed Yuri away from the horse skeleton and took one last look at the unidentified bones, trying to figure out if they belonged to one of the missing pieces of the horse skeleton or to the skeleton of a woman. Were they what was left of Katya? Perhaps she had been eaten nearly entirely, bones and all. The larger and more robust ogres seemed to be built large enough to crack bones with their teeth.

My heart sank.

I dropped the collection of smaller bones into the hole Yuri had dug and allowed myself to cry a little while. Then I looked up at the branch, its tell-tale reddish-brown stain tinted a little more red by the light of the setting sun, and stood up suddenly, cursing my stupidity and inattention. I had not given careful thought to how the blood had gotten there; I had merely taken steps to confirm it belonged to Katya. The stain was on the top side of the branch and was not accompanied by a spatter of smaller drops.

Blood does not drip upward; it drips down toward the earth. Like a fool, I had not looked up from the branch. I did so now and was soon climbing up into the tree toward a suspiciously solid lump of branches and browning leaves. It looked too small to hide a person, but I climbed up anyway, knowing that appearances can be deceiving.

It was her. Katya had escaped captivity and hid herself up the tree. The lump, however, was very still, not moving as I approached it, and after I pushed away her makeshift blind I wondered for a moment if she was alive or dead; a question resolved once I touched her face, finding it feverishly hot and her pulse fast but weak. She was alive; but only barely.

Her injuries had brought fever with them, and they were severe injuries indeed. Her right leg ended mid-thigh in a ragged wound, likely infected. Whatever force had taken her leg off (I imagined the giant mouth of the largest ogre and shuddered) had snapped her femur like a twig. Her left arm had been severed cleanly, ending in a nearly smooth plane, and the surface of the wound burned by something hot, either to torment her or to crudely cauterize the wound. The untreated nature of the wound to her leg suggested the former.

I was proud, angry, sad, ashamed, and happy all at once. Small wet spots dripped down onto Katya, tears released by the overwhelming emotions surging through me. I was proud because with only two intact limbs to her name, Katya had somehow cut herself free and escaped her captors. Angry, at those who had done this to her. Ashamed, for the way I had left her dying in the branches as I rode off to inflict vengeance. Happy, that I had found her, and happier still that she was alive. Sad that she might not stay that way for long.

It was remarkable that she had survived. I carefully carried her down from the tree. She was frighteningly light. She groaned softly as I carried her down; and when I laid a blanket on the ground and laid her on top of it, her eyes were open, and she was looking at me, rasping out some croaking noises as an attempt at speech.

I carefully brought her up to a sitting position and put my canteen up to her lips, tilting it slowly for her, spilling a little between her parched lips at a time. After several careful swallows, she spoke, very quietly.

"You came back. I thought you rode away."

My first order of business was carefully watering, feeding, and trying to treat Katya's wounds, which involved a great deal of patience and vodka. A certain amount of the liquor I poured down her throat to help with the pain, but most of it I used for cleaning her wounds before bundling her up in a blanket. After the sun had set, I came to the conclusion that I had done everything I could to make sure she stayed alive through the rest of the ride, but that I should get her to a surgeon, and quickly. I am not particularly given to religion or superstition, but I found myself praying to whoever might be listening: *Let her live through this.*

I pushed my horse hard. He was a good horse. Yuri had trouble keeping up; riding with my armor half-open to hold Katya, there was not enough room to sit Yuri on top of the horse. I told him to take a rest and catch up to us later at his own pace. It was fully dark by the time I rode into camp, to a mixture of surprise and concern. Evidently, the returning Lieutenant Kransky had not been certain that I would show up, much less when. An unofficial conference of officers had congregated to discuss the incident with the ogres, the mission as a whole, and what to do if I didn't show up that night—would they press on in the morning, turn back to Avaria, or wait in the woods?

There was a crowd of people surrounding me when I dismounted. I tried to disperse them, citing Katya's need for a surgeon. They seemed surprised to see her, especially Fyodor, who had seen the ogres' campsite. The artillery lieutenant stared wide-eyed; the other officers looked at him, then back at me. I told them we could talk at greater length in the morning but to fortify the camp in case of a retaliatory raid. The great ogre who had fled might have had more kin somewhere nearby. Then they dispersed, and I marched into the infirmary tent they had set up to deal with the wounded from the battle.

After I laid Katya down on an empty cot, Vitold brought over our better surgeon and directed his attention to Katya. We had two who could be considered professional sawbones, and Vitold had gone to wake up the better of the two when he saw her situation. His prognosis was pessimistic; he doubted she would live through another day, and felt that she would be better served by an overdose of analgesic and a quiet merciful death.

I convinced him to act otherwise.

I held Katya's good hand but turned my head away as he started to go to work, trying to ignore the sounds of his knives and his bone saw. She came to consciousness and started thrashing around halfway through the procedure, which brought matters to a temporary halt and spattered both myself and the surgeon with blood. In spite of another two shots of vodka, she remained conscious through the rest of the surgery, conscious enough, at least, to grip my hand tightly. Though, through either determination or exhaustion, she managed to refrain from screaming aloud or moving her leg again.

The clean cut of the arm was easier to deal with. The surgeon, taking a close look at it, declared his work mostly done. "Mostly," as it turned out, still involved a little bit of cutting with knives, disinfecting the wound with more vodka, and quite a bit of sewing. I could barely stand to watch.

The varyingly tight grip on my hand and the irregular hissing of breath in and out of clenched teeth let me know that Katya was still conscious through that ordeal as well, though not for much long after. After her breathing evened out and her hand relaxed, the surgeon came back over and talked to me, quietly. She had a fever, and though he had removed the dead and infected flesh from her thigh and sewn it back up, he felt sure infection had spread to her bloodstream and that she would die.

He didn't want me to blame him when she died; which he thought was as likely to be tonight, from loss of blood, as the next day, when the infection would have likely taken hold. At normal volume, I reassured him that I thought he had done the best job he could and added a little louder that I had every faith in Katya recovering in record time.

She was a remarkable woman and remarkably tough, I added. Inside, I hoped that Katya might hear and take heart, or that at least it would penetrate her dreams. Inside, I was less confident, but for the sake of the surgeon, and for whatever consciousness the apparently sleeping Katya might have, I tried to paint the best face on the situation that I could.

Vitold came back, and we had a very quiet conversation. Staying in one place was ill-advised in terms of the probability that more ogres would appear with vengeance on their minds, but well-advised due to other circumstances. We would spend an extra day camped here. The mules were exhausted from all the unaccustomed galloping, I did not want to move Katya immediately, and the extra day manufacturing charcoal would bring our supply back up to slightly less dangerously low levels. The other wounded, as well, would probably benefit from the extra rest.

Perhaps I should have thought of the other wounded first, as there were more of them; but Katya, and the delicate balance she walked between life and death, was in the center of my mind.

After Vitold went forth and distributed orders, he came back again with a tray of food and wine. We had another very quiet conversation as I slowly ate and the both of us drank. I say slowly because I used only one hand; the other was still occupied holding Katya's. This conversation was a more personal one; we didn't touch upon business after his announcement that my orders had been passed on to all the appropriate officers. We traded worries, making their weight a little lighter by the sharing, and dreams, which grew a little as we passed them back and forth.

We talked about little shops for making and repairing mechanical things. About bakeries and farms, towns and villages. After Vitold left, I stayed; and in the morning, when I woke with a sore neck in my chair, I still held Katya's hand in mine. It was limp but warm; I could feel her pulse faintly, so she still lived.

I gave silent thanks.

CHAPTER THIRTY-FOUR

In Which I Connect Death to Courtship

M ikolai, wake up!"

As these words penetrated my unconsciousness, I came to two conclusions almost simultaneously. First, I had fallen asleep in my vigil over Katya; and second, I had an unexpected visitor. The visitor was a familiar little old lady.

I greeted her warmly with a hug and a smile, as well as a mixture of concern and relief. The last time I had seen the little old lady, she had been wandering around by herself in one of the less safe parts of the territory, formerly known as the kingdom of Wallachia. I had been involved in a mission to suppress rebel activity in the area under the command of the (in)famous General Ognyan Spitignov, and the area. I had been quite worried for her safety; seeing that she had gone unmolested by rebels or bandits was a relief.

On the other hand, she had apparently taken a wrong turn and was now wandering around the deepest and darkest woods in Europe. Had she gone senile? I didn't ask that aloud, mind you. It would have been impolite, and I had not yet found a good reason to be rude to little old ladies, especially ones lost in the woods. When I tried to ask what she was doing in the woods, she countered by opening up a line of inquiry about my health and well-being, simply ignoring the question as if I had not asked it at all. The elderly can be very stubborn sometimes.

The supply colonel entered carrying a kettle of hot water in one hand and balancing a tray of breakfast food in the other. He was polite and obedient to the point of obsequiousness (a most unusual attitude for him) and appeared completely sober—a most unusual state for him.

Evidently, before she decided to wake me up, the old lady had asked him to fetch breakfast; for some puzzling reason, he decided to obey. Perhaps he had grown up with an overbearing elderly relative and obeyed out of trained reflex.

There were three cups for hot tea, I noticed, though the supply colonel (lieutenant now, I thought to myself, correcting my mental mistake) did not linger after announcing that another member of the kitchen staff would be along shortly with food. By process of elimination, I discerned this was a subtle hint that the old woman wanted Katya to take tea along with the two of us. I therefore excused myself from my conversation with my visitor to gently wake Katya and attend to various necessities, the last of which was propping Katya up into a sitting position with the aid of several pillows.

It was only a few moments later that the acolyte entered the tent, carrying a tray with eggs, toast, and tea. She had not gotten more than three steps into the infirmary tent when she screamed. The piercing shriek startled me, and I flinched involuntarily. Katya, too, was startled and nearly fell over as a result, tightening her grip on my arm violently. When I looked at the source of the disturbance, I saw eggs, toast, and a mug with some tea remaining in it scattered on the ground, surrounding an upended tray. I could also see the rapidly retreating rear end of the acolyte disappearing through the tent flap.

Lieutenant Gavreau had been seriously injured in the battle, pulled off his horse when his lance lodged in an ogre's rib cage, which explained the young weather-witch's decision to pay the infirmary tent an early-morning visit; after all, Quentin was one of the two charming lieutenants vying for her affection. However, that did not explain the scream. I peered over at the lieutenant. He didn't seem any worse than he had been the night before. Perhaps she had not seen the extent of his injuries before? If so, she was both a more sensitive person and more attached to the cavalry lieutenant than I had thought.

The surgeon, sharing my puzzlement, griped in his native Venetian tongue as he looked at the mess. He thought the spilled food would attract flies and was unsanitary. He was a very finicky fellow, always insisting that the infirmary tent be kept as clean and as neat as possible, to the point of driving his subordinates to distraction. However, his skill had earned him ample respect, and even the most patriotic of the imperial soldiers had to admit he had a steadier hand than any of the alternatives.

The old woman appeared to share in the surgeon's disapproval of the intruding girl's erratic behavior, frowning dourly in the general direction of the fleeing disturbance, though she refrained from commenting. She handed Katya and me each a cup of hot water, first sprinkling some leaves in my cup, and then fiddling around in her pouch before coming up with tea leaves for Katya. A practical woman, she had already served herself a cup.

"Grandmother, let me send an escort with you. I can surely spare a few men to see you back to Ruthenia," I said as I waited for the leaves to steep and the water to cool to a drinkable temperature.

She demurred, telling me there was no need for such a thing and that she would be just fine. Then she cleared her throat pointedly, looking at Katya.

"I'm sorry, Grandmother, I should have introduced you. This is Katya; she's—" I hesitated. "A soldier in my company here," I continued, erring on the side of respectability and vagueness. "She was in the group the last time you visited us," I added, trying to reassure her obliquely without violating the protocols I had set up regarding mission security.

The old woman snorted, made a few pointed comments about the importance of honesty, lies of omission, something about how she hadn't been born yesterday, and that if I intended to pull wool over her eyes, I had better get up earlier in the morning than I had managed today. And, moreover, I had better not sleep in late in the morning while clinging to Katya's hand like a mother clutching her babe to her breast. She then said several things that I think are inappropriate to quote, adding some speculative inferences that were in some ways uncomfortably accurate. Katya, who had been silent and nervous the entire time, blushed and looked away.

"Grandmother! Please!" I exclaimed, then lowered my voice. "Yes, we have become lovers, and she has become very dear to me. And . . ." I gestured at her bandaged stumps, searching for the words. I didn't want to say that Katya was probably sitting on her deathbed right now, not out loud and within Katya's hearing. Hope is a precious analgesic, and in some cases seems to have curative properties as well.

The old woman let out a sound that was halfway between a derisive snort and a thoughtful hum. Katya stammered out something about liking me very much; the old woman gave her a look sharp enough to cut glass. Katya looked down and sipped at her tea. After a moment of uncomfortable silence, I asked about the weather, and the three of us eased back into a more casual conversation. Katya said very little. Not a voluble woman at the best of times, she was injured and intimidated into a silence that only broke when she was asked questions directly by myself or the old lady.

After a bit of meandering between seemingly unrelated topics, I told the old woman that I owed her a favor or three, intending to take another try at convincing her to accept some helpful escorts to ensure her safety in her ill-advised trip through the deep forest. At this point, the conversation took a strange turn.

"Yes, I suppose you will owe me another favor after this morning," she said. "I do have something I would like you to do for me." She pulled a dirty rock out of her bag. "Here."

I took the rock, eyeing it dubiously. The stone around my neck, the last rock she had given me, felt cold.

"What's special about this rock?" I asked.

Surely the rock was important in some way. It didn't appear to be a valuable mineral. I turned it over, looking for inscriptions and finding none. It was a hunk of some kind of opaque crystal, not particularly pretty looking. Rough quartz by the looks of it. Perhaps it was some kind of rare mineral that I wasn't familiar with? Geology had never been my strong suit.

"Not much," she said. "It just looks like it's supposed to be an important rock."

"Um. Grandmother, what do you want me to do with it?" I stared down at it.

It didn't look like an important rock to me, and I couldn't think of many important rocks that would look like a hunk of rough quartz. Perhaps the old lady was getting delusional in her old age. I gritted my teeth.

"Oh, nothing really. Just take it with you. Someone will probably try to steal it. It looks like the sort of rock that people want to steal." She sighed.

"Of course, if that's too much of a favor to ask from you . . ." She put on a martyr-like air, and I suppressed a groan.

"No, no, I can carry the rock around, it's no trouble, really. But what do you want me to do if someone tries to steal it?" I was dubious that anyone would want to steal what looked like a fairly ordinary hunk of rock.

She shrugged. "Whatever you think seems appropriate, dear. I'm sure you'll figure out something. It's not a very important rock, so don't kill yourself over it. And don't just carry it in your pocket or leave it in a crate somewhere. Make sure to lock it up in something that looks nice and secure, and take it out to check on it fairly often. Give it a little sunlight and a little moonlight."

"That tea tasted awful," Katya told me as I fussed over her, tidying up in the wake of breakfast.

Eating and conversation mix messily enough when you have two working hands and aren't in pain. I paused in thought, realizing how difficult breakfast must have been for Katya, and opened my mouth to apologize.

"Bitter and strange," Katya added, yawning. "I feel so tired. Sleepy."

I turned my head to the old woman to apologize for Katya's critique of her tea-making skills, but she had already left without my noticing. Turning back to Katya, I could see that my precious wounded woman was starting to sway a little in her seat, lending extra weight to the statement she had just made. I helped her lie down without falling over, covered her with a blanket, and then kissed her fevered forehead. She closed her eyes.

Then I hustled out of the infirmary tent, determined to catch up to the little old woman and try, one more time, to convince her to accept an escort to protect her as she traveled through the forest, but I didn't see her, and nobody I asked seemed to have noticed her leaving the infirmary.

Indeed, nobody I talked to seemed to have seen her outside the tent before or after breakfast; the surgeon had been going through his rounds of inspecting the aftermath of his work, the supply colonel had made himself scarce gathering mushrooms, and as for the young weather-witch . . . well, the girl wasn't in a mood for conversation. She was sitting on the ground a dozen yards away behind a tree stump, clutching her knees and rocking back and forth as she shivered, eyes round as saucers, staring blankly into space as she breathed in and out rapidly. Her face was as white as a sheet.

When she didn't react to my waving a hand in front of her face, I walked off to search the perimeter of the camp. There was no point in trying to reason with a lovelorn adolescent, especially not one in the grip of an irrational attack of panic or premature mourning, but the old woman might have left some sign of which way she had gone. I say "might," because it turned out she hadn't; after walking one circuit around the perimeter of camp, I gave up.

Heading back into camp, I crossed paths with the acolyte again, who was now unsteadily walking and clinging to Fyodor's arm like a drowning sailor to a rope. She flinched and ducked behind him when she saw me, peering around in every direction frantically, looking for something or someone (perhaps Quentin? I was not sure) before settling back down and standing up. I tactfully refrained from remarking on how quickly she had gone from fretting over Lieutenant Gavreau to clinging desperately to Lieutenant Kransky.

On later reflection, I came up with two possible explanations for why the acolyte might be deeply upset by Quentin's injury and yet be clinging to Fyodor later. The first explanation that came to mind was the order that had educated her made a fetish out of the survival of the strong. Perhaps she was not upset by the risk of Quentin's death as much as the proof that he was weak; by contrast, Fyodor, returning triumphantly uninjured, proved he was strong.

The second explanation that came to mind was simpler and substantially more plausible, making me wish I had thought of it first: She liked both Fyodor and Quentin very much; so if she was convinced Quentin was going to die, she would be very unhappy and yet also be left a very simple choice as to what to do now. It did occur to me that rather than casting a panicked gaze about looking around for Quentin, she might have been looking around for crows. Given prior experience, I couldn't fault her for reacting that way after seeing the man she called "Colonel Raven" approach in a foul mood. The last time she had seen me particularly upset, there had been a number of angry birds present, after all, and it had left an impression of sorts.

From the diary of Quentin Gavreau

It has been some time since I last wrote, but Ragnar has been so kind as to fetch me my journal and writing materials, and I find myself in need of distraction as I recover from my injuries. The Swedes were not among the troops selected to go on what Ragnar calls "the great troll hunt," and the lieutenant has been keenly interested in the details of our encounter with the great and terrifying man-like beings he only knows from storybooks. Apparently, these creatures are well-known in the north.

I am sure it is an adventure that my little sister, Septima, would find interesting, and after telling the tale several times to Ragnar, I feel sure of the details, so I will write on that. I will begin by saying that I am grateful our mother insisted that I practice my lance work before going east along the Istros.

The colonel was concerned over the fact that his woman had not returned and asked me to personally retrace her trail as far as she had marked it along the way, which was to a thicket of blackberry bushes. Searching all the way around the thicket, we found that on the far side of her markings, there were broken and torn bushes and deep gouges in the earth, signs of a violent disturbance.

We followed the trail out until it became harder to track, then sent scouts in all directions. The one who found the campsite was none other than Banneret Teushpa, the Cimmerian who had wanted my honeycomb pistol for a trophy after my shameful defeat. We have since become friends of a sort; he is of good breeding and a skilled illusionist, and he is the third-ranked officer of the cavalry after myself and the colonel's woman.

The troll camp was full of bones, gruesome evidence of their appetites, singed and gnawed upon, and footprints much like those of men, only much larger. I could recognize among the many bones a horse's skull, and it seemed likely that the colonel's woman had met her end there, eaten by forest trolls. While the colonel dealt with his grief, I rode ahead with my men, following the trail of the trolls to their next campsite. There were many of them, and the trail was much easier to follow than the one that had led to the campsite in the first place.

The smallest was at least seven feet tall, and the largest easily ten, and there were thirteen of them, an unlucky number that boded ill. As we waited for the colonel on his plodding draft horse to approach, bringing with him several squads of infantrymen mounted on equally slow mules, the forest grew darker and quieter. The only sound I could hear was a faint susurrus that grew in volume until the colonel came into view.

I looked up; there were many crows in the trees and flying about, though none of them were cawing, a fact that disturbed me greatly. The colonel told us that his woman was likely still alive and captive in the camp. He would ride down to negotiate; but if the negotiations went poorly, we were to come down in force.

Banneret Teushpa volunteered to ride into their camp unseen and see if she was there at all, to save us the trouble; he turned himself and his horse invisible with a flourish.

"Stop," the colonel said, holding up his hand and looking at a spot a few yards downhill from where the Cimmerian had vanished. "I know you think well of your ability to move quietly, but if you are seen, it will go badly. I will ride in myself openly to negotiate instead."

Banneret Teushpa's voice responded from the empty air. "Sir, are you sure?"

"Yes," the colonel said. "Your horse may be sure-footed with a quiet gait, but all it takes is one of them looking in the wrong direction and they will react poorly. It is better I approach them openly and appeal to their reason, for they can be reasonable creatures from what I have read of the matter. If they prove unreasonable, I will give a signal, and you can ride down from the hill."

As Banneret Teushpa reappeared in his new position, a disappointed look on his face, Lieutenant Kransky raised his objections to the plan for a general charge. The infantry officer said that his men were mainly arquebusiers and *wasted in a pointless charge, whether they did it afoot or attempted to spur the mules into an act against their nature.*

He himself had brought several explosive rockets and had nothing better than an officer's one-handed sword for close combat, countering that I and my men should charge while his held the top of the hill, raking the camp with fire. To me, this sounded like a recipe for getting myself and my men shot by friendly infantrymen along with the trolls.

After some negotiation between us with the colonel moderating, we compromised. Most of the infantry should charge on foot behind us, but we would begin with a single concerted volley of gunfire to soften them. That the colonel would be in the middle of such a volley didn't seem to concern anyone, least of all himself. The sky darkened with more nearly silent wingbeats as the colonel crested the hill, taking his first direct look at the trolls.

Then there was total silence for the space of three heartbeats. He pointed his sword down the hill at the smallest of the trolls. The air filled with the sounds of cawing, and the colonel began to run down the hill. I looked over at my fellow officers. There was a rush to fire such guns as had been readied, and then I raised my lance and called the charge over the crest and down the hill.

The man to my left let his lance tip dip as he tried to keep control of his mount downhill and was yanked right out of his saddle; to my right, a horse stumbled, both mount and rider tumbling down into the stream. My mount leaped across the stream cleanly at my signal, and I arrived with space to either side of me, my tip held true and level and piercing a nine-foot troll through the heart. Importantly, I gripped the lance well as it pierced the creature's rib cage, or the blow would not have had enough force to pierce the creature through; the skin of trolls is very thick and their bones massive.

I was unhorsed but not without means to fight, even if the impact with the ground took the wind out of my lungs and left me unable to stand. I fired all six shots from my honeycomb pistol, and I think at least three shots landed home, though with all the feathers and fury and pain it was difficult to discern matters clearly.

We paid a steep price riding to avenge the colonel's woman—eight men dead and five injured, three seriously. He stayed by their first campsite, the one with the bones, seeking to bury what he could. To my surprise, he somehow found her there, horribly wounded but still alive, one arm missing and a leg ending in a ragged mess. I was there in the infirmary tent resting from my own injuries when he brought her in, the surgeon working at a nauseating rate.

The next morning, an unfamiliar old hag barged into the tent. I woke to the sounds of the colonel and the hag talking in some dialect of Slavonic and the clink of teacups. I only understood a scattering of words, but from her tone of voice, the old woman seemed to think she'd done the colonel some sort of favor and was about to demand payment.

Then she surprised me by pulling out a most remarkable object. It was ovoid and smooth, irregularly black and red but also glittering with gold and the iridescent colors of the rainbow. In the dim tent, it seemed to glow on its own. She held it out to the colonel, saying something in the sort of insistent and querulous tone that old women take when they're demanding that you give them something.

The colonel shrugged and accepted the object with a look somewhere between puzzlement and boredom, as if the object was nothing special and asked her a question; the two of them talked for a while, the colonel nodding politely, and I stared at the object sitting on the breakfast tray for a long while, trying to discern a pattern in the irregular red and black blotches, the gold flecks, the shimmering bits of rainbow tucked into it. Then the colonel's hand covered it, and I realized suddenly that the old hag was no longer around.

Maestro Zilioli was, though, and he made a careful inspection of my ribs before saying I should stay at rest for several days and to keep my chest stiffly wrapped so that nothing moved out of place. I have never before met a surgeon who is also a physician, or rather a physician who decided to take up surgery; based on his results, his surgical technique seems a great improvement on the usual barbers. I have decided that he is a truly wonderful person, even if he does not speak much on his reasons for departing his home city.

CHAPTER THIRTY-FIVE

In Which I Take Pains to Care

As I passed by the acolyte and Fyodor, I was suddenly reminded that with us setting camp for an extra day, a latrine ditch was a necessity. The wind must have blown in from the wrong direction at that particular moment. Thus, reminded of my responsibilities, I roamed around the encampment, which had been set up in my absence, checking the depth of the latrine ditch and looking for other problems.

Partway through my circuit, I ran into Vitold. I gave him the rock and the head-sized box whose lock I had smashed open, leaving him with instructions to fix or replace the lock and put the rock in the box. When he asked me what the rock was for, I shrugged, then relayed the old woman's instructions—namely, telling him that it wasn't particularly important, but she wanted me to haul it around for her, at least for a little while. He suggested that I bury the rock in a hole outside of camp, as it was probably something that would bring bad luck. I chided him for his superstition and told him that I would keep my promise to the little old lady.

What I intended as a brief stop at the mess tent turned into an impromptu officer's meeting, which was not brief. With the scouts in fairly poor condition and both Quentin and Katya out of action, the patrol schedule was more or less completely wrecked, and this is when I learned that each of the captains thought Quentin and the scouts were unofficially their direct subordinates in the chain of command. All of them had been giving him orders on a regular basis and were annoyed that he hadn't been especially good at fulfilling them all promptly.

I had, I realized, set up this situation when I had drawn up our table of organization and undercut the then-absent Katya by telling each of the other three captains that I expected Lieutenant Gavreau to work with them closely. I temporarily delegated responsibility for putting together patrol teams to the infantry captain and resolved to sort out the situation more clearly later, once it was clear that I still had surviving cavalry officers of a rank higher than banneret.

Thus reminded of Katya's mortality, I made an executive decision to cut the meeting short and stalked off in a foul mood.

Leaving the mess tent, I passed the artillery lieutenant and the acolyte yet again. The acolyte was walking a little oddly and was wearing Fyodor's parade formal pants in place of the skirt and leggings she had been wearing earlier. Her hair was damp. Why would a young woman be walking oddly while clinging to a man's arm and wearing a pair of his pants, very shortly after the two of them had gone off together somewhere private? The answer was fairly obvious, although I didn't see how the damp hair connected to the rest of it.

If their fraternization caused problems, I would deal with them later, I told myself. Or, better yet, the infantry captain would deal with them first, and I would handle any leftovers that got kicked further up the chain of command. I returned to the infirmary tent.

The cavalry lieutenant was awake and complaining to the surgeon—a positive sign, really, even if Quentin's eventual recovery might lead to further drama.

The surgeon looked over at me when I walked in, then looked away, biting his lip. Katya lay motionless on her cot, not stirring as I approached. Her eyes were still closed, though her face had relaxed, and she looked peaceful. When I felt her forehead, it was no longer feverishly hot. She didn't respond to my touch; she just lay there, as still as a wooden doll. The conversation between the lieutenant and the surgeon ended, and the surgeon walked over to me, wringing his hands nervously.

He spent time hemming and hawing before getting to the point. Evidently, having me looming around made him nervous. He repeated his prognosis from earlier, which is to say he expected Katya to die from infection and suggested, in fact, that this had already happened. She hadn't groaned or writhed around since I'd left, and for someone in as much pain as she probably was, and as fevered as she had been, that was unbelievable.

If her forehead was warm and not hot, well, it had to become merely warm at some point as her body cooled from burning hot to the temperature of a corpse, he told me. Once the infection passes into the bloodstream and into a burning fever, such as the one he had observed, a patient is in for a long period of suffering, he added, saying that she had grown too quiet too quickly for it to be anything but her final point of expiration. His mulish certainty was tempered only by his evident nervousness.

I didn't believe him and told him as much. He flinched and begged me not to kill him, reminding me he'd done as good a job with the amputation as possible. I told him that I wasn't going to kill him. He didn't seem to believe me at first, and after a little while I realized that he was drunk. The smell of strong drink lingered on his breath, his coordination was impaired, and his sense of proportion was clearly distorted.

The profession of sawbones tends to be one surrounded by liquor; used as a disinfectant and anesthetic, surgeons tend to be alcoholics. One of the reasons the surgeon I was talking to was better than most, at least better than the Ruthenian surgeon we'd had to rely on before impressing the mercenaries into our unit, was that he had the sense not to anesthetize himself before performing surgery. When he'd amputated the ragged end of Katya's leg, he'd been sober.

With no surgeries left to perform, just the task of waiting to see if his patients lived or died, he had turned to the bottle to try to ease his nerves. I considered pulling out my knife to prove my point but then realized he might misinterpret my drawing of a blade in his nervous state. Another reflective surface would be a better choice. I went over to the cavalry lieutenant, borrowed the small hand-sized mirror he kept with him for use in signaling, and held it in front of Katya's lips. After a few seconds, it fogged with her breath, and I showed the surgeon.

He felt her forehead. Yes, the fever was gone. After a little bit of fumbling, he found her pulse, which seemed to him to be in a normal range. He pronounced it a miracle, asking what sort of medication she might have been given. Of course, she'd had nothing of the sort, simply getting down a little breakfast and drinking the tea the little old lady had pressed upon her, so I simply told him to keep his voice down so as not to disturb Katya's rest.

He told me that the infirmary wouldn't be the best place for her in that case, being that his other patients were at times quite noisy. I could see that my staying around the infirmary unsettled him, so I didn't press the point. Some people work best when not constantly supervised.

I went to Captain Rimehammer to arrange for a private tent to be set up for Katya and then went back to the infirmary tent and carried Katya out on her cot, careful not to jostle her awake. Arriving at the tent, I found that there was already one cot set up inside; so I simply set the new one next to the old one, shut the tent, and lay down next to Katya on the other cot. I, too, could use some rest, I realized. She stirred, rolling toward me and reaching for me with her good arm, then flinching back when doing so brought her weight on her now-armless shoulder. I reached over her and took her hand in mine, then pulled a blanket over the two of us and went to sleep.

Katya woke me up several hours later, sprawled horizontally across both cots, her head in my lap. I think she was reassuring herself that I was still there; still whole, even if she wasn't; and that I still loved her. I propped myself up on an elbow and stroked her hair.

"Feeling a little better now?" I asked, my breath hitching involuntarily.

"Mmm-hm," she hummed in reply.

"I love you," I told her, running my hand down from the crown of her head to the top of her thigh, stopping well short of the bandages that marked its end. I tried to instill reassurance into my hand as I slowly continued to stroke her. She was warm, but not fevered. Her eyes were twinkling, and she seemed in surprisingly good humor for someone who had been just short of delirious the morning before and so tired that she had fallen asleep immediately after drinking a freshly brewed cup of tea.

"Do you feel well enough to go get lunch? A little fresh air? Not that I'm not enjoying your company, but healing is hard work, and you barely picked at breakfast. I think you might be hungry," I said. The angle and intensity of the sunlight beating down on the tent suggested it was closer to dinnertime than lunchtime.

"Mmm-hm." She wiggled her derriere suggestively, then froze in sudden pain when the motion pushed the stump of her thigh against the hard edge in the middle of the two cots I'd pulled together.

"After you've had more time to heal," I promised. "Not that you aren't tempting me severely at the moment."

I gently pulled her head out of my lap and carefully unwrapped the bandages around her stump to inspect the progress of her healing. Once we were both fully dressed and I had changed Katya's bandages for clean ones, we hobbled down to the mess tent. With Katya's one good arm wrapped around me, we soon reached a good three-legged rhythm; still, I was glad when Vitold scurried over with a crutch for Katya.

We were too early for dinner; the cooks hadn't quite started making it, in fact, and the mess tent was only still set up because we were spending the day at rest. Vitold, however, scrounged up a cold luncheon for us and started a pot of stew cooking, citing the privileges of rank. He seemed exuberant, cheerful for some reason.

Then Ehrhart peered into the mess tent, looking around for a quick moment before cautiously edging away. Strange. Katya and I nibbled our way cautiously through cold sandwiches. The stew was starting to smell good when someone else walked into the mess tent. Lieutenant Fyodor Kransky, looking formal and awkward, and a well-dressed woman hanging onto his arm. I looked at her again and blinked, but she didn't become more familiar.

I had never seen her before in my life.

CHAPTER THIRTY-SIX

In Which I Unravel a Loose Thread

There are times when it is wise to speak. There are times when it is wiser to wait and listen to see what someone else has to say, even if you are bursting with questions. I identified this as one of the latter, then picked my mug back up and sipped.

Katya didn't want to wait; her hand dropped down into my lap. For a moment, I misread her motives, recalling the mood she had woken up in; and then I felt her grasp the unloaded pistol I had attached to my officer's belt to balance my sword. She pulled it out of its holster and deposited it in her own lap, keeping it low and underneath the table. Then she began the difficult task of loading it one-handed.

Fyodor gave a small bow.

"This is Captain Helen Winslow," he announced, then continued. "Her men are waiting outside of the camp. She has questions, which I have told her are best answered by you."

I took the name, the features, and the attire into consideration, and immediately concluded I was dealing with a Loegrian officer. In particular, by the boots and cloak, a Loegrian officer in charge of a reconnaissance company. I wondered if she was an exile or a loyal subject of Leon I, but I didn't know enough about the politics of the far western realms to guess.

Regardless, by the keen-eyed looks she was casting about, she was a sharp-witted woman whose suspicions had been aroused. There were two possible reasons why her company would be waiting outside of our camp: First, she was suspicious of us and unwilling to let her guard down. Second, my officers had decided not to let a large body of armed enemies into our camp, which similarly would lead to the arousal of her suspicions.

Her presence here by herself suggested several additional possibilities. She was not the commanding officer; she was confident in her force's ability to extract her or wreak revenge in the event of trouble; or she was reckless. None of these possibilities were particularly comforting. She probably had a partner or bodyguard waiting outside; with that thought, I glimpsed the shadow of a figure outside the mess tent. A large shadow, with several irregular protrusions marking weapons. Bodyguard then.

"Thank you, Lieutenant," I said, standing up from the table. It occurred to me that the woman may not have been told my name, so I continued by introducing myself, taking a moment first to recall the correct name and title to give her. I decided to try addressing her in French. "I am Colonel Marcus Raven. How may I be of service to you, Captain?"

"You run a very tight operation here, Colonel," she said. Her French was fluent, though the accent was different from Quentin's. "Your men wouldn't tell me more than the time of day. Most unusual in a mercenary company. As far as service goes, it is more important you are at the margrave's service than my own." She frowned.

I said nothing, waiting patiently.

She continued. "I've never heard of you before, I've no idea who your company is working for, and I've no idea what you're doing marching west into these borderlands. Explain."

It was not good news that she already knew the direction of our travel, though good news that we were near enough to the edge of the great forest that one of the Gothic Empire's margraves would have soldiers patrolling it. I asked her to take a seat across the table from me, signaled for Vitold to go fetch Captain Rimehammer and some paperwork, and started laying out our cover story.

We were a free company formed from the remains of several that had been all but destroyed in the recent fighting, I explained, gesturing in the general direction of the distant Sarmatian mountains. I had folded the remnants of several other mercenary companies into my own after recent fighting against the encroaching forces of the Golden Empire. My former employer had refused to reimburse the destroyed companies for their lost equipment or pay death benefits, and we had decided to seek new employment.

We were in need of rest, recuperation, and reorganization, and had chosen this route through the forest on the theory that it was a shortcut and that the dark rumors surrounding this particular bit of geography were overrated.

I felt like a very unconvincing liar. My gut churned the whole time, even though much of what I said touched on the truth.

"I see," she said, not appearing to. "I noticed you have more recent injuries," she added. "Your surgeon was sharpening his tools and complaining of the fresh wear on them when we passed by your infirmary on the way here."

I revised my estimate of her intelligence upward again and felt my gut try to creep lower another inch. "The deep forest has some fairly savage inhabitants, as you must understand, having patrolled it for some time yourself," I said. "It turned out to be harder to pass through unmolested than I had originally anticipated."

She gave me a hard look, clearly thinking carefully. Under the table, I could feel Katya adjusting her aim.

"We only defended ourselves, I assure you," I said. "As I said, we need some rest and recuperation before we take up a new contract." I gently pushed downward on Katya's hand, trying to discourage her from pointing the gun at the captain under the table. "We had an encounter with some ogres, as well as some men led by white-cloaked wizards."

"I see," she said, curiosity glinting in her eyes. She may have wanted to ask more questions about our travels, but Captain Rimehammer walked into the tent just then, necessitating another round of introductions.

The Swedish captain followed up aggressively on the introduction with a barrage of paperwork. Out came charters, contracts, letters of credit, and expense records; some partly or mostly genuine, some entirely fabricated. The table was soon mostly covered with documentary evidence supporting my account.

"Colonel Raven, you are remarkably well organized. I'm all the more surprised I haven't heard of you," she said. She seemed slightly intimidated by the volume of paperwork backing up my account of our history. "Not many mercenaries would see fit to keep their file clerks this busy while evacuating through a war zone."

"It would be difficult to negotiate for expense reimbursements without good documentation," I told her. "We hoped to be thoroughly compensated for the work we've done."

"Not that you weren't already being paid generously," she said sourly, looking at a contract. "Any chance we could convince you to sign on at a reasonable rate? The margrave is hiring."

I could think of three very different reasons she would ask that. Any of the three would mean I was treading on very dangerous ground in this conversation. I needed to answer this very carefully and very deliberately.

"Ordinarily," I lied, "I would be quite happy to take you up on the offer." I shifted back to technically true statements. "We are battered right now, though, and we need rest and repairs before we take on any commitments. I like to take my commitments seriously."

I paused, then added another lie as I tried to sound greedy and short-sighted. "I suppose it depends on what you could offer us." I would not be a convincing mercenary if I simply dismissed the possibility of a paycheck without first looking at how large it was, I thought to myself. More difficult circumstances usually simply meant holding out for a higher price. "We could discuss the matter further over dinner and drinks, perhaps share the campsite for the night and swap some stories."

Making that offer was risky; allowing her to stay in camp longer increased the probability that she would spot some crack in my cover as a mercenary, but I didn't see any alternative other than trying to act my role as best as possible. I hoped that she would decline the offer. I waved Vitold back over and told him to fetch a bottle of brandy.

The Loegrian woman, for her part, whistled loudly. A large and extraordinarily solid-looking man that I suspected of being at least part ogre ducked into the mess tent. The captain gave a series of hand signals; the giant man saluted and then ducked back out of the tent, jogging off.

"I suppose I may as well take advantage of your hospitality," she said. "The other officers will be joining me shortly."

Katya bristled wordlessly next to me, reminding me of a sheepdog staring at a wolf through a fence. I squeezed her knee in what I hoped was a calming manner, hoping to communicate my intention that she not shoot the Loegrian. Then I excused myself from the table. If my camp was going to be full of wandering Loegrian soldiers in the service of a Gothic margrave, I wanted to go check on a few things to make sure our cover was solidly in place.

This was going to be a serious test of my army's ability to act like mercenaries. True, a significant fraction of them were mercenaries, and I had been trying to integrate the mercenaries into my force on their terms, rather than on the terms of standard imperial military protocol. I had also taken measures to try to disguise our most distinctive equipment. Nevertheless, I was nervous.

There were a few people I had specific concerns about. After I mentioned the white-cloaked wizards, it occurred to me that I should check on the acolyte and ask her to keep out of the way. I didn't want the Loegrian officer suspecting me of having a friendly connection with the weather-wizards. They were almost certainly enemies of the margrave.

I was pretending, after all, to be the sort of mercenary that had been working for Avaria and would be perfectly willing to take a job with a margrave of the Gothic Empire. While I was not actually associated with the white-cloaks, it would be easy enough for Captain Winslow to arrive at that misunderstanding, rather than the misunderstandings that I wanted her to arrive at. The acolyte was a loose cannon rolling across the decks of our disguised vessel.

Further, if the acolyte had loyalty to her former masters, she could cause serious trouble for us by saying the wrong thing to Captain Winslow. My half-baked plan to win her loyalty by waving handsome young men in front of her nose seemed to have worked, but it paid to be paranoid. And thinking of that plan . . . if Fyodor paid too much polite attention to the Loegrian captain, the acolyte might act disruptively out of jealousy. He had been very gallant and formal in escorting Captain Winslow into the mess tent.

Since I had assigned Ehrhart and Fyodor the task of keeping an eye on the weather-witch and I didn't spot the weather-witch, I settled for finding Ehrhart, who turned out, conveniently enough, to be fiddling with something on his cart. He jumped and spun around to face me when I greeted him. Very excitable fellow. His voice cracked an octave higher than I thought it could, and his startled jump brought him up to eye level with me for a brief moment.

Ehrhart told me that the young weather-witch wasn't around anymore and had snuck off somewhere. When I pressed for details, I learned that the last person she had talked to at any length was Vitold. She had wandered her way to where Vitold was working on some project, picked up a rock that was sitting around nearby, spent a little while looking at it, and then Vitold had waved a pistol at her and had some variety of angry conversation with her.

After she put the rock down and backed up with her hands in the air, Ehrhart told me, Vitold calmed down a bit and stopped threatening her with the pistol. Then the acolyte had thrown a bit of a theatrical temper tantrum (Ehrhart thought she was acting) and then stormed off to Fyodor's tent. (Fyodor wasn't in it at the time.) Then she snuck out the back with a small bag slung over her shoulder and left. A sentry stopped her at the edge of camp but decided to let her pass.

Later, I located the sentry. The sentry pointed out, quite reasonably, that I had said quite publicly after unchaining her that she was free to leave. I could hardly object to that, and for all I knew, she was doing exactly what I wanted her to do: lay low while we had visitors in our camp. I just wasn't sure, suspecting she might be up to some variety of mischief instead.

Ehrhart pointed out that she didn't have to be present to cause mischief, and continued his account. After she left, Fyodor had gone looking for her; eventually, he did talk to the sentry and then went over to Vitold to vent his upset. Vitold seemed to be surprised but pleased. Fyodor seemed not to have any idea why the weather-witch might have left, so went over to the infirmary tent to talk with Quentin about it.

Ehrhart, who confessed he had found the unfolding drama of the love triangle fascinating, followed Fyodor to the infirmary tent. From just outside the tent, he listened to the artillery lieutenant question the cavalry lieutenant vigorously (and more than a little threateningly) and then apologize profusely after learning that Quentin hadn't known of the girl's departure until Fyodor had showed up to ask questions about it. The two of them then shared a longer and much quieter conversation as they passed a bottle back and forth; unable to overhear more without being obvious about his eavesdropping, Ehrhart had reluctantly left them to it.

Later, I would deeply regret my failure to question Fyodor and Quentin about their conversation.

CHAPTER THIRTY-SEVEN

In Which I Watch Watchers

After questioning Ehrhart one last time and then making sure that my troops were well informed about the fact that we had visitors dining with us (and about the importance of being on their best behavior), I returned to the mess tent, leaving energetic chaos in my wake.

If looks could kill, Katya would have been rinsing Loegrian blood off her face, but her eyes were only metaphorical daggers. She was not making any motion to finish the last piece of the sandwich on her plate, leaving her hand in her lap under the table.

When I came around to her side of the table, I saw the reason why; she was still holding the pistol in her lap, cocked and ready to fire, concealed by the tablecloth. I appreciated the dedication to duty that left her ready to shoot the Loegrian officer at the drop of a hat, but on the other hand, I didn't want it to happen accidentally. How could I defuse the situation without revealing that Katya had been a trigger pull away from killing Captain Winslow the entire time?

Rather than immediately taking my seat, I first walked behind Katya's chair, then bent over to whisper in her ear. I told her that I was confident that she could draw, ready, and fire the pistol quickly enough if something went wrong, so she could afford to relax a little. Then, on impulse, I nibbled on her earlobe as I reached down into her lap, gently uncocked the pistol, and helped her stick it in a loop on her belt, which was usually used for a cleaning rod. As she was not toting her rifle and its accessories currently, said loop was conveniently empty.

In my defense, while I whispered, that earlobe was right next to my mouth. It was a cute earlobe, and I had nibbled on it before; its owner usually reacted well to having an earlobe nibbled upon. And she didn't react poorly this time, either; she smiled at the compliment regarding her skill with guns and blushed fetchingly at the affectionate gesture.

I realized too late that the Loegrian officer, sitting across the table, had her eyes locked on my hand as I withdrew it from Katya's lap and seated myself. For a moment, I thought she might have developed suspicions about me; then I took into account the embarrassed way she looked away when I met her gaze and thought about what she would have seen from her perspective. The mercenary colonel whispering something flattering in his female subordinate's ear, then reaching down between her legs, causing her to flush bright pink in what could easily be taken as a combination of pleasure and shame.

A crude and unseemly display, in other words, of our status as lovers. I sighed to myself; Captain Winslow's alternate interpretation of my actions had probably lowered her opinion of me and my dear redheaded sniper, but it was fairly innocuous compared to the truth. It was no secret that Katya and I were lovers, after all, and better to be taken for an exhibitionist than for the captain to realize how much danger she was in.

The bodyguard returned with three normal-sized Loegrian soldiers and then went over to the corner, where he loomed discreetly. If Katya decided to shoot Captain Winslow, or vice versa, we could expect a rapid response from the bodyguard. As Captain Winslow introduced her three subordinates, I assessed them carefully, first with an eye toward immediate danger, and then with an eye toward trying to determine their backgrounds.

The first was named Caleb Pendley. He looked old and hard-bitten enough to be a veteran of the Century War, with a trio of missing fingers on his right hand suggesting he'd been an archer on the losing side of one of that war's bitter battles before seeking his fortune in the Gothic Empire. He had a longsword with a pistol barrel running along the forte strapped across his back, a pair of knives in each boot, and the brightly colored puffy sleeves of his outfit, likely concealing additional weapons. His eyes flitted around the tent often, a display of professional paranoia.

The second was Jacob Fairfax. He was armed only with a brightly polished pistol and a dress sword that looked like it would bend if I glared at it, a more normal practice for someone simply attending dinner in friendly military company. With his bright blond hair and his dress sword, he looked more like a young noble dressed up as a soldier for a masquerade than the genuine article; he looked too young and his uniform too new and too well tailored to belong in a war zone.

The third was introduced as Alan Gant. He was a weathered man of average height, medium build, and an indistinctly muddy hair color. Next to the other two, he looked drab; his clothes were well-worn, with stains that looked as if they had been ground in over the course of several years and plainly had not been tailored to his particular build originally. His features were so remarkably forgettable that it would be hard to place him in a crowd; from his boots and equipage, I guessed him to be a scout. He entered the tent with a rifle over his shoulder, which he politely handed off to the bodyguard as he entered.

If dinner ended violently, the odds were not in the favor of the five Loegrians in the mess tent; besides, it was not certain we were enemies, even if we were not allies. In the meantime, we dueled with our wits over dinner. Caleb Pendley had been a mercenary for some time in the Gothic lands before joining his fellow Loegrians in Captain Winslow's company, and he was the main weapon in the captain's arsenal as she fought to convince me that the margrave was reliable and trustworthy, with a policy of treating mercenaries well. After all, his association with her company was both recent and voluntary.

If the veteran mercenary was Captain Winslow's principal weapon, mine was Katya. Though remarkably hale for someone who'd had the ragged remains of her leg amputated a day ago, Katya's injuries were a vivid illustration of the need of military units for rest, recuperation, and the occasional replacement of limbs and/or persons. When the conversation veered back to the margrave's need for soldiers, Katya would start to glower, as is natural for a patriotic citizen of the Golden Empire considering service with a foreign prince. Then I would fuss over her and her injuries, playing up the role of the concerned lover to the best of my ability. (This was not difficult, as I was in fact both her lover and also concerned about her injuries.)

A few verbal nudges from Captain Winslow, and Jacob Fairfax was discussing the training of their medics, talking about how Leon the Usurper had spearheaded reforms in military medical practice, and that their medics were as good as those in Leon's military service. Partway through what was sure to be a lengthy lecture, I spied Katya yawning out of the corner of my eye and pounced upon the excuse to cut short my attendance. I cited Katya's need for rest. Then I picked up Katya, caught Vitold's eye, and motioned to the crutch and the box with the rock in it; the three of us departed the mess tent on four legs with full arms.

As I walked away into the night, Captain Winslow turned, casting a quick glance in my direction. For the space of a single, unguarded heartbeat, her expression fell, sadness crashing across her face like a wave over battered rocks in a storm. Disappointment, perhaps even outright despair; I would not have found it out of place on a mourner at a funeral. Then she fixed a bright and artificially cheerful smile back on her face and turned back to the table, gesturing for a refill of her drink.

I awoke shortly before dawn and watched the light change from pale gray to warm reddish-orange to the bright yellow of full day as I tended to Katya. Her wounds looked much better than they had the day before; the speed of her recovery was, on the whole, quite impressive. She was in pain still, though she tried her best to hide it when she thought someone else might see.

It was my intention to get my army moving again early in the morning, but one delay led into another, and it was nearly noon before I was watching a familiar draft horse's rear end plod away as the wagons I sat in bounced and rattled over roots and rocks. I had taken one of our better-sprung wagons and installed a padded cot in it so Katya could lie down and rest with minimum jostling; that was the cause of one of the delays. That minimum of jostling was probably still quite uncomfortable. The cart was large enough to hold my own suit and one of my jury-rigged mechs, so it did; it would have fit more if I hadn't made space for Katya, a collection of spare parts, and a small workbench.

Minor complications included the fact that two of our lieutenants (Fyodor and Quentin) were, in fact, still drunk at the crack of dawn, and were absolutely no good for organizing anything until they were sober. We strapped the injured one onto another cot and threw both of them into a wagon filled with lots of charcoal and absolutely no more liquor. The root cause of their mutual inebriation had not returned, and I was not inclined to wait for her. The acolyte would either catch back up to us or she wouldn't. I would be content with either case, as long as she didn't bring along her master or another army of savage bear-warriors.

Another source of delays: The Swedish mobile cannons had to be unloaded and then loaded back up; the walking guns had been placed in carts parked on softer ground, and in two nights' time, the heavy load had pressed the wheels a third of the way into said softer ground. After enduring one last half-hearted attempt at recruitment into the margrave's service, we bid the Loegrians farewell and headed westward out of the forest, down a trail that Captain Winslow promised would lead to a real road within no more than three days' march. I could sense the captain's sad gaze on us as we rode off.

The draft horse told me he was much happier to pull two modified steam suits, a heavy wagon, and assorted supplies than to carry a single rider in heavy armor. Not that I blamed him; pulling heavy things was something he was more accustomed to. It was calming to watch the draft horse cheerfully pull close to two tons of metal and wood with nary a word of complaint.

Then Katya woke up with a groan. Half-woke, really; the task of resting and letting her body heal was an exhausting one, and I had aided her pursuit of that task by applying more vodka to her body both internally (through her mouth, along with a measure of laudanum) and externally (to ensure her wounds were thoroughly cleaned). Her groans took on the edge of a whine, an uncomfortable tone laced with insecurity and unhappiness, and I worried that she was reliving her recent trauma in her dreams.

She calmed when I held her hand, but I could not both attend to her and direct the draft horse at the same time. She needed something familiar to hold on to in her pain-ridden vodka-numbed exhaustion, so I made a snap decision that saved my life later that afternoon: I unpacked the pair of beautiful runed pistols I had taken from the ogre, an ammunition pouch, and several silk-wrapped premeasured charges for her to snuggle up with under her blankets.

I would have brought out her rifle, but I thought it might get damaged if she dropped it and it went rattling around the cart, and she loved that rifle very dearly. The comforting feel of gunmetal and the familiar scent of ammunition served to relax her; she hugged the guns with her arm like they were cloth dolls, and nuzzled her face into the ammunition pouch like it was a lover's shoulder.

It was both adorable and a little sad.

I climbed back into the front of the cart. We were near the head of the column, so there was not too much dust, and the weather was pleasant. Yuri, bored of riding, paced alongside, easily matching the draft horse's slow plodding pace. Remembering the request of the old woman that I should show the rock she'd given me some daylight, I took it out of the box and set it next to me for the ride. The rock looked a little less dirty and dingy in the sunlight, a hunk of plain white quartz. Humoring the old woman's request seemed harmless enough.

CHAPTER THIRTY-EIGHT

In Which I Am Spooked

With Katya sleeping fairly peacefully, I entertained myself with the daydream that I was simply going for a ride through the countryside—some landed farmer taking his wife, dog, and horse out for a short (and idyllic!) trip to town. The dark and dangerous woods were behind us; I could see fields and farms. My daydream was interrupted when I went temporarily deaf in my right ear, the right side of my face hot from the muzzle flash of Katya's pistol, the sharp crack of her gun shattering any illusions. A ghastly shriek responded.

When I turned, I saw a skull-faced wraith hanging onto the side of the wagon, a hole torn straight through its middle; then, remarkably, there was a second shot from Katya. It collapsed, leaving behind a fading patch of glimmering darkness and a scattering of disconnected bones. Several scraps of fabrics suggested a shirt; a real but heavily rusted saber rolled away.

"Man down on the left flank! They're on both sides of us!" Katya's voice was oddly muddled as if her mouth were full of bread, and her cry was followed by a loud thump; turning, I saw she had fallen off the cot. A ring-shaped burn over her lips and several distinct round bulges in her left cheek showed how she had reloaded the pistol one-handed so quickly and explained why she was having trouble articulating consonants clearly. As I set the hunk of crystal back down in the box and rushed for the back of the wagon, she rolled underneath the cot, beginning the awkward process of reloading again. She had dropped deliberately to seek cover, rather than lurching off accidentally.

I flung myself into my open armor, reaching out with my mind to jump-start my mechs as I closed the armor around myself. As I reached out with my mind, I sensed a pair of unfamiliar presences to the north—to our right—heading toward us under the cover of an orchard of apple trees. A riderless horse bolted off back toward the woods, panicked by the loss of its rider but not having the good sense to stay near the friendly humans who had been feeding and caring for it for the past several months. I made a quick calculation of the speed of our column, its size, and the probability that we would be able to escape the ambush intact by trying to ride past it. It was a depressingly easy calculation.

"To arms! We fight where we stand!" With that order shouted, I snapped my helmet shut, hoping that the protective magic of my armor was good against the dead.

Partially armored phantom warriors, skull-faced and deadly, armed with everything from rusted pistols to bearded axes, floated toward our wagon from the south in ranks. The draft horse stopped in his tracks, obeying half of my command to the army. He nickered nervously, not particularly interested in the "fight" part of "fight while we stand." That was okay; I and Ilya's old steam suit were ready to greet their charge. The inside of my helmet flickered with turquoise light as they slammed into us with force out of proportion to their weight, and the shrieking of venting steam beside me announced that the mech next to me had taken a blow that would have been indirectly lethal to a human inhabitant of a steam suit. Their axes dented my shield and ripped at my armor even through the protective power field.

I held and fought back conservatively, chopping in short sharp sweeps. The cough of a self-propelled gun from the east announced that the Swedes in the pair of wagons behind mine had been ready for action; the deeper roar from the west let me know that the vanguard of our force had taken notice and that the heavy mech that had been leading the column at the moment would soon enter the fray. Hopefully, it had enough charcoal, or it would not be able to fight for long.

Their numbers were small. They must have meant to slay the unwary, or grab and swiftly make off with treasure; I simply had to hold out long enough. The other three of my personal mechs had been already on their way to my position. Feeling confident now that my armor was tested and was holding, I directed two of them to the north, readying them against the presences I had felt in that direction. The third, the mech that had once been Misha's steam suit, dove into the ranks of warriors in a manner much like an ox whose tail had been tied with an oil-soaked rag and then lit afire barging into a dance hall.

Yuri's barking and the cawing of crows added to the sense of animalistic panic; we, the living, had come unwelcome into the dance of the dead, and the dead were gripped by a frenzied determination to set our heartbeats to their tune.

Much like the father of a bride at a certain wedding whose reception had been disrupted by a flaming bovine, each of the skull-faced warriors seemed to be in the mood to murder me (as much as they could be said to have a mood). Unlike said gentleman, however, the motives leading to that sentiment were wholly unclear. What had I done to offend these undead warriors? I knew I had offended an undead king not too recently, but I doubted there was any direct connection.

These undead warriors had arms and armor that seemed much too modern in style to be connected to the king whose rest I had disturbed. The wraith-like skirmishers had steel sabers or pistols, gone only a little bit to rust; the bearded axes didn't look much different from the smaller ones that some of the Swedes favored; and lurching out of the apple orchard was a six-limbed semi-mechanical monstrosity with a billowing smokestack, strangely unheeded by the soldiers who rushed by it. It had, for reasons that defied rational engineering choices, been constructed largely of bone, the bones glowing a dull orange, barely visible in the bright, cheerful sunlight.

The dead king had come from an age when the worship of Christ was a novel cult. He had been buried long enough to miss the invention of guns, the firebox arcane engine and, consequentially, steam power, and he'd displayed that unfamiliarity freely during our encounter. The bronze tubes mounted on the monstrosity looked suspiciously like cannons.

So why were we being attacked?

A shriek behind me marked the demise of another wraith, its insubstantial body torn by a bullet fired from a runed pistol. The wraith waved a pistol of its own in the air as it collapsed, the shadowy echo of a bullet passing through the canvas of the cot and leaving a smoking hole behind.

A greater ghostly shadow loomed among the trees, wafting through them like smoke, an insubstantial being that looked like an armored giant wading waist-deep through the earth, wicked arms and head larger than that of any of the ogres we had fought. Most bullets passed through it, but Katya's shot bounced off its insubstantial armor instead. As ranks of soldiers formed around me, I stepped back, wondering how to deal with the threat. My fingers twitched in the pattern I had learned.

Moments later, I was trying to wrap a rope of magical force around it, but it resisted the pull with an insubstantial mass somehow far greater than my own, fading back into the woods as my heels were dragged forward through the mud. I had done little more than bend one of its limbs.

"Only a magic weapon will hurt it," Katya shouted. "Ragnar! Help him!"

I wasn't sure what Ragnar could do against a ghost-machine, but I thought my bronze sword might have some small magic associated with it. I had, after all, somehow changed its appearance with my abilities; it had been touched by magic at the very least. Perhaps that would suffice. Six of us advanced forward into the woods after the retreating insubstantial hulk: myself, two mechs, Yuri, the Swedish lieutenant, and one of the Swedes' self-propelled guns, trotting quickly behind Ragnar on stubby legs.

For a little while, I thought I saw glints of solid metal, but as it turned mockingly to meet us, it faded to ghostly again, the poleaxes of my mechs swishing through it without contact. My weapon, though, made contact with the massive apparition, tearing through its ghostly armor. The rent in its midsection solidified briefly, and it frantically swung back at me with its massive claws as I followed through with a second strike. As my armor strained against the impact, I heard a loud ring of metal on metal and the crackling of ice.

There was now a massive dent in its head, ice spiraling outward, damaged but not destroyed. It raked away angrily with its claws, one catching Ragnar in a glancing blow that nevertheless sent him staggering. Wherever the ice from the hammer touched, black metal came clearly into view. Where the black metal came clearly into view, my mechs' blows landed solidly. Soon, the untouchable monstrosity was a battered piece of machinery, its inner cage of runed bones smashed, and its actual propulsion system revealed: A pair of wheels. As the wheels turned solid, they dug into the ground more deeply, then cracked under our blows.

What kind of deranged wizard builds a mech that moves on two wheels? Getting it to stay upright alone must have been a difficult challenge.

Ragnar's timing must have been amazing to strike it just as it was starting to turn solid but before it attacked, I thought to myself, and then considered the possibility that a hammer wrested by force from the hands of a king dead for over two thousand years probably was, if not enchanted, at least made of something that would feel as solid to ectoplasm as flesh. Such a thing would have been very rare and special, especially back then; but it was a royal treasure, after all.

I spent a moment contemplating the play of sunlight on the frosted fragments of the machine's head and then brought myself back to the present. My column had been ambushed; I needed to return to it, not chase shadowy monsters through the woods. In the distance, I felt a flare of magic receding; there had been a wizard behind this attack, but a canny one and a cautious one who had kept a prudent distance from the action.

We had proven ourselves too deadly, I thought to myself. Looking over at Ragnar, drenched in his own blood and barely standing, I amended my thought: We had seemed too deadly when our actions were viewed at a distance. Had the mechs' master been brighter and bolder, we might not have survived our reckless rush, but the enemy commander's nerve had faltered.

When we returned to the column, the fighting was all but over. The junior most of my three cavalry officers was being clapped on the back and celebrated by his peers—evidently the alleged illusionist had found some particularly effective way of harming the phantoms. Perhaps one or more of the weapons in his collection had been enchanted particularly against phantoms.

I noticed that the blade of my sword was coated with some disgusting fluid. It usually dripped itself clean. In the case of the battle with the ogres, the gore had run so thick and deep that it ran down to cover the crow-like grip, and I had to scrub the grip afterward, but not the blade. I assumed the gory coating had cracked off after drying while I was preoccupied with riding after Yuri to catch up to Katya. Fighting a necromantic machine, though . . . whatever fluid had been in its hydraulic tubes, it was not coming off by itself. I had to scrub.

We burned the bodies, theirs and ours, in a great pyre. We had not lost many in the ambush, fortunately. My jury-rigged mechs had absorbed a great deal of the violent effort, as had the heavy mech at the front of the column. It would be some time before any of them were functional again, and there could be no confusing the fact that there had been no bodies inside of them.

I thought the last fact would have shaken the surviving steam knights, who had reverently referred to Ilya, Misha, and Gregor as if they were still alive, but they were more bothered by the fact that one of their number had managed to cook himself alive, a casualty of rushing to jump-start the steam engine on his suit without checking all the safety valves first.

They held a strange little memorial service for him, speaking quietly of the departed man (Sergei Popov) and praying his soul might become the spark of wisdom in the machine, whatever that meant. I resolved to check my own safety valves and wondered exactly what strange vein their theology had gone down. I decided to ask Vitold more about the matter. What had begun with a simple deception to keep ourselves in the good graces of General Spitignov had grown into something deeply strange, and Vitold seemed likely to know a bit more about it than I did.

Before I tended to my suit, however, I tended to Katya. She had burst some of her stitches in her dive for cover; I saw to the bleeding and stitched it back up myself, as the surgeons were both very busy with fresher injuries. I spent some time fussing over her, but I could hardly complain about her conduct. For one, she had once again saved my life; and for another, I had poured more laudanum and vodka into her to ease the pain until she was no longer in much of a state to understand any complaints I might have spoken on the subject of not overexerting herself.

Another thing I did before tending to my suit was clean and load the runed pistols. They were clearly blessed with some kind of enchantment, not merely decorative. If one of the insubstantial wraiths returned in the night, I would be ready for it. We posted double watches around our camp that night. After going over my suit, I sat by Katya, propped my feet up on the box containing the rock the old woman had given me, and kept my eyes and ears peeled as I returned to the question at hand: Why had we been attacked?

I was already confident that the dead king was not the culprit.

These were freshly equipped dead, with relatively modern weapons, accompanied by advanced necromantic machinery. It pointed to an opponent with machinations in the present and aspirations toward the future, not a fragment of the past stirred up by our passage. So, too, did the fact that my wagon was attacked, rather than the vanguard of the column on its way through. It did not make sense to commit to a full attack against the middle of a column with an inferior force. Perhaps our enemy had underestimated our capabilities, but if they wanted to destroy our army, they would have been better served by striking at our supply wagons first, killing horses and mules with their skirmisher wraiths.

They had chosen to attack my wagon specifically. What had been in the wagon? Myself, Katya, and some mechanical odds and ends. I lifted the box. The box had formerly contained a large quantity of currency and now contained a worthless hunk of rock. I opened the box and pulled out the rough hunk of crystal, examining the inside of the box closely. I had emptied it completely. No false bottom. I did a few quick mental sums, trying to recall the full value of the currency and papers that had been in the box. Had they perhaps been after money?

I compared that sum to the price of an ordinary mech, and then multiplied by ten to account for the ethereal monstrosity. I didn't know the cost of an armored skeletal warrior, but that could not be cheap either. The letters of credit were theoretically quite valuable if they could be redeemed at full face value, but even their full face value did not rationally merit the risk of the resources that had been thrown at us—even assuming the attackers had known about the letters of credit, which would require either scrying or spying on their part.

If they were not trying to rob us and weren't trying to wear down, delay, or destroy our army, then the ambush must have been an assassination mission. I put the rock back in the box and closed it up. As much as I loved Katya, I doubted they were aiming to assassinate her, and neither Yuri nor the draft horse were in a habit of making enemies. As the commander of a mercenary battalion, I was the logical target.

That was the question of "what," but it still left behind "who" and "why." After a long while of thinking, my fingers tracing the decorative patterns on the box, I failed to come up with a single likely suspect, and the only reason I could think of was that someone wanted to have a band of desperate, confused, and leaderless mercenaries wandering around the Gothic countryside in a bad mood. I locked the box, put it back on the floor of the wagon, and laid my hands on Katya instead.

Her breathing was regular. She was warm, but not feverishly so. Impulsively, I gave her a kiss and told her that I loved her, and then I spent the rest of the night sitting by her side on the cot, waiting to see if the undead would return to kill us in the darkness.

CHAPTER THIRTY-NINE

In Which I Swiftly Sleep

The dawn came. I was still alive. Tired, though, and a substantial breakfast with Katya didn't help any. I told her to wake me if someone or something required me to be awake, told the draft horse to be good and plod quickly, and then bedded down in the back of the cart on a bedroll. I was asleep before the morning fog finished clearing, and when I woke again, the rosy fingers of sunset were clasping the distant trees.

Katya was sitting on a pile of blankets next to me, awake but relaxed, a row of guns next to her: both of the runed pistols, a blunderbuss, five arquebuses, and the smaller pistol she had appropriated after Radu Odobescu had tried to kill me. (I was a little surprised to see that pistol. I had not seen it for a while; she hadn't had it when I took her down from the tree.) From the looks of things, she was halfway through breaking down and cleaning a second blunderbuss.

I wondered who was driving the cart, so after exchanging a few sweet nothings with Katya, I peered forward. I could see Yuri napping contentedly on the driver's seat, and beyond Yuri, the draft horse was plodding forward on his own. I looked back and was reassured to discover that the rest of the army was indeed behind me. I woke Yuri and had a quick conversation with the horse. I discovered that the horse had set forth immediately upon my ordering him to plod forth, and had been obediently plodding forth in a straight line since then. He was grateful that I had gone to the trouble of helping him find his way through the woods (not quite sure what the horse meant by that) but was getting a little tired after the long march. Walking dawn to dusk without a break is quite impressive.

He seemed to think we had covered about five times the distance we had the previous day, though as that number was greater than the number of hooves he had to count on, I would not place too much confidence in his precision. Horses are not noted for their grasp of mathematics or even a good sense of spatial perspective; I think it comes from having eyes that don't look straight forward at once, but one off to each side. In my adolescence, I tried several times to teach one or another draft horse the famous theorem of Pythagoras so as to plow my father's fields more efficiently, but that never ended well.

When it was definitely dark, I called for a halt, and the rest of the army slowly caught up. They, too, looked tired, but worked quickly to set up camp, knowing that dark would be coming soon. Or rather, the enlisted soldiers of my force did; most of the officers were swarming me all at once. Each had some pressing issue needing my attention.

These pressing issues had evidently not been urgent enough to spur the officers into braving Katya, who was in a murderous mood and guarding me with a large arsenal of loaded guns, but now that I was awake, they were all suddenly urgent. I would almost rather they had not waited a whole day to wake me, but I was feeling a little drained, even after having slept the entire day. Perhaps they sensed I was tired because they approached me very respectfully and were full of effusive flattery.

The gray-bearded captain in charge of the heavy armor started off by telling me that my display of magic had been very impressive to an experienced campaigner before hemming and hawing his way around to asking me for a favor. He wanted to poach a couple of the mechanics from Captain Rimehammer's command and train them up to be skilled combat mech commanders, but Felix Rimehammer had been keeping them too busy on repairs and maintenance and outranked the other captain outside of combat.

The infantry captain looked like she had a complaint about the acolyte, who had reappeared. I sidestepped her, Fyodor, the acolyte, a limping Quentin, and a fuming supply colonel (lieutenant, I corrected myself, as I wondered how he had become involved) for the moment, suggesting that we could settle various personal and personnel problems after dinner. People would at that point be in a better mood to talk to each other and less prone to snappishness. Captain Rimehammer had a sheaf of papers for me to look over; I promised to read them and stuffed them in a coat pocket for later. Then I reached Vitold.

Vitold started off by expressing awe about how much ground we had covered, and how easily, before eventually getting around to his point. It saddened me a little that he felt the need to butter me up before delivering what was clearly unwelcome news. I had to push him a little to put it to me directly: Ehrhart was dead. Vitold had opened up the heavy boiler of a damaged mech (the one that had been breaking trail during the ambush the other day) and found a very thoroughly boiled corpse inside.

Could I see it? Well, yes, we had been driving forward at a punishing pace, so there hadn't been time to stop and dig a grave. He had simply reclosed the boiler and moved on to other necessary tasks.

When we opened up the boiler, the corpse was in a rather nauseating state. I steeled myself and took a closer look, puzzled.

"That's not Ehrhart," I told Vitold.

He looked at me blankly. I explained the obvious, patiently.

"The arms are too short, for one, even accounting for the state of the connective tissue. I doubt Ehrhart would have fit inside the boiler. Second, I don't recall having seen that tattoo before, and I would have noticed it. Third, that's a wooden foot. Fourth, look at the teeth—they very clearly belong to a much younger man, or one who's had better dental care in his life."

There were more subtle physical differences that could easily be overlooked, but those were all grossly obvious at a glance.

"If you say so," Vitold said, dubiously. "I never saw him without boots on."

Neither had I, but a wooden prosthetic simply isn't very flexible, unlike a mechanical prosthetic, giving it a characteristic effect on the gait of the user. They are much cheaper, though.

"You haven't seen him around, have you?" I asked.

"Not since we were having dinner with the Loegrians. At first, I figured he was just sleeping off a hangover, then I forgot about it with all the excitement." Vitold seemed glum. "You sure that isn't him?"

"Positive," I told him. "There's not even a passing resemblance between the two of them. Go and check if he's just napping out of sight in one of the wagons somewhere. I'll deal with this. If we have one missing mechanic and one unexpected corpse, we have two mysteries to resolve. The mysteries may well be related, though."

Extracting the remains from the boiler, examining them more closely, burying them, and then flushing out the boiler to clean it was a sequence of unpleasant tasks that I couldn't imagine a regular colonel (let alone a real general) lowering themselves to do. I simply couldn't bring myself to dump the job on someone else, and I felt vaguely responsible. Whoever had killed this man, whoever he was, his death was ultimately partially my fault.

In fairy tales told to children, when there are two rivals for a maiden's hand, there are three things you can rely on. First, she only loves one of them. Second, only one of them deserves her love. Third, at the end of the story, only one of her suitors will be alive and free, with the other having been killed, eaten, sucked into the netherworld, imprisoned by the Mongols, fired out of a mortar, committed suicide, exiled after a horrid embarrassment, mysteriously disappeared after being rude to some little old peasant lady, et cetera. At this point in the story, the remaining suitor will both be loved by the maiden and deserve her hand in marriage. Then they get married and they live happily ever after.

I now understand the irritation some adults show when children beg them to entertain them with fairy tales. It had been a long night. Because I had slept through the day, I did not sleep much in the night, and in the brief few hours I did sleep, I dreamed of a poor, innocent man dying a dozen awful deaths, several involving steam engines. I tore myself from my dreams just as the sun began to peek through the branches and heard a phrase that belonged in a fairy tale.

"And who stands as your second in the resolution of this grievance?"

It was a high and clear voice. The infantry captain I had placed in charge of half of my men. My eyes went from half-lidded to fully open, and I pinched my arm to make sure I was awake and not simply dreaming up another way for the one-time thief to die. What was going on?

"Vitold Szpak, ma'am. Lieutenant of the mechanics." Fyodor Kransky's voice.

Katya made a puzzled sleepy noise as I went from horizontal to sprinting in the space of a heartbeat, dashing off in the direction of the voices.

"Very well, gentlemen," continued the infantry captain, and began to count.

Lieutenants Kransky and Gavreau were walking away from each other, stiffly, each holding a pistol. The cavalry lieutenant moved more stiffly than the artillery lieutenant because he was still injured from the battle with the ogres, but not by much. Two other lieutenants—Ragnar and Vitold—were present, both looking a little apprehensive as I approached. The two of them together showed less worry than the young weather-witch, who was anxiously biting her nails. The infantry captain was holding a handkerchief out. There were several other soldiers standing around, one of them holding an engraved and padded (but presently empty) box.

"Stop!" I shouted this word with the intent for it to sound authoritative.

I succeeded well enough that the soldier carrying the box (a large ox-like man, particularly notable for his steadiness and even temperament) flinched, dropping the box. The young weather-witch, who evidently hadn't noticed my approach, jumped, her head momentarily the highest in the crowd. Yuri, who had been racing to catch up with me, stopped so quickly he tripped over his own paws and fell over.

Having gotten their attention, I spoke in a conversational tone. "There will be no duel. I thought I expressly forbade dueling."

The captain twisted her foot uncomfortably, much like a child caught with paintbrush in hand and a half-painted sheep not a dozen yards off. She paused, licked her lips, and then added to the impression by adopting a pleading tone. "Sir, last night, I thought you said you wanted us to settle the matter permanently . . ."

"I did," I said. "I should have been more explicit." I noticed the acolyte edging slowly away, and speared her in place with a look. "You're at the center of this matter, girl. Stay."

She froze and turned white.

"I'm not going to shoot you, girl. I want to settle this without anyone dying, and that includes you."

I looked at all four lieutenants in turn. Ragnar looked embarrassed. Vitold gave a shrug, silently announcing he didn't feel responsible for the situation. Both Fyodor and Quentin managed to mix relief and indignation in equal parts.

"Girl," I said, deliberately trying to sound like a disdainful village elder. "Pick one."

She looked back and forth, her gaze flitting between me, Lieutenant Fyodor Kransky of the artillery, and Lieutenant Quentin Gavreau of the cavalry. She stammered and started a couple times, blurted out that she couldn't, and then broke down into tears.

At that point, I realized she was being honest. Unlike the fair maidens of the fairy tales, she really did like both of them, and she just had no idea how she might pick just one of them. She had very little life experience to draw on, and that life experience had been spent in training to become a white-cloak rather than in a normal childhood and adolescence. Which meant . . . well, I felt bad for her, and a little guilty for making her cry.

I lowered my voice.

"Captain, if you would . . . um . . ." I gestured at the crying girl, hoping that the captain could deal with settling her down.

"You two, come with me," I said, pointing at the two would-be duelists, walking them toward the privacy of the command tent.

I met Katya hobbling the other way with her crutch, looking like a very unstable redheaded gun rack. She had hung quite a collection of firearms around her neck, shoulders, waist, and arm, ready to try to assist me with whatever had gotten me so alarmed. I slipped my arm around her waist, steadying her, glad for her loyalty and dedication, even if I wished she would take it a little easier on herself. The degree to which she had recovered from her injuries was astonishing, but she still needed to rest and recover.

In the command tent, we had a frank discussion. Which is to say, I talked angrily at the two fretful lieutenants for quite some time until I began to notice myself repeating some of my earlier statements, then asked the both of them about their feelings on the topic. Naturally, both of them claimed an interest in the young woman, and both claimed to be the acolyte's sole beloved suitor.

I didn't want to seem unfair to either of them. I was tempted to declare the girl off-limits to both of them, but I doubted that would work, and I needed some way of breaking the impasse that didn't leave one or both of them feeling resentful. Then I looked over at Katya, seated next to me, and at the nest of guns and straps that mostly obscured her torso from view.

"In the battle with the ogres, both of you served valiantly and well."

I reached over to Katya and drew the two runed pistols out of their holsters.

"You, Quentin, led the charge that broke them. You, Fyodor, landed a most impressive shot with a rocket, leaving them ready to be broken. Both of you can say you have earned these guns."

The runes glimmered as I turned them over in my hands.

"They are a matched pair, and it would be a shame to separate them. Today, I give them to one of you, as a matched pair. The other will remain free to court the young woman, for however long her path parallels ours. However long that may be."

They looked at each other hesitantly for a moment. Then Quentin stepped forward to claim the pistols.

When I walked out of the tent, Katya murmured to me, very quietly, "That was a very nice thing you did. But those were very nice pistols you just gave away." She let out a wistful sigh.

I gave her hip a consoling caress and silently resolved to buy her something nice when we arrived in town.

CHAPTER FORTY

In Which I Learn a Lesson

The fair maiden at the center of our little drama was hiding in a wagon. Specifically, the wagon that Katya and I had been traveling in and using as a tent. (It is a good idea to keep wounded persons elevated above the ground while they recover, lest they catch an infection.) She was in the process of moving the little locked box (the one with the old lady's rock in it) out of her way in order to better conceal herself when we came across her, returning to drop off some of Katya's excess firepower. (I had strongly encouraged Katya to take it a little easier on herself.)

A clicking sound to my left announced that Katya had cocked the striker hammer of the blunderbuss. One small twitch of the trigger, and the hammer would strike the phoenix stone, sparking off an alchemical reaction energetic enough to perforate the acolyte with a full load of shot. The acolyte—the maiden fair, if you will—froze on her hands and knees, the locked box in one hand.

"I know I told them that she might not be with us for long," I told Katya, referring back to our recent conversation with the fair maiden's two suitors. "However, that was not a suggestion that you kill her."

Katya gave me a strange look. While she was doing that, the young weather-witch put the box down and began slowly edging her way back out of the wagon, looking somewhat fearful and guilty.

Poor girl. She was still worried about Quentin and Fyodor. "Don't worry," I told her in my most reassuring voice. "They're both still alive. I talked some sense into them. It's all fixed now." I made shooing motions with my left hand, and the weather-witch obeyed both me and her natural instinct for self-preservation by running off.

"Thief," grumbled Katya. "You should have let me shoot her. She'll steal it sooner or later."

"Steal what?" As the words left my mouth, I remembered what was in the box, and what I had been told about it. The old lady had told me that someone would probably try to steal the rock. She'd also said that the rock looked like the sort of rock that people want to steal. I had ignored it as being more likely the product of senility than knowledge, but perhaps that hunk of crystal did look like something that was somehow valuable.

"The magic glowing rock," Katya said. "Big round thing the size of a baby's head, glitters like Koschei's treasure, throbs like it has a heartbeat when you hold it up in the sunlight?"

I unlocked and opened the box and looked at the vaguely rectangular rough hunk of quartz crystal, holding it up to the sunlight. While the rough quartz did arguably glitter a bit and it was about half the size of a baby's head, it failed to glow at all, let alone with a pulsing heartbeat. Maybe she meant a different rock. "What rock?" I asked, cautiously.

She pointed at the one in my hand, giving me a puzzled look.

I tightened my lips in worry. While Katya had seemed to be recovering well, she was clearly out of her head with pain and beginning to hallucinate. I was lucky that she hadn't shot anyone yet, aside from the undead attackers who had come to assassinate me. I put the rock away, felt Katya's forehead to check for fever (if she had one, it was mild) and urged her to take it easy on herself. I wrapped her back up in blankets over her protestations that she was perfectly fine, and tucked her in with the pillows.

"I could ask the surgeon," I told her. "I'm sure he would say exactly the same thing: Stop pretending you aren't hurt, so you don't pop your stitches and need more attention from him. Rest as much as you can until you're all the way better."

Her protests subsided. She knew as well as I did that the surgeon was still astonished at her continued survival and expected her to drop dead at any minute. I promised to fetch her breakfast, then went off to fulfill that promise. While I was fetching breakfast, Vitold and I talked more about the mysterious death. It was unsettling, bad for morale. Someone had murdered one man in a most foul fashion, and someone had caused another to disappear entirely. I brought the matter up with Katya as we ate breakfast.

"Maybe one of the Loegrian mages shot someone in the camp," she said. "Magically silenced pistol."

"Pistol?" I frowned. "Why not a rifle?"

"They say a rifle is too hard to muffle. I asked Banneret Teushpa and he said he could not do much to make mine quieter, even if he had the time and orichalcum to do a proper try of it," Katya said.

I frowned. "Are you suggesting that the Loegrians snuck into our camp while their officers supped with us? They wanted to hire us, not kill us."

Katya looked at me, dumbfounded. "The Loegrian captain was a thaumaturge. So was one of her lieutenants. Either could have silenced their pistols with magic. And everybody knows that Loegrians are savages that kill for fun." Seeing my puzzled look, she took pity on me and explained further. "She had metal cartridges." She waited patiently for me to make the connection.

I looked back blankly at her, baffled. Why would metal cartridges be significant? I didn't understand. Little brass containers to hold the charge and ball of a gun seemed extravagant, but nobles often engaged in extravagance.

"Metal cartridges are very expensive and silly," she explained. "Thaumaturges need special cartridges so they can do magic things to the powder and shot right before they drop it out of the cartridge and down the barrel. Normal people do not use metal cartridges to hold their ammunition because if they are just a little too small, you might drop them into the barrel and then they become stuck to the barrel with the blast. Silk or paper just burn up and go away."

She made a strange gesture, holding one arm across her chest, which I later realized was her trying to cross her arms across her chest to display her exasperation with my ignorance. It is difficult to cross your arms in exasperation when you only have one of them.

"Oh." I filed away the useful piece of information for future reference. I hadn't noticed that they were carrying metal cartridges; nor would I have known what that meant. "Anything else I should know?"

"If that ranger officer comes back, and we kill him, I want his gun," she told me, a dreamy expression flitting onto her face, all thoughts of murder mysteries displaced by the discussion of guns.

"It is a very nice gun. Triple phoenix stones, resistant iron receiver, royal walnut stock, Damascus steel barrel. I once saw a boyar with a pistol like it. It was from a master smith in Cyprus." She let out an intimate sound, about halfway between a sigh and a moan, her eyes glazed over with desire.

I refrained from commenting on her lust for exotic foreign armaments, and instead simply promised Katya that if, indeed, I had the opportunity to give her that gun as part of the spoils of battle, it would be hers. Her eyes misted as she looked at me, and her passion for the Loegrian's gun turned to a very convincing demonstration of her gratitude, at which point I, too, forgot about the puzzle of the missing mechanic, at least for the moment.

It's thought that the custom of dueling to resolve disputes dates back indefinitely, but was formalized into law and custom in its current form by none other than the Romans. It remains quite popular in the Romance countries where Rome's influence persists. This includes Wallachia, as well as much of the coastline of the Axine Sea, in spite of the Emperor's attempts to outlaw it as wasteful. No less than five separate regulations of the Imperial Army expressly forbid dueling.

Given the pernicious persistence of dueling, even to this day, it should come as no surprise that my decision to ban dueling within my army would be received poorly in certain quarters. I expected this; I expected objections from many of the mercenaries hailing from the areas where duels were traditional. What I did not anticipate was just how wholeheartedly otherwise sensible men from the Golden Empire embraced the idea of dueling. Evidently, five separate regulations against dueling were not sufficient to actually eliminate the practice in the Imperial Army.

I suppose there is something of the idea of trial by combat that survives in the mind of the modern soldier; whether you are charged with hacking the enemy limb from limb with an axe or blasting them with shot, you need something to appease your conscience. What is a war if not a duel between nations? There has to be something appealing about saying to yourself that your victory, or at least your continued survival, proves you to be in the right.

This comparison of war and dueling passed through my mind as three of my captains came to speak in its defense. My fourth captain stayed silent on the subject and quite still, hidden beneath a pile of blankets and pillows which concealed both her and most of the lower half of my body from view. The conference had come upon us unannounced, and she had decided stealth was the better part of discretion.

None of them made the connection explicitly, but each found excuses for condoning duels so readily that I could not help but suspect it had to do with the profession of soldier more than anything specific to them individually. Dueling is not a legal method of resolving disputes in the Golden Empire, and I thought I remembered reading that the holmgang, the Norse version of the duel, had been banned in Sweden quite some time ago.

The captain of the armor was the most surprising to me; the man was as traditional as they come and an old veteran of the campaign trail. He advocated for it as a convenient way for us to eliminate disputes and what he referred to obliquely as "troublesome personnel." Since only unreliable sorts of soldiers would get themselves into a duel against someone liable to kill them, it would weed out weak, undisciplined, and stupid soldiers from our ranks. I had thought that the staid gentleman would have reliably endorsed the official stance of the Imperial Army on dueling; while conservative and cautious, he was more flexible and pragmatic than I had anticipated.

The captain of the infantry, not surprisingly, felt I had undercut her authority when I had canceled the duel that she had helped to arrange. It was bad enough that I caused the problem for her in the first place by enchanting the young weather-witch with lust for her subordinate. This was news to me; I had thought only perfectly natural human inclinations had been involved. Then, worse, I had turned around and publicly trampled all over her solution to said problem.

Her complaint was more about status and respect than about the issue of dueling itself. She did, of course, also think that a duel had been an exceptionally suitable method of resolving the particular issue at hand, as well as being perfectly equitable and rewarding virtue. She also added the elder captain's argument to her own, commenting that she didn't think we would much miss the French cavalryman, who she presumed would have lost the duel.

The Swedish captain, my second-in-command, had a slightly different perspective, one with less bloodthirstiness and more nuance. He felt that while dueling was wasteful, it was clearly the local custom, and our troops might get in the habit of disobeying orders if we issued orders they were not inclined to follow. In the interests of keeping our force unified and coherent, we should permit dueling; otherwise, dueling would happen regardless, and doubtless in a messier fashion. Then we would see not only waste but also insubordination, gambling, and the general growth of vice.

I could see his point about not giving orders that you do not expect to be enforced. I was not convinced of his premise; that is to say, not convinced that a ban on dueling would not be respected by our troops. I tried to keep a calm and level face throughout, sipping my tea. It would not do to look angry, petulant, or interrupt my captains. I did not even argue their points with them, however much I wanted to.

I patiently waited for them to run out of reasons and metaphorical steam, nodded thoughtfully, and then told them that I expected them to try their best to enforce my order and prevent duels between our own soldiers for the time being and expected them to stand by my decision if I changed my mind. I had complete confidence in their abilities to do so effectively and told them I valued their suggestions. In fact, their points on the merits of dueling had some substance, so they ought to write up a detailed proposal as to how we might systematize dueling to resolve not only occasional personal disputes, but perhaps also disputes over promotions and demotions among the officer corps, as well as the assignment of more or less desirable duties.

After the other three captains left, the fourth bestirred herself, peeking out of the blankets to ask quietly if I was serious. I told her I hadn't technically lied but had no intention of changing my mind on dueling either. I wanted them to think long and hard about the prospect of some displeased subordinate challenging them to a duel; one need not be a fan of dueling to be subjected to a challenge.

Dueling made for exciting stories, but was absolutely terrible for military discipline and efficiency, and was wasteful in the extreme. Not to mention unjust; there is no relationship between skill at arms and other virtues. The good may be weak, and the evil may be strong.

At the end of my monologue, Katya looked down and was silent and still for a while. I thought that perhaps she had fallen asleep. Then she spoke. "Mikolai, are we good?"

I wasn't sure how to answer that question.

INTERLUDE

From the diary of Helen Maude Victoria Winslow

March 3

We have arrived at the rendezvous point a day early. There is no sign of the cartography team we are supposed to meet here, which seems a poor sign; surely the rangers would be here a day early if they could be? Alan assures me that there is little cause for worry, but if there is one thing I have learned this month, it is that absolutely nothing goes well in the deep woods.

March 5

The rendezvous itself went smoothly yesterday, but now that I have slept on matters, I wish urgently that we had traded more than bad news. Morale is becoming a serious problem; the deep wild forest is a thoroughly depressing region to patrol at the best of times. In the best of times, the rail lines would be complete, the Lithuanians would keep to their side of the border, and undead bogeymen wouldn't leave experienced woods-wise rangers quivering in their boots.

These aren't the best of times.

As for my bad news, I can at least hope that the difficulties in Opole are temporary. The massacre was horrible news to pass on, but I felt obliged to do so. The margrave's new recruits are getting slaughtered in the middle of the night by soldiers who are supposed to serve the same emperor, and his map makers are getting slaughtered in the middle of the night by undead monsters. I'm not sure which is more depressing.

Could it get worse? We could run into the Lithuanians in force. The border isn't that far, and the war has spent most of its time on our side of it. Now that spring is here, it's fine campaign weather, as the generals would say, and the chill that the winter put on the war has been replaced with a terrifying freneticism with the warmer weather.

<u>Addendum:</u> Alan has found signs of a large force passing through from the east. They have heavy mechs with them and were moving in some haste. We will investigate. I pray to Saint George that they are not Lithuanians, for we are outnumbered and have only light mechs for mechanical support.

March 6

My protégé came up with the bright idea of sending our men all the way around the camp of the unknown force. They outnumber us about three to one in men and have heavy mechs, as well as some of the new Swedish-style walking guns. In spite of the haste evident in their force's trail, they appear to have been camped there all day, and for all their wealth of machinery, they don't seem to have many sentries or scouts. We are not sure what they are doing here or who they are working for. They could be mercenaries or bandits.

After some discussion, I have sent a pair of fast riders back with news of their presence and a rough accounting of their numbers—one west to the margrave, and another north to the more loyal of the Silesian dukes—and have decided to approach them openly.

<u>Addendum:</u> They have not shot at us. I am going in to talk to them.

March 6

Yes, I took a new page. It is [brief illegible section of diary] and the joke is, the duck never had an acorn in the first place, right? I will have a headache in the morning. But I want to write this all down while it is fresh, which it won't be in the morning. The mercenaries are very heavy drinkers, and the brandy sort of snuck up on me. There is a lot to say.

The mercenaries are led by a man called Colonel Marcus Corvus. Mark the Crow. Caw, caw. This is probably a pseudonym. He has the strangest accent; his diction is very formal and stilted, with the vowels slightly off, and if he's distracted, he slips into language that is just positively archaic.

His French has too many consonants and sometimes gains complex Latin declensions. He also uses a lot of strange metaphors and phrases without explanation, as if they're idioms I'm supposed to be familiar with. Listening to him is like listening to a priest read liturgy.

I gathered that he has the Gift, though nobody would tell me where he came from or what his native language is. I don't think his origins are a mystery to his officers, but they are very jealous of his privacy. He is followed by a small monastic order of men vowed to silence, who all go into battle in steam armor, which apparently is his practice as well. (They filed in, prayed, ate sparingly, prayed again, and left.)

His woman has bright red hair and said nothing the entire dinner. She looks like she lost a couple of limbs a month ago; she also looked at me like she wanted to reduce me to the same state. Slowly. With a rusty knife. Her death stares directed at me were occasionally interrupted by eating or giving Marcus doe eyes. The two of them are very affectionate.

The officer who initially greeted me has a very thick Slavonic accent. He skipped dinner. We found him later on our way back from the dinner, he and Quentin Gavreau. Yes, those Gavreaus—he's a stepson, and therefore, only one by marriage, but he has the same exact way of curling his lip and the same boring tendency to recite bits of his family tree by way of small talk. I remember enough of his and Mathilde's recitations to be confident he is indeed the adopted second cousin once removed of Mathilde Gavreau, either that or a very dedicated impersonator.

Alan thinks the mercenaries are an undercover force operating under orders from a paymaster somewhere in the Golden Empire, possibly the Imperial Army or one of Koschei's many ministries. In the eastern half of the Gothic Empire and in Lithuania, steam horses are far more popular than infantry steam suits, and Avaria hardly has any of either at all. Many of the soldiers have a Slavic look to them and speak French poorly, if at all. Furthermore, they have several mechs, which Alan says look as if they were made somewhere in the Golden Empire, though the signs are subtler than I could tell at a glance.

Alan has a keener eye than I do, and he thinks the boilers and hip joints are dead giveaways that they come from the southeast. Still, it's hard to credit a Gavreau as willingly pledging allegiance to an emperor who contests Leon I's claim to being Emperor of Rome based on what some exiled senators from Byzantium said after it fell. Even if Quentin is an adopted Gavreau with a claim to land in faraway Wallachia.

The most puzzling part are the steam knights: They are clearly a monastic order, devoutly religious, the kind of fanatics that you see defending Emperor Leon's easternmost holdings. What religious fanatic, though, would follow a man who openly paws his unmarried lover in front of everyone? It is such an odd assemblage. Perhaps the company is just what it looks like, a varied collection of fragmented mercenary companies welded together by a combination of necessity and charisma.

The man has a sort of peculiar magnetism to him. Christ! I would feel much better about it if he had responded positively to our overtures; if he is what he seems to be, his aid would be helpful in reinforcing the border region, and if he is indeed a mercenary, he ought to see the business sense in not turning down good paying work. And if he isn't what he seems . . . shouldn't he be jumping at the chance to backstab us?

There is something very confusing about this. I will think about it again in the morning, if I am still alive.

March 7

Unsettling dreams last night, of both good and bad varieties. Committing them to paper seems improper.

Am a fool if I do not order Alan to stop me if I look like I'm voluntarily drinking brandy ever again. Burgheard certainly won't—he seems to find his "little mistress" very entertaining while drunk.

In spite of suspicions from Alan, cannot see a good reason for trying to detain Col. Raven & company, nor think it practical. They are heading west today.

March 8

Alan begged that we ride in a circle for a day investigating the area, and then stop back at the mercenaries' campsite to give him and his trackers a chance to turn the remains of the campsite inside out to learn more about Col. Raven's battalion. I acceded to his wishes.

<u>Addendum:</u> Chief Wofford told me that the local civilian mechanic auxiliaries are worried about one of their number being missing. I could swear I counted eight of them running around here, and I am certain that's how many we started with, but he says they're insistent that one's missing. Now we're searching for clues and missing mechanics. Caleb has gotten it

into his mind to check the latrine ditches. Christ preserve us from enthusiastic men with shovels. I'm staying well away from the digging. I know! I'll go pour some shots, go make some noise about teaching Jacob how to pour his own shots.

    <u>Extra addendum:</u> Jacob has never poured shots before. Blood-quenching to prepare the shot for his aura was only a theory to him, and he nearly ruined my mold. They're really rushing them through training these days. I really did need to teach him about that, though. No thaumaturge ought to be commissioned without knowing the fundamentals. Perhaps fate frowns upon my fabricating excuses to avoid work . . .

CHAPTER FORTY-ONE

In Which I Duel with Wits

Katya surprised me by insisting I needed another guard to watch over "the wagon" (i.e., over me) while she rested. Looking back on it now, I think it might have been that she felt if she was going to be put to bed like a child, I would suffer through being watched like one, but it's also possible that she understood the danger I was in better than I did. I find it similarly difficult to look back on that day and credit Katya with having had either great foresight or, alternately, to credit her with the capacity for acts of small petty revenge. Perhaps it was simply intuition at work.

I had Quentin come over to drive the wagon, reasoning that if he was well enough to attempt a duel, he was well enough to sit, watch, and fight. Besides, his new pistols were proven effective against ghosts, and by requesting his aid in this manner, I helped ensure that he would stick to the terms of our agreement. It was like striking two birds with a single stone, only without the part where you risk having two angry birds twittering avian obscenities at you and knocking your mother's second-best blouse off the drying line because you only clipped the both of them.

I had a great deal to read through, and at the request of Captain Rimehammer, several reports to write. I never thought of the post of commanding officer as a literary one, but sifting through written reports, accounts of supplies, et cetera takes a surprising amount of time if you're trying to understand everything that's going on and improve upon it, especially when your second in command has a seemingly endless supply of paper. (Did I mention he had a paper press put together? I believe I did.)

There was also the issue of trying to figure out where we were. I was having trouble believing the distance we had supposedly covered the previous day, but we seemed to be coming close to a major habitation. After a while studying the map, I guessed we were probably headed downhill toward Starezamky. (I was wrong.)

Around noon, I took the rock out to see if Katya had stopped hallucinating yet. She again described it as having a pulsing glow. Increasingly worried for her mental stability, I coaxed her into taking another dose of our vanishing supply of laudanum. Then, just as she began to lay back down and relax, I heard shouts of alarm. We were, this time, ready for the attackers; though we had not expected them to come from above.

Our attackers were flying. They had webbed bat-like wings and were dark against the background of the light sky. The first man to see them announced them as birds; the second, as they drew nearer, called them dragons. Neither claim seemed quite suitable to me; their skin was smooth and pale, lined with faint runes rather than scales. Perspective, speed, and their unfamiliar shape made judging their size in the air difficult.

One dove down at me (or so I thought) but both Katya and Quentin shot it in the head before it reached the wagon. It was already dead with most of its head missing when I ducked away from its claws and speared it through with a hastily borrowed swordstaff on its way to the ground. Katya was staring quizzically at the blunderbuss in her hand, muttering something under her breath, the laudanum already taking effect.

The beast flopped around in the wagon in its death throes, knocking tools off of crates with abandon. In silhouette it may have looked like a dragon, but up close it looked all too human. Its pallid skin tattooed with faint runes had no more hair on it than a man's body and was no thicker than a man's, scratched and bloodied easily by splinters and nails. Nor was there anything serpentine about it, as there had been about the three-headed serpents we had fought in the deep dark woods.

After landing, it was clear that it was barely man-sized but for the stretched length of its wings. A bronze collar hung around the base of a neck no thicker than my own, and the wagon's axle wasn't the slightest bit strained at its man-like weight. At one point, this had been a man (or perhaps woman), warped into a new shape by grievously unnatural magics. The brains that had been blasted out of its skull didn't even direct its will anymore; that direction belonged to whoever owned the bronze collar.

In its death throes, the abomination scrabbled blindly in the general direction of the dull hunk of crystal, loose bits of brain spattering the ground. My heart sank, and I remembered again what the little grandmother had said. She'd told me that it looked like an important rock, and looked like the sort of rock that people would want to steal, and the acolyte had looked like she had been trying to steal it. I reminded myself that the old woman also said something else I had better keep in mind: "It's not a very important rock, so don't kill yourself over it."

My memory flashed back to the wraiths, ghostly forms barely visible in the sunlight, making a beeline for the wagon I was in, which was also the wagon the rock had been in. At the time, I had assumed that I was the target of the attack, just as my first thought had been that these abominations also had been sent to attack me, for whatever reason. But I was just a deserter, an officer of the Golden Empire who had wandered away from his assigned post and dragged a short battalion with me.

The rock, on the other hand, "looked like an important rock." The wraiths had gone straight for it; the abominations had gone straight for it; and I was simply in the way. Even Katya and some of the other soldiers seemed fascinated by the rock for reasons that weren't clear to me. Perhaps the rock was the anchor of some kind of curse or spell that drew greed.

Whatever the root cause, though, the little old lady had somehow gotten her hands on a magnet for death and destruction. It was something that people not only wanted to steal but that people would kill to possess. I dropped my polearm, grabbed the rock, and jumped out of the wagon, running back toward the wagons used by the artillerists. Fyodor was there, slinging around powder, shot, and orders with alacrity.

"I need a mortar set up and loaded with a double charge of powder but no shot," I said, shouting at the top of my lungs to be heard. I could see the face of another not-quite-human monster turn to track me as I moved, weathered, sun-browned skin forming the webbing of its wings. No, not me; it was tracking the rock. I needed a distraction.

All the crows in the woods had come out to see the battle; as one, they took wing and started tearing at the unnatural creatures, delaying them. From somewhere out of my sight, I could hear an angry voice cursing the birds in Greek. Fyodor hastened to obey my order, directing the setup of a mortar and personally packing it with a dangerous quantity of powder. I shoved the dull hunk of crystal into the barrel and the rest of the soldiers stepped back. Afraid, presumably, of what might happen with an overloaded mortar.

"What am I shooting that at, sir?" Fyodor shouted back at me, his voice just audible through the racket.

"You're shooting it away!" I said, matching gestures to my words. "Far away!"

He tipped the mortar up to an angle halfway between vertical and horizontal, then adjusted the tiniest fraction downward to correct for the resistance of the wind. Artillerists know their trigonometry far better than horses. Then he set it off. There was a loud bang. A woman screamed—at least I think it was a woman. The high-pitched shriek managed to be audible in the wake of the mortar firing next to me and through the cawing of the crows.

After the loud report of the mortar rang out, the abominations' heads raised as one up to the sky, the uncanny unison motion of their motion suggesting they were all under the control of a single master (or mistress) somewhere nearby. It also confirmed my suspicion about why they were here—for the stone, not for us. Or, more precisely, they were here for whatever their controller believed the stone to be. The old woman had simply said it looked like an important stone; she hadn't said that it actually was one. It looked like a very ordinary stone to me, but perhaps it looked different to the abominations, wraiths, and even Katya.

More than half of the abominations took to the sky after the stone. Half of the remainder were already dead or disabled; the others simply went berserk. One of them spat at me in anger, black saliva hissing and smoking where it landed in the dirt. Then I was busy again, hacking, blocking, trying to kill the monsters before they killed too many of my men. The abominations still fighting flung themselves at us with great passion but little signs of intelligence; I could only assume they'd been ordered to perform a holding action to keep us occupied or to punish us for some stone-related transgression. Even that lingering fraction of their forces killed ten soldiers and left another seven seriously wounded.

I felt no exhilaration during that battle, no rush of wild sensation as I cut and stabbed the enemy with the swordstaff. I just slowly became more tired and sickened by the carnage. We set a fortified camp early, and not that far from the site of the battle, to gather the mules and horses back in, repair broken wheels, bury the dead, and tend to the wounded. The beasts did not return that night, nor did we see them again as we reached the river and headed downstream.

In the aftermath of the battle, the young weather-witch preferred to avoid me as much as she could, including eye contact and conversation. For my part, I thought it was embarrassment or annoyance related to her love life; Katya thought it was a sign of guilt. Katya was once again in favor of shooting the acolyte, on the grounds that the weather-witch had probably done something to cause the monsters to attack us.

Katya had heard how most of them left when the stone was fired in the air, and she felt the circumstantial association between the monsters being interested in the stone and the acolyte being interested in the stone were enough to convict the latter of conspiring with the former. I refrained from mentioning Katya's odd stone-related hallucinations and her own unusual interest in the stone.

Instead, I took this renewed interest in executions as a sign of improving health and put her in charge of organizing patrol and sentry schedules. We camped a short distance from the field of battle and spent the next day at rest, burying the dead and treating the wounded as Katya organized scouting missions to be sent up and down the river, as well as picket patrols in pairs around the edges of our camp. With only one arm and at best one and a half legs, she recognized she was not fit to go on patrol herself and compensated by driving the scouts harder.

As scouts returned, she began sketching a map of the area, one that disagreed vigorously with the estimates of our location I'd made from the maps we had. We were not near Starezamky; orienting our winding way through the woods and estimating the true distances we'd traveled was no mean feat.

I soon wished I had put Katya in charge of patrols earlier; people seemed afraid to disappoint her, in a way they were not afraid of disappointing Lieutenant Quentin Gavreau. I am not sure if this was because of her renewed interest in executions, the fact that she was much closer to me, or the interaction between those two properties. Perhaps threats issued by the commander's woman are credible in a way that the threats of other officers are not.

Katya didn't hallucinate throbbing glows on any more mundane items like the rock. Perhaps she shared some special sense with the abominations, and it was how she interpreted it. I did not like to think my lovely limb-lacking lady had anything in common with abominations, though, so I soon settled with myself that the hallucinations were instead linked to laudanum.

Our nights since leaving the woods had been full of sudden starts from sound sleep and dreams filled with terror, but Katya's dreams faded when she woke up, just as mine did. They didn't intrude on her waking hours— not as far as I knew—but they robbed her of rest, just as they robbed me of rest.

Nor were Katya and I the only ones near the end of our wits. Our sentries sometimes fired into the night, thinking they saw the motion of more horrors. We had been in the field too long and fought too many fights, with each enemy less human than the last. The bear-cloaked men of the forest had seemed bestial and magical to many of my soldiers. Then there had been the ogres, man-shaped and alive but monstrous. Then we had fought foes that were already dead. Then, after we had left the deep of the woods behind and started to see cultivated fields around us, horror had struck once more as we were attacked by twisted, eyeless horrors.

Being attacked in the bright daylight and open sky was the last straw. Any shadow, any passing motion in a clump of trees or shrubs, anything at all could look like a dark engine of destruction or new twisted horror. A few times we saw peasants in the distance, but more often we found vacant farmhouses and barns. We were strangers, a whole army of them, and that was as frightening to them as the twisted horrors had been to us.

Still, as we marched along the little river, the vacant farmhouses and barns became more common, the peering eyes behind trees and hills closer and more numerous. We were out of the deep, dark woods and had reached civilized lands, where the risks came from wars and less formal raiding activity. We were the frightening monsters now.

If the border between Lithuania and the Gothic Empire was like the border between Lithuania and the Golden Empire, raids would only rarely be deliberate incursions by one side against another. More often, they would be bandits outlawed on both sides of the border, living in the nooks and crannies between uneasily coexisting polities.

Later, I learned it was not unusual for raiders to be thinly disguised men-at-arms belonging to nobles who were supposed to be on the same side. The periphery of an empire tends to be a very loose arrangement with little intervention of central authorities in local disputes.

Less than two days after I put Katya in charge of patrols, scouts reported we were coming up on a city—a real walled town, not a village or hamlet that could empty itself within scant minutes of our being sighted by a nervous peasant on a horse. The next day, as we drew nearer, the scouts brought reports of other towns in the near distance, towns clustered closely together. On the opposite side of the river, there was a railroad.

There were no more abominations, no more wraiths, no more ogres or three-headed serpents. We had left both war and wilderness behind and reached civilization.

We stopped and set camp early, and I called a meeting of officers to discuss matters. Two weeks earlier, we had been a band of deserters lost in the deep, dark woods, fending off the vicious attacks of wild men and monsters; tomorrow, we needed to be a mercenary battalion traveling around the great Gothic Empire as we looked for work. We sent a messenger, a well-born scout with the rank of banneret who volunteered for the duty. He returned to tell us that the name of the town was Dab and that our presence had been reported several days earlier by anxious farmers.

Dab was unmarked on the maps I'd been consulting; the whole cluster of towns had been growing substantially and hadn't been thought noteworthy by mapmakers in the Golden Empire. We were actually not that far from Krukov, the city of crows. If we had turned northeast instead of northwest, we might have ended up there, placing us in Lithuania instead of the Gothic Empire.

The Dab council recognized the name of Captain Helen Winslow, and the banneret had claimed (helpfully, if perhaps not honestly) that we were considering entering the margrave's service. Entry into the town still required a small amount of negotiation, in which we reassured the townsfolk, posted a nominal bond, and paid in advance for the rental of a building to house our heavy equipment.

For now, though, it was time to rest. Our long journey out of Avaria was at an end. We had fled a hostile kingdom in the wrong direction and come out of it on the other side in a different empire from the one we had started in.

About the Author

Tomas J. McIntee is the author of the Accidental War Mage series, originally released on Royal Road. He is a lifelong lover of science fiction, fantasy, and alternate history. When not preoccupied with dancing, data science, medical research, recreational reading, long walks with his dogs, or voting systems, he quietly writes fiction of his own. McIntee's work is inspired by his interests and an eclectic education comprised of diverse degrees in mathematics, physics, philosophy, and the social sciences. He lives in Chapel Hill, North Carolina.